Martin Booth was born in 1944 and educated in
Hong Kong. He has written for television and the
cinema and is the biographer of Jim Corbett, the
tiger conservationist.

He has also written documentaries for television.
His first novel, *Hiroshima Joe*, was an international bestseller, the *Daily Telegraph* calling
it 'an outstanding achievement' and *The Times*
nominating it as one of the ten best novels of
its year. His second novel, *The Jade Pavilion*,
appeared in 1987, his third *Black Chameleon*, the
following year.

Martin Booth lives in Somerset.

ALSO BY MARTIN BOOTH

Black Chameleon
Hiroshima Joe
The Jade Pavilion

Martin Booth

DREAMING OF
SAMARKAND

ARROW BOOKS

Arrow Books Limited
20 Vauxhall Bridge Road, London SW1V 2SA

An imprint of Random Century Group

London Melbourne Sydney Auckland Johannesburg
and agencies throughout the world

First published in Great Britain by Hutchinson 1989

Arrow edition 1990

© 1989 by Martin Booth

Phototypeset by Input Typesetting Ltd, London

Printed and bound in Great Britain by
Courier International Ltd, Tiptree, Essex

ISBN 0 09 963510 0

To Tony and Ulli

Contents

1   Beirut: 5–10 December 1911   9

2   Aleppo, Syria: 12–14 February 1912   43

3   Beirut: late February/early March 1912   65

4   Areiya: May 1912   92

5   Carchemish: May 1912   112

6   Areiya, Aleppo and Carchemish: June/July 1912   128

7   Beirut and Areiya: July/October 1912   168

8   At sea, France and England: the Winter of 1912/13   210

9   At sea, Beirut, Halfati and Carchemish: January/March 1913   246

10   Beirut: the second week of March 1913   302

11   At sea, Beirut and Brumana, and Switzerland: March-June 1913   307

12   Switzerland: June-September 1913   347

13   Montana and Locarno, Switzerland: January and Spring 1914   380

1

Beirut: 5–10 December 1911

She could hear him coughing, spasmodically, from somewhere in the dark recesses of the house. Every so often he would stop, half-heartedly mumbling his Turkish exercise for the morning and she would wait, her own breathing suspended momentarily in sympathy, for the hiss of his breath and the raw rasp of his throat. Listening to him, she thought, was like listening to her mother snoring in the next room when she was a child. The calm silences between her mother's snores, filled only by the sound of night crickets, were worse than the snores themselves, for they were filled with frustration and anticipation – a longing for quietude yet with the expectant knowledge that it would not come.

Hellé put down the copy of Wordsworth she had been reading. Here on the verandah, the sun was hot, the air dry and motionless. In these hot hours, when the shade of the cypress was most deep, there was no bird-song. She had noticed the absence as soon as they had arrived in the Lebanon.

Out in the garden, nothing moved except for the cat in the shadow of the cypress tree. Every so often, it flicked its tail from within its sleep, and she pondered whether the animal was dreaming or if this was a reflex action to drive ants or fleas from its fur. Every twitch of the tail brought up a soft puff of dust which did not blow away but settled on the cat's hindquarters, lightening its chocolate brown coat.

'I've had enough! There's no beauty in it.'

She turned to see her husband standing in the doorway. His light grey flannel trousers hung limply from his belt and his shirtsleeves were rolled up. He wore no collar, having snatched it off, but the stud remained in the white cotton. It was, she thought, like a tiny jewel at his throat.

'What has no beauty?'

'Turkish!'

'Surely you can find some in it,' she suggested, trying as always to encourage him in his studies.

The Consular Service examinations were so important to him, to the future of his career, to their whole future. A pass would bring about a promotion which, in its turn, would produce a rise in salary. They had only been married for six months, but already it was clear they desperately needed more money, as she still had no buyer for the house she owned in Athens.

He was so careless with money; even on their honeymoon they had been forced to stay the night in a decrepit inn at Chalcis – and return to Athens on the train, without tickets, because he had miscalculated their spending. In Corfu he had actually lost their money: not spent it, just mislaid it.

'I cannot understand,' he continued, sitting on the bench under the vine, brushing aside the remaining yellowish, fallen leaves with a cursory sweep of his hand, 'how something which has taken so long to create can be so ugly. Everything has beauty. I'm certain of it . . . Yet I just cannot, for the life of me, find beauty in the Turkish language. The land, yes. The desert, yes. The people, perhaps. But the language . . .! It's unbearable.' He paused to breathe. 'I don't *like* the land, you understand. The desert is detestable for its banality and bleakness. The people . . . Less said there . . . But I do accept they have a beauty. Like or dislike it, it does exist. And

I don't like their faith – Islam is a sham, a religion of bellicosity and antagonism with no human love in it at all. It's the religion of the scimitar-wielding hypocrite, the believer in might as right.'

He was left quite without breath after his outburst.

'That's not what you said last week.'

'Then I was different.'

He stood up, leaning against the stone pillar at the end of the verandah, his right hand raised to grip the beam over his head. In silhouette against the hot sun and the dry land, the cypress and olive groves, he was curved, she thought, like the new moon.

He had stood like that, she remembered, when they had stayed at Chalcis. They had strolled hand in hand in the early evening, just as the sun was setting. The air was growing chilled: they could hear the stones clicking as they cooled. When sunset came, they stopped and watched the sun turn orange over Thermopylae. Later, time running them by as it always does with lovers, they watched a new moon rise cold and sedate across Greece, across all history, the moon shadows bending out from the buildings. Somewhere in a hidden court-yard a nightingale fluted, enthralling them with its solitary song.

He had been in love, not just with her, she realised, but with her country too. He revelled in treading the same earth as the ancient Greeks: the classical poets and philosophers, the thinkers and makers of civilisation. Every ruin, every timeworn road, every mountain track or span of seashore, every town or village or hillside hamlet held for him a complete drama from the pages of history. He had only to close his eyes to see and hear the march of Spartan troops or the dip and wash of galley oars in the tides of the Aegean, the gasping for breath – so much like his own breathing – of the messenger from Marathon.

'What are you writing?' she enquired. If she could draw his attention away from his academic drudgery, she might rekindle the fire in him. He was so moody whenever he faced his studies.

'Nothing much.' He turned, the sun shining round him like an aura.

'Are you ever not writing something? Show it to me.'

'It's nothing,' he said dismissively.

'Do you remember where you first read me your poetry?'

'The Straits of Messina,' he replied quickly.

'No,' she chided gently. 'It was the next day.'

'In that case,' he challenged her in his most pedantic tone, 'if you know so much, tell me which poem it was.'

She turned in her chair like a child preparing to recite, straightening her back, resting her hands in her lap where her fingers looped over the spine of the volume of Wordsworth, preventing it from slipping to the floor.

' "Pillage",' she began, 'a poem by James Elroy Flecker . . .

> . . . we are dumb but a song of our State
> Will roam in the desert and wait, with its
>   burden of long, long ago,
> Till a scholar from sea-bright lands unearth
>   from the years and the sands
> Some image with beautiful hands, and know what
>   we want him to know.'

'Bravo! You speak my poem like an actress.'

The cat abandoned the shade, crossed nimbly through the sunlight and curled itself around his feet. He let go of the beam and bent to rub the knuckle of his index finger between its shoulder-blades.

'Roy, what would you want him to know?' she asked.

'Who?'

'The scholar.'

'Which scholar?'

Already his voice was dour. The lifting of his spirits by the poem had been so temporary that it scared her. He was sliding into one of his melancholy moods, away from the sunlight and away from her.

'The one from the sea-bright lands?'

He straightened up, not immediately answering. The cat raised its tail against his trousers, twining it round the material but to no avail. Realising it was to receive no more attention it jumped down into the sunlight, returning to the dust under the cypress.

'I should want him to know what beauty the image held in its hands. It is not only the hands that are beautiful, but also what they contain.' He paused and wheezed upon his next breath, his mouth tightening momentarily in a tiny wince of pain. 'They are your hands,' he said.

'You wrote the poem before you knew me.'

'Only by a few days. It was one of those moments where art inspires reality. It happens all the time.'

She turned again in her chair and faced the sunlight. From beyond the stone wall came the clonking and tinny chiming of sheep's bells.

He came and stood behind her, resting his hands upon the back of the chair.

'You flatter me,' she said quietly.

'I love you, my Pallas Athene,' he replied and kissed the top of her head, her springy hair tickling his cheeks. She reached up and pressed her fingers against his neck. Under the skin a vein was throbbing and she knew, from times watching him asleep, that soon he would cough once more.

She opened the Wordsworth again, remembering as she did so the Straits of Messina.

The *Crimée* had been steaming slowly, close in to the coast, past the town, and all the passengers were lining

13

the rails to gaze at the devastation on shore. Many of the houses were mere piles of rubble, while those still standing had gaping holes in their roofs or a matchwork of beams exposed to the sun. Already, on the more substantial buildings, repair work had commenced.

She had, she recalled, still felt queasy. They had had a rough passage across the Gulf of Lyons and she had stayed in her cabin. The sight of the earthquake damage on shore further upset her.

'Quite an awful sight, is it not? It makes one glad to live in England where such catastrophes do not occur.'

She could not take her eyes off the devastation to look at the passenger standing beside her, could not stop thinking of the tiny figures she had seen clambering over the wreckage of their homes. From one building a drift of dust was blowing on the sea breeze.

'I am Greek,' she replied, 'and to me such disasters are not uncommon.'

The ship altered course towards the centre of the channel, listing slightly as she turned. Hellé felt the motion of the vessel and gripped the deck rail tightly. She had yet to find her sea legs.

'Can I help you?' the man at her side asked, noticing her knuckles whiten on the varnished wood. 'You look a little unsteady.'

She moved to face him, not letting go of the rail. 'It was the passage from Marseilles . . .' she began.

He was smiling. His eyes flashed with the reflection of the sun off the zinc-coloured sea. His hair was thick and black and blown back from his brow, his skin deeply tanned. His hands looked strong. He was wearing a greenish Norfolk jacket over dark brown trousers.

'Can I assist you in to the saloon?' he offered. 'Perhaps if you were to sit down for a moment . . .'

'No, thank you. I shall be all right in a minute.'

The ship levelled after the turn and Hellé felt less discomfort now that the vessel was on a straight course.

'Are you English?' she asked.

'Yes. May I introduce myself – James Elroy Flecker.'

'Hellé Skiadaressi.'

She looked away briefly at the sea. His gaze was sharp and penetrating, yet gently so.

'And are you going home?'

'No. I live in Paris now with my mother. My father, who was a doctor, is dead.'

'I'm sorry.'

'It was some years ago ... And you, Mr Flecker? What are you doing aboard?'

'Travelling,' he replied non-committally. 'I am in the British Consular Service. In Turkey.'

'You do not look like a diplomat.'

He grinned with an air of almost boyhood mischief. 'No.' Then, turning, he said, 'You must excuse me. I must go below and make myself beautiful.'

Later he had rejoined her on deck, looking now somehow less tanned and, if anything, more handsome. They had sat side by side on upright folding chairs and she happened to mention, in their small talk, that she was reading Rossetti's poems. Immediately her companion showed his pleasure.

'There was a very good pocket edition brought out a few years ago,' he said with authority. 'Published by Ellis – '

'And edited by William Rossetti,' she interrupted. 'It is that which I have in my cabin. He is my favourite poet.'

Flecker laughed gaily and said, 'A like soul on a tramp steamer to Thrace! What exquisite luck!'

The coast of Calabria slid by and the ship sailed on across a calm Adriatic. The evening swept over them from the east and soon a young moon appeared from behind clouds in a deep jade sky. The ship's wake was a ghost trail on the surface of the sea.

It was not until the morning after that he showed her 'Pillage'. She had read it sitting in the same upright chair as the evening before.

'But this is extraordinarily good for an amateur!' she had exclaimed.

'Well, I'm not quite an amateur, you know,' he answered with a wry smile.

'Really?'

'I have published four books to date – my latest is *Thirty-Six Poems*. I'll lend you a copy of my *The Bridge of Fire*, if you like. I have one in my cabin.'

That afternoon the *Crimée* steamed past Cythera. At midnight, it rounded Cape Maléa. They were still up, on deck, talking into the early hours.

He told her of his childhood in England, his father a priest and headmaster in Cheltenham. He recounted his schooldays when, he admitted, he had been unmercifully teased for his Jewish looks, snubbed for his cleverness and rebuked by both his fellow pupils and the masters for his lacklustre attitude to games.

'I didn't think you Jewish when we first met,' she said. 'I thought you were an Irishman.'

'It must have been my green homespun jacket,' he laughed.

He also admitted, in such a forthright way that it took her aback, that he had fallen in love a few times at school but they were repressive relationships – expulsions were common for what the headmaster termed 'the corrupting confluence of the manly body and the bestial soul' – and the restraints put pressures upon him he could vent only in anger. Once, he declared, he had hit a boy so hard he had cracked his nose; he heard it fracture like a snapping knuckle. Now, he stated, love was something more wonderful and free.

They remained on deck all that night. Together they shared the brilliant explosion of the sunrise before docking in Piraeus and, that day, with a party of half a dozen others, they took a landau to the Acropolis.

'I love Greece,' Flecker professed to her in a moment when they were alone, 'and all things Greek.'

In the high heat of the day he had insisted on walking through the town to the Zappeion. The white marble pavements glared up at them, blinding them just as he was now blinding her with love. When he took the train for the short ride back to Piraeus and the boat, she felt unutterably sad. His promise to write did nothing to assuage her grief.

Yet he did write – from Constantinople, a long letter telling her of his office work, and of how he kept the consular accounts with their fascinating tidy rows of figures. Then, by chance, that August she was invited to stay with friends on the Bosphorus and met him once more.

He was thinner than when she had last seen him and suffering from a sore throat; but he was in good spirits, living happily in a house at Candilli which he shared with fellow consular officers.

She remembered the wooden house with its printed wall hangings and cool sitting room, on the sill of which squatted a green dragon made of Dardanelles earthenware. How she had coveted that dragon; and it would, she thought, have made such a pretty ornament for their Beirut home.

The pages of the Wordsworth glared in the sunlight and she closed her eyes.

The air in the city was not good for him. Hellé was only too aware herself of how dusty Beirut could be, how dirty. From time to time she coughed herself – and whenever she blew her nose there was always a thin grey smudge on her silk handkerchief. Whenever she had been for a walk in the city, the collar and cuffs of her blouse were grimed with dirt when she removed them. If this was what her clothes were like, she wondered, what must her husband's lungs be like? Or her own?

In the streets there was a perpetual taint of sewage. The city had no organised system and, after rain, the ground in some parts reeked of effluent. The centre of every thoroughfare was invariably littered with horse and camel dung, some of it wet and malodorous, much of it dry and dusting on the wind.

A move of house might help him. They could try to rent another set of rooms nearer the seashore, where the wind coming off the sea would be less laden with dust and would contain the ozone which she had been led to believe was beneficial to someone with a weak chest. Alternatively they could perhaps move to the hills where the air, she was reliably informed, was cleaner and always moving, even in the hottest of the summer months. Either would give him some relief.

As she strolled along the corniche, the sea changing its noise as the tide turned, she thought over the options. A house in the hills would be expensive, certainly more costly than their present home. Not only would the rent be higher but living out of town would incur added transport costs. A house by the sea would be less expensive and not far from the Consulate offices; but it would still be a strain upon their meagre purse. Her savings would not last for long if they were extravagant but, she assessed, they might just manage the rent of a house near the shore if they were careful. That of course, she reasoned, was an aspect of their married life she would have to control. At times, he could be not only careless but quite prodigal with money.

On the other hand, just for her own part, she quite fancied the idea of living in the hills. They had seen a very pretty house at Areiya, surrounded by jasmine and pomegranate trees, which she would have loved to rent. They had visited it once when they had first arrived, going there for dinner with the Consulate officer whom her husband replaced. His wife adored the house but, Hellé remembered, they had had a private income to supplement their diplomatic service salary.

Unlocking the front door to their home, she considered the various ways in which she might broach the subject to her husband when he returned late that afternoon.

The fire had been smoking for most of the morning. Flecker called in the elderly messenger who usually sat on a plain Windsor chair at the end of the corridor; he prodded the embers and puffed the bellows at the base of the grate, but this did little either to build up the blaze or to stop the smoke eddying into the room. With every contraction of the bellows a small cloud of wood-ash floated across the floor.

'*C'est impossible!*' Flecker exclaimed. '*J'ai beaucoup de travail aujourd'hui et cette . . .*'

He waved his hands despairingly at the hearth, and the messenger, his waistcoat besmirched with flecks of ash, laid down the bellows, propping them against the fireplace. He shrugged resignedly.

'If you can do no better than that,' Flecker said with exasperation, resorting to English, 'then let the damned thing go out.'

The messenger nodded and left the room. He shuffled as he walked, his soft shoes worn through at the heels.

Once the sound of the messenger's faltering gait could no longer be heard, Flecker put down his pen and stretched his arms before him, opening and shutting his fingers. He closed his eyes and let his thoughts control him. He was tired. The night before he had barely slept.

They had made love just before midnight, hesitantly and gently. Hellé had begun the overtures by caressing his chest, touching him lightly with her fingertips, running them from his sternum to his solar plexus, her long rounded nails snagging in the hair and tickling him. He had tried, by way of teasing her, to ignore her, but she persisted and her fingers gradually made his skin more and more sensitive until, finally, he had surrendered and clasped at her hand.

It was then she kissed him on his throat, in the hollow where his chest began, and her kiss was like a shard of ice. The irritation in his throat was instantly soothed away as if he were her child, not her husband, and she not his wife but a nurse or his mother.

She had lain upon him at first and then, later, he upon her; but their love-making soon exhausted him and he began to rasp, each gulp of air being snatched at with increasing urgency. For the rest of the night he had gasped and sucked.

He would have preferred their special love-making, but it was too cold to be out of the bed. The darkness in the room was chilled – there was snow reported falling in the mountains – and his breathing not only hurt his throat but also his head. It was like drinking freezing water on a day of virulent sun.

A curt knock on his office door brought an abrupt end to his reverie. He opened his eyes and stared at the panelling as if in disbelief that someone should want to speak to him, then shuffled the papers on his desk into a hurried semblance of having been read.

'Do come in,' he called.

'Morning, Flecker.' The voice greeted him before the door was open more than a foot.

'Morning, Robbins.'

The door banged against the upright chair, upon which were draped a camel-hair overcoat and navy blue knitted comforter.

'You've been here a while from the look of your desk. Much happening?'

Flecker thumbed through the papers.

'Not much. There's a report down from Constantinople that the Old Man should see. German railway ciphers again. I've just finished transcribing them, but they've yet to be typed.'

His handwriting was small and orderly, yet straggled across the page with loops and curls. Some words were linked to each other by arabesques as if the pen, hurrying, was trying to keep abreast of his thoughts. Robbins picked up one of the transcriptions.

'See what I mean? Berlin to Baghdad in six days, they say . . .'

'I wasn't actually reading the text, Flecker. I was looking at the writing. You really do have a most intriguing hand.'

The fire, dying in the grate, crackled and flicked a chip of glowing kindling on to the floorboards, where it began to burn yet another black mark in the polished wood. A delicate perfume of singeing varnish impinged upon the room.

'What do you mean, I've an intriguing hand? Either the words are of interest or they're not . . .'

Robbins pulled over the chair from behind the door, at the same time removing the overcoat and flinging it across the top of a wooden filing cabinet beneath a faded portrait of the King.

'See here, Flecker!' He spoke with the enthusiasm of a junior schoolmaster. 'Writing is an art. Just like painting and sculpture . . .'

'Of course it is,' Flecker remonstrated, on the defensive.

A competent consular officer, Robbins was a good sort. They had met, briefly, when up at Cambridge University; both had been members of a literary society. Yet Robbins had no love for modern literature and read no poetry. Flecker was conscious with Robbins, as he was with many of his peers in the service, that they were a little uneasy with him – with his Mediterranean, almost Jewish features; his having been to both Oxford and Cambridge; his poor showing in the examinations; his Greek wife, more than two years his senior; his being a published poet; his almost regular absences with illness. It was not that they despised him. It was rather that they would not miss him when he was posted on. Indeed, the higher-ranking officers, as he knew from his periodic assessments, would be secretly pleased. His superiors had no time for a poetic diplomat. The work demanded an appreciation of the arts, of course, but someone who was positively artistic – and had published verse and had it reviewed – was not really the type they required.

'. . . so, much as you can tell an artist's character from brush-strokes, or a sculptor's from the mark of the chisel or lines in the clay, so can you tell the character of a writer from his hand.'

'Show me, then.'

'Right-o. Look at this memo here. Don't concern yourself with what it's about; look at the way it's made. Note the phrasing – that's standard Foreign Office. Look instead . . . See this *I*. Notice the small initial loop? That means you're jealous. Not very, because your *h* lacks the loop, as does your *t*. Now take the open *a* and *o* in *anomalous* . . .'

He turned the memo around, allowed Flecker a brief

glance at the word by his finger and then spun the paper back.

'They suggest you're talkative. And you are, dammit! The small dots on the *i*s make you out to be loyal and the short *t* and *d* have you as independently minded. But the low bar on the *t* tells me you underestimate yourself, and the loop on the inside right of the *o* in *good* and *doubt* says you are secretive – and the tapering ends of the words that you are diplomatic. I would say too that you can be indecisive, for some of your *d*s slope leftwards like a *delta* and some are upright. So, all in all, Flecker old man, you are a bit of a confused chap and therefore ideally suited to the career you have chosen.'

Flecker pulled the memo round. Before him he saw no interpretations of character, only a report on the developing facilities at the railway tunnel near Baghche and the problems the Germans were having building it.

'It's tosh. You can't tell a man's character from his handwriting.' He slipped out from beneath the pile of papers before him a note from the Consul-General. 'He writes his letter *t* with a low bar. You can't tell me the Consul-General is one to underestimate himself.'

'Why not? Who knows?'

'How do you work all this out?'

'My aunt. She's an expert graphologist. Picked it up in Italy – from an Austrian doctor, I seem to recall. She's writing a book on it, you know. A new science in the making.'

Robbins stood up. The chair scraped over the floor. 'Shall I take those through for typing?'

'I'll send them along shortly.'

Robbins left and Flecker leaned back, staring at the fire. A flame had appeared at the corner of the log and, even as he watched, it spread up the side, engulfing the saw marks and the dry, peeling bark. A small wisp of smoke curled under the mantel and rose, almost invisibly, towards the ceiling.

Cumberpatch, the Consul-General, sat down next to Flecker, easing himself into the second armchair.

'Just a chat, Flecker, now that you've fully settled in to the routine here.' He flexed his fingers. 'All this writing – gives one finger cramp. How's your wife?'

'Well, thank you, sir.'

'I was told she was a bit under the weather. All passed?'

'It seems so, sir.'

Cumberpatch leaned forward slightly. 'Women's problems? It's often the case when they come out to a rigorous climate. Throws them off-centre a bit.'

'No, sir. It was a fever. The doctor seems to think it is over now, however.'

'And how are your studies coming along?' Cumberpatch changed the subject so abruptly that Flecker wondered if his superior had any real interest in Hellé's welfare.

'I'm working at them, sir. The Arabic and the Turkish are not easy, I must admit. My French . . .'

'Be glad,' Cumberpatch interrupted, 'that you don't have to struggle with other languages. What with the Italians in open hostility to the Turks, the Greeks, Bulgarians and Turks hammering away in the Balkans, the Germans expanding their empire as fast as they can go – well! How long before you get Serbo-Croat and the Lord knows what else to study, just to keep abreast of things . . .'

'It bears no thought,' Flecker replied. 'Three languages are enough.'

'Never mind! Knuckle down to it. Get a mastery of them. And how's your knowledge of Beirut now,

Flecker? Coming to grips with the convolutions of local politics?'

'Fairly, sir. The French have a great influence here . . .'

'. . . which we intend to share; don't forget that.'

'No, sir. And the locals seem to be most antagonistic towards each other. There is certainly no amity between the Shi'ite, the Druse and the Maronite communities.'

'None whatsoever,' the Consul-General agreed. 'They'd massacre each other, given half a chance. Head-strong fanatics to a man – almost all of them. There are a few more level-headed individuals in each grouping, but they don't necessarily have the power to hold sway. It's a melting-pot of religious rivalry, bigotry and deep-rooted hatred. Of course, as you'll know from your briefings, we want to spread our influence in this area, too. Whenever there is strife, we must be seen to be ready to mediate, to pour oil on the rough waters. Naturally, the French are keen to assert their presence, too. And the Germans, up north. Needless to say, our former colonies in the Americas have their representative over here ready to step in where they see a void.'

Cumberpatch paused and Flecker sensed with some apprehension that the conversation was going to take a new direction.

'And tell me,' his superior began, 'how is your own writing career, as it were, coming along? I am led to believe you have a new book either in the immediate offing or just out.'

'Yes, sir – already published. A collection of verse.'

'Title?'

'*Forty-Two Poems*, sir,' Flecker said, sensing as he spoke that Cumberpatch already knew the title.

'Strange art, poetry.' Cumberpatch wove his fingers together, his hands resting over his stomach, his thumbs hooked into a gold watch-chain. 'Neither fish nor fowl.

Hasn't the solidity of prose, but similarly hasn't the chaos of mere jumbling words. How long have you been writing it?'

'Since I was a schoolboy. I first published when I was up at Oxford. It was just a privately printed, slim thing.' He decided to mention it dismissively; this might please Cumberpatch.

'When was that?'

'1906, sir.'

Cumberpatch made no reply. He sat quiet for a moment, gathering his thoughts. When he did at last speak, his tone was brisk.

'Take a word of advice, Flecker. Play down this poetry business. Not the sort of thing we encourage in the Consular Service, you know. One has to be well-read. An intellectual with a sound academic background is vital to the service. But it's another thing to actually produce the stuff. I imagine it's hard work writing?'

Flecker nodded very slightly and was about to say something in his defence, but his superior continued, 'Thought as much. Know how damnably hard a report can be, never mind an imaginative piece. Take my advice: give all your literary efforts to the job at hand. We'll all benefit from it, I'm sure. Poets have a bad reputation, you know . . .'

'Yes, sir.' Flecker acquiesced but, in his heart, he was determined to ignore what he considered to be such crass counsel.

The oil in his lamp was low. He could see that the dark shadow of the reservoir had dropped half an inch since he had sat down. The top of the glass funnel was sooty. He had altered the wick a fraction when it began to smoke.

The sallow light gave the paper upon which he was

writing a leprous hue. The neat lines of his script upon the paper were like stained flaws in old Carrera marble. Outside a low wind moaned, but no draught succeeded in entering the room. Hellé had packed strips of damp cotton and paper into the loose window casements, pressing the carpet close to the door-jamb, curling the edge up against the crack. The passage of feet on the lintel had worn it away in the centre. With so little air circulating in the room, the atmosphere was muggy and smelled of lamp oil, yet it was warm and prevented him coughing.

She was dozing in her chair. The lamp on the table by her side was guttering and he went across to extinguish it. He was in two minds whether or not to rouse her, but she awoke to the tiny squeak of the lamp screw.

'What time is it?' she enquired drowsily.

'About midnight.'

She pressed her hand against his arm. 'You are tired.' She did not ask him but stated the fact.

'Yes. But only in body. I'm so very alive inside . . .'

She squinted at the circle of yellow light cast over his books.

'You've been writing.'

'Of course.'

'You know what I mean, dearest,' she rebuked him. 'I mean *writing* writing.'

'*Bu hangi istasyon acaba?*' he replied. '*Tren burada ne kadar durur?*'

'Did you learn that tonight?'

'Yes,' he lied.

'What does it mean?'

' "What station is this? How long does the train stop here?" '

'But you are *writing* writing tonight. Your poetry. I can see from here your Turkish vocabulary is shut . . .'

27

'I surrender. Yes, I admit it.' He opened his hands as if beseeching forgiveness of her. 'I was writing. But it is late and I have done enough Turkish for a lifetime. Besides, I shall not pass the examination.'

He moved back to the table, sitting down and taking up his pen. By the lamplight, his dark features took on an even swarthier look. His bushy moustache and black eyebrows seemed to hang over his mouth and eyes, exaggerated by the shadows thrown by the dimming lamp. His hair, combed from left to right, had fallen forward to cover part of his forehead and he restlessly brushed it back. When his pen moved, it scratched upon the paper, sounding like an insect seeking entry to the room through a window-pane.

She watched him for ten minutes, during which time he did not cough, wheeze or struggle at all to breathe. He sat calmly, bent poring over his sheets of paper. Occasionally he pushed one aside to replace it with another, his dark eyes catching the waxen-coloured lamplight as they darted from one sheet to the other, comparing texts.

'Read it to me,' she commanded after he had spent more than a minute motionless except for his eyes, his pen no longer poised but lying on the table. She kept her voice soft and low, afraid that by speaking she might break the thread between him and his muse.

'What?' He was startled.

'I didn't mean to disturb you. It was just you haven't . . .'

'That's all right,' he interrupted, the surprise gone from his face.

'Will you read it to me?'

'It's not done,' he replied cautiously. 'I began it only yesterday. Well, in a manner of speaking . . . I found a fragment and thought I'd work upon it. Nothing's been coming easily of late.'

He sat upright, away from the lamp, the shadows moving and fading on his face. He picked up the sheet of paper, tilting it in the lamplight. The sheet of paper was flimsy and she could see his fingers silhouetted through it.

This place was made divine for love and you and I to dwell;
    This house of brown stones built for us to sleep
      within;
  Those blossoms haunt the boulders that we might see
    and smell;
Those old rocks break the hill that we the slopes might win.

He let the sheet drop into the full circle of the lamp-light.

'Is that all?'

'It's a first verse.'

'Have you the second?'

'I think so.'

'Read that to me, also.'

He gazed at her in the semi-darkness beyond the governance of the lamp. He could not see her; it was as if she were a part of the room, the night, her voice a disembodied spirit.

'No. It is utterly unworked-upon.'

'Do you have a title?'

He nodded slightly and his hair slipped on to his brow. She rose from her chair to stand by him and look over his shoulder. Just as his mother had done so often in the playroom in Cheltenham, she smoothed his way-ward hair up and patted it flat.

'What will you call it, Roy?'

'I thought "The House at Areiya". You know the one.'

For a moment she pictured the house in her mind and wondered if she should not now mention her plan to move their home; but she held back. To talk of such banalities might upset his mood.

'I should like to live there,' was her only remark.

'So should I,' he said pensively.

On one of the other sheets of paper, half scribbled over, were other lines. She bent to look at them, reading one fragment aloud.

' "Beyond it," ' she quoted, ' "red and green, the gay pomegranate tree. Around it, like love's arms, the summer and the rose." I like those lines. Very much. You must use them.'

'Perhaps . . .'

The oil in the reservoir was even lower now, the flame smoking again. He patted his papers into a sheaf and deliberately thrust the Turkish vocabulary beneath his other books.

'You need a good night's rest,' she announced, watching him. 'And you should stop worrying about your examinations. I'm certain you'll succeed in them. This time. And if not – well, let's not think of that.'

'If not . . .' he repeated; and his mind started to scan the scroll of alternatives he had begun, in a disjointed way, to assemble in the early hours when she was asleep and he awake.

If he quit the service he would have to pay his £500 bond and that would put an unbearable strain upon him and Hellé; and there was no immediate way in which he could see himself maintaining their present living standards on his salary, not to mention losing it.

He could try to make a living from writing but it would be precarious, to say the very least. He had published several books of verse and there was much still in him to write – he knew that. He wanted to write for the theatre; he knew there was a blaze of prose in him only waiting to be ignited. He could, he reasoned, write another textbook; after all, his *The Scholar's*

Italian Book was now published and promised well. But he could not get away from the fact that none of his writings had earned him much; indeed, they had cost him money – if not in actual cash, then at least in kind, in time and effort.

Another alternative which had occurred to him was to enter teaching. His father was headmaster of a reputable, if small, public school and he was a graduate of Oxford. He was sure he could do it, could discipline boys and impart knowledge. If he could obtain a position in a small school in the shires, with a school tied house, he and Hellé could live together in rural peace. He would have time to write, would be living in an atmosphere of intellectual industry. It could not fail to help him. The salary would not be good, not at first. He would, he thought, be lucky to earn £150 per annum. But their house would be free. And there would be the long holidays in which to dream and polish his writing.

That night, as he slept, his head tossing slowly on the pillow, his fingers twitching as his dreams pushed his pen across virgin pages, she watched him by the light of the moon. He was, she considered, so full of energy, so bursting with poetry and life.

The room was filled with conversation. The Consulate was holding one of its regulation parties for its fellow diplomats in Beirut. Cigarette smoke drifted upwards with the words to form a haze below the ceiling. Despite it being December, someone had switched the fans on to their lowest speed to dissipate the blue fog, but to no avail. Flecker snapped up the brass rheostat by the door another notch, the connector clicking and sparking, but it made little difference.

'Ah, there you are!'

Flecker turned. Behind him stood Mr R. A. Fontana, His Britannic Majesty's Consul from Aleppo.

'Let me introduce you to Tom Lawrence.'

Flecker's gaze turned to the man standing beside Fontana.

He was not a tall man – Flecker judged him to be about five foot six, with legs which were too short – yet he seemed larger, more impressive than his diminutive height might demand. His head was too big, slightly out of proportion to the rest of his body. His forehead was high, topped with a wave of mousey-coloured hair; his chin was rounded, of the sort one expected to find more on bare-knuckle boxing champions at a fairground than on the face of a man at a diplomatic gathering. Also, unlike those others in the gathering who were wearing suits and high collars – with college, club or regimental ties – or the uniforms of their military service, Lawrence was dressed in baggy trousers, a shirt with no tie and a dust-stained collar, and a shapeless jacket, the pockets of which sagged as if they were used to carrying stones rather than a handkerchief. Fleetingly and irrationally, Flecker wondered if they were accustomed also to carrying a pistol.

There was something raffish about him and yet, at the same time, he was distinctly unmeretricious. A prince incognito at a gathering of commoners might, Flecker considered, carry a similar bearing.

The newcomer remained quite still, looking at him intently. He had the most beautiful blue eyes Flecker had ever seen. For a moment, Flecker did not react to the introduction. It was as if he was held by some indefinable sorcery. He was strangely scared but simultaneously exhilarated. Then he reached out, offering his hand. Disconcertingly, Lawrence raised his own in a kind of wave, an acknowledgement of their meeting but an avoidance of contact. He then loosely lowered his arms below his chest, tucking his elbows in and placing one small and delicate hand over the other in the middle of his stomach, his wrists pushing his jacket open.

Fontana noted Flecker's discomfiture. He had seen other men unnerved at their first meeting with his companion; he had been so himself in 1909.

'I understand you are now a man of family, Flecker,' he said. 'Nothing like a staunch confidante in our line of trade. What is her name?'

The Consul's question gave Flecker the chance to turn away from Lawrence's gaze.

'Hellé. She's Greek.'

'Ah-ha! You poets! You can't escape from Parnassus, no matter how hard you try. If you can't live on the slopes in a goat-herder's hovel, you steal one of the nymphs from the grottoes – is she an oracle from Delphi?'

'As beautiful. Not as oracular,' Flecker answered.

Lawrence suddenly laughed – very quietly. It was more a chuckle than a laugh.

'That was the poet speaking,' he said.

Flecker could not take his eyes off the man's face as he spoke. His mouth was sensuous yet not sensual, his smile disarming and his words filled with the most extraordinary charm.

'I admired your book . . .' Lawrence put his hands together, interlocking them and pointing the index fingers together. Flecker noticed he held no glass. 'I'm searching for . . . *The Bridge of Fire* it was.' His hands parted and hung by his sides again.

'You read it?'

'You sound astonished.'

'It was only a slim volume. Sixty or so pages.'

'I know of many books which are slim and yet have two hundred pages.'

Lawrence smiled.

'I remember best,' he continued, 'a few lines from the ending of your title poem. They went something like:

> The wheels of Time are turning, turning,
>   turning;
> The slow Stream waits for thee, the stagnant
>   Mire.
>   The Dreamer and his Dream
>   Shall struggle in the Stream
> Sunless and unredeemable for ever,
>   Since this the Gods command,
>   That he who leaves their land
> Shall travel down to that relentless River.

'I apologise if I have dragged your words through mud. I am no reciter of verse.'

'You quote it exactly.'

'You are, I understand from Raff,' Lawrence said, ignoring Flecker's compliment, 'an Oxford *and* a Cambridge man. Quite an achievement.'

'Not really,' Flecker explained. 'I was up at Trinity. A Third at Greats, I'm afraid. Then I went to Cambridge for the student interpreter course, and the ICS examinations for the Foreign Office . . . although I actually lived mostly in lodgings in Jesus Lane. I wasn't too good at attending lectures.'

'I only a-spired to the former establishment, some four years after you,' Lawrence said, breaking the verb into two. It took Flecker a moment to appreciate the humour.

'My spires were all on ivory towers,' he rejoined.

Fontana took the moment to excuse himself from their company, saying he had to have a word with one of the consular staff. Lawrence nodded, then turned back to Flecker.

'You knew Jack Beazley, didn't you?'

'Yes,' Flecker admitted cautiously.

34

'I, too. He is a fine poet. Or was. I'm afraid the world of shards and bones has him now. A love of Greek and Greece got him, too. As it has you.'

At first Flecker made no answer but, quick to realise reticence might be misconstrued, said, 'He was a wonderful boy poet.'

'You loved him.'

Lawrence's statement was so forthright that it stunned Flecker. 'We were very good friends,' he said simply.

His ambiguity was not lost on Lawrence. 'Yes,' the other man responded. 'We have a number of us been good friends of Jack. You also founded the Praxiteles Club with him – not to mention the Narcissus Club . . .'

'They were just japes,' Flecker said quickly. 'We were the only two members of the Praxiteles, and the latter was a joke on a fresher.'

Lawrence looked around: Fontana was now busily engaged with the head of chancery.

'Let us leave this gathering and discuss a new business venture. What do you say?'

Reduced to silence by the extraordinary turn events were taking, Flecker simply nodded and followed Lawrence from the room. He noticed, as they left, that Fontana had turned to watch them.

Along the corridor was an office usually occupied by one of the naval staff who was, however, absent on a mission to Cairo. Lawrence pushed the door open and held it back for Flecker. Once inside, he shut the door firmly, turning the key which had been left in the lock.

'Don't want anyone barging in.' Lawrence's face was serene but solemn. 'It wouldn't do. Please,' he indicated a chair before the desk.

Flecker sat on the hard chair, while Lawrence perched on the end of the solid mahogany desk.

'This won't take long, but I need to ask you a few

questions. Rather serious, I'm afraid. We'll try to make some fun of it a bit later.'

Through the window came a slight whistle of draught. It was late and the wind was rising.

'How important is the Empire to you?'

The suddenness of the question startled Flecker. 'Important?' he stammered. 'I can't see . . .'

'You don't need to. We are concerned with but the most basic of ideals here. Do you consider British spheres of influence important? Very important?'

'Of course. Doesn't that go without saying?'

Lawrence's brow furrowed momentarily, and Flecker realised he was no longer staring at his eyes but keeping his glance averted, only occasionally allowing it to settle on his face.

'I'm not interested in how you feel you fit into the order – into the Levant Consular Service – but what you *believe*. Are you being true to yourself?'

Flecker had no immediate answer. This line of questioning was perplexing. He realised he was still holding his glass, a quarter of an inch of whisky in the bottom. He placed it under the chair.

For a moment, he wondered if Lawrence was one of the Foreign Office staff who travelled around, like inspectors on the railways, checking on and chivvying junior staff who were slacking in their studies. It could be, he thought, they had spies out watching how hard he was at work on his Turkish and Arabic, ascertaining that he did not over-indulge in poetry-making.

'I was questioned like this when I first joined the service,' he said. 'Are you from London . . .?'

'No. I'm not – not directly, I suppose . . .' He looked briefly out of the window. It was getting towards twilight. 'I'm actually from Oxford.'

'Shall I put the light on?' Flecker suggested.

'I think not. We shan't be long. Best we stay in the dark.'

'I'm in the dark as it is,' Flecker replied, a hint of frustration in his voice.

'Up at Cambridge, didn't you join the Fabian Society?'

'It was just a passing phase. Social reasons, really. I had friends . . .'

'Still your friends?'

'Not really. They were poets. I'm not in touch with them now.'

'Nor with their ideals? The socialisms or left-wing concepts?'

'Good Lord, no! Our friendship was social, not socialist. Besides, I was a lot younger then.'

'It was only a few years ago.'

Flecker said nothing.

'And you knew Rupert Brooke, didn't you?'

Flecker nodded and said, 'Yes, I knew him . . . know him. He was in the literary circles at Cambridge.'

'Another fine poet in the making.'

Lawrence spoke in short, terse sentences. He did not raise his voice, nor did he fire the questions at Flecker as if to catch him out, yet there was somehow a crucial, near desperate immediacy in his words. It was as if time were limited for them both, not just in their borrowed use of the office but in their lives.

'Do you remember Hogarth?'

Just the name immediately conjured up for Flecker the panorama of the High Street, the bend in the road by Long Wall Street and the view of Magdalen Tower by the bridge over the Cherwell. He could even hear, as clearly as if they were ringing out over the Lebanon, the bells.

'Yes, I remember him.'

He could visualise the ugly man, his portentous beard

solid upon his rounded bulk of a face, his simian body hunched in a leather armchair.

'You visited his rooms or his home?' Lawrence asked.

'Both. Mostly his rooms.'

'Can you recall what he spoke of?'

Casting his mind back, Flecker replied, 'The usual.'

'What was that?'

'He was a good conversationalist,' said Flecker. 'We talked of archaeology, politics. And there were the thematic meetings. We all came together to rethink some great historical moment – the Magna Carta, the passing of the Corn Laws, the battles of Jericho, or Waterloo, or Agincourt. He taught one how to think . . .'

The office was growing darker and Flecker leaned forward. Lawrence moved from the edge of the desk and sat behind it in the naval staff officer's chair, folding his arms on the blotter.

'Go on.'

'There's not much more. He was a sardonic character, autocratic. The world was a chess-board to him, to be played with; he liked controlling pawns as well as bishops and knights – or thought he did. He believed democracy was a sham . . .'

' "A nation requires – no, demands – a band of dedicated men of special ability who will strive for that nation, seeking neither pay nor honours but only the personal satisfaction and belief that they are shaping history for the sake of itself." Have you heard him say that?'

'Yes. Or words to that effect. Often.'

Flecker smiled in the gathering darkness but Lawrence did not notice. He was looking at the blotter with such intensity that Flecker wondered if, as well as talking with him, he was also trying to decipher the back-to-front writing on the paper.

'Would you say you are one of his band of dedicated men?'

'I hadn't thought of it that way . . .'

'Of what?'

'It – of my work here. I suppose I just work for the service and, through it, the country.'

'If you are not one of that band, would you become one if the opportunity arose?'

'Naturally. We are all in the service of our country.'

'Good.'

Lawrence paused. Footsteps were slowly approaching. A light came on under the door as someone illuminated the corridor outside.

'One last question: would you work with me?'

'I don't know what you do. We've not met . . .'

He procrastinated but the question, almost a request, filled Flecker with the thrill of anticipation. To have the opportunity to get to know this fascinating – this beautiful – man was one he could not afford to pass over.

'I'm sure I could . . .'

He was interrupted by a gentle knock on the door. A knuckle rapped twice, stopped, then rapped twice again.

'Raff,' Lawrence explained, rising from the desk and unlocking the door.

Fontana stepped quickly inside. The light from the passageway stung Flecker's eyes and put moving bands of light between himself and the other two men.

'Well?' Fontana enquired.

Lawrence nodded.

'Excellent!' The Consul turned to Flecker, who got to his feet. 'Glad you've agreed.'

'I'm not quite sure what I've agreed to, sir.'

'Raff!' Fontana admonished. 'Let us drop the *sir*, now that it seems we shall be seeing a lot of each other in the months to come. I'll arrange with your Consulate for you to visit me in Aleppo. Your role will be explained to you there.'

'We must have a total commitment,' Lawrence said. 'Are you prepared for that?'

'Yes,' Flecker answered, still puzzled yet unequivocal.

'And you must inform no one of this,' Fontana went on. 'Not even your Consul. He will be told a tale to satisfy him.'

'This will be your second bridge of fire, James,' Lawrence said. 'To paraphrase your poem, you are now between your own "red Death and radiant Desire". You are your own god now.'

The cigar and cigarette smoke had aggravated Flecker's throat once they had left the naval officer's room. The whisky had taken its toll, too. He had started to wheeze just after Lawrence and Fontana left, well before the gathering broke up, but the first fit of coughing did not occur until he was back at their house. Hellé had bathed his forehead with water and given him warm milk to drink. It soothed the soreness; yet still he could not sleep.

In the early hours, he left their bed and sat, huddled in a shawl, in the central arch of the verandah. It was cold, but the wind had shifted direction and was blowing on to the rear of the building. The cypress was tossing about but he was in calm air.

His sore throat and aching lungs were not the cause of his insomnia; he was unable to put aside his meeting with Lawrence and Fontana. The former's charm, his discreet discussion and Fontana's personal informality nagged at him. He could not stop recapitulating the events of the evening.

He had no idea what he had let himself in for. Obvi-

ously, it was official work – Fontana was involved –
but there were so many imponderables. What would
his responsibilities be? What extra work would he have
in addition to his everyday tasks? Would he have to
forfeit some of his writing time? How would he be able
to carry on swotting for the examinations? Then there
was the mention of Hogarth: he was an archaeologist,
Keeper of the Ashmolean Museum in Oxford, university
don and intellectual. What had he to do with it?

Perhaps, he pondered, Lawrence and Fontana had
made a major archaeological discovery and Flecker was
somehow to help them get it shipped back, through
diplomatic bags, to London. Like the Elgin Marbles.
Perhaps they had unearthed one of the fabled tombs of
the Pharaohs, or found Joshua's trumpet or the Ark of
the Covenant. If this were the case it would at least
account for Lawrence's secretiveness.

He had another area of worry – that they knew so
much about him – his politics and his joining the Fabi-
ans, if only to get into their social circle; his university
career; his poetry; even his sexual history, his relationship with Jack Beazley and their founding of the Praxiteles Club – not to mention the supposedly homosexual
Narcissus Club. . . . Between them, Fontana and Lawrence knew more about him than his mother. Or his
wife.

One other detail bothered him – slight but intriguing.
As they had left the naval staff officer's room Lawrence
had picked up Flecker's whisky glass from under the
chair and said, 'Don't forget this. We must be careful
not to leave a hint behind.'

At the time he had given it little thought but now,
sitting in the solitude of the verandah, he wondered
about it. After all, the cleaners would be the first to find
it and they would simply take the glass to the kitchen
for washing. No one would know whose it was.

It was then he remembered, although he could not explain why the memory returned to him at that precise instant, a statement of Hogarth's at one of the discussion meetings in Magdalen. He was sure it was in college; he could recollect being surrounded by books and Attic vases at the time. Hogarth had made an outrageous statement which they had all seriously debated without arriving at a conclusion.

He could hear the man's words, spoken with cynical, dogmatic conviction:

Information and knowledge are the most important and powerful of weapons. And why, gentlemen? Because they can be used not only in war but also in peace, and not only against our enemies but also our allies. No alliance is ever permanent. The sands of politics and history are shifting all the while, and the only safe and solid position in that insecure place is the rock of wisdom.

2

Aleppo, Syria:
12–14 February 1912

At the end of the narrow street, as if squatting over the heads of the grey, dusty asses sandwiched between the lattice-wood walls of the three-storey buildings, was the ruin of the citadel of Aleppo.

As Flecker walked along the street, avoiding the laden baskets on the donkeys, the dirt whipped into tiny eddies at his feet. A fine floss of wool drifted, like the down of summer seeds, from a doorway where a man was beating a fleece with a long and wiry whip.

Flecker watched the castle shaped against the leaden sky. It was a legendary fortress, solid and austere: built by Malik es-Zaher, a son of Saladin, even the zealous Crusaders had balked at attacking it. Now, balanced on the sky, it was moving like the rainbow's end, always there, seemingly unattainable.

The street was not busy. It was afternoon, a time for prayer, and many were either in the mosques or the privacy of their courtyard houses. Only the donkey boys were about, and an old man emptying his hookah on to the cobbles a hundred yards ahead. The boys were shouting and cajoling their beasts, prodding them with sticks or futilely striking their rumps. No matter how hard they were beaten, their animals refused to move either faster or slower. Time had decreed for them their own allotted speed, and neither man nor moment could alter it.

Flecker's meeting with Fontana had been detailed,

fascinating and somewhat daunting. They had sat in his office in the Consulate, a wrought-iron stove burning in the corner and radiating a comfortable warmth. Between them was a desk no bigger than a folding card-table, upon which were spread several folders – dossiers with official insignia upon them, tied together with fading pink ribbon. Several bore red wax seals cracked and split by opening. Beneath the folders were a number of maps and sketch plans.

Fontana began their meeting with an informality to which Flecker was unaccustomed.

'Coffee, James? I've managed to pick up some roasted beans from British East Africa. Someone I know is trying to get it to grow there. A cousin of my father . . . Thinks he's on to a winner, but I don't see it. Has to cut down acres of jungle to get a crop in and, soon as it's leafed, either a herd of antelope or the local elephants or a swarm of blessed locusts home in on it like pigeons to a loft and strip it bare in hours. Apparently these beans survived only because he has a twenty-four-hour guard on them. Do try them. A quite new taste. . . . Have you been to Aleppo before?'

Flecker shook his head as Fontana poured two cups from a pot on the stove and returned to the table. He handed one to his guest and gently stirred his own with a silver pilgrim spoon, the metal ringing dully on the china.

'Black with sugar: only way to take coffee.'

Flecker made no reply. The scent of the coffee rose from the cup: delicate, not aromatic like Turkish coffee.

'Now – I'll try to be brief – this can be an awfully complicated business. In any case, Tom Lawrence will fill you in on the detail. It's all to do with the railways . . .'

'I thought it might be,' Flecker answered. 'There's been a lot of ciphers through to Beirut.'

'Quite! Well, I'll put you in the picture a bit, as I'm sure you're not completely *au fait* with the situation. In short, the Germans are building a railway from Berlin to Baghdad. The ultimate destination isn't there: it's Basra on the Gulf. They're planning, of course, to by-pass Suez, break our monopoly – as they put it – on sea trade and somehow mould the Ottoman Empire into their own India. Not an unambitious plan, is it?'

Flecker shook his head.

'In 1902,' Fontana continued, staring at a closed dossier before him as if able to scan the pages through the covers, 'the route was agreed through the Toros Mountains – the Germans' partners in the scheme are a French firm and the Imperial Ottoman Bank. The plan was to build through to Aleppo, then on to Nusaybin and Mosul. Three and a half years ago, Sultan Abdul Hamid gave permission to carry on beyond Aleppo and to bridge the Euphrates. They've got that far up to now. The bridge is under construction.

'All along, we've kept an eye on the project, as you will know. But what we really need is a close view, a point of contact to listen in, appreciate, understand, pick up gossip . . . All the paraphernalia of knowledge. That's been the hard part. The Germans, understandably, have been wary of us. However, we now have the ideal opportunity and at the bridge site.'

There was a knock on the door and Fontana looked up, covering the sketch plans and maps with a dossier.

'Come,' he said authoritatively.

A young Englishman wearing a chalk-grey suit and a wing collar entered briskly, his polished shoes tapping on the floorboards.

'I believe you requested CH1200–stroke-11, sir?' He held out yet another folder tied with reddish ribbon.

'Yes, I did.' Fontana stood up and accepted the folder. It was thick, quite heavy and his arm dropped an inch or two as he received it. 'Thank you, Braymell. That will be all. See we're not disturbed, will you?'

'Of course, sir,' the young man replied and closed the door quietly behind him.

Fontana slid the new folder under the maps and sketches.

'Where was I? Yes – the opportunity. They're bridging the river just north of Jerablus. The British Museum has part ownership of an archaeological mound there on the west bank – believed to be the ancient Hittite city of Carchemish. Lawrence visited the site in 1909 on a reconnaissance both of the potential for the dig and the intentions of the Germans.

'Last year, HM Government was persuaded to get permission to dig after the railway was built, which would give us a perfect close view of the traffic which we'd need. Apparently the railway company – that is, the Germans – had previously been given . . .' – he opened one of the folders and thumbed through several sheaves of papers before extracting a single page – '. . . a ten-kilometre zone down either side of the track. Now that would have scotched us good and proper! Anyway, we've got permission and Lawrence is now operating the dig; has been since last year. Even by the time he arrived the Germans already had half a dozen engineers on site with two dozen tents and a labour force collected.'

'Is Lawrence an archaeologist?' Flecker enquired.

'Sort of. He's a great admirer of churches, I'm told, and he's visited Crusader castles all over the Middle East. I dare say Hogarth's taught him a good bit, too.'

Fontana raised his coffee cup and Flecker did likewise, noticing as he drank that Fontana was watching him. His thoughts returned briefly to his meeting with Lawrence two months ago. Then he had been asked if he had known Hogarth, and of the meetings in his rooms in Magdalen.

'You should know a few things about Hogarth,' Fontana said, breaking into his thoughts.

'I know a good bit already.'

'That's as maybe. He's a complex man and you know only the autocratic don and antiquarian. He has a few other facets to his diadem. For example . . .' Fontana looked at Flecker's cup. 'More coffee?'

'Thank you, no.'

'Don't mind if I do?'

Fontana rose and went to the stove where the coffee pot was burbling quietly. He removed it and stood holding it in his right hand, the cup in his left. He made no immediate attempt to pour.

'Without a doubt, David George Hogarth is a highly complex character. Let me give you a fact or two for background. He's in overall charge of the Carchemish dig, but not just in a search for Hittite pots and relics. He's also in Intelligence. He runs a network or two here and there, in the Middle East and Eastern Europe.'

'A network?'

'Groups of people who gather information. Some quite obviously, some covertly, as it were.'

Flecker could hear Hogarth in his mind: 'Information and knowledge are the most powerful of weapons. The rock of wisdom, the rock of wisdom.'

'You mean sort of spies?' he asked.

'I mean exactly that.'

Fontana poured his coffee and dropped two generous pinches of brown and gold sugar crystals into the liquid before replacing the pot on the stove.

'So Hogarth is . . .'

'Exactly. He was out here last February, early March. Stayed at Baron's. Where you are staying. One of the best hotels in this part of the world. Of course, he does want finds – preferably exciting antikas, objects he can pack off back to Britain to keep his patrons satisfied. He's not really after close archaeological analysis . . .'

His words faded and he studied Flecker's face.

'I think I see,' Flecker responded pensively.

'I was sure you would. But to put you fully in the picture. Briefly, Lawrence is no use unless he can get his information back – as well as his Hittite bits and bobs, of course. This is where you come in. There are four of us in on all of this – Lawrence is the operator in the field, myself a kind of overall manager in the area, Hogarth's the top man in charge and you are the field officer. Not something you're quite used to, I dare say?'

'No. Nothing like it. I'm used to a somewhat longer chain of command.'

'We – the four of us – have no use for secretaries, under-secretaries, attachés, ambassadors and all that rigamarole. We are a small self-reliant network.'

From somewhere across the city a muezzin was calling the faithful to prayer. Fontana looked at his watch and gazed at the leather-bound travelling clock on his desk for reassurance.

'I'm going to let you take these to the hotel.' He patted the maps and folders. 'These two hold background reading – the maps are self-explanatory, as are Lawrence's drawings and outline plans. This' – he picked up the dossier the cipher clerk had brought in – 'contains photographs. You have to sign them out, naturally. And I want them back here, read and understood, before dark. If you've any questions ask me when you return them. I'll be here. Oh, and give them back to me personally. Not to one of the others. All quite clear?'

Picking up the folders and maps and sliding them into his leather portfolio, Flecker replied, 'Yes, I think

I've got the general idea. However, I'm still somewhat hazy as to my own specific responsibilities.'

'You are the front man, so to speak. You contact Lawrence, liaise with him, assess and sort his information, send it on to me. And to Hogarth. You may have to ship back some of his finds as well. You'll need to use your initiative a good deal.'

'Why do we not work through Latakia?' Flecker asked as he stood to leave. 'It's a port far nearer to Aleppo than Beirut.'

'Too close to the Turks, too close to the Germans. Both have plenty of spies in Latakia,' Fontana replied.

As he placed his hand upon the knob of the door, Flecker turned and asked, simply, 'Why me, sir?'

'Raff!'

'Why me, Raff?' he repeated. 'As you must know, my service hasn't been exactly free of blemishes. My examinations . . .'

'Hogarth selected you. You aren't his first, by a long chalk. He's been doing this sort of thing off and on since the turn of the century, and he had his eye on you when you were up at Oxford, as he has had on many another.

'It's not your academic prowess, but you're like the rest of us, James. Many-sided. A poet, a writer, a diplomat . . .' He paused for a brief moment before going on, 'One not cast in a mould. Take Braymell. King's School, Gloucester, followed by King's College, Cantab. A king's man through and through. I'd not be surprised to discover a birthmark like a royal monogram emblazoned on his buttocks. He doesn't question which king so long as it's an English one. He treads the straight and narrow like a nun. He's the backbone of the service. You are not, James. The service can exist without you. Yet it needs your sort – Lawrence's sort

– from time to time. Can't do without it, in fact. And one of those times is now.'

'I've received no training . . .' Flecker began.

'You don't need training. Just native guile, a sharp wit, an adaptable character, the ability to keep yourself – your true self – hidden. Just as you do . . . so well.'

Flecker smiled. 'My wife?'

'Needless to say, she must know none of this. Your trips up here will be just official business.'

Flecker had left the Consulate fired with thoughts of the task ahead, although it was not for this that he had entered the Consular Service. At times, he anticipated a career in a more senior position but then, at others, he wondered what had motivated him to join in the first place. Acting Vice-Consul, to which rank he had been promoted on his posting to Beirut, was, for all its apparent grandeur of title, a comparatively junior position. He had no ambition to be an attaché, certainly none to be a consul or ambassador. After a few tours of duty he had expected to be returned to London to perhaps live an innocuous and quiet life as a civil servant in Whitehall: lunch in his club off Trafalgar Square, a night a week at the theatre with Hellé, literary meetings with fellow poets. If that did not work out, then he'd become a schoolmaster like his father, sunk into the worlds of academe and literature. If he failed his examinations a few months hence, he would anyway have to recourse to that alternative career.

For the moment, however, he reasoned, life would be a good deal more exciting, not merely because of the nature of his new duties but also because they would involve Lawrence.

Ever since they had met in the Beirut Consulate, Flecker had been unable to shift the other man from his thoughts. Struggling with a rhyme or a metaphor, grappling with his Turkish verbs and pronunciation, he would find his mind recapitulating their meeting, Lawrence's appearance and charisma, Lawrence's intimate knowledge of his own thoughts – thoughts to which, he now appreciated, Fontana was also privy.

With a finickiness more suited to an Arab stallion, one of the donkeys side-stepped the wet patch on the cobbles where the old man had emptied his hookah, the pannier on its side bumping into Flecker, jarring his arm and jolting his train of thought. His fingers involuntarily tightened on the portfolio as he crossed behind the donkey into the Rue Baron and entered his hotel.

'There is a letter for you, sir.' The concierge leaned across the reception desk and proffered an envelope.

Flecker knew before he opened it that it was from Hellé. Her firm handwriting was on the cover and the stamp was clearly postmarked Beirut. He took it to his room, lay on the bed, propped himself on his elbow and ran his finger down the seal. The glue was of a poor quality and it opened easily.

Dearest darling Tiger, [she had written]
  I do pray this finds you well and not too cold. Here the weather has become very cold indeed and I think of you and fear you are not wrapping yourself well. You must. Keep the muffler to your neck and be sure your room in the hotel is well warmed. Drink warm milk. Well – you know all this but I feel I must remind you for you are careless of yourself sometimes, dearest.
  A package has come for you from England. I took the liberty of opening it. It is from Frank Savery and contains a copy of a magazine entitled *Poetry Review*. This is edited by Harold Monro who has also written a letter to you, come today. He is very interested in your poetry and would like to publish some. Isn't this grand news!
  I am burning with unhappiness at your absence and am longing to see you returned safely to Beirut, to me. I will cover

you with my love when you arrive. Think of my hands upon
you as you read.

> Your only loving,
> Pussy.

His eye skipped her signature. She used his pet name
for her, and even to read it with her being so far away
pained him.

There was a postscript: 'Some poems have been
received back, also. It matters not. . . .'

He folded the letter and pushed it beneath his pillow.
On the table before the window was a bundle of manuscript. He stared at it desultorily, lifting the first page.

' "*The King of Alsander*. Chapter One – Blaindon.
The writer of these simple lines, now sadly dead, was
a man of the soil . . ." ' He read the words out loud,
then sighed, dropping the page once more. 'Unhappily,'
he said quietly, 'not sadly.'

He opened the portfolio and balanced the folders
upon the pages of his novel. Settling at the table, he
opened the first folder, and began to read.

For three hours he turned the pages avidly, captivated
by the reports, signals, details of railway construction,
interpretations of activities. Copies of documents –
some of them were not merely manuscript versions but
photographs of the originals – from German embassy
officials to their respective ministries in Berlin, military
maps and topographical studies began to litter the table
top and spread on to the bed. To each was pinned
or appended a typewritten translation with the salient
points underlined neatly in red ink. It was only when
the light coming through the shutters began to fail that
he realised it was time to return to the Consulate.

Before leaving his room he wrote a hurried note to
Hellé confirming that he was keeping warm, that the
cold was not bothering him, and asking her to drop a

card to Monro to say he would reply as soon as he was able.

Fontana was seated at his desk as Flecker was shown in.

'Well, James? A good afternoon's reading?'

'Yes. A quite captivating one. I had no idea it was all so . . .' He searched for the word.

'Conspiratorial? They're devious little beggars, aren't they?'

As the Consul laughed briefly, Flecker thought of how he had once described Fontana in a letter to a friend as a glorious specimen of worn-out aesthetic Genoese aristocracy. It still fitted.

'Any other questions, now you've read it through?'

'A score or more, but they'll come clear in due course, I expect. One or two I should like to ask now, though.'

'Carry on.'

'It would seem, reading through the dossiers, as if we have quite a number of spies in the German camp . . .'

'We have. Just as they have in ours – but you're not to know that, so mum's the word. By the way – not *spies*. Intelligence gatherers, Hogarth calls them.'

It was Flecker's turn to laugh mutedly. 'So I am to be an intelligence gatherer,' he said thoughtfully.

'In a manner of speaking. You're really a sifter and assimilator, a decider and reader and interpreter of the facts. Lawrence will gather it – harvest it. You may occasionally help with the scythe . . .'

Flecker made no response and Fontana studied him, deducing his silence to be a sign of reluctance, of second thoughts.

'You have some fine literary antecedents,' Fontana remarked finally, breaking the lull. 'A good many writers have served our country so – Defoe, Marlowe, Pepys. Perhaps even the Bard himself. All men, in their own ways, not unlike you . . .' – he paused and watched his tiny flattery work – '. . . with their minds busy with creativity as well as reality and a marriage of the two – isn't that the poet's job? The romancer's task? To meld what is to what might be? The *agent d'espionage* has to do much the same thing. Take realities and extrapolate them – see where they might go.'

'I don't see myself as a Samuel Pepys . . .'

'I once saw Pepys's diaries. In London. Have you seen one?'

Flecker shook his head.

'Written entirely in code. Tachygraphy, a sort of shorthand Pepys adapted to his own ends. Having been accused of treason, he was covering his tracks. As for Defoe, that wasn't even his real name. He was actually Daniel Foe – D. Foe – but he grandified it a touch . . . All men like yourself; dreamers, yet with their feet on the ground.'

Outside Fontana's room someone was turning a key in a lock.

'How long will my assignment last?'

'Can't tell. A few months, maybe. Perhaps longer; it's not like a posting. You'll remain attached to Beirut, but you'll be travelling up here a fair bit.'

'When it's over, then what?'

'You'll go back to normal duties. And, while it's on, you'll still have to carry on in the ordinary way. Keep on studying for the examinations, do your bit about the Consulate. You'll find your work-load reduced a good deal.'

'That will not go amiss,' Flecker replied with a rueful smile.

'The worst thing after one of these assignments is the return to normal working. It seems so innocuously tedious. Until the next time . . .'

Another key jangled in a lock. It was a signal for Fontana to begin clearing his desk. He tapped his files into a pile and rose, taking them to a steel cabinet bolted to the wall of his office.

'May I be frank for a moment?' Flecker asked.

Fontana pushed the files on to a shelf and closed the solid cabinet door.

'Of course.'

'I've been finding the work in Beirut dreary. Stultifying. To be truthful, I've been thinking of leaving the service and going into teaching.'

'I sensed as much.'

'This might be a respite from that boredom.'

'Indeed.' Fontana locked the cabinet. 'I think I would guarantee it.'

'I'm afraid of afterwards . . .'

'Perhaps there will be no afterwards. If you perform well there's always the chance of moving on to other, similar work. And, if anything happens, they'll see you all right.'

For a moment a look of fearful apprehension ghosted across Flecker's face. Fontana saw it.

'I'm not being melodramatic; I don't mean you'll be killed or something. That's highly unlikely, in fact – even for Lawrence. But should you meet with a patch of ill-luck, they – the masters in Whitehall – will see you are cared for. And your wife.' He tugged a gold hunter from the inside pocket of his jacket. 'Speaking of which, if I'm not home soon, my wife will be wondering.'

They parted at the main entrance to the Consulate. There were few people in the street. On the wind were carried the sounds of the *suq* and the noxious stink of fresh camel dung.

'Before you return to Beirut you must come round and dine with us. Winifred's been asking to meet you; she's read your book. And one other thing – stay around the hotel. You should be receiving a visitor; Lawrence is coming down tonight.'

Entry to the castle was by a great stone staircase which led steeply up the sheer limestone slopes of the castle mound, crossing the deep moat on a colonnaded bridge, passing through the forbidding gate built by the Emir Zaher. Set into the massive masonry were arrow-slits; over them projected rock-hewn look-out posts and shelves from which foolish invaders could be stoned or smothered with boiling tar. In the centre of the steps were two smooth slopes, up which wheeled vehicles could be dragged.

Half-way up, Flecker had to step aside to allow a mule and cart to overtake him. A youth in baggy pantaloon trousers was urging his charge onwards. Lawrence, who was walking on one of the stone ramps, also had to get out of the way.

'They're removing stone,' he commented, the mule snorting as it went by. 'It's been going on for centuries, stone robbing. Except that it isn't a crime. It's a re-use of resources. The Normans did it to Roman buildings in Britain, those the Anglo-Saxons hadn't already plundered. Many a parish church in the shires has Roman stones in its tower.' He looked out over the ancient roofs of the city below. 'One wonders how much of the houses began life up here as fortifications.'

Where the vaulted entrance-way reached the first of its sharp angles, changes of direction controlled by iron gates and cut to confuse and slow any invader with the extreme good fortune to have reached so far, Flecker had to pause to catch his breath. He was wheezing with the effort of the climb. Lawrence, who had walked ahead, came back and squatted on the ground like an

Arab, down on his haunches with his forearms resting on his knees.

'We'll wait for a bit. Give you a chance to get your second wind.'

Flecker nodded, gasping an apology. He was bathed in sweat despite the chill wind.

'No need to excuse yourself. It's a steep ascent.'

'You seem to be able to get up it like a chamois,' Flecker replied.

'Practice. I was out here for quite a while in . . . well, a while back. Visiting all the Crusader castles. I've had a lot of experience of scrambling over – and up – such places.'

After Flecker had rested, they set off once more. Through the entrance gate, they came upon a wide, stepped street, to the left of which were three ruins with low domes upon them. Higher up was a larger domed building and, above that, a square minaret; to the right were more ruined, once substantial, buildings.

'It's more a city than a castle,' Flecker remarked, making steady if slow progress. Lawrence kept by his side, obviously eager to be getting on; there was an air of almost innocent excitement about him.

'It was a city. Built in 1183, although there was a settlement here in 2000 BC. Abraham is said to have stayed here to milk his goats. Look, this building was a shop.'

He raised his hand and touched the smooth stone wall. He did not slap the stone as if to reinforce his point, nor simply brush it in a desultory way as if it were a transient proof of his statement. He stroked it as if it were alive and could respond.

Flecker peered inside. Some rubble had recently been shifted, a dark stain on the masonry showing where it had lain hidden for centuries.

'It was a bakery,' Lawrence announced. 'See the urns

57

for flour? Against the far corner. There are several such store-rooms here, and merchants' houses, deep-cut wells – even dungeons. And the mosque . . .' He looked up to the minaret and Flecker followed his eyes. 'The building with the low dome was once a small Byzantine church.'

They walked further up the castle hill, passing the mule tethered to an iron ring jammed temporarily into a crevice. From nearby echoed the thud of a heavy hammer on stone.

'After Zaher, the Egyptian Mamluks took it over until it was conquered by the Mongols in 1260,' Lawrence went on. 'And again, in 1400, by Tamerlane the Turk. He butchered twenty thousand of the city's inhabitants and made hillocks of their heads.'

The two men reached the top of the street of steps. Below them, in the early morning light, was stretched the city of Aleppo. The domes and minarets, the mud-coloured houses upon which the sun had yet to break through high hazed clouds, the courtyards and narrow alleys and the wider thoroughfares rested under a drift of wood-smoke and the first rising of the day's dust. The air was cool but had lost its chill. The wind had died.

'You know so much of the place,' Flecker said admiringly.

'I've studied it. It's a fascinating land. The history is so embedded into our own, so much a part of our cultural background.'

'I have to admit I find it all a bit boring.'

Lawrence, who had been scanning the city with his eyes alert for every detail, turned to face his companion. There was a hint of castigation in his look.

'Boring!' he exclaimed. 'How can you . . .' His voice rose but then fell again immediately. 'I think I can see how you would find it boring out here. At least, in

Beirut – surrounded by the stiff collars and starched shirts, the etiquette and the diplomacy. But away from them . . . Just as it is in any country – get out to the people, explore the land with an open mind, be receptive to the spirit of the country and you can't help being' – he paused – 'enthralled. You must teach yourself to be able to accept . . . suffer . . . the drudgery. Suffering always cleanses the soul.'

'My job's in Beirut,' Flecker said with a touch of dejection.

'Then we shall have to see about that. Get you out from behind your desk and into the desert. With the Bedouin! Now, why don't we climb the minaret? It's a little rickety here and there, but I've been up and the view is quite beyond words.'

'I don't think I could make it,' Flecker admitted. 'But you go on. I'll wait here.'

'Right. I'll not be long.'

A smooth boulder by the side of the ruin of the mosque afforded Flecker a resting place. He lowered himself gingerly on to the stone, the cold quickly seeping through his trousers.

His companion's words echoed in his mind. To go into the desert with Lawrence would be wonderful: to visit the desert tribes and meet them, to see at first hand their way of life, their black, tented encampments. . . .

Yet his motives were not purely literary. They were emotional. He wanted to be there with this man, this friend of dear Jack Beazley, this thinker and archaeologist, climber of castles and wanderer of the desert. This spy.

When he had returned from the Consulate the evening before, Lawrence had already been in Baron's, given the room next to his own, on the front of the building overlooking the street. They had dined together, then sat in Flecker's room and talked well into the night.

Their conversation had ranged from old friends and mutual acquaintances to recently published poetry and to the likelihood that Lawrence's gift to Flecker was genuinely Hittite.

After Lawrence had left Beirut just before Christmas he had sent Flecker a seal upon which was cut a swastika. With the seal had come a terse note: *Hope this reminds you of your Praxiteles Club.*

The message had taken Flecker aback. The club blazer had borne a swastika on the pocket. He remembered then Lawrence's comments at their first meeting, and tried to guess how he had known of the blazer: perhaps, he thought, Jack Beazley had told him. And yet, why should he? However, he found the curio extraordinarily exotic. That it had come from Lawrence's hand gave it an added excitement, and he had used it several times since to seal his personal correspondence.

Certainly, for a while at least, life promised not to be boring and he would be able to thrust aside, if not completely beyond the reach of his thoughts, his fears for his long-term future.

As soon as Lawrence returned from climbing the minaret they left the castle, passed the tomb of the Emir Zaher by the madrassa and made their way through the streets in the direction of the *suq*.

'Have you been into the markets?' Lawrence enquired.

Flecker shook his head.

'Then we'll take a long short cut back to the Consulate.'

'*Ihtæris!*'

The shout came from behind and Flecker started.

A small *arabîyât* was bearing down upon him at some speed, the two ponies pulling it straining at their reins, steam jetting from their nostrils. They had cut a swathe through the people further up the street. Flecker was transfixed, but Lawrence, with an economy of move-ment Flecker marvelled at but to which he could not react, stretched out one arm and pulled Flecker out of the path of the vehicle by his jacket collar. The *arabîyât* jingled and clattered by, the driver cursing loudly.

Flecker was badly shaken by his narrow escape and stuttered his gratitude.

'Don't mention it,' Lawrence said off-handedly before adding more seriously, 'but remember, dear poet, in our line of business it's always best to be alert – eternal vigilance is the price we pay for maintaining a head on our shoulders.'

The covered *suq* was a labyrinth of alleys and sunken passageways with colonnades, stone arches and holes-in-the-wall crowded with merchants, each, according to his trade, in the correct area of the market. In the butchers' *suq* whole sheep's carcasses were being paun-ched, the intestines falling as soft green tentacles to the ground where they slithered, snaking against the bare feet of the butchers. On wooden benches, sheep's heads were being filleted, the joints sawn and chopped. The air was dense with the iron scents of fresh blood and the bitter stink of bile. In the spice *suq* the merchants were offering trays and boxes of cumin and coriander, nutmeg and peppercorns, cloves and henna and aniseed for *arak*; the scents assailed the nostrils like a succession of drugs. In the rope *suq*, the air smelled of hemp. Elsewhere there was the fresh tang of cotton with the oily reek of fleece. Every so often they passed by one of the *caravanserai* opening off the alleys and lanes of the *suq* into grand courtyards in which mules were tethered.

'Khan al-Nahassin,' Lawrence stated as they walked before a grand gateway giving on to a large, flagged courtyard. 'The coppersmiths' *caravanserai*. It was built in 1539 by the Venetians – was their embassy. We had ours in the customs *caravanserai*. Not a lot has changed in four hundred years. And yet, paradoxically, so much has . . .'

'Do you have many Arab friends?' Flecker asked as they left.

'I've many Arab acquaintances,' Lawrence answered. 'Not many friends. But then I have not many European friends either. There is one . . .'

'At Jerablus?'

'At the dig at Carchemish. You will meet him; he is in a way my servant, but . . .'

He said no more and Flecker did not enquire further but, as they reached Rue Baron, Lawrence said, 'His name is Dahoum. You will meet him soon enough.'

Before they parted that evening, Lawrence preferring to travel by night despite the dangers from bands of brigands and being lost in the hilly scrub of the desert, Flecker enquired after the work at Carchemish and his own role.

'Raff will have briefed you well enough,' Lawrence said, 'and what else you need to know will come in time. It is important that the artefacts I send back are re-packaged for the journey home. You'll receive them in an assortment of wrappings. What you must do is wrap everything again in paper, then with straw and finally, if you can get it, with sawdust. Let nothing come within six inches of the outer boxing. Use tea-chests – they are superb. But bind and seal them well. The address . . .'

'. . . is in the file,' Flecker interrupted.

Lawrence frowned briefly and Flecker realised he should not have interjected.

'The work is going well. We are down several layers and I am convinced the site is Hittite. Of course, being a settlement, it's on a hill and gives us a grand view of the railway. Their bridge is coming along famously, too. They use some of our rubble for bedding down the embankment and providing hard core for the track.'

'You mean you are in daily contact with the Germans? The file said you were in communication, but . . .'

Lawrence laughed. It was now his turn to interrupt. 'Oh, goodness me, yes! We often have a jaw together, swap stories. You must meet them when you come up. They are such stolid fellows – thoroughly Teutonic, without a sense of humour or japery. You'll find them very – entertaining: that's the word.'

'When shall I come up?'

'Soon,' Lawrence replied enigmatically. 'Soon.'

The sheet of foolscap was spread before him on the table. Beside it lay his pen, the cap unscrewed, the ink dried on the nib.

He raised the top corner of the paper with his left hand, angled it to catch the light and scanned the writing.

> Where are they, the young man's dreams,
> The statues standing in the darkened streams,
> The ones who search for knowledge, by the night,
> Know only truth and beauty, justice – light:
> Want but to touch the historic shards of earth
> And rattle off their lives in joyous mirth?
>
> Ridden through the glades and gone from home,
> Wondrous as the star o'er the Emir's dome,
> Following their dreamer, blue-eyed, singing
> Into the dun hills beyond the cedars, swinging
> In moonlight, like a lover's . . .

There he had stopped. The lines were becoming tangled with his thoughts, confused with his emotions.

Usually, a poem began with a central theme, an idea of where it was going. This poem would not behave so methodically. It began well enough, but the further it went the more it wanted to draw in – love, passion, anticipation – and the more it suggested a greater landscape of emotions. He was tired, and unable to cope with so wide a vista.

He looked again at the last three lines, crumpled the paper into a ball and, with a flick of his hand, sent it rolling beneath the bed. Then he coughed, pressing his hand to his mouth, his fingers dampening with spittle.

3

Beirut: late February/early March 1912

He could feel the round flesh of her breast nestling beneath his hand, her nipple firm. She was breathing in short, sharp gasps, her ribs lined rigidly against the skin, then softening. He could not see her in the darkness, only feel and hear her.

He lay beside her, letting his hand run from one breast to the other, then off her body altogether. He silently counted to ten, knowing she would be doing the same, then let his right hand slide over her belly and downwards. She held her breath for a moment before sighing deeply. He would have done likewise – they had acted in unison in the first two months after their marriage when such rituals were established – but knew that to do so would have rasped his throat.

She had slept deeply: they had made love once already that night. He could still sense her fingers and nails where they had dug into his back, leaving dark half-moon scars. On his buttocks the deep pink marks of her hands still smarted. He wondered if his own hand-marks were stinging on hers.

Now she was no longer fully asleep but semi-consciously thinking of him, registering his movements as if they were part reality, part fantasy.

Gently he moved his fingers between her thighs. They were plump and he felt her warm moist flesh give at his pushing, only to close again upon his hand as soon as the pressure was halted.

She moved her head in the pitch night and spoke. Her first words were too loud but she soon grew aware of their noise, reducing her voice to a whisper.

'*Quelle heure* . . . What time is it? It's so dark.'

'About four-thirty,' he whispered back. 'The night is always darkest towards the dawn.'

He moved his fingers once more and her stomach tightened, then relaxed. She eased herself up towards his arm, her rough hair rubbing on his wrist. Then she let herself fall again to the warm envelope of the cotton sheets and the mattress.

'Do you want to?' he asked, unsure of how to interpret her movement.

'Oh, yes, Roy . . .'

Her words were so soft they were almost inaudible.

'How?'

'How I like it this time, my Tiger,' she replied.

'Like that,' he answered, and she knew what he meant.

For a moment she did not move. Her pattern of breathing altered. Slowly she turned on to her side, her back to him, then moved again until she was lying flat on her front. He ran his hand along her, felt where her breast was pressed out below her arm, smooth against the sheets. With his other hand he tugged the blankets over them.

'Yes, Roy.'

He had asked no question. It was a part of their ceremony.

He moved his leg over her buttocks and lay down upon her back, his hands thrusting under her hips, his mouth against the loose hair behind her ear. It smelled of the wood-smoke from the fire which had long since extinguished itself. He nuzzled into the hair, searching for her ear with his lips.

'Yes, Roy,' she whispered again.

He drew his legs together and squeezed his knees between her own. She arched herself into the air, raising him upon her as a wave might a bather. He felt her press against him, hot and wet, and he pushed into her, his hands under her guiding him.

'Yes, Tiger!' Her whisper was now hoarse and demanding. She thrust herself up at him, her back bending beneath him. He put his hands on her breasts, clawing his fingers into the softness, his nails like talons.

She moaned softly and he clung to her, slid his hands on to her belly, scouring her skin. She hissed in her breath and groaned.

'Bite, Tiger!'

He bit her shoulder, yet she did not wince.

'Pat me with your paws again,' she whispered.

He let go of her breasts, thrust the bedding off his back and brought his hands hard against her thighs. His hands tingled at the contact with her.

'Growl!' she commanded, her words half-muffled by the pillow. 'Growl to me like a tiger-cat.'

But he did not obey. Instead he forced himself deeper into her. And, within his mind, he saw her in the darkness bowed under him, and, in the air over her head, two piercing blue eyes watching him, scrutinising him with a slightly quizzical stare.

As he woke he heard what at first he thought was someone letting off firecrackers. There was a staccato rattle followed by a silence, then another rattle. He eased his feet out of the bed and tugged his pyjama trousers over his hips, tightening the cord. She stirred as he raised his weight off the mattress but remained asleep.

Flecker tugged aside the curtains and squinted at the daylight. Outside the hotel annex in which were the

Fleckers' quarters, it was a clear day with high, hazy cloud . . . or it might have been that the windows were misty with their night's breath. He went to rub the pane and, as his hand touched the glass, it reverberated like a drum. At the same time came a dull rumble.

Flecker was fully awake now, and knew it was gun-fire: not just small-arms fire but the bass explosion of big guns – naval armament.

He gazed out of the window. Over the flat or low-pitched roofs, over the tousled mops of palm trees, out in the sea roads beyond the harbour were two grey warships. A puff of leaden smoke was drifting astern of them on a gentle, on-shore breeze.

As speedily as he could Flecker dressed, ran his ivory comb through his hair and left the building. Outside he was fortunate enough to spot a passing trap and ordered the driver to go towards the Consulate. The man was loath to take him.

'The Muslims . . . Some people are already dead.' His face was a drab olive hue. 'I am a Christian,' he pleaded in English. 'There will be a massacre.'

'So am I!' Flecker retorted. 'Now turn your horse.'

As they proceeded through the streets, people were milling in groups, waving their arms and shouting. At each explosion they automatically ducked, but did not cease expostulating and gesticulating. The horse bucked and flinched at the noise, but kept on going under the regime of the driver's whip.

The Consulate door was shut but, as the trap slewed to a halt – the driver already half turning his horse for a retreat – the doorman opened it and Flecker rushed in to see Robbins standing in front of him with a crow-bar in his hand. He was pointing it at Flecker's belly.

'What on earth is going on?' Flecker shouted as another explosion echoed over the city.

'It's the Italians . . .' Robbins lowered the metal bar

and it rang on the flagstones. 'Two of their battle-cruisers are bombarding the harbour; they're trying to sink the gunboat at the quay . . .'

'Their whole navy against a bath-tub!' Flecker exclaimed with evident amazement. 'Where's the Consul-General?'

Robbins jerked his thumb upwards. 'I'm guarding the entrance. No one else here.'

Flecker took the stairs three at a time and, at the Consul-General's door, knocked. There was a long pause before he was bidden to enter.

'Flecker reporting for duty, sir.'

Cumberpatch was standing at the window with a large bellows camera mounted on a wooden and brass tripod. The metal glinted in the light.

'Morning, Flecker,' he replied, not turning round. 'What do you make of this, eh? Damned Italians! Why they have to bring their war with the Turks to our doorstep . . . Damnably ironic, them trying to hole that gunboat – it was only recently refitted in a basin in Genoa. God knows what they think they're doing. Half their shots are wide of the target – hitting the quayside and the docks left, right and centre. Must be a bloody scene down there . . . By Jove!'

He quickly undid one of the brass butterfly nuts on the tripod and realigned the camera. After a moment he pressed the black rubber bulb which operated the shutter; there was a metallic snap and hiss as the bulb reflated.

'Don't know what exposure this ought to be on – taken a bit by surprise.'

He removed the plate from the back of the camera and inserted another from a box on a nearby chair.

'Anything I can do, sir?' Flecker enquired.

He knew he would be dismissed. Cumberpatch had a low opinion of Acting Vice-Consul Flecker: he was a poet and therefore not much higher up the human ladder than the Italians themselves, with their romanticism, versifying and screeching operatics.

'Don't think so, but thanks for coming in. Jolly thoughtful of you. Just the sort of action we need from a vice-consul. Robbins is holding the fort.'

Yet another explosion sounded from the direction of the quay. It was somewhat more muffled. Cumberpatch leaned towards the window.

'Got her at last!' he exclaimed. 'A direct hit on the gunboat. About time . . .' He pressed the shutter again. 'Look, I suggest you get on back to your quarters. Take care of your young wife.'

For a moment, Flecker thought he sensed a hint of sarcasm in the Consul-General's voice.

'Are you quite certain, sir?'

'Quite. Nothing you can be doing about here. Take a *cavass* with you – one downstairs somewhere. They sent over a few as soon as the trouble started. And exercise caution as you go, we've heard a number of Europeans have been murdered already. Can't be sure, of course – war's the mother of rumour. See you when it's all died down a bit. Damned Italians . . . Suppose the Druses'll be round here in a few hours, wanting action. Damned Muslims . . .'

He turned back to the window, reaching at the same time for another photographic plate.

Flecker ran along the corridor to his office, slammed open the door and fumbled inside his desk. At the back of the drawer was a revolver. He rapidly thumbed some shells into the magazine and left the office without closing the drawer.

The *cavass* was standing beside Robbins, his fez awry and his hand gripping his revolver which remained in its holster. Without much difficulty Flecker persuaded the Turkish policeman to obtain a carriage and accompany him back to his quarters. The man slipped out of the Consulate door and, within five minutes, returned with a carriage in which was already seated a European in a fedora and overcoat which he had unbuttoned; in his hand was a sword-stick.

Flecker made a dash for the carriage, expecting the street before the Consulate to be crowded, but it was completely empty.

'Russian,' the man with the sword-stick began in a thick accent. 'Vice-Consul Vladimir Ko . . .'

His words were lost in the clamour of the carriage setting off, the horse's hooves sparking on the road cobbles, the driver bellowing at his animal. The *cavass* rocked next to the driver as they turned the first corner.

Ahead of the galloping horse, the people milling in the streets gave way, running to one side and waving cudgels, swords and their fists at the carriage. The Russian waved his sword-stick back until Flecker was able to convince him, in French aided with desperate sign language, that it would be better if he sheathed it and they – as diplomats – did not appear belligerent. At the same time he gripped his revolver in his pocket, determined if it came to it to shoot through the material.

At one sharp corner, the driver was obliged to slow the carriage to avoid turning it over. As they negotiated the right-angle in the street they were faced suddenly with an angry mob, bearing down on them from a side road. The leaders were brandishing rifles and bayonets; those following wielded curved cutlasses and antiquated flintlocks. The entire crowd was screaming and hollering.

'Oh, God!' Flecker cried and cocked his firearm inside his pocket.

The *cavass* spun round in his seat and waved his revolver aimlessly at the mob. It did nothing to deter them, the front runners being pressed on by the weight of numbers behind.

A voice in the crowd shouted above the rest, '*Italya! Italya!*' and the remainder of the horde took it up as a chant.

Flecker knelt up on the seat of the carriage and, mustering all he could of his insubstantial command of Arabic, shouted at the top of his voice, 'English! *Ingiltira!* We are English diplomats.'

His words went unheeded as the crowd surged nearer. Bayonets and cutlasses swung in the air. Flecker saw a rifle raised and pointed vaguely in his direction; it was wavering to and fro as its owner ran.

'*Nous sommes Anglais!*' he bellowed. In the vain hope that someone in the mob might understand English instead, he added, 'We are British!'

The carriage rocked violently to the left and Flecker had hastily to snatch at a metal rod on the side of the folded canopy to prevent himself falling on to the Russian and his sword-stick which, once again, was unsheathed.

'For Christ's sake, put that bloody thing away!' Flecker roared. 'You'll impale one of us on it soon.'

The Russian got the gist of Flecker's outburst and grudgingly replaced the blade.

There suddenly appeared at Flecker's side two Turkish soldiers, rifles in their hands. They leaned over the rear of the carriage and levelled their barrels at the approaching rabble, now less than twenty yards off.

'*Büyük Britanya!*' Flecker shouted, pointing to himself and again almost losing his balance. The Turkish soldier by him nodded and grinned. Flecker sat down heavily in the seat and uncocked the revolver in his pocket.

The driver of the carriage whipped the horse and it lurched forwards, neighing loudly with fear and pain.

Flecker saw a thin rule of blood beginning to ooze from the creature's left flank.

They careered through the side streets at a breakneck speed, the wheels jolting and smashing on kerbs, the iron hoops of the wheels screeching on the cobbles, the springs creaking and the woodwork snapping under the strain.

Eventually they arrived outside the small hotel. Hellé had insisted they move in the New Year to the centre of town, nearer the Consulate, and Flecker – who had at the time considered the change unnecessary for his health and inappropriate for his muse – was now certain it had been ill-advised. The centre of town was near his work and the world he wanted to avoid; now it was also the scene of an impending massacre of Christians, if history was any guide.

As the carriage slewed to a halt Flecker spied Hellé standing in the street, anxiously watching out for him. He bade the Russian vice-consul a hasty farewell and bundled his wife inside, slamming the door and bolting it, saying, 'How foolish can you be? Outside? You've no idea what is going on!'

'I was perfectly safe,' she remonstrated. 'The door porter is at the end of the street keeping watch.'

They walked through to the annex in which they had their small apartment. Flecker's nerves were taut and he was sweating. She saw the beads of perspiration slide down from beneath his hair to melt into his collar.

Once in their rooms he collapsed into a chair, his face flushed. At her enquiry, he told her what had happened.

'Were you afraid?' she asked.

'Yes. I suppose I'm a coward at heart. For all the non-pacifist in me, I was terrified by the . . . They must have been Muslims – bent on a traditional letting of Christian blood, no doubt. I suppose keeping my head saved us. And the soldiers, they deserve medals. The *cavass* was next to useless.'

'I should like,' Hellé said quietly, 'to kill a Turk.'

He looked at her with astonishment. She was standing erect before him, her hands at her sides, her fingers curled in a half-fist.

'I should like to shoot him . . .' she decided philosophically.

'That's because you are a Greek. I think, in the circumstances, I should like to kill a damned Italian.'

'That,' she retorted, 'is because you are English.'

A week later, Flecker and Hellé attended a ceremony at the Consulate. It was brief and polite. The two soldiers who had jumped on to the carriage were each presented with a silver cigarette case and the driver was similarly rewarded.

Cumberpatch stood before the three of them, paraded in a row like schoolboys brought before their headmaster. The cigarette cases were on a tray covered with a damask cloth. The bellows camera on its tripod still stood at the window, pointing in the direction of the harbour.

'It is with great pleasure,' Cumberpatch pronounced, 'that I speak on behalf of all of us and say that we are most grateful to you for saving the life of our Acting Vice-Consul, Mr James Elroy Flecker. Without your coolness of action and bravery of spirit, your courage and dedication to the cause of preserving human life, we should today be mourning him rather than celebrating his liberation from the jaws of death at your stout hands. I should like' – he turned to the tray on his desk – 'on behalf of His Britannic Majesty's government, to present each of you with one of these fine cases in sterling silver, in recognition of your bravery.'

The two soldiers and the driver smiled sheepishly and scuffed their feet with embarrassment as Cumberpatch handed each of them their present with a small certificate. This done, they shook hands with Flecker, who was just as embarrassed.

'To think!' he said to Hellé in a tone of disgust as they made their way back to the hotel. 'A miserable cigarette case each. The Russians gave them each fifty pounds on behalf of their vice-consul.'

'You aren't, perhaps, so valuable,' she replied, laughing at the joke.

'No, I'm sure you're right,' he answered ruefully. 'But that'll change soon enough, even if they don't know it.'

She smiled at him and understood him to refer to his working harder at his consular examinations preparation, a determination to pass them with merit.

The sun was warm. In the trees, their new leaves emerald green against the blue sky, birds chirruped and whistled unseen. The river flowed sparkling in the dappled light. On the banks, beneath the trees and on glades upon the low hillsides there bloomed red anemones, pink primroses and wild orchids.

As they walked Hellé picked a posy for herself, her fingers, sticky with the sap, stroking the waxed petals of the orchids. Flecker strolled by her side, his walking stick switching at the grass. Out of sight, they could hear tinny sheep's bells.

'It is so beautiful here,' she commented, not for the first time, as they came to a wide bend in the river.

They had already gone three miles, following paths on the west bank, and had reached the valley below a small settlement. Here a number of paths came down to the river and, ahead of them, Flecker saw a group of women collecting water in polished brass vessels.

Apart from the group was a young girl rinsing out an earthenware cooking pot and rubbing the inner surfaces with gravel and ash. There must have been food remaining in the pot for, just off the bank from where she was squatting, a number of minuscule fish were jumping in the water.

Flecker looked at the map he had sketched on a piece of onion-skin paper; over the past few weeks, he had taken to drawing hasty outline maps and then following them up. It was something he thought might come in useful.

'Yes, it is quite splendid. Exquisite. Somehow it doesn't seem right there should be such a river, such a valley, in a land one thinks of as largely Biblical desert . . .'

'It is like the Bible.' She took up his allusion. 'I was given a Bible in English by my mother when I was ten years of age. It had coloured pictures in it by the famous artist . . .' She searched for the name. 'Hunt, I think.'

'Holman Hunt?'

Hellé nodded. ' "The Light of the World" with Christ and his lantern. But always where he walks in the paintings there are flowers. Like this.' She waved her posy around her, then held them out for his inspection. 'Like these.'

'The pale orchids are like your skin.'

'I am getting browner now the sun is stronger and we take these strolls.'

'I didn't mean on your hands.'

She smiled coyly. 'Later, then, I shall allow you to touch my orchid skin.'

'And your orchid . . .'

The young girl stepped past them, the sleeves of her baggy blouse dark and wet, the cooking pot banging on her thigh.

'How long do you think,' Flecker suddenly asked,

'would it take for the water now going past this point
to reach the Baie de St Georges?'

'An hour. Two hours? Three? I cannot tell. Why do
you ask such a strange question?'

'I was thinking of time . . .'

They continued in silence upstream until they
reached, half a mile further on, an olive grove bounded
by a wall which ran into the river. The path deviated
up the hillside to skirt the trees.

'Far enough?'

'Yes, let us go back now, Roy. Soon it will be hot.'

They retraced their steps past the watering spot where
the women had now been replaced by others gathering
water, past the herd of sheep they had encountered
before, scurrying away from them through the trees,
past the bank of orchids.

'Roy,' she asked after a long silence, 'what are we
going to do?'

'Do?' he replied, pretending not to know to what she
was referring.

'Yes, dear one. Do.'

'I don't know. I'm not having much luck with the
poetry, am I? The *English Review* seems to have
changed direction – they've taken nothing since they
printed those two last September. That's six months –
more since I submitted. I'm writing good stuff, I know
it. They just don't want to see it. Maybe Monro will
take something for *Poetry Review*.'

'But in the meantime?'

'How is the sale going?'

'My Athenian house,' she sighed. 'People look at it,
but no one wants to buy. I heard from our agent but
yesterday. He suggests we might try to rent it, but rents
are low and once we do that we cannot sell it. I don't
think—'

'Then we shall have to make do,' he interrupted her,

'and I shall have to write even better poems. They are there, in me, building and swelling.'

'But in the meantime,' she said again, 'is there no other way . . . ? Three hundred and fifty pounds per annum is just not enough. Your salary is insufficient now we are two. And my resources are gone – we used all that in Corfu and Athens last year.'

'Don't spoil it,' he replied, his brow darkening.

'I'm sorry. I am worried.'

He took her hand, his fingers clasping hers and adhering to them with the sap of the flower stems.

'Do not worry,' he reassured her. 'Something will come along.'

'I thought when they made you Acting Vice-Consul we might receive a little more.' She stepped over a rivulet running down from a spring in the trees, his hand guiding her over the dry tussocks sprouting from the water. 'Why did they give you a promotion when your work hasn't . . . well, you know?'

'I do not know, for certain. And what I do know I cannot tell you.'

'We have no secrets.'

'No, we do not, but they have and my work forbids me telling you. Or anyone.'

He wanted to tell her the Consul-General was not in the know, that this was a business above Cumberpatch and his damnable camera, that he – James Elroy Flecker, poet – was now a spy, in the tradition of Pepys and Marlowe and Defoe, that he was personally responsible for an agent who was actively in the field, spying on the Germans, their railway, their empire-building. He wanted to tell her about Lawrence.

'I have met a wonderful man,' he began, as if changing the subject. 'An Oxford man. We first came upon each other here, in Beirut, but I later met him when I went up to Aleppo. Fontana introduced us. His name's

78

Tom Lawrence. He knows so much about the Middle East! He's an archaeologist, a thinker and dreamer. He might be a poet. He's read my work and likes it.'

'It is a shame then that he is not an editor,' she commented astutely.

For more than a mile he spoke of Lawrence, described him, outlined his travels to Crusader castles, his knowledge, his common acquaintance with so many friends back in Oxford – Frank Savery, Jack Beazley. He talked of Hogarth and his meetings, of history and archaeological digs.

'When he's next in Beirut,' he said finally, 'you must meet him. He's a ray of intelligence, a beam of wit, a whole planet of intellect in a universe of' – he tightened his lips – 'diplomats.'

For several days, their animosity had been building.

At first their morning greetings had been merely curt, but they quickly deteriorated to silent sneers. The hostility had its roots in the fact that the Fleckers' neighbours across the hall laid claim to the right of way. The husband was a boorish man, often the worse for the lager which he drank every mid-day with the German proprietor; his wife was a thick-skinned woman with a shrill voice. The matter came to a head when Flecker, emerging from his rooms, found the landing cut in two by several heavy screens which, on impulse, he kicked over. The resulting noise brought the wife out of her rooms in a rage, and her indignant husband up the stairs.

'Well, damn you and your attitude, Flecker! You think you are some high and mighty . . . some little god now you are Acting Vice-Consul, but I tell you – you are acting! You are not made up to that position; you are merely filling in until someone better comes along. In the meantime, you can damn well respect others . . .'

They were standing on the landing between the two apartments in the hotel annex. Flecker's face was dark with rage.

'How dare you . . .'

He wanted to continue, but the neighbour butted in.

'You aren't popular, Flecker. You are a finicky and self-possessed little man with a jumped-up opinion of yourself. You have not – as I hear it – much talent for the job, and less inclination. As regards this landing' – the man turned briefly to his wife for support – 'we have as much right to use it as we want. It is not a part of your quarters; it is common to us all. If I want to move the table here, I shall.' He slammed his fist on the varnished top. 'If I want to put an aspidistra on an antimacassar in the middle of the stairs, I will. If I want to hang a picture of Allah on the walls, I can. I will. This landing is not your personal domain.'

'How dare you speak to me like that,' Flecker muttered. He had ignored the man's remarks about the ownership and right of way on the landing. 'Who do you think you are . . .'

'I know just who I am. Who are you? Some schoolmaster's son with a few books of poetry tucked under his belt. Poetry!' He momentarily raised his eyes to the ceiling. 'Good Lord! Nothing so insignificant in the world as a first – and, I would suggest, a second – collection of poetry.'

' "Poets are the unacknowledged legislators of the world",' Flecker rejoined. 'Shelley, one of the greatest thinkers of the last century.'

'Such vanity! "The vain poet is of the opinion that nothing of his can be too much: he sends you basketful after basketful of juiceless fruit, covered with scentless flowers" – Walter Savage Landor. You, Flecker, are certainly an unacknowledged legislator, if ever I saw one. And I'm sure your colleagues would agree.'

' "Not by wisdom do poets form what they compose, but by a gift of nature, an inspiration alike to that of the diviners and oracles." Would you question Socrates, sir?'

'Nietzsche – "The spirit of the poet craves spectators – even if only a herd of buffalo." I – and my wife – do not intend to remain here any longer gazing on you like struck cows. You keep yourself to yourself, Flecker. And bear in mind this landing is not an extension of your rooms. "Ah God! The petty fools of rhyme that shriek and sweat in pygmy wars" – Tennyson, a poet and one who presumably knew a thing or two about his fellow animal.'

'Are you implying I am an animal!'

Behind him, Hellé watched her husband's neck muscles tighten. Soon, she knew, he would commence coughing and she prayed inwardly it would not start before he was back in their apartment.

'Are not animals territorial? Fighting and guarding their own part of a field? I thought we might be above all that, old boy.'

The sarcasm with which their neighbour spoke these last words enraged Flecker and he raised his fist.

'Do not dare to strike me!'

'You are a contemptible man,' Flecker said quietly. 'An arrogant, objectionable man.'

'As you will. But bear in mind I have as much right to this landing as you.' With that he spun on his heel and went in through his door, taking his wife with him. Flecker and Hellé were left on the landing.

'Let's go in and forget this man. He is nothing to us. Perhaps he is a little right.'

'The hell he is! He is a slanderous upstart. If this were a hundred years ago, I'd see we duelled . . .'

'Then I am glad it isn't, for you're a poor shot with a gun and a coward at your own admission in the face of such weapons. I would rather have you alive and angry than dead and honour settled.'

He rasped as he inhaled.

'Now, see!' she went on. 'You have aggravated your throat. I will get you some milk and we shall forget this man. And, next time, dearest Roy, let me deal with these things. They should not bother you. You cannot write when you are angry.'

'All poetry comes from anger,' he murmured defensively.

'From emotion, not from offence.'

'We must move. I shall put in for alternative quarters as soon as I get to the Consulate. I will not remain here a day longer than I have to.'

As she held the cup of milk to his lips – his hands were shaking so from his encounter that he could not hold it without spillage – she watched his face, his angry eyes, his throat pulsing when he swallowed. Flecker was not one, she knew, to let the episode go by the way. He would continue to harbour the resentment and it would affect his throat and his poetry. She pondered upon yet another move. That, too, would annoy him after her insistence on coming to the hotel. On the other hand, if they could move to a small quiet house somewhere – perhaps the house she had so fallen in love with at Areiya – everything might be well.

As quietly as he could he carefully bolted the door and, with a crowbar, began to ease up the lid of the chest. It was no larger than a cabin trunk, but the sides were constructed of stout wooden planks and it had taken two of the burliest of the Consulate messengers to carry it into the store-room at the rear of the building.

The binding ropes loosened with no problem and, as the nails came loose with a shrill squeak, Flecker's excitement mounted. Through the opening gaps wafted the smells of straw and dry earth, mingling with a herbal, pungent scent like that of incense.

On each side of the chest was crudely drawn, in charcoal, a stencilled outline of a camel under which was an instruction in Arabic, French and English: 'Keep this way up.' Flecker recognised Lawrence's writing.

Their hand was not dissimilar: Lawrence's capital *A* was often rounded, an enlargement of the lower case letter, as was Flecker's, and his capital *D* and *E* were also the same. And, like Flecker, he alternated between styles: on occasion, his capital *I* was an upright bar, at other times looped, his *C* sometimes plain and sometimes looped at the top with a tiny curlicue, his *M* sometimes angular and gaunt or rounded like a hammock slung between two poles.

No doubt, Flecker considered as he prised free the last of the planks, Robbins would have conclusions to draw from their scripts. An angular *M* would be interpreted as decisive, an occasional tented *A* would mean the writer was a lonely person, a curled *C* that he was vain. Wavering styles would indicate a complex character and devious mind.

The top removed, Flecker delved into the straw. It was not wheat straw but a mixture of tall, sharp-bladed grasses, tough papyrus-like reeds interspersed with balls of loosely screwed-up newspaper – a few pieces were pages from *The Times*, but the majority was German newsprint with its thick black printing. Flecker wondered as he extracted the balls one by one – opening them to ensure they contained no artefacts – if a nation's character could be divined from its printing as a man's was from his writing; if it were so, then Germany was a brutal, uncouth land.

At first he found nothing in the chest. It was not until he had gone down nearly a foot that he discovered the first item. It was a small bowl about three inches in diameter at the widest point, fashioned of cream clay in which were flecks of fine grit of a darker colour; some of them were deep brown, others sandy yellow. The vessel was crudely made and coarse to the touch yet, in its primitive way, it was very beautiful and caused Flecker to gasp with delight. He lifted it carefully from its nest of grasses. Someone had twined a band of woven stems around the rim to give it added support.

The bowl was so light. He guessed it did not weigh more than an ounce, perhaps two. To Flecker, it was a miracle it had survived for thousands of years in dirt, periodically flooded, heated by the intense sun or frozen by the northerly winter winds coming down from the slopes of the Kurdish hills and the steppes of Russia.

He sat on the rim of the chest and held the bowl to the sunlight, half expecting to discover it was translucent, like glass. If the light had shone through it, as it might through a finger held before a candle-flame, he would not have been at all amazed. With considerable gentleness, he put the bowl on the table, placing it well into the centre.

The next item he discovered was an incomplete vessel resembling the top half of an amphora. It had been broken about half-way down, and at first he could not guess why Lawrence had included it. It was caked with what appeared to be dried mud. Flecker vigorously rubbed at the large shard with his thumb, the earth flaking off and dirtying his trousers. It was then that he understood why the piece had been sent. Engraved into the earthenware neck were a number of designs made, it would seem, with a broad-toothed comb. Beneath them was a script.

He peered at it. It was a series of hieroglyphs, in some

ways not unlike the Egyptian pictographs he had seen in cartouches. He smiled as he removed from the earliest of writings the wrapping of modern German newsprint.

After half an hour Flecker found himself standing ankle-deep in grass, reed stems, leaves and torn paper. On the table were a collection of four or five dozen artefacts, a few made of rust-bubbled iron but the remainder all clay objects of one kind or another.

The most impressive was part of a carved stone relief upon which was cut the profile head of a man. It was too large, out of proportion to the part of the body remaining on the fragment. The nose was stylised, the lips broad and almost negroid, yet the eye wide and Indo-European. Upon the crown of the head was a hat which made Flecker laugh – it looked exactly like those one saw on gnomes in children's book illustrations.

Beneath the carved slab was a small package wrapped in a square of oilskin and tied around with coarse string. This he put aside.

Yet, despite the excitement of such a treasure of arte-facts, it was the fragile little bowl which most caught his emotions. As he repacked the items in sawdust from several sacks in the room and fresh brown paper, he rehearsed in his mind the first lines of a poem he hoped he might write about it.

After he had completed the task, hammered down the lid with fresh nails and re-stencilled the sides for its passage home, he unbolted the door and went to his office with the package. Once seated at his desk, he cut the string and unwrapped the oilskin.

The package contained a seal with a maze design, a letter, two dispatches for Hogarth and a sketch map of the archaeological dig and the nearby railway construc-tion site.

Flecker unfolded the letter. It was brief but warm:

Jerablus (Carchemish)

Dear James,

All is going splendidly here. We have cut into a new building and you see before you the spoils and treasures. The tiny seal, which I am fairly certain is not of Hittite origin, is for you. A gift to make the pair with the swastika one you already have.

We are looking forward to you visiting us and I have passed on a message to F——— to contact you about that.

There is little to entertain you here, yet much, I suspect, to amuse and divert you.

He signed it 'Ned', adding as a postscript, '*I am Ned to my closest and dearest.*'

Flecker next read through the two dispatches. One was entirely concerned with the dig and he decided not to encode it. It would be a waste of his time, for no one needed to be prevented from seeing the text, the list of discoveries and assumptions on dating, building usage, elevations and depths.

The second, however, dealt only with the German railway builders' progress. They were well advanced with their embankment on the west side and had already begun to construct the first pillars for the bridge, ahead of the raised track bed. Two deliveries of steel girders had arrived and had been found to be too long. Some cutting had been necessary and this was done for hours on end by the locally hired labouring force under the chief engineer's personal supervision. The span, it seemed from the width of the first pillar, might be dual tracked, not single as they had previously supposed. Land a mile back from the river had also been raised and levelled. Lawrence suggested there might be a depot there with sidings and buildings. The dispatch referred to the labelled map.

With infinite care, Flecker traced the map on to a fresh sheet of paper, rewriting the labels as he changed the text from English to the relevant code. It took him quite a while and, by the time he had finished, his wrist ached and his eyes were sore through darting from code-pad to text.

He burned Lawrence's original of the map in the grate, crushing the black ashes to powder with his fingers. Then he sealed the dispatch in a diplomatic bag pouch and secured it with red wax, the black wisps of smoke from the wick settling on his shirt cuffs and smearing them. He wetted his new gift in the jug of drinking water on the filing cabinet and pressed it into the hot circle on the pouch. The seal design transferred itself perfectly. It would confuse the London clerks, he considered, who would expect one of the consular seals; yet it would intrigue Hogarth.

He folded Lawrence's letter and put it in the innermost pocket of his jacket, then took a sheet of paper from the rack on his desk and wrote

                                             Beirut
              Dear Ned,
                   All here safely and seen to.
                   I am as below to my friends.
                                             Yours,
                                             Roy.

Their new rented accommodation was uncomfortable. The window in the bedroom had a loose pane in it and the draught at night, after the wind had cooled from the heat of the early summer day, irritated his throat and nostrils. The water in the tap was intermittent and the woman they employed to bring four additional pitchers a day was lazy. The mattress was lumpy and, in the small kitchen, Hellé discovered a colony of cockroaches behind the pantry cupboard. The meat safe had a tiny hole in the wire mesh and, needless to say, the flies quickly discovered it.

After a week Flecker heard that the house at Areiya was recently vacated and now available, but at a higher rent than they could afford. In response to this information, which he kept from Hellé, he demanded permission to rent a new and better quarter. His request was promptly passed by Forsyth, in charge of the consular staff accounts, to Cumberpatch.

'I'm sorry, Flecker,' Forsyth had explained, 'but the CG gave me the strictest orders not to allocate you a higher allowance. He said he'd do it himself.'

Flecker's interview with the Consul-General was not amicable. Cumberpatch began by stating categorically that there was no additional rent allowance available. Two consular quarters were being repaired just around the corner from the Consulate and Flecker and his wife could gladly have one of those; but neither would be ready before late July. Further, should a new officer be posted to them of course he would take precedence. As Flecker was well aware that two new officers were already on their way out from London he understood immediately his superior's game – and said so.

This annoyed Cumberpatch who began 'Now look here!' 'You cannot simply come in here and demand an upgrade in your quartering. If you had not been so damnably rude and churlish to your previous neighbours you wouldn't be in your present predicament. You have only yourself to blame.'

Flecker made to reply, but the Consul-General continued.

'Don't interrupt! I've not finished yet. Your attitude is, frankly, not only to blame for this situation, but for much else. You seem to me to be an arrogant man, one entirely lacking in tact and diplomacy – which, I might add, does not exactly suit you for your present occu-

pation. With your conceit and self-opinionated standing, I should suggest you would be better employed as
a pedantic schoolmaster.

'I fail – quite fail – to understand what made London
appoint you Acting VC. You would not have been my
choice at all. Your examinations in the service have
been poor, to say the very least, your Cambridge showing was not the most brilliant or distinguished, and your
actions – certainly as regards this fiasco in the hotel
annex – are hardly befitting your rank.'

Flecker's own temper was rising fast. He felt the veins
in his temple throb and his hands grow hot. His mouth
was dry with anger.

'You are not,' Cumberpatch went on, 'the sort we
want in the Levant Service. Or any other. You are
autocratic, you think you are quite above your fellows
with your poetry and your esoteric reading. You are a
haughty and pushy man with no future – no future
whatsoever! – in this service, unless you considerably
mend your ways. I appreciate your bouts of absence on
sick leave; that cannot be helped. But any other fellow,
with the good of the service and his King and country
at heart, would try to make up for his times away when
back at his duty.

'I would suggest you would do well to consider seeking a transfer – preferably out of the service. I believe
they require colonial officers and police inspectors in
the Malayan peninsula, and in Hong Kong. You might
find both the Far East and its climate more to your
liking.'

Cumberpatch leaned forward and fixed Flecker with
his eyes as if to make sure to drive in the message.

Flecker was in two minds as to how to reply, but
he took the one of which he knew Hellé would most
approve.

'Thank you, sir,' he said mildly, without any sign of

the contempt he felt, 'for your comments on my abilities. Now may we return to the matter of my quarters? They are quite inadequate for myself and my wife. If you should like to inspect them?'

Cumberpatch's face blanched. 'You, Flecker,' he muttered quietly, 'are one of the most obnoxious of all the young men I think I have ever encountered. Your audacity . . . And as regards your new reduced duties: I don't know exactly what you are up to – I'm aware I'm not privy to all the details – I assume that it has something to do with your former academic studies, but—'

'I am indeed deeply interested in archaeology,' Flecker butted in, 'and my friends working up on the Euphrates require consular contact.'

To give himself a cover within the Consulate, and to guard against the inquisitive, Flecker had developed what his fellow officers took to be an abiding interest in relics. To enhance this deceit, London had arranged for a letter to be sent from one of the keepers at the British Museum to Cumberpatch, instructing him to give his Acting Vice-Consul time off to follow up and acquire, if he could, items of interest to the museum collection. He was in no doubt that the letter had done little to improve his position in Cumberpatch's eyes, and his superior's antagonism was further increased by the fact that he, a mere Acting Vice-Consul, was trusted with knowledge and information to which the Consul-General was most certainly not privy.

Flecker paused to draw breath, but Cumberpatch cut in on him before he could speak. 'Your friends!' His face was red. 'No doubt in high places. Well, Flecker, so have I . . .'

'I fear, sir . . .' Flecker began.

'You – shut up, sir! You— How dare you make underhand threats . . . I don't give a damn for your friends and their grubbing about in holes in the ground searching for broken pots and bits of rusty metal. As pointless an exercise as the writing of rhyming drivel. Poetry! At least they have something to show for it at the end – of little value, doubtless, but better than versified words.

'And I take exception to one of my staff – even you, Flecker – and especially an Acting Vice-Consul with other pressing consular duties – acting as postman to a pick-and-shovel operation up by the border with Turkey.'

How, Flecker thought, he would enjoy introducing into their conversation the truth – that he was a spy, not a desk-bound pen-pusher; but it was of paramount importance that as few people as possible knew that the ostensible digging at Carchemish was in reality a cover.

'If you'll allow me, sir. I fear, sir,' Flecker ventured again, his voice as urbane as he could make it, 'that this is not a position in which the wielding of inter-departmental or consular power will have any great effect. My friends on the Euphrates' – the expression had obviously displeased Cumberpatch and was worth using again – 'are under commission from the British Museum and have direct support from the government, from Westminster, at the highest of levels, and nothing may be allowed to interfere with their activities.'

The Consul-General sat bolt upright in his chair, his face dark with rage. 'Damn your eyes, Flecker!' He rang a little brass handbell on his desk.

'Forsyth!' he addressed the junior officer as he knocked and entered. 'Assign the Fleckers a grade three renting allowance.'

'If you recall, sir, we have our quota of grade threes already—' Forsyth began.

'Just do it!' the Consul-General ordered. 'And change the blasted rota.'

4

Areiya: May 1912

A few nights later, the moon would rise in its hump-backed phase to indicate that Lawrence and his Arab companion of whom Flecker had heard but still knew nothing would soon be with him.

He had warned Hellé of Lawrence's imminent arrival when they had been seated for luncheon together at the table on the verandah. He had only to go to his office three times a week, to check that matters were running smoothly and to see to those duties of a general consular nature which he had retained.

'So you shall soon meet him,' he had said with undisguised elation, after he had read her the message. 'We must have a meal together that first night he is here. Will you prepare something?'

She had given him only a part of her attention during their meal, much of her awareness being taken by two black and white puppies she had just acquired.

'If he is fresh from the desert and riding his camel,' Hellé replied, fondling one of the dogs, 'he will want to rest. Food is not good immediately after a long journey.'

'What camel? He makes no mention of a camel and is not riding on a camel, dearest. He will come on the train from Aleppo by way of Homs and Rayak.'

'I thought desert travel . . .' she protested, lowering the larger of the puppies from her lap on to the floor where it began to tussle with its fellow.

'It is a joke of his,' Flecker explained. 'He is full of fun and high spirits; you shall see.'

'When exactly does he arrive? I cannot prepare a meal unless I know. And what food? And what about his friend . . . ?'

'I don't know exactly when they will arrive. They may get a message to me ahead of time, on the railway telegraph. It doesn't matter. As for food, why not get lamb and cook it in herbs and garlic as only you know how, my darling? A meat fit for the gods when you prepare it.'

She was not to be so easily flattered.

'He will have seen enough of sheep in the desert. It is all they eat except for their goats . . .'

'He won't mind. Your way of seasoning is unique; with honey on the outside; roasted over the flames.'

'It takes time to prepare. If they arrive on an evening train . . .'

'They won't. It will be the morning train.' That much Flecker could guess. The night train from Aleppo to Rayak had several sleeping cars and Lawrence would be sure to take one, for it would afford him privacy.

Flecker rose from the table, wiping his mouth on his napkin before kissing her hair as he passed behind her. She usually reached up to him when he did this but now she did not.

'What's wrong?' he asked.

'You seem too excited,' she replied. 'You'll start to cough again.'

'Don't worry.' He reached his hands over her shoulders and pressed them on her breasts, squeezing her gently and moving his palms in a circular manner.

'I do worry. You must conserve your strength.'

'I do.' He put on a hurt tone. 'I take care of myself in order to give more to you.'

She smiled, and her hands covered his and pushed

his fingers into her. Only the approach of their housekeeper and maid, Anela, caused him to let go of her.

'Now,' she said, 'you must return to your Turkish. You must study, Roy.'

'Yes,' he acquiesced, a seed of sullenness creeping into his voice, 'I must.'

He desultorily scanned the textbook, marked a few lines with a pencil and squinted at his earlier marginalia. The chapters of colloquial Turkish were arranged thematically and Flecker had chanced to open the book at a well-thumbed page, the section dealing with travel: the railway journey was the topic before him.

'*Istasyon nerededir?*' he said out loud, adding, '*Beni istasyona götürün.*'

He skipped several passages and began again.

'*Jerablus için ücret nedir?*'

He thought of Rayak, Homs, Aleppo.

'*Jerablus treni hangi perona giriyor?*'

By now Lawrence and his companion would be well on their way. He let his thoughts drift from the text. The syllables strung on the page became the thrub of wheels on the rails. His pulse was the slow gout of steam and smoke as the locomotive negotiated the bends and inclines north of Baalbek. His fingers drumming impatiently on his papers was the train drumming on the sleepers of wooden trestle bridges over the dry wadis.

Before him moved the desert: clumps of wind- and heat-punched palms moved inexorably by, their scanty fronds and bunches of half-formed dates scattering a meagre shadow over a group of somnolent camels and dusty donkeys, small birds perching on their backs and necks searching for mites and ticks. Around them stood a few black-robed women, water-jugs on their heads, infants tottering at their heels. Beyond the trees he could see black, fly-blown tents squatting in the sun.

In his reverie he could almost smell the scene – the donkey dung, the pungent camel breath, the perfume of human sweat and henna, wood-smoke faintly tainted with hashish. On the back of his hand where it rested on the carriage window sill beat the sun, and into the rhythm of his blood pressed the rhythm of the train wheels.

He re-focused his eyes upon the next sentence.

'Bilet gisesi nerededir?'

Outside, some way off, the puppies were yelping in play. Nearer, one of the last of the day's songbirds was proclaiming its territory around the house.

'Peron dokuz nerededir?' He repeated the phrase. *'Peron dokuz nerededir? Bekleme salonu nerededir?'* Then, like a lament, he wailed softly to himself, *'Nerededir . . . Nerededir . . . Nerededir . . . Lorans nerededir? Lorans nerededir?'*

A small lizard appeared at the end of the verandah, its head cocked alert over the rim of the step, its forelegs squat like those of a bulldog. A slender black thread of tongue flickered in and out of the thin line of its mouth, its eyes beads of jet against the bright sunlight behind, catching the sandy scales on its flank and making them glitter like glass powder. For a few moments it remained quite still, its attention taken by a cricket in the angle of the pillar where sand had collected.

As the reptile was about to whip forward at the insect, the warm breeze blowing from the sea caused a movement of her skirt which distracted and scared it: it flicked backwards over the step and was gone.

Hellé was sad that she had disturbed the lizard. She

had been studying it with mounting anticipation, waiting for the moment when it would seize the cricket, awkwardly cracking its thorax in its mouth. She had seen this very lizard catch a cockroach only a few days before and the gluttony of it, the sheer primitiveness of the hunt had simultaneously repulsed and captivated her.

'Hellé!'

Flecker was calling from the shade of the jasmine. She made no attempt to reply and returned her attention from the vacant step to her book.

'Hellé!' he called again, his voice a little louder.

Still she did not answer, keeping her head bowed as if engrossed in the book.

Footsteps on the stony, dry earth approached.

'Didn't you hear me?'

She looked up quickly, feigning being startled. 'Roy! I didn't see you, dearest. You really shouldn't creep up on me like that. It is so . . . so unnerving.' She put one hand to her bosom. 'You gave me quite a fright.'

'You look like an actress at a fairground drama,' he said caustically.

'I don't understand you.'

'Standing there, your book shut and your hand pressed melodramatically to your heaving breast. Anyone would think I was the villain of the piece. Would you have me wax my moustache and blacken my eyebrows, too?'

'Your moustache is better as it is, dearest. As for your eyebrows – why should you want to darken them?'

He ignored her. When she was like this she was impossible – and she had been like this for the whole of the day.

'I was calling you.' He returned to the point of his summoning her. 'Do we have the jug of lemonade ready? Has the ice been delivered yet?'

'It came an hour or so ago. I have it in the ice-box.'

'Then why didn't you tell us?' he demanded curtly. 'It's as hot as hell itself today, my throat is wretched and we are sitting under the jasmines baking like loaves.'

'I didn't want to disturb you,' Hellé responded sweetly. 'You seemed so wrapped up in your conversation. The three of you ... You do make a funny picture.'

She smiled, but he refused to be drawn.

'You've been in a funny mood ...'

She cut him short. 'Would you like me to serve the lemonade now? I can bring it over. You go back to our guests; I shall be over in a moment.'

'Very well.'

Flecker knew when she had the better of him and he wanted to avoid an argument. Happy now, and afraid of breaking the fragility of his happiness, he was damned if he was going to let her moodiness upset him.

As she went through the doorway into the cool shade of the house she looked over her shoulder. He was striding so positively, so determinedly towards the jasmine in the shadow of which she could see two other figures seated, facing away from the house and in the direction of the mountains dancing in the heat haze. It was good to see him so happy, so contented, so alive.

During the night before, he had coughed only the once but, there on the pillow, was a speck of blood in his spittle. It was only a tiny stain, no more blood in it than might have issued from a pinprick, but it had damped his spirits. They had only risen again with the arrival of Lawrence and his Arab servant.

Preparing the drink, squeezing the lemons and limes into the water, grating the tart-scented peel, Anela crushed the ice with a wooden mallet whilst she thought over their day so far with mixed feelings.

She and Flecker had been completing their breakfast

97

when the guests had arrived, much to her surprise, on foot. Lawrence was carrying a small sack containing a few possessions and a bed-roll over his shoulders, for all the world like one of the nomadic peasants one found on the old mountain road from Levádhia to Arakhova in the summer, gathered round their domed tents with Parnassus in the background, grey and bleak.

Lawrence's manservant was hardly a man. He was a youth in his late teens, she assessed, of average height and muscular build, with a round and not at all Arabian face. His name was Dahoum.

Both were dressed as Arabs. Lawrence was wearing a waistcoat over a white shirt with loose cotton trousers below and a pair of soft Arab shoes. Over this he had on a *kaftan* with a dark blue *hezâm* wrapped about the waist. His outer coat was a flowing black *benish*. On his head he wore a white-and-blue patterned *keffiyeh* held in place by a black *ogal* twisted with silver threads and wound twice around his head. Dahoum was dressed similarly. They looked like mountain shepherds down from the hills to sell their flock, but when they sat at the table she noticed a shocking difference. Under Lawrence's *kaftan* and stuck into his *hezâm* was a revolver in an unpolished leather holster. Where Lawrence had a gun, Dahoum had a dagger.

'You look quite the desert brigand, Mr Lawrence,' she had commented as she poured them both a cup of coffee.

He had nonchalantly smoothed the hem of his *benish* over the revolver and replied, 'Not really, Mrs Flecker . . .'

'Do call her Hellé,' Flecker had interjected.

'Not really,' Lawrence repeated. 'Brigands thieve from everyone and can, therefore, be selective. And they often wear the best whereas these – ' he tugged at his *kaftan* ' – are not exactly the equivalent of the desert Bond Street.'

As he spoke she found herself held by his words. He was a clumsy-looking man seated at her table drinking coffee – his head too large and weather-beaten, his hands somehow effeminate, his frame slight even in the abundance of native costume. And yet, once he spoke, his face came alive, his eyes shone and his lips took on a lasciviousness she had never before seen in a man. She could almost feel him kissing her, so strong was his charisma.

She had offered both him and his manservant, who said nothing at all and whom she was not sure how to treat – as a friend, a servant, a comrade? – the use of the bedroom and bathroom in which to wash and change after their journey. Both had accepted and gone together into the room, closing the door behind them. They had not remained there long; within ten minutes they were out, their hands and faces refreshed by water, the dust removed. However, Lawrence had not, as she had expected him to do, changed from his Arab dress into European clothes.

Since then, this strange couple and her husband had sat under the jasmine trees and talked ceaselessly. Occasionally snatches of their conversation had drifted across to her. They were speaking of Oxford; she plainly heard mention of Magdalen College, of several professors, of Hogarth and 'dear Jack', whom she knew to be Jack Beazley. They spoke also of poetry, of Swinburne, Tennyson and Keats. She heard them talk of India and Forster and Kipling, of the British Empire and Imperial Rome, of Greek and Arthurian legends, of the hill forts of southern England and the tels of Mesopotamia, of the Phoenicians and the Minoans, the Philistines, the Sumerians, the Akkadians and the Hittites.

The range of their conversation had surprised her. Her husband appeared knowledgeable in so many of the subjects and, when the talk shifted to discussing pots and amphorae, hieroglyphs and iron smelting, she was amazed to hear him holding forth on design and shape and practical techniques.

Dahoum continued to speak very little, and then only in Arabic, but the other two paid him close attention; her husband even spoke falteringly, from time to time, in Arabic, much to the general amusement. It was Lawrence, of course, who dominated the conversation, and whenever he looked in her direction – even though it was merely a glance and he did not necessarily see her sitting in the verandah shade – she felt an odd thrill, almost a chill, pass through her. There was something magical but also frightening about him.

That he held Flecker entranced was beyond doubt; he hardly took his eyes from Lawrence's face, and Hellé knew the cause. Her husband was in love with the newcomer. She recognised it just as she recognised his love for her. The reason of friendship had been suborned by the illogicality of love.

Her mother had warned her against Flecker. A poet, the old lady had declared, was hardly a reliable soul upon which to build the structure of a marriage. It was like building on sand. Emotions are sand, she had stated: all emotion is a shifting base. Better, she had suggested forcibly, to build on a rock and sprinkle it with sand to hide the hard core of practical foundations.

At the time, Hellé had chided her mother, taken the assessment light-heartedly. Even when Flecker was on half-pay in Corfu and she had had to use her savings to keep them both alive, she had disregarded her mother's warning. She was swept up by his emotion, his attention to her, his poetry and his extraordinary love-making.

Yet now, as she carried the tray of lemonade out into

the blazing heat of the garden, with one of the puppies trying to bite the swinging hem of her dress, she suddenly felt cold with fear. She knew she would not lose her husband to another woman: she was giving him all he wanted from a woman. What she had never considered, until today, was that she might lose him to a man.

She stood on the verandah, back from the line of bright sun where the shadows were deepest, and watched them. They were not talking so loudly now; there was no laughter, no sign of the previous conviviality. They were bending forward towards each other, deep in conversation.

As she stepped into the sunlight they stopped talking. Lawrence leaned back in his chair, tilting it on to its rear legs, while his servant stood up to take the tray from her.

The Arab then placed the tray on his own chair and squatted cross-legged on the ground by his master. 'We are having some success in teaching Dahoum the ways of the civilised man,' Lawrence observed wryly.

She avoided Lawrence's gaze.

The lamp had attracted a swarm of insects. Some were tiny, insignificant leaf hoppers and moths which banged against the glass and fell, either stunned or burned, on to the bare wood of the table where they fluttered or flickered. A few were crickets, wiser than the others, which sat in the circle of the light and bathed in its warmth. One was a huge moth with a wing-span of several inches. It, too, did not venture close to the lamp but spread itself on the ceiling, the hot air from the flame rising to a spot beside the insect.

'When shall you be returning to your archaeological site?' Hellé enquired. 'Surely your workmen may uncover something of value whilst you are away and perhaps damage it through their ignorance? I know this happened to some Frenchmen who were excavating a temple near Xilokastron. I was a girl on holiday there with my aunt . . .'

'No, they will do no harm. While I am away they are merely clearing rubble, sending some to the railway and back-filling several holes we don't wish to fall into on a dark night.'

Lawrence chuckled quietly, his laughter exciting her. She was glad the lamp was burning low and she could not see his eyes.

'How is your life at Carchemish?'

'Hectic. We are digging well into the mound. The soil . . .'

'I mean,' Hellé interrupted, 'how do you live? Do you have a house?'

'Leonard Woolley and I are working on one, and it will be quite civilised very soon. Leonard came out to work with me this year. Last year was not so promising. I and Campbell Thompson were billeted in the Liquorice Company warehouse, a ramshackle dump like a derelict *caravanserai* in a desert ghost town. A dried-up oasis. The walls were holed as if the building had been bombarded. More like a colander! Every night the birds came to roost there. Rats scurried about and the local canines came in to chase them or to sleep. It was not hygienic – but it was fun.'

'How did you get to sleep?' Hellé marvelled. 'Couldn't the rats or dogs have given you rabies?'

'Perhaps. I gave it no thought. Leave well alone.'

'How did you cook?'

'Last year, we – that's myself and Campbell Thompson; our governor, Prof. Hogarth . . .' he gave a slight glance in Flecker's direction before continuing '. . . had

gone by then – took lessons in cooking from Miss
Holmes who lives at Jebail – whom you may have met?'

Hellé shook her head.

Lawrence went on, 'She's a missionary schoolmis-
tress. Quite a remarkable woman in her way. Evangel-
istic but sensible. She knows it's pointless trying to
convert the Muslims. Instead she's shaping their children, gradually bending them, progressively un-teaching
those aspects of Islam that are "not acceptable, Mister
Lawrence!" – I can hear her now. But she is doing a
grand job. I would prophesy that, within a decade,
English will be the *lingua franca* of Syria, supplanting
French. And that will be a triumph over the Catholics
and their French missionaries.'

His hands, folded in his lap, lifted an inch or two
and opened as if to support his claim.

'But I'm straying somewhat from your question! How
did we cook? Well, Miss Holmes had a cook in Jebail
and I studied his operations and attempted to teach our
camp cook – one Haj Waheed – the same techniques.
It was, I fear, an unmitigated disaster. He was unused
to our flour and his bread was thin and elastic. His
cakes, purporting to be sponge, were very much like
the original of that form from the sea, or else so liquid
as to be more suited to invalids. We had no oven, you
see. I attempted to improvise one but it was a dismal
failure. Finally Hogarth struck a deal with the Turkish
army commander at Birejik and we were supplied with
the thick, wholemeal bread the soldiers had. Like the
bread of the Limousin, yet much browner and not sour
like the French. The rest of the time we ate from tins
we had brought, mixed with local produce. Most of it
was poorly prepared, to say the least. I contracted a
worm, but shifted it with liquorice. Not from the warehouse!'

'It sounds a terrible existence!' Hellé exclaimed.

'Not a bit of it. It was quite jolly fun. And besides, that's behind us now.'

'How much have you uncovered?' Flecker asked. He knew the answer from the reports and the crates he had re-packed and shipped onwards, and was merely making conversation for his wife's benefit. Her apparent interest in Lawrence pleased him hugely.

'A good deal. The remains are not all that deep. The site has built up – the strata of the soil, that is – under successive occupations, and must once have been even higher. It is, Mrs Flecker,' he turned to Hellé again, 'a hill. But erosion has stripped some of the surface off and so we don't have to dig so far down as, say, those working in Egypt have to. Also, we are digging in earth rather than sand and this reduces the danger; we do not have to shore up any but the deepest of our holes. The occupation layers are fascinating – Ottoman on the top, then the centuries of the Arabian Baghdad caliphate, then Roman. Below that a mish-mash of time all scrabbled about by those since who cannibalised the site, robbed the stone and remains. Below that, the Hittites.'

'Robbed stone?' Hellé questioned.

'Robbery of sites is a long tradition the world over, as we saw at Aleppo,' said Lawrence, turning to Flecker. 'Indeed, at Carchemish local robbers have looted a necropolis not far away from the site – there is a Hittite cemetery there with Roman shaft tombs cut into it. We've had some fine Roman glass and Greek imported pottery, come up with coins, fibulæ, bronze jewellery, some unusual little pots, sculpted slabs. Some fine Hittite seals have come to light from our mound, not to mention reliefs of lion-headed humans, basalt slabs of warriors with decapitated prisoners, as well as the usual iron axes and sword-blades one somehow expects to discover. One of the latter had a wooden hilt, but a workman has pinched it ... to sell in the Aleppo bazaar, no doubt. We have to keep an eagle eye out for disappearances ...'

The moth on the ceiling shifted itself, oscillating its wings and vibrating its feathery antennæ. Dahoum watched it with a studied gaze.

'Perhaps you should come to see Carchemish for yourself?' Lawrence suggested. 'You may find it of great interest and, I'm sure, we could allow you to find some bauble you might keep. The Hittites made quite beautiful little beads and they imported lapis lazuli and faience from the south. At least, we assume it was they ... Would you care to come?'

'I should, but it is not easy to leave Beirut. My husband needs me here. He is ...' She turned towards Flecker. His eyes were closed and his lips pressed to his steepled fingers. He might have been praying.

'... not so busy as he might be,' he interrupted, not opening his eyes. 'I'm sure in a few months something could be arranged if you wanted it, dearest. In the meantime, I shall have to go on my own – on consular business.'

She leaned forward to look him in the face but still his eyes remained shut.

It was Lawrence who explained. 'We are foreigners in a foreign land, Mrs Flecker. Diplomatic permissions and exchanges have to be arranged, re-assessed and re-negotiated all the while. We are never without our tame Consul on hand to smooth the way with the authorities. On this occasion it is with the Turks. And your husband's time in Constantinople makes him amply suited to dealing with the problem we have at present.'

'But my husband is ...' she began.

Flecker sensed what she was about to mention. 'Lawrence knows I get short of breath from time to time.' He spoke tersely, with little patience. 'It was so when I was in Aleppo. Carchemish will pose no strain upon me.'

Hellé was obliged to give way. If he had made up his mind to go he would. She tried just one other ploy.

'Will you get time off from the Consulate . . . ?'

'This is official business,' Lawrence reminded her, his voice gentle and persuasive. 'It is all square with the Consul here.'

'When will you leave?' she enquired, her heart sinking.

'The day after tomorrow,' Flecker answered. 'There are some things to sort out here first. I'll be gone a fortnight . . .'

'At the very most,' said Lawrence. 'And I assure you we will look after your husband as if he were a sheikh.'

She could not sleep. Her husband was breathing deeply, his throat unusually clear, but beyond the door she could hear light snoring and, every so often, someone turning over. Lawrence and his manservant were sleeping on the Persian carpet in the centre of the living room.

Her thoughts spun as if she was drunk. Every idea formed but refused to develop, spinning off into another before she could expand it. She knew she was afraid, but not of what.

So many anxieties flicked through her head, flashed their warnings to her and then disappeared before they could deliver their message.

First and foremost, she was afraid, terribly afraid, that her husband was dying. Gradually. She had no proof to substantiate her fear. The doctor diagnosed him as bronchitic. Bronchitis! He had consumption; she was sure of it, although she could not understand or justify her certainty.

The physical signs, she felt, were there regardless of what the doctor stated. The coughs, the rasping breath, the sore throat and now the damning fleck of blood.

They never talked of it. He made no mention of his coughing and laboured breathing, accepting the doctor's judgement. When the tiny spots of blood appeared on his handkerchief or upon the pillow, he either ignored them or explained them away: he must have bitten his tongue in his sleep, he had cut his gum cleaning his teeth, his lips were dry and cracked – he needed vaseline for them, would she be so good as to buy him a jar?

When they made love she gave herself to him utterly. Her every muscle concentrated on giving him the ecstasy she wanted for him, taking from him the same raptures she wanted for herself. Yet, recently, although she concentrated hard, she was unable to give him every tiny essence of herself. In her mind lingered, ever so small yet startlingly bright like a single living coal in a dark grate, the fear that time was short.

She tried to think how long it took to die from the appearance of blood, tried to remember how long Keats had lasted before dying in his rooms over the crash-box of the Piazza d'Espana. No sooner did she think of this than she tried to recall if that was where he had died. Perhaps it was in a friend's house, at Leghorn, by the sea. She sought to tug her thoughts back to her husband and his predicament – her predicament – but they would insist on considering the setting of John Keats's ultimate breath.

Then she wondered where he would die. In Beirut, in the Lebanon which he claimed he so hated yet so curiously loved? In Athens or back on Corfu? In a sanatorium in Switzerland or in the shadow of the rugged Italian Alps? Back in his own room in Chelten-

ham with his gentle Cotswold Hills, of which he had
told her so much? At Carchemish?

This prompted her speculations about his imminent
trip. Yet no sooner was she giving this her consideration
than his illness faded to insignificance against the threat
she believed Lawrence and his manservant posed.

The snorer in the next room went silent. There was
a shuffle of cloth and a muted groan, a brief whisper
and then the snoring began once more, somewhat faster
than before.

Her husband was so obviously captivated by the pair.
She was certain he was in love. This being so, would
he leave her? Surely not – but she could not assume it
to be so, for no sooner had she dismissed the idea as
ridiculous than her doubts returned. He could not leave
her because of his job, the scandal – but he did not like
his job, he wanted to write. He wanted so much to be
a successful poet, not merely a man with a few books
behind him but a writer of stature, of position in the
world of letters. He was not a brilliant poet, not Shelley,
not Byron, not Keats. Yet he was good.

She wondered how she might scotch the intended trip
and started to formulate means of preventing him from
going, but then she remembered. It was an official journey. It was not just for the sake of it, to see the ruins
being unearthed, to be with Lawrence and his native
boy. It was not for love.

She reached under the sheet and touched the small of
his back. The cord of his pyjamas had worked loose
and she slipped her hand on to his buttocks. They were
cold, almost clammily so, and she shivered.

The camera was warm. 'I trust the film will hold good
in the heat,' Flecker remarked.

'It should do,' Lawrence answered. 'I've five cameras

at the dig and we do have problems – it seems only Cristoid films can withstand the temperatures – but it's far hotter there than here.'

Flecker was wearing his Praxiteles Club blazer, the trimming dark and the clockwise swastika on the pocket stark in the bright sunlight. Above his left ear he had balanced a blossom plucked in the garden, the short stalk pushed into his hair. It was a white flower, contrasting with his swarthy, almost Mediterranean features.

'Would you take our photograph?' Lawrence asked Hellé. 'Your husband looks quite dashing in his jacket.'

She took the camera and steadied it against her bosom as she peered into the prism of the viewfinder. There, in the little window, stood her husband and his friend. Lawrence was the shorter of the pair yet through the camera, in his flowing Arab robes, seemed taller.

'Hold still!' she ordered and pressed the lever. The shutter clicked.

'Now with Dahoum,' Lawrence suggested. He beckoned to the Arab boy who joined them, standing between the two men and grinning broadly. Again Hellé snapped the shutter.

'Next I shall photograph you two with Hellé,' Flecker announced, walking down the length of the verandah. 'Come along, dearest. Down you go . . .'

She positioned herself between the boy and Lawrence and looked coyly towards the lens. Lawrence made no attempt to draw her near, to put his arm around her or make any other common sign of momentary familiarity. He simply stood by her. His desert clothing smelt faintly of camels, of old perspiration and wool.

The photograph taken, Lawrence left her side and spoke quietly to Flecker who put the camera down on the verandah table. Then, together, they went into the house, leaving her and Dahoum outside. Neither gave her so much as a glance.

The fear she had felt in the night gripped her again. She wanted to go into the house, to see what they were doing. Yet she was afraid to. She was terrified she might find them caressing each other or stealing a brief kiss. She was so scared of the possible truth. Yet she wanted to know, to be sure of her worries, for once a worry is known it can be acted upon; while still unknown, unformed, it is a thing of terror.

When Dahoum sneezed she was almost glad of the distraction. The boy beamed at her and spoke in Arabic, but she did not understand and merely smiled back.

The door opened and Lawrence appeared dressed in a pair of khaki shorts, a collarless shirt and Flecker's blazer. He picked up the camera from the table.

'May I present the Sultan el-Roy!' he proclaimed.

Flecker appeared from the doorway dressed in Lawrence's Arab clothing. Around his head was Lawrence's *ogal*, beneath which was a dark blue *keffiyeh* woven with broad bands of cream silk. His outer, full-length garment was dark brown.

'The carpet.'

Lawrence pointed to a patterned Persian rug they placed on the verandah during the day and spoke to Dahoum in Arabic.

The boy scooped it up and hung it at the end of the verandah.

'Good,' Lawrence exclaimed. 'Now we have a suitable backdrop. Can't take a good photograph against the glare.'

Flecker leaned against the verandah pillar, the *keffiyeh* hanging loose over his right shoulder. Beneath the outer garment he was wearing his own shirt, the collar tucked in. His legs were incongruously white below the hem of the outer garment. On his feet were a pair of brown leather slippers.

The picture taken, Lawrence walked briskly to Flecker's side and wrapped the *keffiyeh* around his head, flicking it over his left shoulder. Flecker then sat cross-legged on the floor and peered at the camera from the shadows of the head-dress. He looked sinister and full of foreboding.

Hellé watched the proceedings, her emotions in turmoil. Once, not long after they had moved to Beirut, Flecker had slipped on her nightdress while she was washing and had surprised her, creeping up on her in their bedroom and wailing in a poor imitation of a tormented spirit. She had turned, seen him and laughed aloud at the ridiculousness of the sight. Yet this game of his had drawn them somehow closer together. When she came to their bed that night she could feel him still inhabiting her clothes, his skin her skin.

Now he was wearing Lawrence's clothes. That night, she knew, as she slept with him she would be thinking of Lawrence being there, between them.

5
Carchemish: May 1912

From Aleppo, they went on horseback by way of Bâb.
Flecker rode most of the time, while Lawrence preferred
to walk with Dahoum. The only occasion on which
both he and the boy took to their mounts was when
they had to cross a tributary of the Euphrates which
was sluggishly running with the remnants of the day's
storms in the Kurdish mountains which, for the second
day of their journey, were ever-present in the hazy distance.

The air was dry and the gusting wind whipped the
dust into small clouds, but Flecker – a *keffiyeh* borrowed from Dahoum wrapped bandit-mask fashion
around his mouth – had no discomfort.

Apart from the mountains ahead of them, stretching
away to the west, the land was monotonous and flat.
To the east and south stretched the deserts which spread
as far as Arabia; to the south-east was the Euphrates
running to the vast depression through which that river
and the Tigris ran on into the Persian Gulf.

Occasionally the flatness of the scenery was alleviated
by mounds, the tels of towns and villages long lost,
around which had settled recent villages of low and
squalid mud hovels and the black tents of the desert
nomads. Camels sat in the shade of the hovels, working
their jaws and snorting with boredom. Smoke rose from
the camp-sites, to be whisked away on the sporadic
breeze. Whenever they passed downwind of the settle-

ments Flecker could scent the burning of the fires and the stench of the camels.

Half-way between Bâb and their destination the dull plateau began to drop towards the river, every mile indicating a different stratum eroded millennia before by the far-off river.

At Jerablus, near the Carchemish site, Flecker was surprised to see a new village of some fifty mud buildings arranged around a spring of good water. Obviously the railway and the archaeologists had brought some increased wealth to the region. Half a mile to the east of the village flowed the mud-brown Euphrates.

They did not halt in the village but skirted around it, Dahoum holding tightly on to the reins of their three pack animals. Lawrence led his horse by the nose and Flecker dismounted to follow on behind.

The house Lawrence was building was only a quarter of an hour's walk from the village, close to the scrubby grass-grown mound of Carchemish which Flecker had been told by Lawrence was known as *Kalaat* by the locals who still referred to themselves as the 'people of the mound'.

As they approached the site, the sun setting and the shadows of the undulations in the land already dark, Flecker felt a sense of the timelessness of the place. The mound itself was not as impressive as he had expected. He had thought it would have been higher, more imposing, more mystical. In truth, it was nothing much more than a low hill, for all the world like an old spoil tip outside a long-defunct mine. Had it been accompanied by a granite chimney it might have been the remains of a tin mine in Cornwall.

The house was, if anything, the most impressive object of the whole place. Flecker arrived with emotions of elation – he was at last at the end of the journey, and in Lawrence's own home – which quickly metamorphosed into amazement.

The building was low, single-storeyed and constructed of roughly cut stone. The flat roof was made of mud and the whole place shaped like three sides of a quadrangle. The top of the square consisted of a huge living room with a timbered ceiling. To the left were rooms for Hogarth whenever he visited, the kitchen, and a store-room into which Dahoum unloaded the pack animals. Opposite were a photographic dark-room, a small museum room, a bathroom and bedrooms for Lawrence, Woolley and Gregori, Hogarth's Cypriot headman. To one side several Bedouin tents had been erected but they were unoccupied, their flaps closed and weighted against the wind with stones.

Flecker handed the bridle of his horse to an Arab youth of about the same age as Dahoum, who bowed slightly and led the beast away.

'So!' Lawrence exclaimed as they entered the living room. 'Welcome to the *serai* of El-Orans, as they call me. You are an honoured and esteemed guest, dear Poet of the Eastern Star.'

The room was vast. From the timbered rafters hung oil lamps, all brightly yellow, the glass funnels clear of soot. By their light Flecker saw whitewashed walls hung with Persian rugs and a William Morris tapestry, and decorated here and there with Damascus tiles. Upon a set of bookshelves he could clearly make out the titles of the books – a *Complete Works* of Shakespeare, another of Dante and a *Complete Spenser* leaned against French novels, books by Francis Thompson, Rabelais, Lucretius, Charles Doughty and Virgil. At one end of the shelf, propping up the others, was a copy of Robert Louis Stevensons's *Treasure Island* whilst at the other end of the top shelf – acting as a book-end – was a slab of stone with cuneiform writing etched into it.

Before the shelves were two armchairs made of white leather and wood so black it might have been ebony.

The door mouldings and pillars supporting the timbers were made of basalt – some of them plainly cut in antiquity – and a fire with a copper hood burned slowly to one side. The smoke had drifted into the room and settled in a layer above the level of the lamps.

Flecker sniffed.

'Are you well?' Lawrence enquired. 'Will you rest now? It's been a hard day . . .'

'No. I'm all right. It is the wood . . .'

'The smoke soon goes.'

'I mean the scent . . .'

'It's olive. We purchase it from boatmen on the river. What do you think of our floor?'

Flecker looked down; the room was paved with a beautiful mosaic.

'We are going to rub it smooth and get it waxed,' Lawrence said. 'You aren't seeing it at its best.'

It was a two-panelled design: in the lower was an orange tree on either side of which were antelopes and waterfowl; in the topmost was a vase from which twined and curled a vine filled with birds, on whose highest point was perched a Glossy Ibis, the bird unmistakable from its haughty demeanour and distinctive plumage.

'Nearly one hundred and fifty thousand tesseræ,' Lawrence proclaimed proudly. 'It is third century and we uncovered it a mile away. I supervised its lifting in sections and we had it re-set here. A grand stone carpet, you agree?'

'Indeed I do.'

Flecker turned around. Wherever his eye rested there were artefacts of value – Hittite bowls, Katuchia pots, a green, blue and red Rhodian vase.

'The vase is for my mother. I purchased it in the *suq*

in Damascus and intended to take it back with me last August but my illness . . . It slipped my mind. From time to time I buy her small gifts. My family are very good about subbing me an advance on my salary . . . as you would know . . .'

'Yes.'

On several occasions Flecker had received Lawrence's payment from Hogarth, sent in the form of gold sovereigns and half-sovereigns; but he had also received other sums from another source in Oxford which he had assumed to be his family.

'Well, let us wash the dust of the desert from our skins and settle down to a meal.' Lawrence gazed briefly out of the door. 'It won't be long before Woolley gets back. They'll be packed up and he'll be seeing to the guards.'

'Guards?'

'We put guards on the mound; it stops pilfering. Well, in fact, we had the platoon placed here by the Turks at the end of the last season's digging. There are just a dozen or so Ottoman soldiers under an *onbashi*.'

Dahoum appeared at the door with a galvanised bucket of water.

'That's all for you. We have other bucketsful on the way,' Lawrence said, and he guided Flecker to the bathroom and left him.

Leonard Woolley was Lawrence's superior at the Carchemish site, and eight years his senior. They had met at Oxford, where Woolley had been a junior assistant keeper at the Ashmolean Museum; it had been Hogarth who had introduced them to each other, and to spying. Woolley had had a good deal of experience digging in Egypt and had even brought two Egyptians with him to Carchemish as photographers – much to Lawrence's chagrin – but they had been unpopular with the locals, an unpopularity Lawrence was ready to exploit. Just before Flecker's arrival the two Egyptians had decided to leave, their departure putting Lawrence in high spirits. It was in such a mood that he introduced Flecker to his fellow archaeologist in the living room.

Leonard Woolley, dressed in a grey flannel shirt and golf trousers, with dusty and scarred leather brogues on his feet, shook Flecker's hand firmly. He had a squarish head and long, broad nose: his hair was brushed flat to his skull, while his eyes were cool and touched with arrogance.

'How do you do,' he said formally. 'I know your work, Flecker, but I don't think we've ever met. You know Jack Beazley.' It was a statement, not a polite rhetoricism, and he gave Flecker no opportunity to accept or deny the fact. 'How are things in Beirut? All going smoothly?'

'Yes, I think so. All shipments are going through on time. Messages and reports are in London with all speed.'

Woolley had raised his eyebrows at the apparent uncertainty of Flecker's first sentence.

'You must go over the full structure of our channels from Aleppo to London. I haven't had time to be briefed as thoroughly as I might have liked.'

'There's not much to it,' Flecker began, but Dahoum entered the room at that juncture to announce that the cook was ready with their meal, and he stopped speaking.

'Let me know later,' Woolley said abruptly. 'I am *au fait* with the outline of course from Hogarth, but not the details you've arranged.'

It had been with a degree of misgiving that Flecker had anticipated the food at Carchemish. Lawrence's stories of rubbery bread had not been forgotten; yet their dinner was excellent. Haj Waheed had obviously improved since the previous year and the mutton he served was tender and rich with herbs. It was accompanied by asparagus and carrots and was sprinkled with caviare. For dessert they were given a light sponge pudding covered in melted chocolate.

'This is not quite what I expected,' Flecker announced as they left the table. He and Woolley sat in the armchairs, while Lawrence squatted cross-legged on the mosaic. 'You seem to eat as well as in a London club.'

'Our stocks are considerable,' Woolley explained. 'Most of it is tinned, of course – the asparagus and carrots, for example. We've Cooper's Oxford marmalade, loganberry and plum preserves, Edinburgh shortbread and wheatmeal biscuits, sardines and anchovies and curry powder. The caviare is Russian. Fish, eggs and meat we buy locally – and some vegetables. Fruit too, of course. Our only major problem is getting decent salt; the sale of it is a government monopoly and it's shoddy stuff. We get tins of Cerebos salt brought in, labelled as preserving chemical. Lord knows what they think we are preserving, but you know the Turk!'

They had eaten using almost entirely Hittite crockery and Roman glassware. The sugar bowl was made of a dark grey clay, and the salt was stored in a small juglike vessel decorated with a wavy line pattern, a cork placed in the top. They drank wine from un-matched Roman tumblers.

'Everything will one day be in the British Museum,' Lawrence remarked jovially, watching Flecker admiring the sugar bowl. 'You'll be able to tell your grandchildren how you once dined from these oddments in the middle of the desert, accompanied by a famous archaeologist and a less famous writer of books and jottings . . .' Outside in the darkness, one of the pack animals snorted. '. . . And a snoring horse,' he added.

They spent the evening before the olive-wood fire, talking of Oxford and poetry, of the Germans and the Hittites.

'Even our grate is Hittite,' Woolley admitted. 'This room, from floor to ceiling, spans three thousand years . . .'

After a while they drifted into silence, then Woolley bade his companions good night and left Lawrence and Flecker in the flickering light of the dying fire.

The two men did not speak. Lawrence lay on his side on the Bokhara carpet in front of the grate and Flecker slumped in the nearest armchair. The lamps were put out by Haj Waheed.

Flecker watched Lawrence. He was breathing shallowly and slowly, though he was wide awake, his eyes fixed on the embers. His hair was worn longer than was the fashion and curled at the ends, giving him a tousled appearance. Over his white shirt and shorts he was wearing an Arab waistcoat of white and gold and, covering that, a cloak of gold and silver thread.

After some time he sat up. 'Tomorrow, I'll show you the dig. And we'll have a little scout about. The day after, we're to have a party.'

'Who's invited?' Flecker enquired. 'Local chiefs?'

'Not local. I'll be here, and Woolley and you. And Raff and Winifred. And Hogarth. They're paying us a visit.'

Flecker was given one of the tents in which to sleep. It was warm within, a fire of charcoal glowing in a grate of stones at its centre. The little smoke it generated was blowing through a hole in the roof. He lay down on a folding military bed and was soon deeply asleep.

To go to the site Lawrence wore his working clothes — a fresh white shirt, a French grey blazer trimmed with pink braid and a pair of white shorts with a garish Arab tasselled belt. His legs were covered by knee-length grey stockings and on his feet he wore a pair of red Arab slippers. Over this attire he wore a reddish-brown woollen cloak. Despite the heat of the sun, he remained looking cool as he strode purposefully from excavation to excavation, pointing out where they had discovered a certain Roman coin, iron artefact, bowl or shard. His memory for even the tiniest of details was prodigious. The entire site was some acres in extent, yet he knew every nook and cranny and what each had yielded by way of knowledge or object.

Woolley, who was opening up a new hole as they arrived just after nine in the morning, showed Flecker their first find, a mere seven feet below the surface. It was half of an unglazed bowl.

'Was this a house?' Flecker asked, looking around at the slabs of hewn stone starting to appear under the shovels of the workmen.

'Hard to say. Could have been a dwelling, pure and simple. Might have been a shop. Possibly a small shrine. Have you seen the Little Shrine yet?'

'Not yet,' Lawrence interrupted. 'Thought we'd take a look at it from the top. Going up there next . . .'

The climb up the mound was gentle and did not make Flecker wheeze or gasp. Lawrence watched him, not obviously but carefully.

Just below the summit Lawrence jumped in to a trench lined with stones and paved with slabs of basalt. At one point along the rim of the trench a shelf had been constructed, just below the soil level. The rear of the trench, and one end of it, were bare earth which had loosened and fallen in. Flecker followed.

'What is this site?' he asked.

'Nothing,' Lawrence answered. 'It might look like it but it's nothing. You have to go down eighteen or twenty feet more to hit anything of interest. Maybe some Ottoman bits and bobs . . .' He tugged at a tiny fragment of earthenware sticking out of the side of the trench and handed it to Flecker; it was no bigger than his thumbnail. 'Otherwise it's of no archaeological interest. It is, however, of considerable railway interest.'

He smirked like a schoolboy and nodded his head towards the horizon. Flecker looked in that direction and saw the beginnings of the railway bridge. Groups of what looked at this distance like ants were toiling along the embankment.

'Here.' Lawrence produced a pair of field glasses from under his cloak. 'Have a closer look – but keep your head down to the rim of the trench. You'll find that shelf handy for resting your elbows. Balance the glasses on that smooth stone.' He patted a rock set on to the shelf. 'But keep them tilted down a bit. Don't want the sun catching on the lens; flash like a signal mirror otherwise and the Germans are no fools.'

Flecker did as suggested and adjusted the knurled knob before his nose. The bridge site and embankment came into focus. The heat haze was not yet high and there was little distortion.

The ants became miniature men, working in lines. They were passing panniers of earth from a tip at the base of the embankment up to the top, where a group of others emptied the earth under the supervision of a European. He was only distinguished from the labourers by the fact that he was not working.

Shifting the field glasses, Flecker studied the bridge-head, the short lattice-work of girders patterning the cut stone of the first pier around which muddy water swirled and sliced into the bank. Far up the pier, Flecker could see the high-water mark to which the river had risen when flooded.

'They're doing rather well, don't you think?'

'Yes, they are.'

Flecker passed the binoculars to Lawrence, who bent down and expertly scanned the whole scene in one motion.

'They're having a problem with the pier on the western bank. As I predicted and, I think, reported?'

Flecker nodded.

'That's why they're asking for more stone from us, not just rubble. The current's going to erode the pier and will be a huge problem for them. The only way they can stem it is to make a massive stone breakwater – roll hundreds of tons of stone into the river and cause it to flow outwards. And they'll need to back it some way up the bank, too. Otherwise the river'll simply cut in behind it.'

'It seems strange we're helping them.'

'Not at all. They'll get on with it one way or another and, besides, it'll be a while before we see a locomotive on this stretch. They've had problems with their tunnels . . .'

They walked back down the mound, the dry grass blades snagging at Flecker's trousers and catching on Lawrence's cloak. He pointed out the site of the Little Shrine which Woolley had mentioned: to Flecker, it was yet another hole in the ground lined haphazardly with stones. It was only different from most of the other holes in that it was also paved.

Woolley was fully occupied. Dahoum passed by with a bucket of water, on the surface of which floated a large ladle. He grinned expansively at Lawrence, who patted his shoulder as he went by but did not speak.

'Why don't you grub about the digging for a bit?' Lawrence suggested. 'You'll find your eye soon picks up things. It's just a matter of practice. Look by your foot!'

Gazing down, Flecker saw a few stones, dusty earth

and a line made by the feet of what might have been a lizard.

'Do you see it?'

'Well,' Flecker replied, 'something's been along here. A reptile?'

Lawrence laughed quietly and pointed to the ground, moving his finger so that its shadow rested against one of the stones. 'There! Turn over the stone. Gently now.'

Beneath the stone, the dust falling upon it, was the rim of a substantial pot. Flecker prised it free. 'How on earth did you know it was there?' he exclaimed.

'I saw the end of it protruding from beneath the stone. You'll soon pick up the knack. If you're enough of a poet to see the right words – and, dear Roy, you are and have proved it so – you'll soon catch on.'

Until the midday sun drove him and the Arab labourers away from the dig. Flecker rooted about in the soil of areas of the site now abandoned by Woolley. He found a number of potsherds and several fragments of Roman pale blue-green glass – one the complete neck and lip of a lachrymatory.

He searched in a semi-daze. He was happy just to be at Carchemish with no responsibilities save to observe the place, and so to have a better idea of it when reading, encoding and transmitting reports. He was even happier that, despite the barren land around, despite the inconvenience of the journey, the roughness of his throat and the nagging ache in the left side of his chest, he was here with Lawrence who, only a short time before, had addressed him as 'dear Roy'.

The party was, Flecker thought, extraordinary.

The Fontanas and Hogarth arrived in the late afternoon and, while Winifred Fontana sat in the shade of the living room with a cup of Earl Grey tea, sketching the interior of the room, her husband and Hogarth, with Lawrence, Woolley and Flecker, went directly to the dig. Once there, the conversation was exclusively scientific, and Flecker ignored. For an hour the group traversed the site, prodding and raising stones, scraping at the ground with a trowel Hogarth had produced from his pocket, pacing distances from point to point, discussing trenching and transverse sectioning, strata and burn lines, skeuomorphology and the Ugarites. Eventually Hogarth made a few curt suggestions, Woolley debated them with him and Lawrence, and they all strode to the top of the mound. Once there they dropped into Lawrence's trench and surveyed the progress of the railway embankment dancing in the heat below them. Flecker's opinion of the railway was sought and he gave it, Hogarth nodding approvingly at the salient points.

Their expedition over, they returned to the house as the twilight developed, and an hour later sat together in the mosaic-floored living room for a meal which Flecker would have considered fine in a good quality hotel in the shires.

Haj Waheed first served beef consommé with crisp croûtons lining the rim of the bowl. This was followed by a delicately flavoured river fish smothered in spiced yoghurt, a rack of lamb and four varieties of vegetable, and finally a flan of fresh peaches doused in cognac. Every dish was taken from Hittite or Roman vessels, the wine – a creditable claret – being poured from an Ottoman jug.

'Well, Flecker,' Hogarth said as Dahoum handed round Hittite cups of Turkish coffee, 'what do you make of Carchemish?'

'The site or the situation, sir?'

'Both.'

'I find the site quite spectacular – the river flowing

by, the uncovered buildings and the sense all the time of something great about to be discovered in the next shovelful of dirt. I'm afraid I can't draw any scientific conclusions. I suppose the magic of the history excites me.'

'Magic,' Hogarth said distantly. 'Yes, it has a certain pull. And what of the situation?'

Flecker lowered his cup carefully to the table.

'The railway seems to be progressing well, but we did see today how they're going to have problems with erosion.' He glanced at Lawrence. 'And I think they are making fairly slow progress. At this rate they will take some time to reach Baghdad, never mind the shores of the Gulf.'

'How much of a threat do you think they pose here?'

'Militarily, slight. Politically, they may well carry much more influence. The Turks are favourably disposed towards them and are not over-fond of us. As you will know from the reports . . .'

Hogarth cut in impatiently, autocratically silencing him with a wave of his hand. 'Anything further come about as a result of that business at Birejik, Leonard?'

Flecker raised his cup to his lips and thought over the matter. He had read and re-drafted the report on it which Fontana had sent on to him.

The *onbashi* had refused Woolley permission to dig, the permit being in Hogarth's name. To settle the matter, Woolley and Lawrence had gone to the local Turkish governor in Birejik, twenty-five miles up-river. The governor was not interested in the matter – if the permit was in Hogarth's name, then so be it. The words of Woolley's report came back to him:

The *kaimmakam* treated us with disdain and gave us the cold shoulder. I decided to bluff him, assessing that he was not one to succumb to reason. I drew my revolver and, positioning myself beside his chair, placed the barrel to his head. Through our cook, who was acting as interpreter, I said that unless permission to commence work the next day was forthcoming I would shoot him and accept the consequences. At this, the Turk immediately capitulated . . .

Woolley stood up to poke the fire and place another handful of olive-tree roots on the flames.

'Some problems but nothing I think we can't sur-mount. Hassan Agha, a local headman, has laid claim to a third of the mound. He's issued a writ against Tom here, and we've been up to the Islamic court in Birejik. I signed a document to say I was responsible for the dig and up it went with Tom on his next trip. He got there ready to do battle, but the case was adjourned.'

'You'll be called to book for this,' Hogarth warned. 'Can you provide any help, Raff?'

'I was ready to accompany Tom to the court for the second hearing . . .'

'But I went instead.' Woolley sat down again. 'It was a farce. We travelled all the way up there to find the date changed again and all the papers impounded. I told the judge I'd blow his head off if he didn't get things sorted out and we left.'

'You can't be imperious with Johnny Turk,' Hogarth advised sardonically. He frowned and puffed on his pipe, careful to blow the smoke away from Winifred Fontana. 'I'll lay odds you'll have another riposte before long. Give them a week or two.'

'How was your meeting in April, David?' Fontana enquired, changing the subject. He knew the signs; Hogarth was considering a riposte of his own.

'Interesting. You others know nothing of this. I took luncheon with the Kaiser on his private yacht, anchored off Corfu. He was very interested in the dig here – especially taken by your photographs of the dig and my list of finds. He's grateful you're supplying his engineers with rubble and has guaranteed the site safe from possible depredations by the railway.'

Flecker listened. This was far removed from his Turkish studies, his accursed consular exams and the banality of life in Beirut. This was real life. And he was sharing it with Lawrence.

As the table was cleared and they sat around the fire, Winifred Fontana produced her sketch-book and began to rough out pencil studies of the men. Flecker watched her with a calm detachment as she sketched first Woolley, then Hogarth and, finally, a sharp profile of Lawrence.

6

Areiya, Aleppo and Carchemish: June/July 1912

Her playing of *Greensleeves* soothed him, the notes from the piano drifting into the darker reaches of the ceiling, he thought, like the smoke had in Lawrence's house. He lay back in his chair and stretched his legs before him, simultaneously raising his arms over his head. As he flexed his muscles the dull ache in his chest sharpened; he sucked in his breath but she did not hear. From the kitchen came the sound of Anela singing softly to herself as she cleared up prior to leaving.

'You've spoken little of your trip,' Hellé observed as the final bar faded away and she closed the lid of the keyboard.

'There's not much more I can say. It was interesting – the dig, and the finds they keep in their little museum. Meals are served on priceless antiquities. The food is good and the conversation better.'

'What did you talk of?'

'Nothing much. Other than official matters, we chatted about Oxford, poetry, archaeology. History, too.'

'What official matter took you up there?'

Flecker paused for a moment as if considering what it was circumspect to let her know.

'Lawrence has had a spot of bother with the Turkish authorities,' he pretended to confide, referring obliquely to the episode in Birejik. 'Last Sunday it all came to a head with Woolley having to pay thirty pounds in compensation over a legal wrangle. It's all settled now.'

'Did you not have to return?'

She spoke quietly, yet with an edge of shrewdness to her words which she could not quite disguise. He recognised it and his reply was curt.

'Raff Fontana saw to it.'

'Why couldn't he have looked to the earlier business?'

Her continual questioning was beginning to irritate him.

'He looks after his aspect of the dig and I look after mine.'

'What is your share of the work?'

'Enough!' He sat up abruptly and let his hand fall heavily on to the table by his chair. The sound startled one of the puppies at his feet which sat up and growled twice before sinking back to sleep. 'You know better, Hellé, than to question my work. We can't discuss consular affairs even with our wives.'

'I was only trying to understand,' she excused herself, her voice softening. 'You're working so hard these days. So much travelling isn't good for you.'

'On the contrary,' he retorted acerbically, 'it does me a world of good. I get away from the trivial arguments and pettinesses of the Consulate here, Cumberpatch's continual oblique carping criticisms, and worrying about these bloody examinations.'

'I think you will do very well this time,' she said, placing her hand upon him as if the contact could somehow give him a benediction of encouragement.

'I think not. My Turkish is atrocious. I tried out a little on the guards at Carchemish; they laughed and nodded, but I'm sure they understood not a jot of it. And my Arabic's little better.' He glanced up at her. 'Lawrence has had only a year at Arabic, yet he's practically fluent. All he had was a preliminary lesson or two in Oxford and a short stint at the American Mission School at Jebail. And he's got it. Me? I just can't . . .'

'Shush!' she silenced him. 'You simply haven't had the practice. You don't live in the desert as he does, always in contact with the Arab tribesmen and the Turks. You will do well. It's a written test, after all.'

'Yes. But all the same Lawrence has their languages off pat and I'm struggling. It's as if, putting on a *kaftan*, he puts on the language and customs as well. All in one movement. Do you know he wears Arabic costume – or a good deal of it – all the time? At the dig, grubbing about in the earth, in the house they've built, when he's out walking or taking his photographs. All the time . . .'

'I think I do not want to speak of him any more,' she replied, but he did not hear her.

'It's as if he *is* an Arab sometimes. To see him eating with his left hand like a Muslim . . . We were on our way to Jerablus and stopped in a small settlement to take water from their spring. Lawrence was invited . . .'

'*En voilá, assez!*'

She had risen from the piano and was standing before him. 'Enough!' she repeated in English. 'I want to know nothing more of him.'

Flabbergasted, her husband made no immediate response. He gazed at her and his dark eyes took on the fire of the temper that lived suppressed inside him, the temper he had fought to control ever since he was a boy.

Now, his wife's high-pitched demand that he stop speaking of his friend had made his anger rise: it manifested itself in his eyes, not his actions. He rested his hands palm down on the table. The best way, he knew, was to turn rage into argument. An argument he could win, a tantrum he could not; she was less adroit at argument than he was and he knew he would triumph in the end.

'Why?' he asked, feigning mildness.

'Because I do not wish it. You talk nothing but of

Lawrence. Lawrence and his official business. Lawrence and his ancient plates. Lawrence and his boy-servant. It is enough now.'

'He is our friend and I have been away with him. Why shouldn't I want to tell you of him and my journey?'

'You have. Several times. I know it and I want to know no more of it.'

'Is this reasonable?'

He kept his voice quiet, aware this ploy would enrage her further. There was some part of him which enjoyed wielding such power; perhaps, he considered, this was an underlying reason for his boredom with the Consulate in Beirut – he had no authority, none he could be seen exercising, yet in secret he did have a power at his command far greater than that of his peers in the service. He was a spy in a network and they were merely pen-pushers.

'I am not wanting reasonable,' she retorted, her English slipping. She knew she was going to lose but she would not surrender without a struggle.

'I've not seen you like this since . . .'

In exasperation, she stamped her right foot. It was only a small movement and because of her long dress he could not see her shoe as it struck the floorboard and dully thudded the cedar planking.

'. . . since the docks at Marseilles. You last stamped your foot there when the *chasseur* from the hotel attempted to extort a larger than average tip and was prepared to stay his ground. "*Vos bagages, madame, sont trés lourds. Je demande un plus grand pourboire.*" How that "*demande*" fired you! Your foot positively tattooed upon the flagstones . . .'

He looked up at her. Her face was white.

'Please,' she appealed, 'I do not want to talk of him. Or of your journey to see him.'

'This isn't like you. And why shouldn't I speak of my

friends? When I was in Carchemish I was living again. A room with a mosaic floor two thousand years old. The desert night a sparkle of stars. The river, one of the veins of the lifeblood of mankind, sliding silently by as it has ever since man invented civilisation there. I spent a morning on my hands and knees, looking for remains. I went to the top of the mound there and . . .'

He paused. He could not tell her why, of the German railway and the espionage, but she took his pause as hiding something else. On top of a mountain, as she knew from a dalliance she had once had as a girl, no one can overlook you. No one at all.

'I will not hear more!' she shouted. 'You are in love with him, I know this . . .'

It was said. She had not meant to, to admit her fear, to admit she knew. Yet she had. He had forced it from her.

Flecker made no answer. It was true; he could do nothing about it. He could do no more about it than he could dam the Euphrates itself. The river was like love, he thought, older than men, inexorable, unequivocal.

'I suppose you are right. I am . . .'

His admission chilled her and she felt her face, already white with her anger, drain. The tension in her cheeks, the tension in her jaw, relaxed and she believed for a brief moment that she was about to faint. Yet she did not, she remained standing.

There was a long silence. Nothing stirred in the room. Not even the flame in the lamp wavered.

'So what hope is there for us, now?' she asked finally.

'Every hope!' Flecker's words were almost enthusiastic. 'I am not leaving you for him. He is not a woman . . .'

'He has more power than a woman,' she interjected,

her voice brooding. 'He has more influence over you than ever I could have.'

'That is not true.'

'I believe it is. I see you when you are with him. The . . .' – in her agony she searched for her words and could not find them, reverting to French – '. . . *le fond de l'affaire* . . .'

'. . . is that I like him. He has everything I want in a man. But he is not you; we have other special things he could not replace.'

'Yet you love him. You want him. And you want me. How can this be? You cannot love twice at once. *C'est impossible!*'

She threw one hand in the air and let it drop back to her side. Once more she was losing her self-control.

'If you believe this,' her husband replied calmly, 'then do not fight it but join it. Share him with me. Be one of his friends, too. Listen to my stories of him, allow yourself to grow close to him.'

'I cannot.'

'Why not?'

'He makes me afraid. He looks at me and his charm and his . . . his dominance trap me. It's as if he can weave magics. *Il est un homme ravissant.*'

She turned, her eyes moist with tears, and walked to the door. Flecker made no move to follow her. 'I am going to bed,' she announced from the doorway. 'Will you see Anela out.' It was not a question but a command.

'I will be along shortly.'

'If you wish . . . if you want to be with me.'

He watched the door close, the latch clicking loudly in the stillness.

The moonlight was pallid, filtered by clouds blowing in from the sea. Flecker stood in the grey shade of the jasmine and listened to the cicadas in the trees. The insects, he thought, were so like people. At the approach of any movement they fell mute, hiding themselves in a cloak of silence. They did not want to run any risk; it was better to hide than to come out into the open and seek the unknown. Hellé, he considered, was just like that.

She moved against him. His hand was pressed between her spine and his stomach and he felt her buttocks squeeze smoothly against his groin. He extricated his hand and ran it over her hips and down her belly. She made no further movement and he could tell from her breathing that she was still asleep.

The first light of dawn was edging the curtains, and a soft breeze, draughting in through a crack in the casement, ruffled the material. A bird began to sing in the jasmine. From across the valley came one, very faint, human call.

He bent his left arm under the pillow and edged his body closer in to the curve of her back. She grunted in her sleep as his right hand pushed between her legs, the ball of his thumb nuzzling into her. He could feel himself hard against her buttocks, hot against her comparatively cool skin.

'No, Roy,' she murmured, her mind on the verges of consciousness.

He said nothing but pushed harder and harder against her, all the while seeing in his mind's eye the Glossy Ibis atop its vine, the lower end of which was covered by a hem of gold and silver weave catching the gathering dawn light.

'Don't, Roy,' she murmured, awakening slowly to the pressure of him moving inside her. 'Don't, Roy.'

'Don't?'

'Don't,' she repeated.

'Don't what? Don't what . . .'

He was breathing harshly, in quicker bursts.

'Don't,' she pleaded in rhythm to his breath. 'Don't . . . Don't . . . Don't go. Don't go away.'

The room was sweltering. Outside in Rue de Baron, Aleppo's morning din of street vendors' calls, rattle of pony tackle and clopping of hoofs, chatter of conversation and occasional jangle of carts had disappeared. Even the wind had vanished, as if seeking a shady comfort from the blaring sun. The red level in the alcohol thermometer by the window read 91°.

Flecker mopped his brow. The humidity was low and his throat correspondingly raw, as if he had been chewing on sand. He had almost lost his voice. Open before him on the table, the high sun striping it with brilliant bars of light, was his dossier.

'What's this entry?'

Lawrence leaned over his shoulder and tapped the last line of the column with a pencil. Flecker ran his finger down the list until it touched the pencil.

'Film stock . . .'

Flecker was about to add the make chosen, but Lawrence was now reading ahead of him and interrupted.

'That's no good. The surface gelatine is affected by the heat and the resulting pictures have no definition. No use whatsoever when I'm trying to get accurate snapshots of the girder construction. The lines go fuzzy and you end up with an Impressionist photograph.' He laughed briefly, then became business-like once more. 'You'll have to let London know I need something more reliable. Tell them what temperatures we face.' He tapped the thermometer. 'Tell them I must have those Cristoid films – or something close to that in specification.'

Flecker noted the request on a pad.

'We're also dropping a little low on ammunition, particularly revolver. I doubt we've two hundred rounds left.'

Flecker studied his copy of the original supply manifest and said, 'I shall need to know why you've expended so much. London's sure to ask, especially as your reports don't mention having to repulse hordes of mounted Bedouin thirsting for blood.'

'Tell them Woolley's shot a few *kaimmakams* . . .'

Lawrence dissolved into a fit of laughter and Flecker joined him. He dropped his pen on the message pad and hugged his sides.

'Shall I say,' he stuttered through his laughter, 'that it's been an open season on Turkish governors?'

As their mirth subsided, Flecker said, 'Do you think Woolley's going to get stick for that?'

'I expect so. They'll have him account for himself and he'll need to be a good deal less imperious with Their Lordships. Raff informed me that a pretty stiff memo came through to Aleppo about it. The Old Man in Constantinople's been fending off diplomatic complaints . . .'

'I know, I read it,' Flecker said. 'Indeed, I encoded it.'

'With glee, I trust?'

'With some degree of . . .'

'What a master of litotes you are!' snorted Lawrence. 'But how have you used so much?'

'When Woolley arrived, we had a spot of bother with the labourers. Some of the headmen started to stir up trouble. Woolley mounted his high horse, we dismissed three dozen of the leaders, just to show we could, and then – in order to gee up the remainder – we made it a rule that every find be heralded by the firing of our pistols. You know how the Arabs love to do that sort

of thing. Well, all went perfectly for a day or two and
then we came upon what must have been a merchant's
dwelling. Pot after jug after bowl came to light. It
sounded like a battle . . . that's where it all went.'

'What do you suggest I put in the report?'

Lawrence thought for a while, then advised, 'Put
down that we had to pay our guards in bullets. That
can't really be questioned and it sounds logical.'

Again, Flecker made a note.

'And that's it, I think,' Lawrence said, stuffing the
pencil into a pocket in his shorts. 'I fancy now a cool
drink and a lie-down. We'll set off just after four and,
as there're just the two of us with no encumbrances,
we should make Bâb by nightfall.'

They left Flecker's room and went downstairs. The
foyer and bar were deserted save for a dog which had
inveigled its way in and was lying on its side just within
the door. It was asleep but, on hearing Lawrence's footsteps, quickly got up and slunk away into the scorching
sunlight.

'No one about,' Lawrence declared but, at the sound
of his voice, one of the hotel servants appeared. He
wore a fez which tipped slightly to one side. The tassel
swung as he approached them.

'*Orid assir fœkihœ min fadlak?*' Lawrence ordered.
'*Bortokal.*'

'*Æywœ.*'

'*Orid sœndœwitsh rozbif . . . wœ gibnœ.*'

'*Æywœ,*' the servant repeated and left them, shuffling
softly away on his slippered feet.

'Will that do you?' Lawrence asked as they sat in two
of the wicker armchairs by the bar.

'Yes,' Flecker croaked, his voice cracked. He decided
an affirmative was the best reply; the Arabic had been
too quick for him to follow.

'Are you all right?' Lawrence was concerned and

looked over the bar to see if there was a carafe of water there.

'I'm fine,' Flecker whispered. 'Just a bit of a frog in my throat.'

'You're sure?'

'Quite . . .'

'Nothing worse than a Frenchie in the windpipe,' Lawrence retorted. 'Best thing to do with the French is spit them out.'

They did not speak for some time. The servant brought a jug of fresh orange juice and two plates of sandwiches made of the local coarse bread.

As the time passed the sun grew less strong and the street outside began to come once more to life. The first sound to establish itself was the beating of a metal-worker's hammer. The noise did not come from one of the shops but from a tiny stall in the street operated by a Soleyb coppersmith, a nomad earning money on his way through the town. Soon the sound of the shops grew – more hammering, bargaining and heckling, the swish of passing pack animals.

'One day,' Lawrence declared, 'I'm going to write a grand travel book about the cities of the Middle East. Not just a book of guide instructions – a kind of personal Baedeker – but a real study. A look at the history and life of the cities, a volume that captures them for all time. And here, Aleppo, will be one of those cities.'

Flecker drank his orange juice and sucked his teeth. Fragments of the stringy roast beef from the sandwiches were wedged between them.

'This is a fascinating place, quite unlike any other,' Lawrence continued. 'It was – it still is – a melting-pot, a whirlygig of customs and creeds and languages all coming together in the spirit of compromise. That's just it! The spirit of compromise. Look about you, Roy. Even though the city speaks predominantly Arabic, I'm sure you could find fifty tongues spoken within a half-mile radius of this very hotel. Jews, Kurds, Armenians, Turks, Arabs, Christians and Gnostics, Muslims and atheists, Jains and Parsees . . . You and I! They all mingle here. And the Aleppines have absorbed elements of every single type. They're shrewder, more fanatical, more beautiful, stronger. Yet they lack a conviction, a self-consciousness. Which is why Aleppo is what it is – a kaleidoscope of ever-changing patterns rather than a fixed entity with a purpose. I believe that, but for this terrible deficit, Aleppo would have been the Venice of the desert, the trading citadel of the seas of sand . . .'

'You know so much,' Flecker said with evident admiration, his voice less husky now he had drunk the juice.

'Only because I immerse myself in it. Arabia is a place of excitement for me. Here is all I want at present out of life. The wonders of its past, the insecurity of its future . . . I hope, one day, to be able to help the Arabs stand on their own feet. They're too naturally proud to be continually buffeted from side to side by the greater powers – by the French, the Germans, the Italians. We must help them to be themselves. They may come under our sphere of influence – that's Hogarth's aim – but it can only be good in the long run for all concerned. We're benevolent, whereas the French and Germans are merely colonial exploiters.'

The dog came to the door again, poked its head in and retreated to the street.

'I like the Arabic way of life. The comradeship, the morality . . .'

'Dahoum?' Flecker ventured.

'Yes, and him. Perhaps especially him.' Lawrence paused. 'Did you know Vyvyan Richards up at Oxford?'

'We met,' Flecker answered.

'He's a good friend,' Lawrence replied enigmatically and fell silent for some minutes before going to his room to rest.

Between their two rooms was an adjoining door. Under normal circumstances it was kept bolted, but as the rooms were permanently booked by the Consulate for use as quarters – more specifically as a meeting place for espionage staff beyond the ears of the Turkish spies amongst the Consul's local staff – the bolts were seldom slid across.

In his room, Flecker lay on his bed and watched a hornet patrolling the ceiling, on guard for smaller insects upon which it might prey. It made no sound as it hovered, then flew on to its next station. With a methodicity that would have been laudable in a human mind, it worked up and down the ceiling in flight patterns about three inches apart. From studying its behaviour, Flecker realised its range of accurate eyesight must have been about two inches.

He concentrated on the hornet only in order to quash his thoughts of Lawrence in the next room, lying stripped to the waist, perhaps naked, sweating in the oppressive heat and semi-darkness produced by the shutters.

He toyed with excuses he might use to go to the adjoining door, turn the polished brass knob and enter the next room. Perhaps, he pondered, he could go in to ask once more just how many rounds of revolver ammunition they had expended in Carchemish. Or how many rounds of rifle ammunition were required – had they, possibly, fired their rifles in jubilation as well? Were they in need of more salt? Woolley had said the local stuff was of poor quality; had their supply of Cerebos lasted? Would it see out the season? He could ask again for the date of Woolley's departure, just to be sure he would be gone by the time they reached the site. He knew the answer – Woolley was already on his way home on leave, breaking his journey at Constantinople in order to visit the British ambassador there.

They were alone here in Aleppo. Fontana and his family were in Beilan, the hill resort to which they retired for the hottest of the summer months. With them had gone the expatriate staffs of the other Aleppo embassies and consulates. The town itself was under quarantine for an outbreak of cholera, but that had not deterred Lawrence – and where he went Flecker was prepared to follow.

Through the slats of the shutters came the distant cry of a *muezzin* calling the faithful to prayer.

The hornet, having entirely traversed the ceiling, was now flying up and down the wall behind the table. When it arrived at a crack above the skirting-board it landed and tentatively probed the crevice.

Flecker swung his legs slowly off his bed. His slippers were over by the table but he ignored them, walking barefoot to the door. He put his hand on the knob and twisted it and the mechanism clicked loudly.

'That you, Roy?'

'Yes. Are you awake?'

'More or less. Come on in.'

Flecker pushed the door open. Lawrence was lying on the floor with his feet in the barred sunlight. His chest was bare and tanned, his arms limp by his sides. His legs were splayed apart and his midriff covered by a towel embroidered with the hotel's motif. His eyes were closed, long hair damp with perspiration and adhering to his cheeks. Without opening his eyes, he stroked the hair aside.

'I should get it cut. Once it starts to flail your face and get near your mouth it's a blessed nuisance. I say,' he opened his eyes and looked up at Flecker, 'you wouldn't give me a trim, would you? There's a pair of scissors in my attaché case.'

Flecker looked down at Lawrence, feeling his pulse quicken rapidly. He had been wondering how to excuse his entrance and now Lawrence, as if by design, had given him his reason.

'I've never cut hair before. Don't know the first thing about it.'

'Doesn't matter. It only has to be neat; I'm not looking for a perfect gents' coiffure.' He pointed to the table by his bed. 'The case is under there.'

His hand shaking, Flecker opened the flap on the well-travelled case and rummaged about in the papers and photographs for the scissors, eventually finding them in a pocket at the side. They were long bladed, ideal for a barber's work.

Lawrence got up, wrapped the towel around himself and tucked in the loose end at his waist. Then he sat on the upright chair by his table and faced the window.

'Cut away!'

'How much?'

'Just snip it back to the nape. It doesn't have to look pretty.'

Flecker began to cut, the curling mousey-fair hair dropping to the floor where, if it landed on his feet, it tickled and he had to twitch his toes to flick it off. Touching Lawrence's hair, he realised it was the first time they had had any form of other than accidental physical contact. It was soft and damp with sweat and stray hairs clung to his fingers, caught under his nails. He wanted to caress the hair, not ruthlessly cut it short.

When Flecker had finished Lawrence pulled the small dressing mirror along the table and turned his head from side to side.

'Do you think you can remove a bit more? Another inch or so? In the winter, it's warming to keep it long, but now . . . I suppose it prevents sunburn to the back of the neck, like the Foreign Legion *kepi* does, but as I wear a *keffiyeh* most of the time anyway . . .'

Standing behind him once more, Flecker continued to cut the hair, attempting to give it some shape. The curling ends made this awkward.

When he was almost done, Flecker – affecting nonchalance – rested his hand on Lawrence's shoulder and close to his neck. He made the action seem as if he was holding Lawrence's head still while he cut back a few loose strands.

'There! I think I'm done,' he announced. 'It's not exactly an expert cut, but it's fairly neat.'

He put the scissors on the table but did not move his hand. Instead, he let it slide a fraction of an inch away from the neck and then back again, as if the motion had been in error.

Lawrence gazed into the mirror but instead of twisting his head about to inspect his hair-cut, he looked directly at Flecker, his blue eyes cool yet not cruel.

'I know,' he said quietly, 'yet it's not possible.' He put his own hand on Flecker's and moved it away without holding it.

'Why not?' Flecker asked, just as quietly.

'It just is not. It's not that I . . . It is not my way, Roy. There's nothing wrong with you; I like you hugely. But I'm not able . . . We are good chums, you know that. And we must stay so for the sake of both ourselves and the cause of our work. But nothing else . . .'

'I do not understand . . .' Flecker began, hurt.

'I do not expect you to,' Lawrence interposed. 'I do not always myself.'

'I am willing to share anything with you. My life and poetry, my interests . . . Like Jack did.'

'I am no Jack Beazley,' Lawrence said.

'And Hellé . . .' Flecker went on.

'No, I cannot. Accept me for what I am, for what we are together, and ask nothing more. And don't be hurt, Roy. You are not the first I have had to reject, nor will you be the last.'

'Is there nothing I can do?'

'Not now. Maybe later.'

Flecker stepped away towards the door, then turned and asked bluntly, 'What of Dahoum?'

'That is different,' Lawrence answered, somewhat sharply. 'Very different indeed.'

His brusqueness was intended to put an end to their conversation and Flecker made no further comment. He went through the door and closed it softly behind him. Then, very quietly, he began to weep.

When they mounted their horses a few hours later, neither man made any reference to the episode. Flecker was glad they were leaving the city. Although they had eaten no vegetables whilst in Aleppo and had drunk only fruit juice or water they knew for certain had been boiled, he was still afraid of contracting the cholera. Lawrence was excited; Flecker put this exhilaration down to the fact that they were returning to Carchemish, and Dahoum.

In the starlight, the temporary track which had been laid to take the dump cart shone brightly. It ran for only a few hundred yards, from the beginning of the bridge to the point where the labourers had organised a heap of debris brought over from the archaeological dig. The sleepers beneath the rails were black against the grey hues of sand and gravel.

Flecker gripped the rail nearest him. It was, to his surprise, very cold despite the fact that the night was unusually warm. As he pulled himself over the earth, the rail clicked slightly against the bolts and mountings holding it in place.

Ahead of him, across the rails, he could see the dark bump which was Lawrence's head silhouetted against the starlit landscape. Below him he could feel Dahoum's hands pressing upwards on the soles of his shoes.

'Here!'

The word was barely audible despite its issuing from only a few feet in front of him.

Reaching forward, Flecker's hand was grasped by Lawrence who tugged evenly on it. Dahoum thrust upward. Flecker slid over the rim of the embankment and lay beside the nearest rail. Lawrence slithered past him and leaned over the edge. Within a moment, the Arab boy was with them.

Flecker was breathless, yet not with exertion or illness.

Lawrence's hand touched his ear and he was instantly alert, straining his hearing.

There were footsteps approaching them. They were not advancing at speed, having the rhythm of a man out for a stroll. Several times they halted, scuffed about on the track bed gravels and then continued, always towards them.

Once again Lawrence's hand touched him, this time on the thigh.

From instructions given him before they left the house, Flecker knew what to do: very carefully he manoeuvred himself so that his body was against the rail, his hands on the nearest wooden sleeper. He could smell the creosote in which the wood was steeped. Then, with the pressure of one arm and one leg – Lawrence had shown him how to do it on the mosaic floor – he rolled silently over the rail, across the space to the next, over that and on to the gravel at the far side. He made virtually no sound and felt smug.

The footsteps had halted and he heard a soft voice speak in German. His heart raced and his wrist, pressed against the protruding end of one of the sleepers, pulsed with each beat of blood.

The voice spoke again. He readied himself to run. Lawrence had made it quite clear that confrontation – his euphemism for anything from 'a smart punch on the hooter' to a knife in the ribs – was to be avoided at all costs. The Germans were not at all popular with their Arab labourers, despite the fact that they paid good wages – better than the British, in fact. They beat, abused and exploited them; yet there was no circumstance in which an Arab would actually murder one of them. The repercussions would be too great. Therefore, Lawrence had explained, there would be no way in which, if they did 'confront' one of the Germans, the crime could be adequately disguised. If they were cornered, they would have to run for it.

Flecker was not a little worried that this eventuality might have to be faced. He was sure he could run, but only for a short distance; after that, his breath would come only in gasps and he would slow down. Dressed as he was in an Arab cloak and *keffiyeh*, with an *ogal* around his brow, his confidence in his being able to run even a short way was considerably undermined.

As these thoughts raced through his mind, his ears alert for Lawrence's curt command to run, he heard a German voice begin to sing. It was a tuneless noise, a hum interspersed with muttered words which sounded incongruously guttural.

A hand touched his wrist and a finger tapped his palm twice, rapidly. This was the signal to lie still.

The footsteps started up again, receded slightly and then halted. There was the scratching of a match.

Flecker knew he should have lowered his face; tanned though it was, it would still present a lighter than average disc if illuminated by even a flimsy source of light – even a glowing cigarette. Yet he did not move his head, but looked in the direction of the match.

It was then he realised the German was very close to them. He had reckoned the man to be at least twenty yards away, but he was barely seven. His singing had seemed distant because most of the sound was going over Flecker and out into the darkness of the night. In truth, the man had stopped virtually beside them.

The close proximity of the German was frightening. Flecker felt sweat break out on his forehead and the *keffiyeh*, though made of good quality cotton, started to itch his scalp. The cloak, where it came in contact with his bare arms, also irritated his skin. His throat was soured with bile – he dared not swallow for fear the bitterness would make him cough.

The breeze blowing from the river was not strong enough to extinguish the match, but it flickered. The German turned his back on them to cup the flame to a cigarette.

There was an infinitesimal rustle beside Flecker. He only just heard it; a grass blade shifting in the breeze could not have been louder. Turning his head, he discovered he was alone on the trackside. The other two shadows which had been his companions had vanished as if by some trick of sorcery.

The German faced the river once more. He took two steps towards Flecker, the red tip of his cigarette glowing as he inhaled. The two steps brought him still closer. He exhaled and Flecker saw, as if it was a dreadful threat in the worst of his nightmares, the cigarette smoke wraithing in the starlight. He took another step. Then another.

Flecker knew that he should run. He should get up and flee. Dive over the track, spring down the drop to the river bank, sprint for the cover of the reeds growing

thirty yards away and from which they had first spied
the German, trying to assess if he were a guard or just
an engineer out for a night-time stroll. Lawrence had
analysed the latter; he was apparently unarmed, seemed
not to be paying much attention to his surroundings
and, besides, they seldom put a sentry on their work-
ings. The only bother they really faced was from the
Aleppine Arabs creeping back at night to go through
the recently tipped spoil from the mound in the hope
of finding Roman coins or relics they might then sell to
Lawrence, or the Germans, or to other Europeans when
they returned to Aleppo.

There was a series of tiny thuds from the embankment. The German turned round abruptly.

'*Ja?*' he asked, tentatively.

There was no further sound.

'*Kommen Sie hierher! Tæælæ honæ!*' he ordered, his
Arabic strongly accentuated by his mother tongue.

He was not answered.

'*Mæn . . .*'

He cupped his hands to his mouth and called, '*Hast
du etwas Ungewöhnliches in der Nähe gehört?*'

'*Nein!*' replied a far-off voice. '*Gar nichts. Vor fünf
Minuten hab' ich einen Hund gehört.*'

'*Ach so!*'

He reached under his jacket and Flecker heard rather
than saw him draw a pistol. There was a metallic snap
as he cocked it.

'*Min?*' the German asked.

Cautiously, he walked to the edge of the embankment
and peered down. He leaned over slightly, bent from
the waist as if bowing politely.

To be mistaken and shot for a desert mongrel, Flecker
thought, was not a fate he relished. In a moment of
light-headed farcicality prompted by his terror, he won-

dered how Hogarth might contrive to write his obituary in *The Times*.

A hand touched Flecker's ankle and lightly tugged at it. As he rolled over very slowly, every pebble of gravel seemed to explode beneath him like a squib, yet the German did not hear them.

After a minute, the German strolled off, replacing his pistol in its holster. When he was no longer in sight, Lawrence whispered in to Flecker's ear, 'Well done, Roy! A good clear head. That's just the ticket for a spy.'

'I was frozen stiff with fear.'

Lawrence patted his hand.

'How did you distract him?' Flecker asked.

'Loose stone, rolling down the slope . . . Let's get on with it.'

Carefully they made their way towards the river bank. Just short of the beginning of the stonework for the first pier, they stopped. Lawrence pointed ahead of them.

In the embankment was a culvert. Before it, the earth had been dug away and the fan-shaped area so formed had been lined with square-cut boulders.

'From near the Little Shrine,' he whispered, touching one of the stones with his foot. 'In we go!'

The culvert was pitch-dark, a circle of blackness against the embankment. The starlight penetrated it for only a few feet. Dahoum bent down and went in first and, once well inside, struck a match. It flared, a pin-prick of light, and Flecker, at the entrance with Lawrence, smelled the burning sulphur. Dahoum made a plosive noise and Lawrence pushed Flecker ahead of him into the culvert.

It was a tunnel, about four feet in diameter. Twenty feet under the embankment, it passed through a forty-five-degree angle. At the curve, they stopped and

Dahoum struck another match; its tiny explosion of light in such a confined space temporarily blinded Flecker.

By the third match, his eyes had become accustomed to the sudden light. Lawrence spent the duration of each match studying the culvert roof, pushing his fingers into the crevices between the stones, testing the mortar and measuring each stone with his hands.

'What are we...?' Flecker began to whisper, but Lawrence quickly placed his fingers to his lips.

Their task done they continued through the culvert to the other end, where Dahoum crept out and climbed the embankment before returning to signal the all-clear. Together they walked, crouched as if in the tunnel still, to the reed-bed and slipped into its cover.

'Never speak in an enclosed space,' Lawrence advised quietly. 'Sound travels down a tunnel like a megaphone.'

'I'm sorry,' Flecker started to apologise, but Lawrence once more silenced him.

'No need; you weren't to know. Just a trick of the trade.'

They set off in single file along the river bank in the direction of the mound. The further they went from the railway bridge, the slower became the beat of Flecker's heart. His clothing no longer annoyed him and he was able to breathe more easily. The bile subsided in his throat, and his head, so full alternately of intense fear and muddled thoughts, cleared.

Once they reached the well-used pathway the labourers and their donkeys had trodden going to and from the embankment with their panniers of soil, Lawrence began to talk.

'Why was the culvert so important?' Flecker enquired.

'I wanted to see how long it was, how it was made,

also how many of them there were in a set stretch of the embankment.'

'Couldn't photographs give you that?'

'Up to a point. But you saw how they've built sluices. Those low walls of cut boulders, angled like that to guide the flood waters in and under the embankment, actually hide them from our sight from the mound.'

'And what exactly have you deduced from your findings?'

'Simple, Roy. At the bend in the centre would be the best place to set a hefty charge. When – and if – the time comes.'

Dahoum, walking by their side, reached into the folds of his clothes and withdrew a revolver which he handed to Lawrence. Lawrence accepted it, thrusting it into his belt alongside his own.

'I might have needed one of those,' Flecker said. He had not realised his companions had been armed.

'No, you wouldn't,' Lawrence assured him. 'If it had come to it two would have been ample.'

As they left the pathway to go in the direction of the house, Flecker noticed Lawrence was walking holding Dahoum's hand. He felt an instant pang of envy, of rejection. He wanted so much to be a part of this relationship, and knew he could not.

Sweat was running down Flecker's face. His lips stung and his tongue was sore with the taste of his own salt. His eyes ached from the glare of the sun, and smarted. The tops of his ears were reddened by sunburn. Where a sand fly had bitten him on the wrist was a drying bubble of straw-coloured matter.

In the soil before him, projecting from the side of the trench, was the corner of a tablet upon which was an inscribed relief. He could see only a few square inches of it, but it was already exciting. It had thrilled Lawrence when the workman excavating the trench had come upon it, his trained eye holding his shovel back just before it struck the stone.

'If this had been a while back,' Lawrence had exclaimed to Flecker on being shown the find, 'it would have meant quite a heavy expenditure of ammunition.'

Provided by Lawrence with a stiff-bristled brush of the kind Flecker was more accustomed to seeing his parents' maid use to sweep the fireplace in their house in Cheltenham, he set to work uncovering the relief, brushing at the soil above and below it. When he came to a stone or extra hard section of soil he scraped at it with a pointed trowel of the sort used by plasterers and bricklayers.

His most important instruction was to go slowly. There was no hurry, he kept telling himself. It had been in the ground for three and a half millennia; another hour or two would do no harm. But he knew he had to get it free by dusk. Any major find such as this, left after dark, was sure to vanish in the night.

Gradually more and more of the tablet appeared. At first it seemed only lightly inscribed but, as he uncovered a wider area, so Flecker could see it was heavily decorated.

The hieroglyphs were unintelligible to him: squiggles, blocks, arrows and bars with, in the centre of them, a crudely drawn human face in profile.

As more of the tablet came to light, so Flecker's excitement rose. He exposed first the outline of a pointed-toed boot; then another appeared. The legs above them were clad in baggy trousers and, above that, a folded sarong-like garment of the sort found on Egyptian paintings and carvings. The effigy's face, when he reached it – brushing the sand and grit away from it with heightened anticipation – was almost humorous.

It had a huge, stylised nose, as big and exaggerated as a clown's but pointed. On its head it wore a pointed hat of the kind depicted more commonly on gnomes and elves or Irish hobgoblins. Around its neck the effigy was carrying a deer – possibly a dog, a sheep or a hornless goat – while at its waist hung a sword, the hilt of which was shaped in outline exactly like an erect penis and testicles. He thought of the carved slab of stone in Lawrence's first crate of finds sent to him in Beirut, and wondered if this might share the same provenance. The figure was similar.

The tablet once free of the earth, Flecker propped it against the side of the trench and hailed one of the labourers passing by above him, laden down with a basket of dirt.

'*El Orans!*' he ordered. '*Otlob El Orans!*'

The labourer lowered his burden with evident delight and disappeared from sight. Flecker could hear him calling and, within a minute, Lawrence was at the end of the trench and bounding along it, stepping over fallen boulders.

Together the two men studied the tablet. Both of them laughed at the vigorous wit of the artist.

'A man with some talent to amuse,' Lawrence proclaimed. 'These Hittites seem to have been jolly fellows – and jolly well endowed, too, from the state of his dagger. An interesting metaphor that – the member as a weapon. How fascinating that the image has survived all these years; you only have to read the pornographic literature of the last thirty or forty to see it still holds good. "He thrust his weapon at her", or "Venus's battering ram" or something of the sort.'

He picked up the tablet. It was not so heavy that one man could not lift it.

Later that afternoon, Lawrence photographed their find and personally supervised its packing for transport.

'Look after it, Roy. It's the best of its kind we've found here. Hogarth will be very pleased when he unwraps this one.'

As dusk fell the labourers began to gather at the house, forming a crowd in front of Flecker's room. He had the use of the quarter vacated by Leonard Woolley and opened the door to be confronted by the crowd, squatting on their haunches and suddenly falling silent at his appearance.

'*Masa'il kher*,' he greeted the assembly.

A few replied to his greeting, but the majority said nothing; they just watched him. He felt their stares, and was afraid. He had not felt such fear all the time he had been in the Middle East. Here, in the desert, he was aware of his vulnerability and the precariousness of Lawrence's situation. And, he thought, when he was gone Lawrence would be on his own.

His apprehension was dispelled by the appearance of Lawrence at the living-room door, calling out in fluent Arabic to the men who slowly rose and began to shuffle into some semblance of a line.

'What do they want?' Flecker asked.

'Paying,' was Lawrence's blunt reply.

He went in to Flecker's room. There he opened – it was unlocked, with not so much as a stick through the hasp – the large chest, and Flecker saw to his horror and surprise that it was half-full of silver coins.

'I have been sleeping in the treasury . . .' he began.

'Indeed you have. Safest place about.'

'But it's not even padlocked . . .'

'No need. If one of them were to steal, then it would be short odds all round. They know the supply is finite – and they'd soon know who the thief was, and he would pay for it. Of that you can be certain. Desert justice!'

Lawrence began to pay the labourers, handing the

wages to the headmen who then redistributed them to their own gangs of workers.

Bathed in the warm light of the lowering sun, Flecker watched as his companion passed the money to the Arabs, counting the coins out and noting the transactions in a pocket book. When he was done, he placed the record of payment in the chest and dropped the lid with a thud.

'That's done for a week,' Lawrence said with relief. 'I hate being a paymaster.'

Dahoum brought Lawrence a bucket of hot water, a bar of carbolic soap and a nail-brush with which he energetically scrubbed his hands.

'Nothing as filthy as money, and nothing filthier than money in the Middle East,' he commented, rinsing his hands and studying them closely. 'Blood money, much of it. Touched by slavery but, worse, touched by . . .'

He stopped speaking. There was still, on the end of his thumb, a mark where the silver tarnish had blackened his skin. He set to once more, scrubbing harshly at the offending mark.

'The Arabs keep their money close to their skin,' he announced. 'Sometimes in the groin. The safest place, I suppose. But it . . .' He shivered involuntarily and scoured the nail-brush over and over his thumb, the scent of the carbolic drifting over the sand.

'*Guten Tag, Herr Lawrence!* It is a long time since we last met and yet we are only a few miles apart. How is your digging of holes progressing?'

Lawrence shook the German's proffered hand very briefly, grinning all the while.

'Good evening, Herr Contzen. My hole-digging is progressing nicely and, because of that, I see your embankment grows stronger.' He turned towards

Flecker who was standing in his shadow cast by the blazing fire. 'May I introduce to you Herr Flecker? Not an archaeologist but a poet.'

'*Ach! Ein Dichter!* And tell me, Herr Flecker, how do you like Carchemish?'

They moved towards canvas seats placed upwind of the fire. An Arab servant threw a large piece of driftwood on to the flames, the sparks exploding into the sky.

'It is not the most beautiful of places,' the German engineer continued. 'The sand, the midges, the mosquitoes . . . Everything seems designed to – cause you pain.'

'Cause one pain,' Flecker suggested, 'between the eyes?'

'Yes! That is right. Even the sun has a will to bite.'

The Arab returned with a bottle of schnapps on a tray. Under the German's supervision he poured out three generous measures into glass tumblers.

As he spoke, Flecker watched Lawrence. He did so only fleetingly, looking to him only as he would a friend, to see if he were comfortable. Lawrence was beaming genially at the others but his eyes, pretending to screw against the glare of the fire, were quickly absorbing details of the equipment he saw in the half-darkness on the edge of the firelight's range.

Looking back towards the fire, Lawrence exclaimed, 'You two seem to have struck a common bond in your appreciations of Arabia. Hardly a word from me seems likely to change your opinions of the desert and convince you otherwise.'

The German laughed: it was as harsh a sound, Flecker thought, as his language. It came in bursts like gunfire. He wondered if this had been the man who, only twenty-four hours before, had stood over him on the railway, had lit a cigarette and cocked his side-arm.

'Are you finding many antikas, Herr Lawrence? If the débris you are providing us with is to be judged, then you are doing well and discovering much.'

'It is proving to be a most important site,' Lawrence answered. 'Quite the most important of all the Hittite sites so far discovered. We know this area was the region of their empire, yet I don't think anyone realised to what extent they had settled it. An empire in those days could be a few thousand square miles only.'

'Rather than a few thousand races of peoples today. Such as your own.'

The German did not speak with any rancour, but Lawrence was shrewd enough to know his thoughts.

'A benevolent rulership,' he rejoined, smiling. 'We give and we take as we civilise.'

'Just so. It is also our way, the German way. Now,' he handed the glasses round, 'let us drink not to our nationalities and empire successes but to the ghosts of Carchemish. *Prost!*'

They raised their glasses. Flecker noticed that Lawrence only let the schnapps touch his lips and, when he lowered his glass, he kept his hand around it so as to disguise the fact that he had not drunk.

'I am also glad,' Contzen continued, 'that our difficulties have no more to come between us, Herr Lawrence. We are just people doing our jobs in a strange place, and there is no knowing when we might not need the assistance of the other – apart from you giving us your unwanted earth, of course. It has happened the once already, and we are very grateful . . .'

Flecker watched the fire. The embers glowed scarlet every time the river breeze blew even slightly more strongly. Sparks lifted and drifted across the desert, not dying until they were yards off in the night. He wondered where the other engineers were; Contzen was the man in command.

He considered the difficulties Lawrence and the Germans had encountered. The worst episode was when a German had had Dahoum flogged for interrupting work on the railway. When the boy had sought repayment for a loan he had made to one of the Germans' foremen, an engineer accused him of preventing the men from getting on with their jobs and had had him beaten. Lawrence had been livid with rage and stormed across to the German camp where he had confronted Contzen, who replied that there was nothing wrong with flogging Arabs – they could not be managed without such treatment.

'We thrash at least one man a day,' he had reported. 'It keeps the rest at their work; it does not have them growing lazy or taking advantage of us.'

'You treat them like prisoners. Numbers painted on their cloaks! They are not slaves.'

'Indeed no!' the German had exclaimed. 'We pay them well.'

'I demand an apology be made to the Arab boy.'

The Arab labourers had stopped work to watch the encounter and one of the foremen was translating for their benefit.

'No!'

'Then I shall take the man responsible down to the village and have him flogged,' Lawrence had retorted.

'You could not do this!'

Lawrence calmed his voice.

'Do you not think so, Herr Contzen?'

Contzen had turned to the engineer who was standing behind him. They spoke in German for a moment and the junior man shook his head. 'Apologise!' his superior then demanded loudly, adding in German, '*Sonst kommt es zu einem Aufstand*.'

Understanding no German, Lawrence was provided with an interpretation by the foreman relaying the conversation in Arabic. Feeling inwardly triumphant, he beckoned to Dahoum who came forward and received a formal apology. The boy had struggled, Lawrence had told Flecker, to keep a straight face and afterwards, as the Germans withdrew, he fell into a fit of giggling. To have a European behave in such a manner towards him was unique.

'No damn German,' Lawrence had said, 'is going to have his way with my boy.'

The fire was dying somewhat and the German turned to order more wood be brought. Lawrence quickly poured his schnapps on to the ground and flicked dry sand over the spot with his sandalled foot.

'Do you know of the trouble we had, Herr Flecker? Herr Lawrence – how do you say it in English – saved us by the skin of the teeth.'

'No, I don't know of it,' Flecker said pleasantly, although he was lying. He had read the file and knew to what the German was referring. 'Do tell me.'

'It was the Kurds,' Contzen explained. 'They were dissatisfied with their conditions of employment. Seven hundred of them we had working for us at that time. They decide to . . .' – he punched his thigh to find the word – 'make a mutiny on us. They attacked us in our camp and then they were joined by three hundred others from the archaeology mound. Only Herr Lawrence and Herr Woolley prevented us from being killed.'

'It was nothing.' Lawrence placed his glass on the ground, well away from the damp spot which had soaked up through the dry covering sand.

'It was much. We are in your debt for this.'

As they walked back towards the house – Flecker pulling his cloak closely around him, for it was now cold and seemed more so away from the heat of the German's camp-fire – Lawrence said, 'Those Germans have no idea. One has to admire their tenacity, the scope of their dream – a railway from Berlin to the Gulf is a grand ambition – yet they have so little humanity in them.

'A few months ago we had to dismiss a hundred or so workmen because we could not afford to pay them – and we are obliged to pay less than the Germans. The men preferred to work on for us without pay rather than go over to the railway. There's a good deal of mutual distrust, even hatred, between the Germans and their workers. How can they expect to build an empire on such foundations?'

'It's their way,' Flecker commented philosophically. 'Let's just use it to our benefit.'

'Yes, but we must not make the same mistake,' Lawrence retorted. As his emotions rose so he began to walk faster. 'If we are to rule, we must do so as benevolent rulers. We can be – Hogarth would perhaps say we should be – dictators, but that is not to say we must be cruel. The Arab . . .' His voice trailed away.

Flecker knew what was in Lawrence's mind. It was not merely his feelings towards the Arabs; it was also his love for them, a love personified in Dahoum.

'The local Arabs hate the Germans,' Lawrence mused, his pace slowing again. 'They accuse them of getting drunk on *raki* and of being mean. There is no greater insult from an Arab than to be accused of miserliness. They are, as you will know, the most generous of races . . .'

'Do you hate the Germans?'

'No, Roy, I don't hate them . . . not exactly. They're brutal, an insensitive nation . . . Last year, Dahoum worked for them for some months as a table boy – we couldn't afford to pay him then. They taught him how to serve food, wait, clear plates and so forth. He learns very quickly and, when we met every night, he told me much of what he had picked up – both in the line of waiting and in the line of railway building. The other servants were happy to answer his seemingly innocent questions.

'And they have to be watched. They have grand designs on the world and they must be prevented from executing them. Can you imagine a world run as they organise the building of their embankment? It bears no thought!' Lawrence brought his hands out from under his cloak and swatted his neck. 'These mosquitoes. Real man-eaters . . .'

Dahoum was awaiting their return, sitting on the ground by the door to Lawrence's room. As they approached he stood up and stepped quickly towards them, speaking hurriedly in Arabic.

'What's wrong?' Flecker asked.

'Malaria,' Lawrence answered. 'Haj Waheed's wife has malaria.'

Dahoum's hands were white, almost as blanched as an Englishman's before the sun started its work upon him. His brow was beaded with sweat and his eyelids fluttered. Every few minutes a spasm of shivering passed through his limbs, lasting only seconds but so violent that Lawrence was obliged to lie across him to hold him down to the bed.

When Lawrence grew exhausted Flecker took over. He bathed Dahoum's brow with water and kept his body well covered by blankets – despite the outside temperature going into the nineties. When Dahoum began to have a fit, he too pressed his body upon the boy's, feeling him twitching, shaking under him. On one occasion he had to grip the metal frame of the bed to prevent Dahoum tipping him on to the floor.

Every few hours they gave the boy water to sip, dosing him with quinine and a concoction Lawrence had obtained in the village, made out of an extract of willow leaves from Turkey. It reduced the boy's temperature slightly and helped him to sleep when he was not delirious.

On the third day Dahoum slept with no more than a sporadic muscular twinge. Lawrence, himself now running a slight fever, attended to Haj Waheed's wife and child as well as a number of other Arabs similarly stricken with what he termed autumno-aestival malaria.

In the evening Lawrence and Flecker sat in the living room, the lamplight dancing on the mosaic, half of which had now been thoroughly cleaned and waxed.

'The Glossy Ibis might take to the wing any day,' Lawrence remarked, looking at the Roman bird, his voice tired. 'You should write a poem, dear Roy, about it. I shall photograph the floor when it is done and send you down a picture.'

'A phoenix arising from the ashes of history,' Flecker suggested.

Without taking his eyes from the bird, Lawrence said softly, 'It would have been very difficult had you not been here, Roy. I'm very grateful to you for all you've done. For Dahoum. For me. You have been a capital companion.'

Flecker made no reply; there was nothing to be said.

'I trust this blessed fever will soon die in me,' Lawrence went on. 'There's much to be done.' He looked up. 'I'm sad you will have to go tomorrow. Are you sure you can make the journey without me? I'll send a man with you to Aleppo, of course.'

'I, too, am sad.'

'But you will rejoice to be back with Hellé?'

Again, Flecker did not answer.

'Of course you will. Your wife will be worried . . . for your health.'

'She will also be worried that I am with you.'

'She knows I take good care of you.'

'She knows I love you.'

There was a silence and Lawrence did not move. His head was turned in Flecker's direction, his eyes blue even in the dull yellow of the fire- and lamp-light.

No longer able to take the staring, Flecker averted his face.

'I know how you feel, Roy. I'm sorry I can't return it. It's not you; you are a fine man. Yet it was ever the case with me. With Jack, with Vyvyan . . .'

'But Dahoum?' Flecker asked.

'That's different, I've told you that. I want not only him, but his whole world. His villages and ruins, the castles of the Crusaders, the dunes of the desert, the hot sun . . . You do understand?'

'I think so.'

'Life is good to me in Carchemish. When they take me away from here, a part of me will fade and cease.'

'Take you away?' Flecker was perplexed.

Lawrence smiled wanly. 'Dear Roy, you are such an innocent, for all your travels and consularings. You and your wife live such secure existences – she in you and you in your words and rhymes.'

Flecker dropped a handful of gnarled olive roots on the fire and Lawrence lapsed into silence, staring at the fire as the olive roots caught. The flames spread along their sun-bleached twists and gnarls, blackening the dry wood.

'What do you really want of your life?' Flecker asked after a while.

'A bit of peace, I suppose. Time to reflect, write, travel. Some excitement . . . No! I want a thrilling peace! The Arabs are heading towards such change, such conflict with the world. A conflict that will last a thousand years. I need to be with them for that . . .'

'You can't be here for a thousand years!' Flecker pointed out.

'No, I can't. But the way I shape the future . . .'

Flecker watched him. Lawrence's hands were pressed together before his knees as he hunched forward towards the fire. The light from the flames cast dark shadows between his fingers and made his face shine.

'I'm a servant of history,' Lawrence announced quietly. 'Hogarth's servant.'

'How can you be?' Flecker replied, a hint of irony in his question. 'You are hardly . . .'

'I love him,' Lawrence interrupted. 'He's literally been like a father to me. He piloted me through Oxford, shaped my thinking, formed my ideas and ideologies. He's given me the excitement I need to stave off the blackness of depression. I believe in him, in his ideas of diplomacy, his concepts of empire and rulership. I believe in what he is doing in the world. Yet I'm not without doubts.'

'Doubts?'

'The more dirt I watch being transferred from the dig of the past to the embankment of the future, leading nowhere, then the more I feel we should withdraw to our tent, to our house with a floor of vines and fowls and the Glossy Ibis, and live simply in the knowledge that what will come to pass will happen, with or without our hand to push it.

'You see, dear Roy, I am in a quandary. I want to be on my own, yet I want to be with my boy of the night – did you know Dahoum gets his name from the word *dahüm*, meaning a dark night with no moon? Woolley claims it comes from *Tehôm*, the darkness that hung upon the waters before the beginning of creation in the Babylonian mythology. I think I might agree. Dahoum is my beginning.'

Lawrence sat up in his armchair, pulling his knees in

and, resting his elbows upon them, he leaned forward. The firelight moved the shadows on his face.

'I want to be alone, yet not,' he continued. 'I want peace and yet I want to be challenged. I want to love . . .' He looked again into Flecker's face. Their eyes met and held each other. '. . . Yet I cannot. I cannot surrender myself to anything. Hogarth believes I have a huge role to play, but I'm not so sure . . .'

'Then go away,' Flecker suggested. It was, to him, a simple solution.

'Go where?'

'Wherever you like. Return to Oxford and lock yourself away. Many a don has done that! Go off on your hunt for castles once more. Take Dahoum with you; I'm sure you could.'

'I could, but wherever we might go – there's no escape. There are no corners of the earth beyond the reach of the men of power. Of Hogarth. Of his masters in the Foreign Office. You will know of this.'

'I do not. They don't affect me,' Flecker said assuredly. 'I'm not of interest to them.'

'There, dear Roy, you are wrong, terribly wrong. You're as trapped as I am – perhaps not as deeply enmeshed, but you've taken their shilling.'

Flecker studied Lawrence's face as he peered at his feet, at the vine winding out from its vase. The leaves were waxed, but the vase had not yet been touched.

'What do you mean? I have no debt to them.'

'Oh, but you have. Your being here is sufficient proof. You've joined the club of those with secrets. Do you think your knowledge will ever let you be free of them?'

'My knowledge? What do I know . . . ?'

'More than you realise. You're as much a spy as I am. You are . . .'

'I am,' Flecker said, butting in, 'in their eyes as well

as my own, a failure. You need only see the results of my consular exams.'

'As a consul you may leave much to be desired, but they aren't interested in that. It's not what you are in your office that counts with them; it's what you do, no matter how well or otherwise. Come,' Lawrence pressed down on his knees with his hands and rose to his feet, 'enough of this talk. It tires me and saddens the soul. And it is late. I shall see to Dahoum and then, if I may, call on you.'

It was dawn when Lawrence left Flecker's room. There was a light dew on the grass blades, cool on Flecker's ankles as he stood in the yard of the house to watch Lawrence walk slowly to his own quarters.

They had not spoken after leaving the living room. Not really. Lawrence had come to Flecker an hour after the fire had died in the grate and they had lain together under the thick, coarsely woven blanket Woolley had left behind. They had not touched until just before daybreak when Flecker was awakened by Lawrence's hand seeking out his own, fingers tapping lightly along his chest to where his hand was folded under his cheek. He had felt Lawrence's wrist rub on his stubble.

Once found, Lawrence took a firm grip of Flecker's hand and held it between them. In the weak wash of first light, in the cave of the blanket stretched between them, both men looked at their entwined hands in the space between their bodies as if they were a part not of themselves but of a picture, a play with other actors upon a stage they did not fully recognise.

'Roy?' Lawrence had said.

'Yes.'

'In the future, think of me.'

'I shall.'

'And, whatever you hear of me, whatever others say
– either in condemnation or in praise – do not believe
them.'

'Why not?'

'They won't be telling the truth. They may see it, but
they shan't tell it. Only you and I have the truth.'

'What is that truth?' Flecker asked.

'The truth is what you, dear Roy, think it is. You
will know it, when the moment comes to judge it.'

'Shall I?'

'Think of Carchemish and the mosaic, of me and
Dahoum, of the desert night and the burning sun. Then
you shall know.'

That said, he had left the bed, swinging his feet outwards and feeling for his Morocco leather slippers with
his toes, wrapping his cloak around him, stealing away
like a lover forsaking his mistress's bed before the husband returns.

7

Beirut and Areiya: July/October 1912

The paper was more difficult than Flecker had expected. The Turkish unseen translation was both pedantic and esoteric. He had anticipated a passage containing some direct speech, a good deal of the vocabulary used by him in his work – the kind of Turkish he would be likely to come into contact with in his everyday responsibilities in a consulate. Instead it was a large paragraph drawn, he guessed, from a political tract. There were single words and whole constructions in it which he could not accurately translate. A glossary of the more abstruse words had been added at the end of the paper, but he was still confused and flustered. At the end of the two-hour examination he felt drained and despondent.

There followed an hour's interval before the second paper of the day. This consisted of a series of questions to which each answer was expected to be a thousand words long. A few of the questions were not beyond him, dealing as they did with the topographical geography of the Holy Lands and the political geography of the Ottoman Empire, but the majority were convoluted probings into the structure of Arab and Turkish politics, the influences of the different European powers upon the Middle East and the role played by the British as opposed to that of the French and the Germans.

He struggled to write the answers he knew the adjudicators would want to read. His own thoughts on the merits or otherwise of colonialism, imperialism or national influence were stifled by his desire to please. It was as if he were once more a pupil, striving at his desk at Uppingham to achieve not only a good mark but also the plaudits of his masters.

The result of the examination was in itself of little significance to him. He did not want to remain in the Lebanon, did not wish to reside any longer than he had to in the confines of the Consular Service. He felt only disdain for the Middle East with its cruel climate and its cruel people and their savage history. He wanted to write poetry and prose, to enjoy the company of muse, not man – unless the man was Lawrence.

The second paper lasted three and a half hours and by the time Flecker was through with it, it was mid-afternoon. He had long since shed his jacket, stiff collar and tie; he had rolled up his sleeves, eased his feet out of his shoes, and his handkerchief was wet with perspiration. On the last page of his neat writing, the ink had been blurred several times by his sweating wrist as he hurried to complete the exercise in the allotted time.

There were six papers in all, two a day for three consecutive days, and as he left the room at the end of the first day he was miserable. All the way out to Areiya he sat in the back of the carriage, protected from the sun by the black canvas canopy, and moped. He could have taken the train but, in his melancholy, he was short of patience and unwilling to await the next departure. He preferred to be alone.

By the time the horse was reined in by the house, he was in a deep fit of despondency and could hardly be bothered to drag himself from the shadow of the canopy to the shade of the verandah. It was Hellé who paid off the carriage before hurrying into the house after her husband.

'Not good?' she enquired, seeing his frame draped in a chair by the table on which the tea things were laid.

'Not good,' he confirmed morosely. 'This morning's Turkish unseen was a page of almost indecipherable drivel taken from some scholarly tome. Some Whitehall intellectual must have set it without any knowledge of the needs of the consular officer in the field. Or, in this case, desert.' He smiled wanly at his attempt at humour. 'I botched the whole thing. Magnificently, thoroughly, sensationally bungled it.'

'I'm sure you couldn't have been so bad.'

When he was in a fit of depression he was often so intractable, so utterly intransigent; she could never reach him, and her heart grew heavy with isolation.

'I was. And the afternoon's paper was just as awful. I have no ideas, no opinions ... I simply do not care what the French did in Egypt and the British in Mesopotamia, the Germans in Turkey or why the Dutch have never been successful in the region. I do care, I suppose, about the future, but ... It's all the subterfuge and double-dealing that is so distasteful. The French! The Germans! Who cares?' He paused and wiped his hands on his handkerchief. 'I wonder if they have similar questions about us, the British, in their examinations.' He imagined a question. ' "Discuss the influence of British imperialism upon the court of the Shah im Shah of Persia between 1890 and 1905. To what extent has this in turn influenced French diplomacy in the Persian Gulf region?" Who cares about all that?'

'History shapes the future ...' she suggested, hoping to bring in a bit of reason, a chance to lift him from his languor by argument.

He made no answer.

'Is there tea?' he asked after a long pause.

She nodded and left the room, returning a few

minutes later with the silver pot to discover him sitting
with his eyes shut, his head tipped back.

'I'm not asleep,' he said as she softened her step. 'Just
resting my eyes.'

'How has your throat been today? I was so worried
after you returned from Aleppo . . .'

'It's been just fine. I've been drinking throughout the
examination. Just sipping from a glass of *erkesoos*; it
was allowed. Poor Robbins was downing water like a
fish.'

'There are scones,' she announced. 'I thought you
would like them. I have made them from instructions
in the cookery book. *Mrs Beeton's* – it's a marvellous
volume. The currants are a little small, I think . . .'

He smiled feebly at her, taking her hand as she slid the
tray on to the table. 'That's very kind of you, dearest.'

'I thought you would like this. There is also unsalted
butter and I have a pot of jam – plum preserve, all the
way from England . . .'

She busied herself with a plate and knife, placing
them before him, pouring his tea into a bone china cup.
The scones, piled in a pyramid on a flower-bordered
plate, were hot from the oven, the dough light. He cut
one in half, smoothed a little butter over it and dropped
a spoonful of preserve on to the butter. He put it in his
mouth, eating it slowly.

'It's very good,' he complimented her. 'One would
think you had been making them all your life.'

His words, for all their praise, were bleak and without feeling.

'I followed the instructions. It wasn't difficult.'

He ate another and she watched him. Although he
had commended her and was consuming her handiwork, she could see his mind was elsewhere.

'There's no need to worry,' she advised him. 'I'm sure
you have done well. Better than last time. You've stud-

ied so much since then. And, even if the Turkish wasn't easy, you have the other papers to come . . .'

'The other Turkish papers will be formidable, I know it. My Turkish has got rusty since Constantinople.'

'Well,' she said brightly, 'you will do well in the French, I am certain! You can practise that with me. And your other papers . . .'

'Yes, I'll do satisfactorily at the French.'

'Satisfactorily!' she exclaimed. She lowered her voice and added affectionately, 'You will do brilliantly, my Tiger.'

She moved her chair nearer to his and put her hand on his thigh.

'The administration papers should be all right,' he replied, choosing to ignore her amorousness. 'I think I can do those standing on my head. I'm an efficient administrator,' he declared with muted but defiant arrogance.

'Then don't worry. Nothing can be gained by it.'

He took her hand and kissed it, but there was no life in his kiss.

'I'm going to sit outside and rest,' he said. 'Call me in an hour.'

Like a tired and elderly man, he walked slowly out on to the verandah. He picked up one of the cane chairs and carried it to the nearest pomegranate tree, where he set it down and dropped into it.

As she watched him go, Hellé thought how he would look just like that when they were both old. A chill ran through her and she placed the tea things back on the tray. Most of the scones were still piled on the plate.

An hour later, she went out to where he was sitting. He was dozing, his breath rasping, his head fallen to one side on his shoulder. He did not hear her approach and started when she spoke.

'Roy, a letter has been delivered for you.'

'From where?' he asked dispiritedly.

'By hand.'

He opened his eyes quickly and she held it out to him. The envelope was typed, the flap secured by a circle of red wax bearing a poorly impressed seal.

'Who brought this?'

'One of the Consulate messengers. He arrived on a donkey.'

'When?'

'Half an hour ago.'

'You must wake me if something like this arrives unexpectedly,' he said brusquely. 'Don't wait.'

'You were sleeping, though.'

'Never mind! Just don't wait.'

He did not open the envelope until she was on her way back to the house. As he did so, slicing the paper with his thumbnail, his spirits soared. Even though it was typewritten, he could tell from whom the letter came. The faint imprint in the wax seal was that of the Consulate in Aleppo.

He took out the notepaper. It was a quarto sheet with the Consulate letter-heading, but bore only two lines of handwriting.

Screwing the paper into a ball and thrusting it into his pocket, he left the chair and walked briskly to the house.

'Hellé! Hellé!' he called. 'Lawrence and Dahoum are coming the day after tomorrow.'

She made no reply but came into the room.

'Are they staying?' she asked.

'I don't think so. They're just passing through, it would seem.'

She nodded and said quietly, *'Eh bien . . .'*

The words swam before him. The examination was only

half-way through and Flecker was unable to concentrate at all. The paper concerned the administration, operation and function of an embassy chancery; he was required to answer every one of the five questions. The first, relating to the duties of a head of chancery, was not difficult and he was able to answer it despite his wandering thoughts. The second question about chancery structure and responsibilities he struggled through. The third, much to his surprise and amusement, concerned the position of the chancery officers in covert activities. As he rubbed his wrist to drive the writer's cramp away, he considered how much detail he should give; theory, which the examiner would be expecting in his papers, was one thing, but he had the practical experience.

Yet no sooner did he begin to write than any ideas he might have had dissolved in his mind. His jotted notes lost their relevance and order, and he was unable to string his thoughts together in a coherent form. As soon as he managed to formulate something, his imagination intervened and brought to him not the theory of intelligence-gathering but the actual act as he had experienced it – the German on the embankment, the dark curving tunnel of the culvert, the so-called excavation near the summit of the Carchemish mound with its step for balancing a camera or binoculars. Once these memories had intruded then he found himself thinking of Lawrence lying on the mosaic before the fire of olive wood and roots, the smoke escaping from the chimney to perfume the room and hang in the rafters like mountain mist.

When the time came to put down his pen he had answered only half the paper and that not well. He was positive he had failed again. As he left the room he felt his knees weaken and leaned upon a table in the corridor. His head ached badly and his throat throbbed.

'I say, are you all right, Flecker?'

He looked up to find Robbins standing next to him, one arm out to steady him.

'No, not really. I feel a bit faint. Just the heat, I'm sure.'

Robbins took him by the arm.

'You need a drink. Come along to my office. I've a flask in my desk . . . But do keep mum about it, won't you?'

Flecker staggered along the passage and lurched in to Robbins' room where he dropped himself heavily into a wicker chair by a varnished filing cabinet, his hands gripping the arms. The sun was shining brightly on to the cabinet and the tang of warm polish invaded his nostrils.

'Here, Flecker, have a swig of this.'

He opened his eyes to see a silver-capped hip-flask being offered to him. He took hold of its leather jacket in both hands, sniffed at the mouth, ascertained it contained cognac and put it to his lips. He took only a small amount. It scorched his throat and made him suck his breath; the fumes entered his lungs and he coughed spasmodically for a few moments.

'Thank you, Robbins,' he said hoarsely. 'Do you think I could have a small chaser of water to follow it down? I'm not used to spirits . . .'

Robbins poured a tumbler of water from a jug on a side table. It was covered with a muslin cloth weighted with beads along the fringe of the hem to keep out the flies and dust. The beads rang on the porcelain.

'Take your time, Flecker. You look quite pale.'

'It will pass.'

'It was a bit of a sod of a paper, wasn't it?' Robbins confided. 'That question about spying . . . I mean, that's never been in any of my reading. I must have covered the wrong material or something, but . . . And this morning's paper on Ottoman law – not to mention yesterday's Turkish! That was quite beyond me in places.'

Flecker held up one hand. 'I'd rather not talk about it,' he said. 'I've found all the papers absolutely murderous and I'm sure I've done badly. I just can't put my mind to them in this heat . . .'

'None of us can, really,' Robbins replied, 'so we'll all be on an equal footing. And they can't fail everyone or there'd be no Levant Consular Service.'

Yet Flecker knew Robbins and the other three had done considerably better than him. He had heard them speaking Arabic, conversing with each other in formal Turkish officialese, the sort required by the examiners. He was still trying to master instructions to the railway station while they were discussing the export of spices through trade missions and the niceties of presenting diplomatic credentials.

By the time he reached Areiya, he was washed out. Hellé greeted him as the carriage departed, leaving him in the dust before the house. She kissed him lightly on his cheek, but he sensed no emotion in her action.

'How were your exams?'

'Awful. I just couldn't concentrate. I felt faint at the end. Robbins gave me a brandy.'

'They are here,' she said, showing no immediate concern for his trying day.

'Where?'

'They are walking. They arrived an hour or so ago. I said you would not be back for a while and so they went for a walk.'

'How long are they staying?'

'They are not.'

Flecker reached the verandah and stood against one of the pillars. In the shade he felt less ill and there was a breeze blowing through the jasmine, cooling his hot brow. He undid his collar and removed his tie.

'What do you mean?' he asked.

'They're not staying. They are passing through. Tonight they sleep in Beirut, and tomorrow they go to the American Mission School at Jebail. The boy,' she deliberately avoided using his name, 'has not been well and they are going to have a holiday.'

She had planned this speech, or something very like it. Afraid to be directly antagonistic towards her husband's friend and his youth-cum-servant, yet she was determined to indicate her disapproval of their presence in tiny ways.

'Aren't you going to join them on their walk?' she enquired. 'Lawrence said to tell you they were going uphill, up the river valley.'

'In a moment, perhaps,' Flecker replied, his voice nearly a whisper. 'Let me get my breath. Five minutes . . .'

He sat on the verandah steps, hunching his shoulders; she grew concerned then, taking his hand in hers and kneeling before him on the stone floor. 'Was it very bad?'

'It was.'

'Can you tell me?'

He shook his head.

'Are we in trouble, then?'

'Yes, I think we are,' he answered quietly.

After a quarter of an hour he left her and made his way through the olive groves below the house to the track along which the shepherds drove their flocks in the early morning. The ground was spattered with pellets of sheep- and goat-dung; tufts of fleece were snagged on the thorns and twigs of the wayside bushes.

He crossed the river, walking slowly, the ascent up the valley not steep but more than his breath could allow at any other than a plodding pace. Several times, where boulders protruded smoothly from the hillside, he paused to rest, sitting down and looking away towards the sea, lost in the haze of late afternoon. Vaguely, along the coast, he could see small sailing craft making their way south to Sidon or north to Tripoli.

At his third stop for breath, he saw two Arabs approaching down the hill. They were well dressed, each in an *abâyeh* of silk shot with gold threads, upon their heads white cotton *keffiyehs* held in place by black *ogals* wound with silver and turquoise cord. He gave them no second look, bending forward in an attempt to gain his strength. It was not far to the crown of the hill and he hoped he might discover Lawrence and Dahoum at the top.

'*Hasa'il kher*,' one of the Arabs addressed Flecker.

'*Æywæ,*' he responded. He was barely audible.

The Arabs stopped before him. '*Ælsœæ Kæm?*'

Flecker did not answer. He understood the Arabic, but was so out of breath he chose to ignore it.

'If you don't have the time, my dear chap,' one of the Arabs answered his silence, 'you might at least be so good enough as to tell me. Perhaps your timepiece *ist kaput? Ach so! Ein Englander!*'

Flecker glanced up quickly, bemused. He saw before him two Arabs, then he noticed that one of them was wearing leather boots beneath his cloak.

'Ned!' he exclaimed, standing up, his voice straining. 'Dahoum!'

'Roy,' Lawrence replied, embracing him but not closely, 'what is the matter? You look quite pallid.'

'I'm not well.' Flecker staggered back against the boulder upon which he had been resting.

'Indeed, you're not.' Lawrence turned to Dahoum and spoke rapidly in Arabic. 'We'll take you to the top;

there's a good cool wind up there and it will revive you. The walk down will not be so strenuous for you.'

Taking an arm each around their shoulders, Lawrence and Dahoum half carried Flecker to the summit. There, under a pomegranate tree, they sat together in silence while the wind blew round them and Flecker regained his breath.

'It is good here,' Flecker said at length. He was relaxing, the pressures of the day slipping from him and the pain in his head easing. 'I should come here more often myself.'

'Not if the hill hurts you so. You looked very poorly down there.'

'Maybe I was rushing it,' Flecker lied, 'in my eagerness to catch up with you. Anyway, enough of that! How are you both? Dahoum looks well. I had heard otherwise.'

'The malaria was bad,' Lawrence commented as the boy grinned. 'We are both of us tired. And it was time for a break. We're on our way to Jebail, but we had to call on you. Couldn't not, really . . .'

A bird settled in the pomegranate and began to sing; then, suddenly, it took to the wing and the wind whisked it away before it soared and flew off towards the sea.

'I would have been most upset had you not,' Flecker said. 'And you'll stay to supper?'

'No, we must be getting on. It's not far to Jebail and I want to make an early start, hence our staying in Beirut. But I had to have a word with you on the way. It's about the Germans . . .'

As they walked slowly down the hill, Lawrence passed on his information on the German activities. They were suddenly forging ahead, he reported: more girders had arrived by boat up the Euphrates and he had seen boxes of explosives delivered.

'Dynamite? What do they want dynamite for?'

Lawrence shrugged, his cloak rising from his boots.

'Perhaps to use over the border in Turkey. Difficulties with the tunnels are still proving a considerable hindrance to their progress through the mountains. Of interest to London, don't you think?'

Before they departed, Flecker wrote his dispatch for the bag to London the following day, Lawrence checking it and adding two sealed letters of his own.

'You see,' he said as he gave them to Flecker, 'I had to visit you for other than personal reasons.' He held up one of the envelopes, which was addressed to Hogarth. 'I could hardly give this in to the Consulate, and there was no time to send it through Aleppo. Raff is away still . . .'

They were gone within the hour, Lawrence and Dahoum striding out along the dusty track towards the road, each carrying his own blanket roll and possessions. Watching them depart, Flecker felt an emptiness fill him.

Later, as he lay in bed wheezing stertorously, Hellé at his side, he thought of his friend and his boy, lying together on the floor of a hotel room in Beirut, wrapped in their blanket as if there was not a plaster ceiling above them but an infinite roof bedecked with desert stars.

'I understand,' Hellé said suddenly. She had not spoken for an hour or more and he had assumed she was reading her book.

He placed his pen carefully on the stand and weighted down the page he was writing with a stone picked from the ground beside his chair.

'Understand what?'

'Your feelings. I know you do not like it here. It is a country you do not love.'

'You are correct; I do not like the Levant – the perpetual and unreal beauty of the sunlight and the blossoms, the continual dry wind and the bleak sky. I sometimes yearn for the never-ending drizzle of England, the damp fog and the blighting Cotswold winds. People speak of the East being the birthplace of civilisation, but where is it? In ruins, misruled by usurping and greedy Europeans. The only real civilisation today lies in the grubby back streets around the factories of England. There the people are in touch with life, not existing from one oasis to the next, nomads with no compass. They know where they're going.'

She smiled at him. He had not shown so much life himself since the end of the examinations.

'The Lebanon is dead; civilisation's finished here and we're wasting our time protecting it. We and the French and the Germans and the Italians and all the others. We can make no empire here. Who wants an empire of sand? Turkey – now that's different. Civilisation still lingers there . . .'

He paused as a bat flew over the table before him, diving at insects congregating above the lamp.

'And yet,' he continued, 'these people are happy. You hear them whining like beaten children, wailing from the mosques as if prayer was pain, but they have an innocent *joie de vivre* completely lacking in those other, civilised lands. The man in Manchester, in Sheffield, in the slums of industry, has no happiness by comparison.'

'You – what will you do about this?' she asked, knowing that to draw him on would possibly be to break the melancholy he had been suffering in the days since Lawrence's visit.

'I can do nothing . . . Not here, not in the Consular Service. I can, I think, do something as a writer, as a poet. I can fill English hearts with elation, fill English minds with dreams of paradise. And maybe I can also teach them lessons that they can teach the world. Fight injustice, and right the imbalance of poverty and power. But I don't know . . .'

'Do you not do this through your work here? Is not the bringing of our ways to the Arabs going to relieve them of their poverty?'

He eased his hands, linking his fingers, rubbing his palms together and cracking his knuckles.

'Hellé, we are not here to save them from anything, nor to bring them anything. They are merely people upon the same stage. They occupy a desert in which we – the foreigners, the infidels – are jousting for power, for ownership of what is theirs.'

'How long have you thought like this?'

'Some weeks.'

'Is this an idea from Lawrence?'

'Partly. It was sparked off by him. He wants to save the Arabs . . . to see Britain as an imperial power that will protect them. A benevolent dictatorship, Hogarth would call it. But I'm . . . I'm not so committed. And I wonder if it matters. When it suits us, our race, we'll change tack – just like a yacht in a veering and capricious wind. We'll let them down, sell them out when it's in our interest. Then as ever we shall be looking out for ourselves, and the Arabs and Turks and whole Middle East can go to hell.'

All night long, she shivered and perspired. At first he slept through it, but finally, in the early hours, her moving woke him.

He lit the oil lamp by their bed and his first reaction was that she was having a nightmare. He took hold of her shoulder and gently shook her, saying, 'Wake up, dearest Pussy. It's only a fantasy.'

Yet she was awake. She turned over and her face was wan, the muscles of her neck taut. When she took her hand from under the blanket and grasped his own, she was trembling violently.

'What is it?' he asked, alarmed at her appearance but still thinking she was having a bad dream.

'I have a fever,' Hellé croaked. 'Get the medicine . . .'

He rushed from their bedroom to return a few moments later with their small medicine box. He turned the lamp up fully and rummaged about in the contents until his fingers found the thin steel tube containing the thermometer. Yet he dared not place it between her teeth, which were chattering uncontrollably; instead, he thrust the instrument into her armpit and held her biceps firmly to her side while he slowly counted to sixty. When he removed the thermometer and held it close to the glass of the lamp, he saw the mercury at the 105°C level.

'You have a bit of a temperature,' he said as calmly as he could, 'and I'm going to give you a cool drink to lower it a little.'

He replaced the thermometer in its tube and went quickly to the ice-box from which he took a bottle of chilled water.

'Just wet my mouth,' she whispered as he held a tumbler to her lips. 'I'm thirsty but I daren't drink. I was sick an hour ago.'

'Why didn't you wake me?'

His voice was angry from concern but she did not reply.

In the morning, Hellé was weak but her temperature had dropped to 101°C. Flecker sent word to Beirut for a doctor who arrived in the early afternoon, caked in dust and with his jacket draped over his arm. His black bag was khaki with dust.

He examined Hellé thoroughly, tapping her back, listening to her heart, taking her blood pressure, pressing his stethoscope so hard into her skin that it left a red weal. He requested a urine sample which he tested for sugar, took throat swabs and, finally, drew from her wrist a large blood sample with a chrome and glass syringe, dropping the blood into a small bottle filled with a dull-coloured powder.

'So, Mrs Flecker,' he declared in an almost jolly tone, 'we must now get you fit again. Drink plenty of fluids. Eat only the simplest of foods – nothing rich at all. Unless you can keep it down, avoid milk. It'll be only a matter of time before you're fit again. There's nothing to get unduly worried about, I'm sure.'

Once outside, however, the doctor's comments to Flecker were not as light-hearted.

'I can't be sure, you understand,' he began, 'but it is my opinion that your wife has contracted Malta fever.'

Flecker had never heard of it. 'She's never been to Malta, so far as I know,' he replied lamely, as if this fragment of information might somehow bring about a miraculous cure.

'That has nothing to do with it,' the doctor answered. 'The disease is prevalent throughout the coastal regions of the Mediterranean.'

'Is it . . . ?' Flecker started to say and the doctor interrupted him.

'Serious? Yes. It recurs – like malaria. It weakens the system and it can be fatal. These effects are cumulative. Nevertheless, do not be unnerved by this. Your wife's present bout is not as bad as it might be – not by a long way. Has she previously had a fever?'

'No,' Flecker said and then, 'Yes, but some time ago. Not long after we arrived in the Lebanon.'

'Was it as bad as this?'

'No, it wasn't. A mere chill we thought at the time; it soon passed.'

The doctor was pensive. 'It may have been a precursor. It can linger in the body dormant . . .'

'What is the cure?'

'There is none as such, no actual medication. We do know that the germ cannot survive in the cold. The best advice I can give is for your wife to return to Europe as soon as possible.'

'Is that all you can offer?' Flecker demanded, a quiver of apprehension running up his back.

The doctor nodded.

'What if it isn't? Isn't Malta fever?' Flecker asked. He was clutching at the straws of hope and he knew it, his mind filled with misgiving.

'I am fairly certain of my diagnosis; there have been a number of cases recently. The blood test is simply to ensure there are no complications present.'

After the doctor had departed, Flecker sat quite still on the verandah and sank his head in his hands. He could not live in Beirut without her. What was already unbearable – despite Lawrence and Dahoum, his work for them – would become unmitigated living purgatory.

The sheet of paper bearing the consular examination results lay before him. He had stared at it for some time, and at the one damning sentence which stood out from the report before him like a canker:

I do not believe for a moment that either of these men will ever make a consular officer of the stamp we require. I would not give them another chance.

Appended to the results was a note addressed to him

personally. It was from Cumberpatch and was as terse as the condemnatory memo:

After much consideration and a good deal of intercourse with London, it has been decided to allow you yet a further opportunity to prove yourself. If, however, at the examinations nine months hence you fail to attain the required standard, your resignation will be requested in addition to the settlement of your bond – your surety – of £500. I feel it incumbent upon me to remind you of the matter of this bond. You have received, at the expense of His Majesty's government, a considerable training at an equally considerable cost to the Exchequer and, through this, to the country. Your withdrawal from the service will require the payment of this debt. For a debt it is. And one for which you are, I must remind you, contractually responsible and to which you are so bound. As an English gentleman, you are also morally responsible. I am, furthermore, instructed to make it abundantly obvious to you that there will be no extenuating circumstances which might be considered in the event of a third failure.

There was a knock on the door and Robbins looked in, his face ashen despite his tan.

'He wants to see you now,' he mumbled. 'He's in a foul mood.'

Flecker pushed back his hair and got up, lifting the paper as he went. 'What's to happen to you?' he asked.

Robbins looked down and replied, 'I've been given another chance.'

Cumberpatch was standing at his window.

'Sit down, Flecker.'

His voice was cool and business-like. He was trying to sound detachedly diplomatic, but could not help a touch of disgust in his words which Flecker immediately recognised.

Choosing the seat nearest the door, Flecker did as he was told; it was, he thought, just like being hauled before Dr Selwyn, the headmaster at Uppingham.

'Well, this is a poor showing,' Cumberpatch began, opening the file he was holding and then closing it again without so much as reading a word of the contents. 'A very poor showing indeed. You have let yourself down badly – again – and you have let down me and the service just as shoddily. After your earlier disaster, I had expected to have seen some improvement. Your papers in Turkish and Ottoman law are a disgrace. Last November you received only' – he looked fleetingly at the file – '158 marks out of a possible 450. This time, it's worse. Last time you were ill, and I see from your records that the Ambassador expressed his belief that your ill-health and sick leave had upset your studies. That is not the case now.'

'No, sir,' Flecker agreed, attempting a placatory and humble tone.

'Indeed it is not, sir! Frankly, I was all for your immediate dismissal. I cannot accept a slipshod attitude towards duties. And you, Flecker, are slipshod. You are here in the Consulate but a few hours each week, doing whatever it is London has asked you to do in addition to your regular responsibilities, and the remainder of the time you are in a comfy spot in Areiya, living in the lap of luxury with your wife. And yet you seem to be spending next to no time at all in pursuit of your studies. Some of the while you are *in absentia* in Aleppo with Fontana.'

Throughout their interview so far, Cumberpatch had stood with his back to the window. The glare of the sun behind him forced Flecker to squint. Now, having discomforted Flecker sufficiently, the Consul moved to his desk, dropped the file and leaned upon it, his knuckles whitening on the buff paper cover where it lay in front of the pen stand. Three red adhesive seal labels on the cover stood out in the sunlight on the desk, forming a scarlet triangle.

'What have you to say in your defence, Flecker? For understand this: you are in a sense on trial here. As I have said, you would be out of the service by now if I had had any say in the matter. As it is, I was . . . Well?'

Overruled, Flecker thought, filling in the missing word. This meeting was not merely a carpeting for doing badly in the examinations; it was also a blood-letting, a face-saving exercise.

'I have nothing to say, sir. I have not been well, my illness continuing after my arrival in the Lebanon. There was hope it might ease somewhat upon my posting here, but this has not proved to be the case.'

'So you put it all down to your illness, do you?' Cumberpatch shifted his knuckles wider apart, his hand knocking a blotter with a wooden handle shaped like a torch-flame and set in red leather; it swung to and fro, gradually losing momentum.

'Largely so, yes.'

'Largely so! What else, then?'

'Nothing really, sir. I get tired easily and I sleep badly. My wife has recently been ill.'

'I see.' Cumberpatch ignored Flecker's reference to Hellé's fever. 'Then perhaps I might suggest you spend less time burning the midnight oil on your literary endeavours. Most of your correspondence home deals not with the ordinary intercourse of a son with his parents or family, but with editors of literary journals and friends connected with this somewhat spurious world of *belles lettres*.' He paused momentarily, as if on the defensive himself, then added, 'Or so I understand to be the case.' He scowled and attacked again. 'What have you to say in reply to that, eh?'

Flecker made no immediate response. He realised now that his personal mail was being intercepted and that Cumberpatch was going through it. He resolved no longer to send his post through the Consulate or its messengers, but to place it directly himself in the post office, and he was thankful that his letters to Lawrence, sent internally to Aleppo, or Hogarth, sealed in his boxes or official bags, were beyond tampering.

'My private affairs, unless they affect directly or impinge upon my responsibilities, or are a cause for a failure in security, or bring upon my veracity or trustworthiness an element of doubt' – he was quoting from one of the directives he had skimmed in his studies – 'are irrelevant.'

'I consider otherwise,' Cumberpatch retorted. He sat down and opened the dossier; still, he did not read it. 'As I have told you,' he said, his voice almost indiscernibly softer, 'you are to have yet another chance to make the grade for promotion to Vice-Consul. You must realise this is a last and very final chance, for your own good as well as that of the service. I would, frankly, be somewhat loath to lose you. I feel you might – just might, mind you – have the right stuff in you. I may find some criticism of the writer of the report on you, but . . .'

Flecker kept a straight face. He was inclined to glower at his superior; suddenly, his tone had changed and his hypocrisy gave him away. Anyone, Flecker thought, who had gone through a grilling with Selwyn – or any astute schoolmaster, come to that – would see the direction in which the meeting was going.

'So I commend you most seriously to apply yourself to your studies. A man of your intellect and education can be an asset to the service no matter where his posting may take him.'

'Yes, sir,' Flecker replied. 'I shall . . .'

He was seized by a fit of coughing, tugged his handkerchief from his pocket and smothered his mouth with it. The spasms came from deep in the lungs, not merely from the back of his throat. He went red in the face and his brow burst out in beads of sweat.

Cumberpatch remained behind his desk, a look of perplexed concern upon his face.

When the fit subsided, Flecker carefully folded his handkerchief in such a way that Cumberpatch might not see it.

'Will you take a glass of water, Flecker?'

He nodded and Cumberpatch poured one from a decanter on a shelf behind his chair, handing it across the desk.

'Thank you, sir,' Flecker said. 'I need only a sip. I think an insect must have flown into my mouth.'

'Quite. These small midges are most annoying. Well, I think this can be the end of our meeting, don't you? I think we have a mutual understanding?'

'Yes, sir.'

As Flecker turned the door-knob, Cumberpatch said, 'Tell me, Flecker, what is it you are busy with at Aleppo? Fontana's not short-handed up there, is he?'

'No, sir. The Consulate seems to be fully comple-mented.'

He turned the knob further and the mechanism clicked.

'Then what is it? Something to do with that young Lawrence? A most amiable man, if a bit of a cold fish at times . . .'

'I'm afraid I cannot say, sir. I must refer you to Mr Fontana. I am under strict control of communication.'

'I see.' Cumberpatch sounded slightly peeved.

'But I appreciate your testing me, sir. I hope in a small way that my answer might restore a little of your faith in me.'

'How do you mean, Flecker?'

'Asking me, sir, to divulge what you know I cannot.'

'Yes, quite,' Cumberpatch answered. 'I am glad you keep to your orders. Quite. An admirable stand.'

Flecker left the room and closed the door, smiling as he made his way down the corridor.

The letter was bonded with wax which had chipped at one corner. The indented design was not one Flecker recognised. He tested the paste on the flap and scrutinised the joins in the paper; it appeared not to have been opened.

His slid his ivory paper-knife under the flap and slit the envelope. Within was a single sheet of Magdalen College stationery; the letter was handwritten and undated.

He smoothed it out on his desk, weighting down the top of the stiff parchment-like paper with the inkwell.

Dear James [he read]

I am writing to inform you that I have successfully manoeuvred your remaining in the Levant Service until at least the end of your current tour. You will appreciate that this was not so easily accomplished in view of your repeated inadequacy in examination.

I realise your work for L at C may be partly to blame, and this was the mitigating circumstance with which I was able to persuade Their Lordships.

Furthermore, I realise you have other worries at present pressing upon you, of both artistic and financial natures. Do rest assured these will be overcome in due course. Everything has a way of working out.

Flecker turned the page over and replaced the inkwell, putting his elbows on the bottom corners of the sheet and resting his chin in his hands as he read on.

. . . Do know Their Lordships – and myself, to say the least

– are most appreciative of your fulfilment of your duties to date. Your work is of paramount importance to us and you would be most difficult to replace at the present.

A further communication of a less personal nature will reach you shortly, along with supplies requested.

Should you require any assistance in any matter, do not hesitate to contact me.

Yours etc.,
DGH.

A postscript added, in writing condensed to fit the space remaining:

Am delighted to say some of your work is being considered for a major new anthology – but you are not to know of this!

He was trapped, he thought, as he watched the sun setting over the sea, the water changing from light blue to dark azure to black coruscating with gold. It was just as Lawrence had intimated.

He took Hogarth's letter once more from his pocket. The crisp folds were weakened with repeated opening and refolding. Certain phrases stared up at him – 'successfully manoeuvred', 'persuade Their Lordships', 'paramount importance' and 'most difficult to replace' . . .

He was ensnared. He could not resign from the Consular Service, for he was already in debt as a result of their spending and his inadequate salary, and the forfeit of his £500 surety would be more than he or his parents – or his wife – could sustain.

He was bound too by the code of secrecy implicit in his part in Fontana's network, The Aleppo ring, Hogarth's private army of ex-Oxford men who were putting into practice their mentor's – or patron's – play in the game of imperialism.

He wanted to resign, to escape from the hated Levant, but he could not: his debt was not merely one of money but also one of loyalty. Hogarth had promoted him, had introduced him to Lawrence, had at least enlivened in some way his boring existence and had now stood by him, too. To renege on this debt would be to leave Hogarth in the lurch and this he was reluctant to do on moral grounds: he had made a commitment and he must abide by it, see it through. At the same time, he was apprehensive of letting Hogarth down – anyone who could tip 'Their Lordships' ' ears in another's favour was someone to be reckoned with, someone who could as easily break as make him. The postscript to Hogarth's letter suggested the don was able to affect not merely Flecker's consular career.

And he was trapped in love . . . that was perhaps the most terrifying of all. There was Hellé a mile or so away, sitting in their house awaiting his return; and there was Lawrence who was, at that very moment, only twenty miles up the Lebanese coast, so near and yet utterly beyond his touch.

He considered, momentarily, whether or not he should risk travelling up the coast to Jebail. It would incur Hellé's wrath: she was so jealous of Lawrence, so afraid of him. The thought occurred to him – perhaps he also wanted to escape from Hellé, his 'Little Pussy'. Should her 'Tiger' slink off back to the forest from which he had come to stalk her?

Or should he take a longer journey, and join Shelley in the waves? The sea looked so inviting. He had only to walk down to the shore. It would be only a few steps into the water. No one need see him. No one would. Then he would be nearer to Lawrence, the coast running like a line between them.

Was it true, he wondered, that drowning was such a beautiful death? After the panic of being submerged, he had heard it said that the journey into the good and everlasting night was peaceful, gentle as a sleigh ride down a long, smooth hill.

He set off down the hill in the direction of the coast but soon turned back. This was, he reasoned, no solution. And he had poems to write yet. So many poems, so many words. As Hogarth had written, things had a way of working out.

The sea was a sheet of gold light now, the sun touching the horizon, the rim of the world.

'I am not yet ready for such a golden journey,' Flecker told a lizard sunning itself on a boulder by the path, soaking up the last heat of the day. The reptile darted away at the sound of his voice.

At the station at Aley, the crowd of passengers waiting for the down-bound train was animated. Flecker asked the ticket inspector what was happening to cause such a furore.

'There are warships,' he exclaimed, his hand shaking as he punched Flecker's ticket.

'Italian or French?'

The inspector shrugged, but a man standing beside him said, '*Italya!*'

The arrival of the ascending rack-and-pinion hill train gave weight to the bystander's comment. The carriages were packed with Beyroutins: even the roofs had young men squatting on them, gripping the ventilators to retain their seat. When the train set off down the hill towards the city Flecker was one of only three passengers in his carriage.

As the train halted in the lower terminus, Flecker jumped clear of the carriage step, hurried out of the station and down to the harbour quay.

The dockside was packed, the mob surprisingly silent.

Flecker raised himself on to an iron bollard to see over the heads of the crowd. In the harbour was a small launch with a single brass cannon mounted on its bow, manned by Italian sailors in blue jackets. They kept just out of musket range from the quay, moving around the harbour, inspecting all the craft moored there. They slowed by the wreckage of the Turkish gunboat shelled in the attack in March, then headed out through the harbour towards the open sea and their mother ship hove to a mile offshore.

At their departure the crowd began to disperse, suddenly noisy and garrulous. They were congratulating each other at their bravery, at their having stood up to the might of the Italian navy and winning. Flecker noticed most of the spectators were carrying beneath their clothing an assortment of weapons, and he realised then he had left his revolver at home.

In the Consulate all was calm. Cumberpatch was in his office and Flecker reported to him all that he had seen happen. He wrote out a brief report at his desk and then left the building, walking back to the railway station. It would, he considered, be better to take the hill train, for the city's cab and carriage drivers would be otherwise occupied with the warship still in sight.

He did not enjoy the train ride. The compartments were hot in the summer months, often crowded, and the smoke from the engine aggravated his eyes and throat. The rack-and-pinion gearing made a rattling, irritating sound and the whole train rocked on the corners as it followed the Beirut river valley. Flecker held on to the open window, fixing his gaze upon the hillside opposite, fighting the dizziness the train invariably instilled in him.

At each station where the train halted, Flecker noticed there were bands of armed Lebanese, muskets and rifles in their hands, daggers and swords tucked into their belts and cummerbunds. The women and children who only an hour and a half before had been fleeing up the hills to escape an impending bombardment were heading back down the valley, either by the train or on foot along the road and pathways. Yet the men, to Flecker's consternation, were making no effort to join them.

As he arrived home he was met by a squadron of Lebanese cavalry, their horses stamping the ground between the trees and the house, one of the black and white puppies frolicking between their hooves and snapping at their fetlocks. Incongruously, one of the horses was standing quite still and delicately nipping the rosebuds off the bushes at the side of the house, its rider making no attempt to prevent it.

Hellé met him as he entered the living room.

'What is going . . .?'

Flecker stopped. Seated upon the settle were two European women; they were coated with dust and their hair was dishevelled. Each was holding a cup of tea.

'These good ladies have been shot at!' Hellé announced. 'They are . . .'

'We are American missionaries from Abadieh,' announced one of them, her accent thick but her voice high-pitched from emotion. 'There is a lot of shooting there. Our home has come under fire,' she went on melodramatically.

Flecker made no reply, but left the room and hailed the officer in charge of the horsemen. From him, he received details of the background to the fighting. A Druse leader had been attacked on his way from Brumana, and his followers, immediately assuming it was a Christian hand which had struck him, had rallied to attack the Maronites. They had begun shooting indiscriminately, not bothering to ascertain if their target was Christian or Muslim or even human. Stray bullets had struck the missionaries' home and they had fled to the safety of the nearest European dwelling – the Fleckers'.

Even as they spoke, a prolonged burst of rifle fire echoed down the valley. It stopped as abruptly as it began, but sporadic firing continued for several minutes.

'Has someone been sent for?' Flecker demanded. 'This is intolerable.'

'Yes, sir,' the mounted officer informed him. 'The Druse leader has requested British protection. A messenger was sent to your Consul.'

Flecker re-entered the living room. One of the Americans, a woman of his own age with mousey hair and pallid hands, was weeping quietly into one of Hellé's silk handkerchiefs while the other, an older woman, was sipping her tea with all the aplomb of a matron at a vicarage fête. She was paying no attention to her distressed companion.

'It will all be sorted out soon,' Flecker announced with imperious surety. 'We have been called in to mediate.'

'We?' the elder of the missionaries asked. 'Who are you to get this unholy mess untangled?'

'I am the Acting Vice-Consul for the British Legation,' Flecker answered haughtily. 'We shall be seeing to the "unholy mess".' He stared hard at the woman. 'Do you not think, madam, that it would be perspicacious to attend to your friend?'

The companion sobbed more loudly for a moment and pushed away her cup of tea across the polished table top. Anela appeared from the direction of the kitchen with a jug of iced water, the cubes in it rattling.

'Our Good Lord will see to her,' replied the missionary with a temerity to match Flecker's own. 'I'm just curious to know where our representative is. We sent for him some time back.'

'Possibly he too is relying on the Good Lord to inter-
cede on your behalves,' Flecker suggested.

The missionary attempted no response and concentrated on drinking her tea.

Throughout the afternoon the missionaries drank tea,
the younger in time ceasing her weeping, while
infrequent gunfire resounded down the valley. They
complained about the Druses, worried about what
might be happening to their house — they prophesied
looting and vandalism, culminating in a razing to the
ground — tried to assess how they might continue to
live in Abadieh after this, weighed up the chances of
what the younger one termed 'the ultimate feminine
fate' and the older one called 'the ravaging of the flesh',
and were caustic about the non-appearance of any
American diplomat. Flecker noticed with contemptuous
humour that at no time did they pray.

Early in the evening, Cumberpatch arrived with one
of the consular guards and a middle-aged man in a
brown suit, the tone of which matched his tan; had his
shirt not been white, Flecker thought when he saw him
through the window, his head would have appeared to
be an intrinsic part of his clothing. He made a mental
note to record the man's comical appearance on paper
as soon as he was able.

The carriage horses were flaked with foam across
their chests and the board beneath the driver's feet was
glistening with sweat. The animals had evidently been
driven hard up the hill road.

'Flecker!' Cumberpatch called before he had even a
foot on the earth. 'Flecker!'

'Here, sir!'

He ran out on to the verandah, his revolver in his
hand. Although night had fallen, the moonlight was
brilliant and with the carriage lamps illuminated the

whole of the garden and the tethered Lebanese cavalry horses, the soldiers sitting in a group near their mounts.

'A word, Flecker.' Cumberpatch drew him to one side and lowered his voice. 'The johnnie in the carriage is one of the Maronite leaders. I've persuaded his motley crew to remain on the defensive, not to take the initiative and have a go at the Druses. It's bad enough as it is. Now we've got to go and hear what the Druse leaders have to say. And I want you with me.'

'Yes, sir.'

Flecker turned towards the carriage.

'Leave your firearm. We shan't need that,' Cumberpatch said, then ordered the guard out of the carriage, along with the Maronite who was requested to await their return.

Together, Flecker and Cumberpatch set off along the road to Abadieh. To their left the rock gorge of the Beirut River was grey and imposing in the moonlight, the mystical shadows more stark than in the brightest sunlight. Every so often along the road a Lebanese gendarme appeared out of the darkness beneath a tree or boulder, his quaint, comic-opera uniform incandescent like a ghost's mantle.

'Don't know why they bother,' Cumberpatch observed, waving nonchalantly in reply to a salute from one of the 'spirit' policemen. 'If the Druses took it into their heads to make an issue of this business, they'd soon massacre every one of these white knights in shining raiment.'

'Has this furore caused any trouble in the city?' Flecker asked.

'Not really. Though coming on top of the damned Italians snooping about in a row-boat with a brass piece on the front . . . well, it couldn't have happened at a worse time. Emotions running high already. Still, there's some good out of it, I suppose.'

'Some good, sir?' Flecker repeated.

'Certainly.' Cumberpatch's voice was filled with a tone of bombasticity. 'The Druses have looked to us to sort the fiasco out and that's one up on the French, for the Maronites didn't get to their allies first. I approached the Maronite leader before the French *chargé d'affaires* turned up and he agreed to let me settle the discussions. So it's up to you and me, Flecker. Puts the French down a peg or two, eh?'

Another of the policemen loomed up in the night, his uniform gleaming. Flecker acknowledged his salute with an almost royal wave of the hand.

'Will the French not be somewhat aggrieved that we are speaking for their protégés, as it were, sir?'

The sound of the horses' trotting hooves was suddenly muffled as they left the road and took to a dusty side-track.

'Too damned right they'll be aggrieved,' Cumberpatch retorted. 'Serves them right. Should be alert to any diplomatic possibility.' He lowered his voice and spoke in more confidential terms so that the driver should not overhear him. 'The more we can undermine confidence in the French the better. They're causing not a little trouble at the moment. The fewer contacts we have with them – apart, of course, from those of a strictly diplomatic nature – the more I like it . . .'

They were drawing close to a village, the horses slowing to a walking pace. The two men stopped speaking, Cumberpatch now expectantly alert, staring into the night and readying himself for his exercise in diplomacy. Flecker watched the square houses squat in the moonlight like a misconceived Crusader castle perched on the hill: he was nervously anticipating the flash of a muzzle-loader.

The driver reined in the horses beneath a huge chestnut tree. He turned up the flame in the carriage lamps and waited. In the yellow circle of light, Flecker looked at the runes carved on an old tomb under the sanctuary of the branches. Then, to a call from ahead, the horses were put into a walk once more.

They were guided by two men, with muzzle-loaders slung over their shoulders, into a courtyard paved with red tiles and brown flags, the colours prominent despite the monochromatic moonlight.

Cumberpatch alighted first and together he and Flecker were shown in through a narrow wooden door studded with iron rivets. Within, in a large room and surrounded by retainers, all of whom were armed with an assortment of antique and modern weaponry, the wounded Druse leader lay on a couch draped in gold-shot silk and propped upon pink and emerald cushions. The Consul bowed to the old man before advancing to him, Flecker copying his superior.

Formal introductions over, Cumberpatch began his peace mission while Flecker sat with the retainers, talking with them in broken English and Arabic, commiserating over the attack upon their chief.

The retainers were of a mind to wipe out the Maronites: they had enjoyed their day loosing off their firearms up and down the valley. However, the conversation soon turned towards the morning's incursion by the Italian navy.

By midnight, and exercising his most skilful diplomacy, Cumberpatch had secured the peace once more and he and Flecker took their leave of the Druse leader and returned to Areiya.

'You know, Flecker,' Cumberpatch observed, leaning back into the leather upholstery of the carriage seat and letting the moonlight wash over him, 'you've got to admire the Lebanese. Under Turkish domination such as it is, meddled about with by us and the French and Italians – and the Germans, to some extent – and with a government that's a shambles, they still seem to run a pretty secure house. Have done for half a century, since 1864 and the establishment of the *sanjak* of the Lebanon. There're few spots in the Middle East now where you can take your good lady out for a picnic with no fear of violence and let your nanny promenade the little ones with no more protection than her wits and a stick to fend off the odd dog. And I suppose it'll be like this for ever unless we carry on meddling. Bloody stupid the European Commission of '64 laying down that the *mutesarrif* must be a Christian – and not a native Lebanese to boot! You know, Flecker, I sometimes wonder . . .' He opened his eyes as if suddenly becoming aware of what he was saying and stopped speaking.

The carriage dropped Flecker off at his house and Cumberpatch took it on, rejoined by the guard and Maronite. The cavalry unit had departed and the garden was quiet under the moonlight.

Flecker stood beneath the pomegranate trees and listened to the night birds in the valley below. It was peaceful. No more rifle fire resounded in the darkness. He felt calm, more so than for many days.

There was a soft noise behind him and he turned slowly, knowing it could not be one of threat to him.

'Is it over?' Hellé asked.

She was wearing her nightgown beneath an overcoat hanging loosely over her shoulders.

'Yes. Cumberpatch has done a deal.'

She stepped beside him and put her hand under his arm. 'You must be tired. And you shouldn't be out after your recent fever. It's been a long day for you. Come to bed.'

'Where are the two Ladies of the Good Lord?'

'Asleep in the little room. They can return in the morning. I shall walk over with them. I am,' she admitted, squeezing his arm, 'quite curious to see the bullet holes in their house.'

He put his arms around her and pulled her close to him.

'You know,' he admitted, 'I quite enjoyed my outing.' He laughed quietly. 'I felt rather important on a real diplomatic mission.'

Her breasts thrust against his waistcoat and he realised he had not changed his clothes since leaving home that morning.

'I must wash,' he said. 'I have the detritus of a whole day clinging to me like a second skin.'

'I like the smell of you like this,' she whispered.

She pushed her fingers into the waist of his trousers. His hands moved from her shoulders, down her back and round to the front of her body. The overcoat fell to the ground and the moonlight shone through her nightgown on to her pale skin.

Flecker completed his report around noon and delivered it to Cumberpatch personally. In it, he outlined all the conversations he had had with the Druse leader's men and his own opinions of the actions of the day.

Cumberpatch read through the three sheets of foolscap. He commented, 'This seems to be a fair summary of events, and I agree with your conclusions. I feel I must add that you were an asset to me last night – took the heat out of the leader's soldiers by palling up with them. Here,' he tossed his own report across the desk to Flecker, 'you might like to scan this, see if I've made any omissions.'

Taken aback by Cumberpatch being so forthcoming, Flecker read through his superior's account. It contained only one deletion. Cumberpatch's last sentence read:

The deductions to be made from these events are that, owing to its inherent weakness, the Turkish administration enjoys little or no respect from the various sects in the Lebanon, and that the racial hatred between Druse and Christians is still as bitter as ever.

He had crossed out the word 'Turkish' with an indelible pencil.

'Would you agree with all that?'

'Yes, sir.'

Flecker handed the report across the desk.

'Sad, really,' the Consul remarked. 'Such a beautiful country, such in-built animosities. Such a fine people. If only there was but one religion in the world – and, frankly, I don't give a damn which one . . . But there isn't, and this part of the world's going to carry on struggling and fighting and knifing itself in the heart until Armageddon.' He tapped his report into a folder with Flecker's and said, 'Get these typed up, will you, Flecker?'

The cases were unlabelled but Flecker knew what the contents were – the stores that Lawrence had requested. They had not come from Britain but from Cairo, transported to Beirut on a British warship which was, as he checked off the manifest, riding the tide two miles offshore.

It was only when he opened the cases to check the contents, the door to the store-room locked as usual, that he discerned that London had sent far more than Lawrence had asked for. The crates were full of rifles. No signal had arrived referring to arms and ammunition. Flecker was horrified at what he was handling.

The rifles were warm despite being packed in wooden crates, the oil fluid upon the metal. Wherever he touched one, his fingerprint was outlined as if embossed on the steel. Yet, within a minute, the mark had disappeared as the oil settled once more.

He picked one of the rifles out of its wrapping of greased paper. It was heavy and smelled as only guns do, of oil and wood-polish. He put it to his shoulder, pressing his cheek to the stock, looking down the line of the barrel. The sights were not attached, but it made no difference. He aimed at the cupboard across the store-room in which stationery was kept; there was a padlock on the door and he steadied the tip of the barrel over it, his index finger automatically feeling for the trigger. He squeezed it and the metal moved a fraction of an inch towards him but there was no click. The bolts were packed separately.

Yet, in his mind, he heard the discharge and felt the recoil against his shoulder just as if he were a child playing at guns, mimicking the punch on the shoulder as the charge went off. And the steel padlock with its sliding keyhole cover of brass was no longer an inanimate object but the head of a man – perhaps a Druse, maybe a Shi'ite, possibly a Christian – dressed in a *keffiyeh* with a black *ogal* holding the square of cotton in place; his face was in shadow, but his eyes glinted.

He lowered the rifle and wrapped it once more in its paper, snuggling it down into the box with the others. It fitted so neatly, too tidily almost to be an instrument of such destruction.

The smell of the gun oil now clung to his hands, a sweet and sickly scent like that of a poisonous flower.

He replaced the lid of the case and knocked the nails home. Each thud of the hammer was the explosion of a cartridge.

As he checked the other boxes, he thought how he was a part of this killing, how Lawrence – like himself – was also a tool of the power-hunters. They were not in command of anyone's destiny, not even their own, save in the sudden execution of the only inevitable event of anyone's life – the ending of it.

Hogarth's ideals of imperialism and his rejection of democracy, the sum total of all those meetings in Magdalen, the sitting of examinations passed and failed, the travelling to the Levant, the studying of languages and the studying of customs, politics and religions – all culminated in but the final moments in the life of a man, probably a foreigner, most definitely a stranger.

Flecker was disgusted with himself. This was not what he wanted. He had not joined the Foreign Office for this. Somehow he had to escape.

He sat on the last of the cases and stared at the floor. It was littered with sawdust and, by the stationery cupboard, a glossy-backed cockroach, as brown and polished as the stock of one of the guns, reconnoitred the edge of the débris of Flecker's activities.

The longer Flecker sat, quite motionless, the more the turmoil grew in his mind and the more he hated himself for what he was doing, the more he wanted to get out of it all. Yet there were so many obstacles, so many complications – Cumberpatch, the £500 bond, the Foreign Office, Hogarth . . . and Lawrence.

His coughing attack continued now, and then well into the night. He gasped every breath, his hands to his mouth holding a handkerchief in place redolent with gun oil.

He had scoured his hands with the nail-brush, rinsed them over and over, rubbed them with butter, worked Hellé's rosewater soap into them, plunged them in water as hot as he could bear, even doused them in lavender water, yet he could not rid them of the last, faintest taint of the oil. It hung upon him, infiltrating his nostrils. He wondered if it was real or imaginary, lingering to tease him.

All evening he walked to and fro, restlessly pacing the room or sitting at the table, his manuscripts spread before him, his fingers tapping on the wood or bouncing the end of his pen on the paper.

'You are so fidgety tonight,' Hellé said, hoping to comfort him. He made no reply save a grunt of agreement.

Just before they sat down to supper he began to cough uncontrollably. He did not stop for a quarter of an hour except to struggle to catch another breath. His mouth was flecked with sputum and his face red with the effort. He ate nothing, but drank diluted sugared milk instead; Hellé merely picked at her food.

When they went to bed, she nestled his head between her breasts but he continued to cough from time to time, the force of his spasms pushing through her chest and driving the air from her own lungs.

Putting down his stethoscope, the doctor moved to the other side of his surgery and washed his hands with a block of carbolic soap.

'You may get dressed now, Mr Flecker,' he said. 'My examination is completed.'

The strong odour of the soap hung in the air as the doctor dried his hands and rolled down his shirtsleeves, fastening the cuffs with a pair of gold links. He checked the contents of his white enamel refuse bucket before sitting at his desk.

Flecker did not speak as he slipped on his shirt and buttoned his waistcoat over it.

'My diagnosis is not good,' the doctor began. 'Your lungs are much weakened and there is some inflammation of the tracheæ. Your breathing is laboured –

but I hardly need tell you that – and you are somewhat anaemic. I shall arrange for you to have iron pills to overcome the latter problem.'

'What can you put this down to, doctor?'

'Quite clearly you are suffering from bronchitis. The best cure for this, especially with the impending winter, is for you to obtain some leave from the Lebanon. The dry hot air of the summer has exacerbated a delicate balance of health . . .'

His patient made no immediate comment. He sat still in the chair and his eyes had a far-away look.

'Would you be so good as to sign a release for me?' Flecker requested after a moment.

The doctor nodded.

'I think that is essential in this instance. And I suggest two months' leave. I'll see the necessary paperwork is sent to Mr Cumberpatch with all haste. This will also,' he added as an afterthought, 'afford your wife an excellent chance to get away. Most advisable in her state of health. There can be a recurrence of her fever at any time.'

As he walked through the streets to the railway terminus, Flecker's mind was blank. In his heart he knew that bronchitis was a kindly euphemism given him by a well-meaning doctor.

At the station a gust of wind blew in from the direction of the harbour. It set him off coughing once more.

The packing case was one left over from the last shipment of relics from Carchemish. It was dented at the corners, but the metal bindings had held good.

Flecker lined the case with crumpled newspaper and sawdust spilled from the gun boxes: then, in the centre of the case, he piled up his Arabic and Turkish textbooks, his notebooks and papers relating to his studies.

With slow deliberation, he nailed the lid shut, bound wire twine around the sides and pasted on to both the top and side the labels he had prepared which read: 'To — Dr W. H. Flecker, Dean Close School, Cheltenham, Glos. Great Britain. Contents — books.'

He rested upon the packing case and wrote a brief note to his parents on a hand-tinted postcard of the seafront at Nice:

Coming by sea a packing case of books: no longer required here. Please store until I return. We are both well. A letter follows. Love, Roy.

8

At sea, France, and England: the Winter of 1912/13

The smoke billowing from the funnels of the P & O liner alongside the dock in Alexandria was blowing downwards on to the quay, besmirching the white suits of the sailors and dropping smuts of soot on to the baggage waiting to be loaded. Arab stevedores were busy loading cargo into nets to be hoisted by steam crane on to the deck above. Around the ship, seated on planks suspended by ropes from the boat deck, lascars were busy using the hours in port to repaint the hull. At the masthead fluttered the Blue Peter: the vessel was under the harbour pilot's command. From the stern pole hung the Red Ensign.

The Fleckers had seen the liner, their connecting ship for Europe, readying to leave port as they sailed past it aboard the arriving Khedivial Line steamer they had taken from Beirut. Its imminent departure had alarmed Flecker and sent them both into a frenzy of disembarkation, rushing through the docks and re-embarkation. Whatever happened, Flecker was determined not to miss the sailing; another would not become available for nearly a fortnight.

Their short voyage from Beirut had been uneventful. At Jaffa they had gone ashore and lunched on a terrace overlooking orange orchards, the perfume of the blossom headier, Flecker had declared, than sin itself. At Port Said, the Greek crew heard that the Greek army had captured Salonika from the Turks, and there was much rejoicing and patriotic banter against all things Ottoman.

They were hurried along by the P & O boarding officer who checked their tickets in the most perfunctory of manners – he knew who they were, for the agent's cable had informed him of their ship's delay. Despite that, another hour and the purser would have passed the all-clear to sail to the bridge, passengers or no.

Their luggage was considerable. Two cabin trunks, five suitcases and eight assorted packages including a wicker basket in which two chameleons clung to improvised perches, above a floor of cut leaves, and tried to balance against the motion of being carried, their tails curled tightly round the bars.

After much argument and the payment of what Flecker considered to be inordinately large gratuities, their trunks were aboard and stowed as 'Not Wanted on Voyage', the remainder of their belongings delivered to their cabin. The ship's funnel gave three long blasts from its siren and the hawsers were cast off.

On hearing the sound, both Flecker and Hellé left their cabin and went out on deck. Very gradually, the ship drifted away from the dockside. At first the gap was only a few feet but it widened inexorably until, suddenly, Flecker noticed they were twenty or so yards off the shore.

The ship's siren sounded again. A small knot of people on the dock gave their last waves and began to walk away slowly, like guests leaving a particularly tiresome party.

'Good!' Flecker exclaimed.

'I'm sorry . . . ?' Hellé said. 'What did you say, Roy?'

'I said "Good". *Bon! Trés bien! Hæsin! Lyi!* Whichever language you choose. There go the sands of Egypt. We are finally cut loose from – from the Middle East, the Levant, the Lebanon, Beirut . . .' His words were lost in a fifth blast of the siren.

'You're happy?'

'I'm very happy.' He smiled warmly as if to prove it. 'We're going home.'

'But . . .' she began.

'But what, my dearest little girl?'

She believed now she could risk the mention. 'You have had some fine times in Syria. You have written so well there, too. And what of Lawrence? Won't you miss him?'

Flecker looked at the receding shore and she sought to see the expression on his face; it was not one of pain, or parting.

'We shall see him in England,' he said. 'One day.'

'And you must return after our holiday,' she reminded him tentatively, afraid no sooner had she mentioned it that her words might once again prompt his melancholy.

'Perhaps, perhaps not. We shall see. I have some irons in the fire . . .'

Their fellow passengers were expatriates returning from the Far East, civil servants from the Malay States, missionaries and old China hands who had not set foot outside the Orient for years. They were bored by the time they reached the Mediterranean: two months of ship-board life, the monotony of the meals and the incessant rounds of cocktails in each other's cabins, the fancy dress party and the deck quoits championship – not to mention the daily tote on the mileage steamed – had taken its toll.

Flecker was disturbed by them, by their wrinkled skin – 'almost as yellow as a Chinaman's' he would say – by their ignorance of world events, their daily bridge sessions in the smoking lounge and their insularity. They thought Sicily was Sardinia and Sardinia was

Corsica. One old woman, her skin gathered in tucks at her neck like those of a turtle, insisted the Tyrrhenian Sea was the Adriatic and would not be convinced otherwise, even by the atlas in the ship's library which, she asserted vigorously, was shamefully misprinted.

At dinner, or sitting in the lounge with the stewards serving coffee from silver pots, or lazing on deck with the traditional P & O 11 a.m. cup of beef tea, Flecker considered these shells of humans and, one morning as the ship was rounding the northernmost tip of Corsica, he put down the book he was reading and turned to Hellé with tears in his eyes.

'What is the matter?' she enquired. 'Is smoke from the chimney bothering you?'

'Funnel,' he corrected her, 'and no, the wind is blowing away from us. It is . . . it is these shrivelled people.'

He looked past Hellé at a woman standing some way down the deck, a tarred rope quoit in her hand. She was bending at the waist, concentrating on the quoit court painted on the deck planking. Her arms were bare where she had rolled up the sleeves of her jacket and her flesh sagged and wobbled as she swung her arm. She released the quoit, which disappeared beyond the corner of the superstructure, and stood up. Her hair was greyish and wispy where it was being snatched from her bun by the wind.

'Look at her!' Flecker said. 'Her body is broken. Do you know how old she is? Thirty-four. I overheard two other biddies talking about her. Thirty-four! She looks twice that. She's a spinster, a nurse working for the China Missionary Society in Nanking.'

'That is a very laudable profession,' Hellé stated, unsure what point her husband was trying to make.

'Yes, but it has ruined her. Life in a foreign land has ruined her.' He paused and sipped at his beef tea. 'Is that the fate in store for us? Are we to look like that

in ten years? Old before our time, wizened both phys-
ically and spiritually? I can't bear the thought. I should
rather die early than be so corrupted by time.'

'Don't think of them!' Hellé exclaimed. 'We shan't
be like that. I promise you, anyway,' she asserted, 'that
I shall not look like that.'

He smiled feebly and held her hand. 'I should never
want your sweet hand to grow – no, to metamorphose
– into a clutch of spurs.'

As the ship docked in Marseilles, Flecker's spirits rose
once more. Hellé, too, was filled with the anticipated
joy of seeing her mother again, for they would complete
their journey by train, with Hellé staying in Paris with
her mother while Flecker travelled on to London.

It was a cold morning and the weather seemed not
only to invigorate him but give him a new optimism.
Surrounded by their baggage, they settled into a private
compartment on the Marseilles-Lyon-Paris express but,
at the last moment, he decided they would break their
journey at Arles so they unloaded their compartment,
changed trains and arrived only an hour later in Arles
where they obtained rooms in the Hôtel du Forum.

By the time they reached there the weather had hard-
ened to a biting northerly wind and the hotel, despite
its *calorifère*, was little warmer than the streets outside.
However, the room they were given had a fireplace and
Flecker ordered a wood fire be lit which quickly made
the room warm and cosy.

'There is nothing nicer,' Flecker declared, 'than being
in a snug room with a fire ablaze in the grate and the
keen wind whistling by outside.'

He placed the chameleons' basket near to the fire but
for the larger of the two reptiles it was too late. It lay
motionless. Its conical eyes were sunken in their sockets
and its skin was flaking; it looked like some of the

Fleckers' recent fellow passengers. The smaller chameleon was alive but inactive.

'The big one has gone,' Flecker announced sadly.

'Perhaps not. Maybe they sleep in the winter, like tortoises.'

'I'll throw it in the fire,' Flecker decided.

'No, Roy, please not. Let it be until morning.'

He acquiesced, but in the morning it was still in the same position, lying in the débris of leaves at the bottom of the cage, all of which had also died and turned orange or brown.

'It would have preferred to remain in the Lebanon,' Hellé said.

'Yes,' Flecker agreed and said no more.

That morning they wandered in bright sunshine through the cloisters of St Trophime, the former cathedral to Arles. As they walked, Flecker gave Hellé a running commentary on the history of the city: Gibelin of Arles was Patriarch of Jerusalem in 1110, Gervais of Tilbury was made Marshal of Arles by Otto IV, the emperor Constantine II came from the city, Van Gogh had lived there and it was here Frederick Barbarossa was crowned in 1178. From the cloisters they crossed the Place de la République to the museum where Flecker wanted to see the sculptures of Augustus. The mosaics he walked by hurriedly; merely to look at the tesseræ arranged as pictures of Orpheus, Europa and the Bull and other classical themes reminded him of the house at Carchemish.

In the afternoon, Flecker having made the acquaintance of the artist who had decorated the hotel dining room with Provençal paintings, they drove to the ruins at Les Beaux, destroyed by Richelieu. All that remained were crumbling walls atop a boulder-strewn hill, set with gabled doorways and windows, through each of which shone the cold, blue sky and was drawn the thin line of the horizon of the plains towards Avignon.

'The ruins remind me of Greece,' Flecker stated, 'the harsh power of history, the intellectual force of the dead and the turns in the fate of men.'

Yet, in truth, he was reminded not so much of Greece but of the ruined castle of Aleppo and his guide through its dereliction.

The Parisian doctor folded his portmanteau shut and snapped the brass catch with a loud click. The leather of the case squeaked against the black hide of the chair.

'Monsieur Flecker,' he began, speaking in English, 'your wife is not in good health. I cannot give you a complete cure, monsieur and madame. All I can recommend is that Madame Flecker does not return to the Mediterranean region for a long time. The disease must be defeated by being alienated from its place.'

'How long must my wife remain out of the Middle East?'

'It is not a matter of time. She must stay away for ever. Once she is cured, the disease may return. There can be no living for a long period in such places. I am sorry . . . If you are to go to the foreign countries again, monsieur, you must go alone.'

When she heard the doctor's prognosis, Hellé's mother was adamant. Her daughter was not to be put at such risk again; it was out of the question. She hoped, she said, that Flecker would seek to obtain a position in England or, if not, perhaps in Paris.

With the doctor's words and Hellé's mother's dictum swimming in his mind, Flecker left Paris for England. As the train rumbled towards Calais, as the ferry rolled and swayed across the Channel and as the English train dragged slowly through the Kentish countryside, its gouts of smoke lost in the grey leaden skies, he rehearsed his arguments, his pleas, his veiled demands for a new posting, a negotiated resignation or a reassignment of duties.

He wove through the crowds of costermongers outside Covent Garden, the piles of cauliflowers and sacks of potatoes, the wooden flat boxes of apples and pears resting in sawdust, and made his way towards Tavistock Street.

The main door to the *Country Life* magazine building was open, despite the drizzling cold day. Flecker entered and asked for the *English Review* office. He was directed along corridors and through several doors, to come eventually to an office with the magazine's name etched in the glass panelling. He knocked and entered, to be confronted by a clerk seated at a desk.

'Yes, sir?'

'I should like to see Mr Mavrogordato,' Flecker announced.

'May I have your name, sir?'

'James Elroy Flecker,' he said, hoping the name would mean something to the clerk. Somewhere in the office, he knew, was work of his under consideration by Mavrogordato, surely high upon a pile of possible contributions if not already placed in the accepted material stack.

'I'm sorry, Mr Flecker,' the clerk answered, 'but Mr Mavrogordato is no longer with the journal. He resigned some weeks ago, and is now a journalist covering the Balkan War. We believe he is at present in Salonika.'

Flecker could find no reply. Instantly, his hopes were undermined and a bleak sense of mingled failure and frustration filled him, rapidly replaced by a feeling of blank fear. This was not the manner in which to begin a new phase in his career as a writer.

'Would you care to speak to our new editor, Mr Norman Douglas?'

He was shown into a second office where Douglas was seated behind a desk heaped with manuscripts, review copies of recent books and sets of proofs. They shook hands over the débris of editorial copy and submissions.

'I did admire *Bridge of Fire*,' Douglas began. 'A slim volume, but one that I feel was a major contribution and one, what is more, that heralded a great talent in the forming.'

Flecker was nonplussed by such praise and made no response save to mutter his thanks.

'Your *Thirty-Six Poems* was also an excellent collection . . .'

'You were kind enough to review it,' Flecker said, 'and I was most grateful.'

'That was, I believe, my predecessor's responsibility. But, a moment,' Douglas ran his fingers up a stack of books balancing precariously on the corner of his desk, 'your latest volume's here already for review. Yes! Here we are. *Forty-Two Poems*, published by Dent.'

'Will you be covering it?'

'I have no idea as yet. Such a lot of first-rate material is appearing these days, so little space. One is bounded by the confines of the pages . . . But, as you can see, it has reached my desk.' He patted the stack which teetered unstably. 'Now, what can I do for you? I understand you reside in foreign climes, so this must be a visit to London where time is precious and I should not want to waste it for you.'

'I am seeking to return to England to live,' Flecker said, 'and am, quite simply, looking for work – particularly reviewing.'

'I see. Well, I would be delighted to add your name to our list. We do, as I am sure you realise, have a good number of people eager to review for us. But one never knows . . .'

Flecker left Douglas's office in a dejected frame of mind. It was quite plain to him that the editor had little intention of giving him an opening. He entered a coffee house in the Strand and sat quietly with his briefcase on his knees, a coffee pot and cup before him, his order of a plate of pastries untouched. He must now see if the Foreign Office would be more encouraging. He was not optimistic.

Lord Dufferin did not remain seated behind his desk as Douglas had done. He came to the door as Flecker entered and shook his hand warmly, indicating they sit in two leather armchairs set before the window.

'Well, Flecker,' Dufferin began, 'I've heard some sterling reports of your work from some quarters, and some pretty blighting ones from others. You seem to be a bit of a mish-mash, one way or the other.'

'Yes, sir, I would think you have.'

For a few minutes they exchanged the kind of pleasantries that always begin meetings which promise to be awkward, discussing the Italians, the progress of the German railway and the general situation in the Balkans. The preliminaries over, Dufferin asked bluntly what Flecker wanted from his requested meeting.

'I was hoping, sir, to seek a transfer.'

'To what?' Dufferin's tone was curt.

'As you know, sir,' Flecker started, hoping that by padding out his request it might somehow appear more reasonable and stand a better chance of being heard sympathetically, 'I am currently in the Levant Consular Service, as Acting Vice-Consul in Beirut under Mr Cumberpatch. My duties include not only regular consular affairs but also acting in collaboration with Mr Fontana, our Consul in Aleppo . . .'

'I know all about that, Flecker. What can I do for you?'

'I was hoping for a transfer from the Levant Service to the General Service. My health is not good, as you will know from my absences on sick leave, nor is that of my wife who has been recommended by her doctor not to return to the Middle East – she has contracted Malta fever – and I am having difficulty with my examinations. The study of one language whilst living in a country where another is largely spoken I am finding quite hard. My main consideration, however, sir, is my health and that of my wife.'

'I see,' Dufferin mused, shifting in his armchair and pushing his hands over the smooth leather. 'You wish to quit the Levant but you would like to remain in the service. I can see there is no harm in your trying to effect such a change. I would suggest you write in, putting down quite clearly your reasons for wishing to move, and that you seek entry to the General Service without further examination.'

Dufferin paused and looked at Flecker with a shrewd and calculating eye.

'I assume you are seeking to avoid further examination?'

Flecker nodded slightly, evading Dufferin's gaze.

'Well, I see that that is not impossible; it has been done before. The precedent is set and that is important in the Civil Service. However, you must realise, Flecker, the General Service could have you posted wherever the necessity arises – you could conceivably be back in the Levant for a while. With Arabic at least partly at your command you may well find yourself in Egypt, Morocco, anywhere along the North African coast. I am to understand we are at present much in need of a vice-consul in Russia. St Petersburg . . . Once such a posting is made, you will be unable to refuse it. I hope that is clearly understood.'

As Flecker walked along the Embankment, he considered his meeting with Dufferin. Plainly, the man was making it awkward for him. He could risk a change to the General Service, but he would still be at the mercy of the Foreign Office. He would still be far away from the literary world, dependent for his reading upon books six weeks in the coming, magazines months old. And he would possibly be just as far from Hellé. He could survive with delayed books, but not with an absentee wife. It would be bad enough having only one companion with whom to share his thoughts; to have none was beyond thinking.

The Horse Guard sat erect and motionless upon his shining saddle, the silver in his uniform glistening in the wintry sun. Leaves from trees in the Royal Park had drifted into the corner of the sentry arch, swept there by the wintry wind, some adhering to a large heap of horse dung. Looking up, Flecker noticed the soldier's eyes were streaming from the cold, but his sword did not waver so much as a quarter of an inch.

Passing through the archway, Flecker entered the Admiralty and presented himself at the entrance desk. A messenger then led him through the warren of corridors. As he passed the office of the First Lord of the Admiralty, Winston Churchill, Flecker sensed the power emanating from that suite of rooms from which the Royal Navy was controlled, guided, commanded. The man with whom he had an appointment was Churchill's personal private secretary.

'Mr Marsh's office, sir,' the messenger announced

before a heavy, polished door, the brass knob of which shone as if made of burnished gold. 'Just knock, sir.'

Flecker tapped the knuckle of his index finger upon the panelling with an overwhelming sense of occasion and apprehension. By the time he next walked through its portal his life could be irrevocably changed.

'Come in!'

He turned the knob and pushed open the door.

Churchill's outer office was not as austere as Dufferin's had been the day before. It was obviously a governmental one, yet there were signs that someone had attempted to humanise it. Upon the desk stood a lamp with a green glass shade, and the shelves against the wall to the left were lined not only with files and reports but also with novels, books of poetry and history, ornaments and silver-framed photographs. Between the two windows, through which Flecker could see the expanse of Horse Guards Parade and St James's Park beyond, hung a painting about two feet square; it was of a group of Jewish peasants – a child with a peaky, rotund face, a seated old man in a skull-cap with a square-cut beard, a plump wife with big arms and a dark shawl and, in the background, her right side turned to the painter, an older woman with a leer on her face, seen in profile.

'My dear James Elroy Flecker, welcome to London. I see you've spotted my current *pièce de résistance*. The painting's by a young artist called Gertler, Mark Gertler. He's lent it to me. Do take a seat and I'll be with you in a moment.'

Flecker sat down as he was requested and studied Edward Marsh as he finished scribbling marginalia on a file before him on his desk. He was an imposing man even seated. His brown hair was parted on the left and swept across his sloping, aristocratic forehead. His eyes were bright even when reading what Flecker took to be by definition a boring government dossier, and his mouth was curved in a wry, humorous smile. His eye-brows pointed upwards at the outer ends giving him a further slightly comical appearance, and his high collar was loose enough to allow his skin to slip beneath it when he bent forward to sign his name on the memor-andum sheet. In his left hand he held a cigarette, set in an ebony cigarette holder. The air smelled not of Virgi-nian but of Russian tobacco.

Marsh closed the folder and dropped it into a wooden tray.

'How good to meet you at last. No, don't get up,' he insisted as Flecker made to rise. 'I'll come round. Hate to talk over a desk – it's like being at a formal dinner.'

He sat next to Flecker in an easy chair that would have been more suited to a drawing room than a minis-terial office. His hands rested over the arms of the chair, the smoke from his cigarette twisting towards the ceiling.

'It's also very good to meet you, sir.'

'Sir! No. Marsh at least, and Edward to my face.'

Flecker was immediately reminded of Fontana and took an instant liking to the man.

'You'll take a coffee? Of course. Time for one.' Marsh pulled a half-hunter from his waistcoat pocket and quickly glanced at the face. 'Ten-thirty!' He stretched over to his desk and picked up the telephone. 'Two coffees, please, Dobbinet.' He replaced the receiver.

'It's very good of you to see me,' Flecker repeated. 'I'm sure your day is busy enough as it is.'

'I'm delighted. Anything to give me a half-hour from the trials and tribulations of government. And Winnie's out at Chatham today, looking over a new ship – just completed her sea trials. So it's a light day, and I'd not miss the chance to meet a contributor to *Georgian Poetry* – and a fine contributor, at that.'

'It's very flattering of you . . .' Flecker began, but Marsh interrupted him.

'No flattery. Flattery's a cheap emotion. I genuinely liked the work you sent in – had I not, I can assure you, it would not have been accepted for inclusion in the volume. Your poem "The Queen's Song" I found quite enchanting on first reading and powerfully evocative on the second. The stand you take in viewing the boy from the position of the throne is most interesting. And . . . Wait! Let me think . . . "Thus in my love for nations yet unborn, I would remove from our two lives the morn . . ." That's it, I think? The poem, it seems to me, contains a lot of yourself hidden within it.'

'Yes, it does,' Flecker admitted.

'I thought as much. The more of the man that is in the poem, the more the poem speaks to men.'

There was a knock on the door and a stocky man with an anserine face and hairy hands, dressed in the uniform of a messenger, entered carrying a silver tray upon which balanced a silver coffee pot and cream jug, two cups and a sugar bowl.

'Will you like some bisquits, sir?' he enquired.

'I think not. Thank you, Dobbinet.'

The man touched his forehead and obsequiously left the office.

'When does the anthology appear?' Flecker asked.

'In a fortnight or so. I have, in fact, a set of unbound pages here. Would you care to see them? A rhetorical question, no doubt.'

Marsh crossed the room to where his briefcase lay upon a table and withdrew from it a set of pages, handing them to Flecker. They were scented with fresh printer's ink, black tobacco and the leather of the case.

Flecker opened them gingerly. The title page proclaimed the name of the book boldly and simply, as if it were a manifesto for an entirely new movement in

British verse. The contents page surprised him. He was in more elevated company than he had even dared to anticipate – Walter de la Mare, John Masefield, G. K. Chesterton, Gordon Bottomley, T. Sturge Moore. Also present were Rupert Brooke and Lascelles Abercrombie, W. H. Davies and John Drinkwater. They were all names Flecker knew from the magazines he had been sent in Beirut or seen when on leave.

'I'm rather honoured to be in with such a talented and famous host,' he said honestly, but Marsh pooh-poohed him.

'On the contrary, you might say they are honoured by your presence. But, in truth, you are all justly represented. Sadly though, there is generally far less honour amongst poets than there is with thieves! You know versifiers, forever at each other's throats. If all the energies poets expended on reviling each other went into their art, the world would see a three-hundredfold increase in poetic production.'

'What will the cover be?' Flecker asked as he handed back the pages.

'Plain. One colour with the title in gold blocking. And the date beneath – "1911–1912" – for I am hoping this might be the first of a number of annual publications. Brought out by The Poetry Bookshop, of course. As you know.'

The sun momentarily broke through the clouds and shone brilliantly upon the buff gravel of Horse Guards Parade, glinting off the stones where the night's rain had lain in puddles. The bare November trees beyond were a stark contrast to the jasmines and pomegranates of the Lebanon. Flecker felt curiously comforted by their bleakness and dull colouring.

'Now,' Marsh said briskly, 'you want to see me for reasons other than poetry, I understand.'

'Yes.' Flecker hesitated, not sure how to continue.

Marsh recognised his hesitancy and said, 'Just come out with it and I'll see what I can do.'

'In a nutshell,' Flecker began, 'I want to leave the Levant Service, leave the Consular Service altogether. My health is not good and cannot take the rigours of such a climate as that of Syria – nor can my wife now, who has caught Malta fever whilst in the Lebanon with me – and I am finding the whole job crushingly boring. I feel so . . .' – he searched for a phrase to do justice to his feelings of isolation from all he held dear – poetry, art, books and conversation – '. . . so utterly sequestered out there. It's like being cast away on an island, on a prison island. Devil's Island. I have difficulty with my examinations, as a result of my health, and my poetry . . .'

'Enough!' Marsh raised his hand from the arm of his chair. 'Let us not listen to what you do not like. What do you like out there?'

'Very little,' Flecker replied bluntly.

'What of your work for Hogarth?'

Immediately Flecker was quiet. He wondered how much Marsh knew; he was betraying no thoughts, his face turned away as he stubbed out his cigarette in a marble and gold ashtray and put his ebony holder down beside it.

'I know all about it,' Marsh said, answering Flecker's doubt. 'The railway, Lawrence's mission. I know also how valuable a part you have played in this. You are a vital link in the chain. It may seem little to you, but it is not. Tell me – does not Lawrence alleviate some of the crushing boredom?'

'Yes, he does.'

Flecker's change of tone, even in just the three words, was quickly picked up by Marsh.

'I thought you and he would hit it off. He is a man much like yourself. A fine intellect, a bit of a rebel, which you are but won't allow to surface, a fine poet which *he* does not allow to surface. He is a man of action, as are you. Albeit in your case it is suppressed.'

He looked at Flecker as he spoke but not unsympathetically; there was no scepticism or searching in his eyes as there had been in Dufferin's.

'You and Lawrence are much of a muchness. And you are both like me. We are members of the same freemasonry, a far more binding brotherhood than that which meets in its secret lodges in Great Queen Street. No grand temples in our society save perhaps the sanctuary of the soul and, possibly at times, the flesh.'

Flecker smiled briefly, then asked, 'But what shall I do? If I quit the service I lose my bond which neither I nor my parents can afford to pay. If I transfer to the General Service, I can be posted anywhere – Lord Dufferin hinted yesterday at Russia or North Africa. To leave the service means obtaining a good job to support both myself and my wife.'

'What plans have you?'

'I was hoping for a reviewing job or two, but that seems unlikely. My writing is not making me any money, although I am certain I could write a successful novel. I am going to speak to Professor Raleigh at Oxford. Perhaps he would, as Professor of English Literature, consider me for a post. I see education as being my only really viable route.'

For some moments Marsh was silent, his elbows on the sides of his chair, his hands pressed together and his lips just touching his fingertips. All the while, Flecker watched him hopefully.

'Let me suggest a few options,' Marsh recommended, lowering his hands to rest in his lap, one palm in the other as if he were holding Flecker's future tenderly in his care. 'You have the General Service in mind and a possible position in Oxford. Also a possible magazine

job which, I am sure, even you can see will not bring
in sufficient upon which to live. You cannot hope, as
yet, to support yourself from writing. The time may
come – I trust it will – but for the present ... So I
would add to those an inspectorship with the Board of
Education, a plain schoolmastering job – although that
may well not give you a great salary, it will provide you
as like as not with a roof over your head – or a tutorial
position, perhaps with a provincial university or with
the Workers' Educational Association. However, you
will have to accept a reduction in the standards of your
living whichever course you follow. For a while ...'

'Is there anyone to whom you feel I should make
direct approaches?' Flecker asked.

'No, I don't believe so. But I will contact Benson at
the Cambridge University appointments board. He may
well be able to suggest alternatives or know of specific
openings.'

Flecker was somewhat crestfallen. He had hoped Marsh
would be able to pull a few strings for him, rather
than merely suggest possibilities and praise his poetry.

To allay Flecker's evident disappointment, Marsh
went on, 'What writing do you have in progress, as
they say?'

'Poems, always poems. I wrote one on the P & O
from Egypt with which I'm quite pleased. A chance
encounter with an artist in Arles provided an added
impetus to it. It's entitled "The Painter's Mistress".'

'Be sure to send it me,' Marsh encouraged.

'I am also writing a drama in verse to be entitled
Hassan, or *Hassan of Baghdad*. It is a five-act play set
in that city in times past. The main character, the
Hassan of the title, is a middle-aged confectioner with
a curling moustache. I began it in June of 1911 ...'

'What is it about? A five-acter is not a little ambitious.
I admire your stamina in working on such a project.'

'I began,' Flecker said, 'after coming across a book of Turkish farces. I was looking for reading for the examinations . . .'

Marsh laughed and interrupted, 'There! You see, some good comes of consular pressures after all.'

Flecker allowed himself a fleeting smile and continued, 'Hassan is a gullible fellow who is always the butt of practical jokes. I wrote a few poems about the theme with Persian rhyme schemes and then read the Mardrus translation of the *Arabian Nights*. The play grew from there.'

'Send me a copy of it and I'll pop it on to Granville Barker for you. He's the kind of impresario to be moved by such a plot.'

'Granville Barker rejected my play *Don Juan*,' Flecker admitted, 'and so did Trench at the Haymarket Theatre.'

'Don't let that discourage you. It was the play they were against – not you. Never allow the poet's paranoia to get to you. The mistakes learned in *Don Juan* will not be repeated.'

Flecker's spirits rose at such blunt and uncompromising encouragement. 'It is as yet unfinished, though six months should see it through. Then I shall let you have the first typed copy.'

'Capital!' Marsh exclaimed. 'And now, if you will excuse me, I must get on with the banalities of everyday government. And you have a lunch appointment, I believe? I'm sure we shall meet again and, I would hope, soon. Keep me apprised of all you do – both literary and within your career.'

The first draft of his letter was a mixture of anger, despondency and frustration; he perused it a third time, wondering whether or not to send it:

My darling Pussy, [he had written]

It is Friday and I have been in London for three days now, crawling round and round from meeting to office to building. The further I have trailed the more unhappy and hopeless I become.

Mavro has quit the *ER* and gone to the war. Mr *Poetry Review* Monro, he of The Poetry Bookshop, lunched with me and has given me some reviewing work – but a paltry amount in all. Dufferin suggests I try for the General Service, but promises nothing but possible postings to Russia or Morocco, which would be as bad as Syria. And you, my dearest one, would be apart from me there.

I am so lonely in London.

Marsh has suggested a few good ideas and I shall follow them up. He is a charming man and very kind. He is a patron of the arts – but I need a manager, not a benefactor.

Last night, through loneliness for you, I went to the cinema. The films they were showing were of the Balkan war and of Constantinople, Athens, Greece generally and her Armed Forces – which pictures were loudly applauded by the audience, some even standing to an ovation. Seeing the place that we love without you there with me set me into a deeper ditch than I had been in before and I slunk back to bed weeping for you in the darkness.

Do please be certain to arrive here next Wednesday. If you fail to come to your Tiger's den I care not to think what might happen. If you do not arrive I shall throw all to the winds and come straight to Paris. I am in purgatory without my Little Pussy. And I have received no word from you at all. As yet. Please write to me in my desolation.

I cannot abide the loneliness of London another day. Your silence adds to the echoes in the night streets.

Tomorrow I go to Oxford where my address will be care of J. D. Beazley, Christchurch College, Oxford.

Ever your loving and all-alone,
Tiger

He picked up his pen.

'Better to put Jack nearer the head of the letter: it looks too furtive this way,' he said aloud and screwed the paper up, tossing it on to the fire where it flared briefly.

Beazley's claret glass knocked against his dessert spoon and he pressed his finger to the silver to kill the chime.

'So. . . .' he said.

Flecker made no response.

'Lawrence is well, then?'

'Thriving when last I saw him. Dressed like a sheikh and living like a lord.'

'Has he . . .' Beazley raised his glass again and studied it against the candle-flame. 'Tell me, has he acquired himself a boy yet? It seems the done thing.'

'Yes.'

Beazley chuckled and said, 'Trust Ned to find his pleasures even in the wastes of Arabia Deserta.' He turned his attention from his glass to Flecker. 'And have you, too?'

'No.' Flecker shook his head, irritated that Beazley should also know Lawrence as Ned. 'I have a wife, Jack.'

'Ah, yes! But should that make a difference? After all, love is surely not exclusive . . .' He left his words to hang in the air.

'Perhaps not,' Flecker conceded.

'A good pheasant?' Beazley asked, waving the stalk of his glass in the direction of Flecker's plate.

'Very good indeed. Such rich prizes are not to be found in the Levant.'

'So Raleigh has not turned up trumps.' Beazley refilled his glass from a crystal ship's decanter. 'What will you do now?'

'Hellé is due over in a few days. We go together to Cheltenham and there, I imagine, it will be a beating of breasts and a meeting of the clan and a thrashing out of a future. Every other line appears to have drawn a blank.'

'Perhaps Marsh can do something with this play of yours. He seems to be able to do wonders with anthologies of poetry. I've just got hold of an advance copy. Have you seen it? Quite a little time bomb of a book.'

Their conversation drifted aimlessly through pleasantries about books, poetry, archaeology — Beazley wanted to hear as much as he could about Lawrence's digging.

'Have you been to Carchemish yourself?' Beazley enquired.

When his guest replied in the affirmative, Beazley's demeanour perked up a good deal and Flecker, in response, went into some detail about the finds at the site and the history of the mound. He described the area around, mapping it on the table top with cutlery and piles of salt from the cellar. He spoke of Lawrence's house, the mosaic floor, the Roman occupation of Carchemish, the Byzantine relics. . . . and the more he spoke, the more despondent he grew.

Their meal over, Beazley invited Flecker back to his rooms.

'A good port for a night-cap, Roy? Straight from college cellars.'

They trudged up the dark staircase to Beazley's rooms, the door to which he opened with a huge, mediaeval key saying, 'Welcome to the tomb.'

After they had settled down with a glass of port each, Flecker decided the time had come to broach the subject he had hoped would have been raised naturally in the course of their meal.

'Jack?' he said, tentatively.

'Hmm!' Beazley responded, leaning back with his eyes closed.

'Are we no longer friends?'

'Of course we are.' He did not open his eyes. 'Why do you need to ask?'

'Friends as we were in the Praxiteles days?' Flecker went on, ignoring Beazley's question. 'Friends of the *Yellow Book of Japes* days? You taught me so much of the craftsmanship of poetry with your images and ideas. I still go back to them . . .'

'Bosh! I hardly helped you be a poet. You were at it long before we met.'

'But you refined me. And that was not all I was taught with you . . .'

Beazley opened his eyes.

'Those days, those heady hours of youth and exploration are over. We are older men now.'

'Does that mean we can't be close again?'

He reached over and put his hand softly on Beazley's knee. The tweed of his trousers was rough to the touch.

'Aren't we?' Beazley suggested, not making to remove Flecker's hand yet not seeking to take it in his either. 'Aren't we now, in my tombic rooms, with the blood of the muses poured into our hands?'

'You know what I mean.'

'Yes,' Beazley allowed, 'I do. And those days can't return. I have other – how shall I put it? I do not want to offend you – liaisons now. Other friends.'

Beazley's words brought the evening to a glum ending. Flecker left soon afterwards: there was nothing more for them to say. He was immensely saddened, not so much at having lost, as he saw it, an old friend but at the realisation that the past was passed, that the heady hours, as Beazley had termed them, had chimed and the clock moved inexorably and cruelly onwards.

Lying in his bed in a college guest room, his toes cold and a forlorn drizzle running on the leaded window panes, Flecker felt wretched. Nothing was working out. Raleigh was no source of hope; Marsh neither. Beazley was cool towards him. The world, he deemed, was a woeful place. He fell into a restless sleep, hoping Hellé would soon be back with him and that, together, in Cheltenham, he and his wife and his parents might be able to cobble some relief for him from his prison of misery.

The train rattled and jolted over the junction, gathering speed as it chuffed out of Kingham station. The wheels rang hollow as the carriages moved over the bridge across the river, and the wisps of steam slicing past the windows momentarily obscured the promontory of Maugersbury Hill.

'I was very worried for you in Oxford,' Hellé admitted, ending a silence which had fallen between them since just after the train pulled out of Oxford station.

'Why?'

He put his hand on hers where it rested on her lap, glad she had at last spoken.

Ever since her arrival in England she had been somehow distant. It was not that she had held back from him, or refused his caresses, or rejected his love-making. Indeed, they had made love only the night before in his favourite of ways and with a passion he had not experienced with her before. It had left him utterly drained of energy and emotion; he had just lain weakly on the sheets, the blankets pulled up to his neck, and watched her. When she bent over, her back half-turned towards him, he could see the fine curve of her hips and could hear her breathing hard still. The fire in the grate was still merrily alight and the flames danced moving shadows into the folds of her body.

Even so she had, in some inexplicable way, not been with him. Somewhere deep inside her, despite her appetite for him, her pressing him into her with her whole strength, her thrusting up against him, her driving her fingernails hard into his skin, there was a black void he could not enter. It had scared him as he lay afterwards waiting for her to return, readying himself for the sudden chill of her cooled skin against his. He wanted to ask her about it but found he could not.

Over breakfast in a coffee house in Cornmarket, he had thought to broach the subject yet could not bring himself to do so. She was not as talkative as usual, tearing her toast – it seemed to him – in an almost exacting way as if it were, like the communion wafer, flesh. But not his flesh.

Jack Beazley had come to see them off at the station, dressed in his academic gown, the black folds hanging around him like the furled wings of a bat. They shook hands through the carriage window, Beazley then leaving abruptly before the train departed.

'Must get to my tutorial,' he said briskly. Then, lowering his voice, he added in a baritone, 'Back to the tomb. From whence I shall arise at noon. Half a rhyme. Keep at it, Roy!'

As he went through the barrier, handing his platform ticket to the inspector, Beazley raised his left hand in salute and the bat's-wing of his gown flapped in the air. . . .

The train echoed under a bridge and past a neat farmhouse close to the line. Behind it, a lane rose sharply up a hill towards a prehistoric earthwork.

'I was worried because . . . You know why I was worried. I know you so well, dearest Roy.'

Flecker gazed out at the Gloucestershire countryside. He was going home, was already in his home county.

The trees were bare. As the railway line curved towards Bourton-on-the-Water, Flecker saw a copse standing a hundred yards away, bearing the cumbersome blots of a rookery. In the light grey sky above, crows were riding the wind.

He thought of her letters, once they caught up with him in his travels, of how they had lifted his spirits if only temporarily. Certain phrases repeated themselves to him: '. . . you won't forget my love beside your Oxonian friend . . .' – '. . . I am startled you have left London early without having achieved your aims . . .' – '. . . if you can do nothing in London, return here to Paris . . .' – '. . . we must try to be reasonable for future's sake . . .' – '. . . of course, I miss you, O my darling Tiger . . .' – '. . . you must know I am very jealous of your friend, Jack . . .'.

'Couldn't you have trusted me?'

'Yes. But you were lonely and when men are lonely they seek love.'

She slid her hand out from beneath his and placed it upon his arm.

'This lonely man found none until you reached his arms,' Flecker answered.

She took his hand and pressed it to her lips.

'It is in the past. We have the future now. Our future. No more Jacks! And we must plan for it, shape it to accept us.' She pointed out of the window at the landscape. 'The hills are so beautiful! Can we walk in them together?'

'The Cotswolds . . . yes, they are beautiful. And yes, we shall walk in them. Up Leckhampton Hill, across to Coberley, over to Withington, down to Andoversford and back by train. We shall take a whole, sunlit winter's day, dine in a country inn like seventeenth-century trav-

ellers on roast beef and ale and come back to the
warmth of our home revived by the beauty of the hills.
How would you like that?'

'I should like it very much indeed.'

He knew there was little hope. His parents could ill
afford to pay his bond to the Foreign Office. A lec-
turership in Nottingham University was coming vacant,
but not until October of the next year and the salary
was a mere £210 per annum; his parents could hardly
be expected to support him and his wife for the interim
ten months.

It was with a heavy heart he wrote to the Foreign
Office as Lord Dufferin had suggested, requesting a
transfer to the General Consular Service. He stated his
case as strongly as he could, his father advising him in
the drafting of the letter.

Praying his letter would have some effect, he sent
it by registered mail from the General Post Office in
Cheltenham.

The reply was back within ten days. Flecker received
it from the postman at the main entrance to his father's
school. Seated at his father's desk in the study, he slit
the envelope with a carved bone paper-knife and
quickly read the letter. It was brief and to the point.

Dear Sir, [it began, the large, official type-face of the Foreign
Office typewriter looking out of place below the small printing
of the letterhead and the neat government ministry emblem]

With regard to your request for transfer from the Levant
Consular Service to the General Consular Service, I am
instructed by Sir Edward Grey to inform you of the fact that
such a transfer is not to be granted . . .

'I cannot be other than plain speaking, Mr Flecker. It
is my opinion – a considered opinion taking in to

account your past history – that you must seek to leave Britain for a sunnier and warmer clime. Your lungs are not, as you are aware, at all strong. Your recent coughing bouts have weakened them and the chill air of an English winter will aggravate them further. What is more, I do not see you receiving any relief from this bronchial state until you are in a warmer atmosphere.'

'Thank you, doctor,' Flecker said in a near whisper.

'You will, of course, have to choose your climate with a degree of care. However, having said that, and admitting at the same time that I am somewhat ignorant of lands outside of Europe, I would suggest that a return to . . . it is Beirut, is it not, where you work at present?'

Flecker nodded slowly.

'I thought so. Well, Beirut would not go amiss. Indeed, it may well prove to be beneficial to you in both the short and long terms.'

'How serious is it?' Flecker asked as he fastened his collar.

'How serious is this form of laryngitis at any time, Mr Flecker? It is serious. It can develop into other things, can weaken the heart with the burden of perpetual coughing, much as can asthma. It can be generally debilitating and thus allow other infection to gain a foothold in the system.'

'I see. Yet I would want to say that, in the Lebanon this past year, my coughing has not reduced for all the sunshine.'

'Then perhaps,' the doctor advised, 'you should seek to obtain employment in an alternative sunny climate.'

Marsh's flat occupied the top two floors of Number 5, Raymond Buildings. It was approached first through a gateway not unlike that of an Oxford college and down a cul-de-sac, then by a spiral staircase of fifty-nine stone steps, finally by a dark green-painted door. Within, it was furnished comfortably with a mixture of Edwardian and Victorian furniture, those walls not hung with paintings lined with bookshelves. The heavy maroon velvet curtains which kept at bay the coal-smoky fog of the London night shone like rich burgundy in the dim light.

'It was Rupert who put me up to editing the anthology,' Marsh said, extinguishing the last inch of his cigarette in a silver ashtray in the centre of which was set a silver Mexican dollar.

'But you were the one who *did* it. I certainly don't claim any honour by it.'

Flecker looked at Rupert Brooke who was lying on his front on the floor before the fire, his chin cradled in his hands.

Studying his poet friend from Cambridge, Flecker could not prevent himself from admiring his beauty. His whole being radiated a fairness of form and character. His body was perfectly proportioned and his light brown hair, swept straight back across his skull, glistened in the light. His shoulders were broad and strong, his neck sensuously long and his brow wide. His eyes were deep-set and held the attention of anyone upon whom they should glance. He was, Flecker thought, a magical youth, an altogether bewitching boy cast in the same mould as Lawrence.

'I came home late one day from the Admiralty,' Marsh remembered, 'to find Rupert perching on the edge of his bed with hardly anything on. I joined him and our talk, after a while, settled upon modern poetry. He suggested we should shake the public out of their lethargy for modern verse. He proposed, impish boy!' – he nudged Brooke's arm with his slippered foot – 'he write an anthology of poems under twelve pseudonyms and publish it as being the work of a dozen new

unknowns. I suggested there were enough around without the need for subterfuge.'

'And so we sat up, there and then,' Brooke cut in,
'and compiled a list. You were in it, Roy. No doubt
about it.'

'I wanted Rupert to edit it but he said it needed a
more authoritarian hand. One older and more
respected. Me! I settled on the title after we had a bit
of a tiff over naming The New Era. A period of time is
traditionally named after the monarch, so I concocted
my ambiguity – *Georgian Poetry*. And that was it . . .'

'It is selling astoundingly!' Flecker exclaimed. 'I met
Monro but yesterday – The Poetry Bookshop has sold
out. Completely. It is selling in droves.'

'We are reprinting,' Brooke said triumphantly.

There was a discreet tapping on the door and Marsh's
housekeeper came in. She was a homely, middle-aged
woman dressed in a pinafore of the sort that would
have looked more in place in a country farmhouse than
the Holborn apartment of a ministerial private secretary.

'If you gennlemun are dun,' she said with a pronounced Derbyshire accent, 'I'll excuse misel an' be up
t' m' bed.'

'Yes, thank you, Mrs Elgy.' Marsh raised his hand a
few inches in acknowledgement. 'We'll see you in the
morning. And that was an excellent chicken . . .'

She bobbed her head in recognition of her employer's
praise and closed the door quietly.

'A gem,' Marsh commented, once he had heard her
footsteps fade down the passageway to the kitchen. 'A
rough diamond of the best quality. Been with me for
nearly thirteen years now. Can hardly read or write,
except in her own particular way. Let me show you
both something . . .'

Marsh went to a large bureau in the corner and

pushed up the slatted wooden lid which opened with a shuttling sound. From a small drawer he removed a wadge of postcards, extracting one from it.

'This was from her last summer. She leaves notes like this to me in the house. Being a little *au fait* with phonetics, I can interpret them, but I'm sure the Secret Service could use her. You think of her, Roy . . . she may be useful to you . . .'

He handed the card to Brooke who read it, laughed loudly and rolled on to his back, the firelight glistening on the smooth skin of his chest where it showed through his unbuttoned shirt.

Flecker took the card from him. It was a view of Bognor Regis, badly hand-tinted; the blue of the sea had encroached upon the yellow of the beach.

The writing was childish and stated simply: 'i lik it heer but the winds to vishus for wirds wen i prumenad and i no nobudy in the otel.'

It was after midnight when Flecker excused himself. He walked to the end of the cul-de-sac and, as he waited for the gatekeeper to open the padlock on the gate, looked back over his shoulder. The light was on in Brooke's room. As he watched, a figure in silhouette came to the window and drew the heavy curtains across the gauze ones. The outline was plainly that of Marsh.

It was, he thought, just as Lawrence had said. He was trapped. There was no conceivable way out. He had explored every possibility and they had all drawn a blank.

Even a letter to Hogarth had produced no result. He had laid out in it, quite dispassionately, exactly how he stood – he was short of money, in poor health, terrified by what the future might hold in store for him. His wife could not return to Beirut, for the sake of her health, while he was doomed to return. His entreaties for assistance had fallen on deaf ears at the Foreign Office. His writing was getting nowhere, he was unable to place his poems, unable to get more than a few meagre reviewing commissions. The first two acts of his play, he told Hogarth, which he was calling *Hassan*, were in the hands of Edward Marsh who was pressing its case with stage managers and producers, notably Granville Barker. Yet it was hard work writing it. He was at his wits' end.

Hogarth replied in sympathetic but largely distant tones. He would see what could be done, he wrote, but could promise nothing. In the meantime, he advised Flecker to return to Beirut and assume his duties. He would still be responsible for the liaison with Lawrence and would be working in collaboration with Raff Fontana. As before, this was not to be discussed with Cumberpatch, for whom such knowledge might prove compromising: he did not explain why this should be so. Once back in Beirut, Hogarth advised, Flecker should at least go through the motions of studying for his examinations. This would strengthen his – Hogarth's – hand in seeking to act on his behalf in mediation with the Foreign Office.

This was, Flecker knew, the only choice he had. His parents believed his arguments for quitting the service to be illogical; they wanted him to follow the course recommended by Hogarth. Faced with such overwhelming odds, he had to comply. Yet it meant leaving Hellé in Paris with her mother. That more than distressed him and he wondered once more how he could face Beirut again on his own.

The words in the top right corner of the sheet read: 'as

from Chez Madame Skiadaressi, 10 rue de Marché, Neuilly-sur-Seine, France.'

Flecker looked at the address. A month hence, he considered, it would be 'The British Consulate-General, Beirut.'

He began to write.

My dear Marsh,

The Foreign Office having given me an extension of leave for a fortnight, I have fled hither for peace and refreshment. Before we left London we saw *Twelfth Night*, and were overwhelmed by its excellence.

I am definitely going to be an Usher in Nottingham next academic year unless, as I hope, something more cheerful turns up. I am writing to Benson.

The hope of my life, which is *Hassan*, is in your hands. I am longing to hear what Ainley thinks of it, still more to hear what Barker thinks of it, and no less to hear what you think of it. Do not scruple to tell me bad news and bad opinions.

My best love to Rupert, and many thanks to you for your great kindness to one as unfortunate as Ovid.

He signed it: 'James Elroy Flecker'.

The frost glistened like confectioner's sugar upon the countryside along the railway line. The train halted at a signal outside Canterbury. Flecker stared at the clumps of hoary grass, the watery sunlight catching in the crystals at the tips of the leaves.

'That there can be so sombre a beauty in such deathly things,' he remarked.

'They aren't dead,' Hellé reassured him. 'In the spring there will be life.'

'In that case I think they are considerably luckier than I. My spring is long past.'

He moved his gaze upward from the brown miniature spires of the grass-blades and saw, across the fields and hedgerows of winter, the towers of the cathedral with their ornate pinnacles, the stone brown under the pale sky.

'How we imitate nature in our attempts to worship the forces which form it. We think we know so much and yet we know so little. We control the present, or so we think, and we chronicle the past as a series of battles won and lost, but the future . . . We have yet to conquer the future. Even in our hearts.'

The train started forward then slowed, the buffers juddering together, then moved forward steadily. The grass clumps disappeared, to be replaced by a patch of leafless nettle stalks and teazles upon which a finch balanced.

By the time they reached Dover and had embarked on the ferry Flecker's spirits were at their lowest ebb. He was quiet and withdrawn and made none of his usual fuss over the baggage, counting the pieces and muttering – as he generally did – at the exorbitant cost of porters' tips.

Their belongings piled in their day cabin for the crossing to Calais, they went up to the boat deck. Flecker was bundled in a heavy overcoat and chocolate brown woollen scarf, a Homburg hat upon his head and his brown shoes highly polished. His complexion, despite the cold wind, was swarthy.

In an attempt to lift his spirits, Hellé said, 'You do look funny, Roy,' and slipped her hand under his arm. 'Like an Eastern European cantor . . .'

'I am not Jewish,' he said sullenly and with a vicious tone.

As they headed out of the harbour the sea turned a grey-blue with hardly any swell on it. The cliffs were off-white behind the wake of the ship, the tops lined with browny-green where the downlands came to their abrupt stop. In mid-Channel the ship slowed to give passage to a stately square-rigger sailing north under the stiff breeze which had caused Flecker to jam his hat further down his brow. She was riding low in the water, her masts carrying a full complement of sails. The canvas looked bleached even in such weak sunshine.

'Like a royal swan,' he observed, 'yet who knows what lies in her holds? Corrupted gold stolen from temples to the sun, gunpowder and guns, the machineries of war . . .'

As the shore of England faded into gradual invisibility, Flecker said stoically, 'I fear, my darling Pussy, this is the last sight I shall have of Albion.'

9

At sea, Beirut, Halfati and Carchemish: January/March 1913

At the end of the dock loomed Naples' Castel Nuovo, the fortress of Charles I of Anjou. The massive stone corner towers, buttresses and the immense foundations were smeared with black stains as if, over the centuries, the stones had slowly, infinitesimally, bled. It had rained during the night and where the footings leaned inwards the stains were darkly glistening as if the process of bleeding were continuing.

On the quayside a mob of stevedores, vegetable sellers, carters and porters milled about in an effort either to unload passengers' baggage or sell their wares to the purser who stood at the bottom of the gangplank vociferously refusing all offers. Horse-drawn cabs queued by the nearest dock gate, awaiting those passengers who were, at that moment, having their papers scrutinised in the smoking lounge by three officials in starched collars and black suits.

Flecker stood near the immigration officers' tables for more than a quarter of an hour, his hand in his pocket grasping his diplomatic passport and papers. He was in a quandary of anguish and self-doubt.

Every day, in the early evening, a train left Naples for Rome. There, in the early hours, a fast express with sleeping compartments and a restaurant car departed for Paris, arriving at the Gare de l'Est just after dark the following night. This much he had discovered from the *Baedeker* in the ship's library. The edition he had consulted was two years out of date and the fare given was sure to have increased in the meantime, but he reckoned he had enough in his possession to pay for the ticket if not for a sleeper.

All he had to do was take five steps to the nearest desk, present his credentials and go ashore. One of the cabs at the gate would take him directly to the station. Perhaps, he considered, the train might leave directly from the Stazione Marittima at the end of the Piazza Municipio beside the castle. He was not carrying so much luggage that he would be hampered by it. Within thirty-six hours – forty-two at the most – he could be back in Neuilly-sur-Seine with his beloved Pussy.

Quite what her reaction would be when she discovered him standing on the steps of her mother's house he dared not think. After all, he considered, he had done as much once already.

In a state of acute depression, he had parted from Hellé in Paris, catching the train to Marseilles. However, when the train halted in Laroche Flecker got off, booked into a *pension* close to the station for the night and returned first thing the following morning to Paris. His arrival at her mother's house had been emotional. Hellé was in tears, her mother likewise; even the maid, opening the door to find him there surrounded by his bags, wept. He had, he said, decided he could wait another week and take a later sailing.

They spent the week very close to each other. Every night they went to bed early, lying in until ten in the morning, caressing and stroking each other, making love two or three times a night. They were obliged to be quiet, for Hellé did not want to disturb her mother, and so moved as little as possible in the huge creaking bed in the guest room. Making their special love out of bed was out of the question – the floorboards creaked even more than the mattress and springs.

Flecker's second departure had been more upsetting for Hellé than his first for which she had steeled herself. At the last moment she thought to abandon their plans and go with him, but she kept her own counsel on this; if she fell ill again in Beirut she would be such a burden to him, and she was anxious to spare him that.

He was in better spirits as he left the house the second time. At the terminus she kissed him lightly on the cheek and gave him one last word of advice which she intended as a veiled warning, but it was lost on him in his keenness to be on his way.

'Do not forget, dearest Tiger,' she had whispered in his ear, so that the other passengers in his carriage could not hear, 'that if you are lonely then your Pussy is just as lonely, too. And she will not seek any solace in another living creature until she is with her Tiger in his lair once more.'

'I shall not be lonely,' Flecker replied quietly but with forceful determination. 'I shall not be. I shall get on with my play and my novel and my new verse collection and my studies, and that will be the end of it. I shall strive tirelessly to finish all three books and pass those accursed exams with flying colours. Undistracted, I shall work, and work, and work. When you join me, you will see a changed Tiger!'

The guard had blown his whistle then and swung his green lantern. The train had sounded its own whistle and the carriages clanked as the strain of the couplings was taken up. He watched her wave once and returned her salute, then took his seat. He did not see her standing on the platform until the train was out of sight and had been gone for several minutes.

All the way to Marseilles he was resolute. He read, he worked upon a few drafts, he dozed and dined well in the restaurant car on roast lamb cooked with garlic. When the train stopped in Laroche he looked out at the station with an air of self-contempt. He thought how foolish he had been to get off there and return like a milksop to Hellé: he was stronger than that now.

He had felt a slight pang as the ship sailed from Marseilles, but comforted himself with the thoughts that Hellé's health would be safeguarded in Paris and, besides, only the Mediterranean separated them. It was not the Atlantic or the Indian Ocean. If he had been transferred to the General Service he might have been posted to . . . He considered a list of the places he had succeeded in avoiding by remaining in the Levant – Haiti, Ecuador, Chile, Japan. And he had so much writing to do: when next they met he would have achieved so much.

However by the time the vessel docked in Naples he was being torn by misery. Hellé was only another, longer train journey away.

Flecker leaned upon the ship's rail beside one of the lifeboats and looked across at the shore of Italy. He could live in Italy, he decided: the homeland of poetry and Dante, of art and da Vinci, of stories and Boccaccio and sculpture and Michaelangelo. If he could earn just a modicum from his writing they could move to Italy, live in the mountains surrounded by bandits or own a small house in the rolling hills of Tuscany or a small flat in Rome. He would be like Keats, an English expatriate poet.

A steam lorry rattled along the road past the Castel Nuovo. Its hissing and thumping stampeded a horse and its cart left parked at the kerbside while the owner took coffee at a stall. The horse did not career far – the traffic was heavy, and it had only gone a hundred metres when the axle of the cart lodged firmly against a steel bollard – but the furore its short gallop caused was extensive. Other horses bucked and neighed, pedestrians ran for cover, other carters attempted to veer their own vehicles from the path of the runaway. No harm was done by the event and, from Flecker's viewpoint, it had all the humour and fast action of a well-staged farce. Yet he did not laugh.

When the ship sailed on the evening tide, he watched the city of Naples, a twinkling of yellow lights, disappear slowly from view and, as the ship moved across the Bay of Naples, he stood alone on deck and saw a thin twist of smoke lifting from the summit of Vesuvius, stark in the moonlight.

The deck-chair was lowered to its last notch and the sun was warm upon Flecker's face. His head was cradled in a pillow, his hands resting in his lap, knees covered by a tartan blanket. His eyes were shut and he was enjoying eavesdropping upon the conversation of two passengers sitting near him. They were both missionaries bound for British East Africa and were quietly arguing about the condition of the souls they would soon encounter in the Dark Continent.

The younger of the two, a fresh-faced and clean-shaven man in his early twenties with fair hair and deep blue eyes, was insistent that they would be dealing with innocents, with races of negroes beyond sin for they had no conception of it. They could not, he believed, be sinful until they knew the difference between right and wrong. It was the missionaries' role to teach them what was and what was not right. The older priest, however, sporting a pair of Victorian sideboards and a thick moustache, was in total disagreement. He asserted the negroid races were inherently evil. They ate babies, they fornicated with animals and had unnatural sexual unions with themselves; they worshipped idols and they killed indiscriminately and without compassion. They were therefore villainously wicked and ripe for bringing to the Lord. They had, he insisted, a perfectly sound knowledge of what was right, but they chose, through their way of life and so-called religions, to ignore it.

'I do not agree, sir, with your assumption that they kill without compassion,' the younger priest argued. 'Is it not true they treat their enemies with respect?'

'Is it not true, sir,' rejoined the other, 'that the B'uganda tribe most despicably did murder and consume the flesh of their bishop?'

'Is it also not true, sir, that the M'assay tribe kill lions bare-handed, armed with nothing but a short assegai? I say, sir, these peoples are brave and honourable but ignorant. They need education in the Lord.'

'On the contrary, sir, they need to know the Wrath of the Lord . . .'

Flecker was captivated by the two theologians' altercation. He recalled his father's sermons about sin and morality, delivered in a booming voice to the assembled pupils of his school. How he had hated those beratings, had come out from the services feeling not uplifted by the worship but oppressed by the accusations. Even now he could hear his father's voice resounding in chapel, echoing off the walls as if the angels themselves were hidden there and chorusing him. He felt an antipathy growing in him for the priest with the hairy face, his Victorian ideology and outmoded attitudes, his hypocrisy. He was on his way to suborn an entire race with the fist of Man, not the word of God; and Flecker knew that fist would be gloved in the teachings of Christ.

Suddenly, in mid-sentence, the younger of the priests fell silent.

'What is the matter, Jonathan?'

He made no immediate reply, then said, 'Listen.'

Both listened, as did Flecker, opening his eyes.

'Do you hear it?'

'No,' replied the bewhiskered cleric. 'Hear what?'

'Excuse me, but do you hear anything, sir?' the young priest addressed Flecker.

Flecker was about to answer in the negative when he did hear something.

'Thunder?' he ventured.

Together, the three men looked at the sky. Puffs of cumuli hung against the blue. The sun was casting keen-edged shadows from the rigging, striping the deck with black lines which shifted to the movement of the ship.

'It cannot be.'

All three abandoned their deck-chairs and went to the ship's side. To port was the brown, hot coastline of Turkey.

'Whereabouts are we?' Flecker enquired.

'We must be,' the older priest consulted a silver pocket watch, 'somewhere off Smyrna . . .'

Just along the deck from them were three American ladies en route from Athens to Jerusalem; they had, Flecker had been told, visited the altars of culture and were now heading for those of God.

'We are near to the Strait of Mytilene,' one of them said, hearing Flecker's question and the priest's vague answer. 'It is gunfire. Really it is most exciting, wouldn't you say? The war is but a few miles off; a fight against the un-Christian forces of darkness.'

'People are killing each other over there,' Flecker replied sharply. 'Christian against Christian . . .'

'Nonsense!' the woman responded and strode down the deck, herding her two companions before her like a chaperone.

The thunder sounded once more. On the horizon off the starboard bow there rose, gradually, like a blossom opening or a stain spreading through clear still water, a tiny pall of first grey then black smoke.

'The war,' Flecker said. 'The American harpies are correct. It must be the war. People killing people with-

252

out compassion. At least African tribesmen see their victims, know them as they die. They don't sit a mile off and kill them at a distance.'

The older priest glowered and walked away. The younger smiled at Flecker and jauntily winked.

For nearly an hour, Flecker watched the horizon and the arid, dull coastline with its scanty trees and low, impassive hills, its tiny settlements gathered at the water's edge like immobile beasts drinking and the occasional grove of dark green olive trees, and he thought of Mavrogordato scribbling on his pad and getting his despatches back to Constantinople and the telegraph office.

After a while the sounds of artillery fire faded and, later, the smoke dissipated in the distance.

A sickle moon and a bright star just like the Turkish emblem, he thought, gazing up at a sky the texture of velvet, the moon like an eyelash of light. Close to the thin wedge of the new moon, all the stars bar the one of increased brightness were extinguished by its brilliance, but elsewhere in the sky they were scintillating and sharp.

A steward approached him from the doorway to the smoking lounge, the soles of his soft shoes sticking as they lifted from the deck. The tar between the planking was still tacky from the day's heat.

'May I get you another drink, sir? he asked, leaning over Flecker's card table and removing the empty glass.

'A mineral water, please.'

The steward bowed in acknowledgement and proceeded down the deck, gathering orders from the few other passengers who were taking the night air.

On this side of the ship there was barely a hint of wind. Even the forward movement of the vessel was creating a breeze so slight that it merely tickled the corners of his writing paper rather than sought to whisk them aside.

Flecker closed his pen and held the sheet of paper up to the bulkhead lamp. He read the last lines aloud to himself, yet quietly so that the other passengers would not hear him.

'The isle and the island cypresses went sailing on without the gale: and still there moved the moon so pale, a crescent ship without a sail!'

He put it down, holding it to the table with his hand. He was pleased with it. It was a good fragment; not an entire poem perhaps, but it would do. He slid it beneath the book he was using as a paperweight and extracted another which had been worked upon at some length, the margins filled with alternative words and phrases. He was certain that it was not completed, but it promised so well. His favourite verse was the penultimate, the one of which he was most sure. Once again, he opened his pen and ran the nib over the lines.

> That old Greek day was all thy history:
>   For that did Ocean pose thee as a flower.
> Farewell: this boat attends not such as thee:
> Farewell: I was thy lover for an hour!

The steward returned with half a dozen glasses on a silver tray and, as he placed Flecker's alongside the book, Flecker asked, 'That island we passed so very close to today, do you know it?'

'Yes, sir. We go well inshore there most trips, sir.'

'What is it called?'

'I don't know, sir. Would you care for me to find out?'

Flecker shook his head and answered, 'No, thank
you. It was only a passing thought.'

And yet, the following morning, he sought out an
officer and asked the same question.

'That island? Yes, we sail close to avoid a tricky set
of currents south of Nisiros – and we cut off a good
bit of time by doing so. Gives us a short cut to Rhodes.
Of course, we can't do that in a storm and have then
to sail right round the islands and up again. The island's
called Hyali . . .'

Back in his cabin, Flecker pulled out the writing shelf
from the panelling above the stack of brass-handled
drawers, took the sheets of paper bearing the poem
from his briefcase and wrote the name as the title of the
piece. Then he copied it into his notebook for further
consideration.

'Island in blue of summer floating on,' he recited to
himself, 'Little brave sister of the Sporades, Hail and
farewell! I pass, and thou art gone, So fast in fire the
great boat beats the sea.'

He was proud of the verse, glad at the alliteration in
the last line, the words mimicking the thrub and drum
of the propellers churning the Mediterranean aside and
behind.

He lay back in his bunk, his eyes open and fixed on the
nozzle of the cabin ventilator over his head. He had
switched it off and instead had opened the brass-ringed
porthole through which came the incessant hiss of the
sea. The breeze was cooling, occasionally salted with
spume.

On the sheet beside him lay the book he had been
reading. It was arched up like a paper tent, the pages
inside bent and crammed together. It reminded him of
a game his mother had taught him as a child, a trick

with his hands and fingers. He clasped his hands together before his face, interlocked his fingers; then he pointed his index fingers upward, opened his thumbs wide and wiggled the remaining fingers against the palms.

'Here is the church and here is the steeple,' he whispered. 'Open the door and here are the people.' His voice was almost non-existent and had a painful croakiness.

He turned on to his side and moaned, 'Oh, God! Oh, God!' then reached for the glass of warmed milk the cabin steward had brought. It had cooled and there was a crinkled layer floating on the surface like that of flayed skin.

The *pension* in which Flecker rented a room was in the city, not fifteen minutes' walk from the Consulate. Around him, day and night, the bustle of Beirut followed its course but he ignored it. As soon as his day's work was done, usually by noon, he returned to sit at his table in his room in semi-darkness, the only light provided by the white sun searing in through the slats of the shutters. There, an Arab shawl around his shoulders and his feet in fleece-lined slippers, he worked on his poems, on his novel and, when the muses were absent, he struggled with his Turkish.

His first thought on moving in to the *pension* was to write to Lawrence and this he did, sending the letter under seal in the diplomatic bag to Aleppo. It was not just that he longed to be in contact again but he was also under orders from Hogarth – which had awaited him in Athens and had been brought on to the boat by a diplomatic courier – to continue surveillance upon the Germans and begin to establish what Hogarth termed 'mutually fulfilling relationships' with desert tribes.

Within forty-eight hours he received in reply a note from Fontana: Lawrence was in the desert, with a band of Bedouin, and would not return for a week or so. Flecker reasoned that Lawrence had received a similar set of orders to his own.

Realising there was nothing he could do but wait for Lawrence to get in touch with him, Flecker closeted himself inside his house. His desire to write was becoming insatiable. The novel was coming more easily than he had expected and words welled up in him, spilling over as fast as he could write them down.

He had first drafted the story as an undergraduate seven years before and, in manuscript, it had travelled with him from posting to posting, all the while considered unpublishable. Thanks to support from Mavrogordato, it had been finally accepted by a London publisher in the summer of 1911 but the publisher had insisted upon extensive tightenings, rewritings and revisions which Flecker had feared would block him from the story – and yet, in a frenzy of creativity, he was now finding them falling in to place.

When not working on the novel he strove to polish up his poems and draft new ones. And when these began to pall he turned to the script of *Hassan* which demanded poetic skills of him and kept his brain thinking in terms of verse.

The opening of the third scene of Act Three required a band of soldiers to enter the Great Hall of the palace, intoning 'The War Song of the Saracens', and Flecker thought at first to write this as a series of couplets. He struggled with the song all one afternoon, working and re-working it. At first the rhyme came easily, but the result looked facile. Then the rhyme was corrupted but the text read well, had a dramatic power so grand he wondered if it was not too strong for the soldiers. At the end, he reached a compromise with a tight but not regular rhyme scheme and the couplets joined into long single lines.

Several times, he read the song out loud, intoning it as he hoped the soldiers would when the play was produced, only to stop half-way through and revise again. It had pace; he knew that. It read dramatically and it had meaning, but was it right, was it good enough? He was plagued by his indecision for several hours, the drive to create burning in him like a fever but his mind doubting the result. He struggled with his own work as if it was an illness he had to overcome, a disease to which he had to find a cure in order to survive.

Eventually, towards evening, as the room darkened, he made a final attempt to complete the song. In the twilight, he read through what he believed was, as near as it needed to be, an acceptable finish. Again, he read it aloud to capture the effect, chanting in a deep voice:

'From the lands where the elephants are to the forts of Merou and Balghar. Our steel we have brought and our star to shine on the ruins of Rum. We have marched from the Indus to Spain, and by God we will go there again; We have stood on the shore of the plain where the Waters of Destiny boom. . . .'

He dropped his pen, a speck of ink flicking from the nib on to the page of manuscript, and he rubbed his eyes. They were sore. His head was aching, his throat dry. He could do with a drink and poured himself a tumbler of lukewarm water from the jug on the chest of drawers; the ice had long since melted.

Then he coughed, a raucous bark which hurt. He screwed up his eyes, awaiting the next tearing of his throat, but it did not come and he smiled at himself with relief in the mirror. Although occasionally painful, his larynx seemed much better and he was coughing far less, even at night. There was little phlegm collecting in his lungs and he only had to clear his throat once or twice in the mornings. He gargled daily with a mild solution of disinfectant mixed with a little mint cordial to kill the foul taste. It seemed to be the remedy he sought.

To allay Hellé's fears and to put an end to what he considered her insistent nagging in her every letter, Flecker booked an appointment with a doctor. His repeatedly telling her that his throat was much improved seemed to be cutting no ice. She wanted an expert's opinion, not a self-diagnosis.

The doctor thoroughly examined Flecker and, at the end of the session, pronounced his larynx as being in top-rate condition.

'Seldom seen a better one, Mr Flecker. Your gargling has done the trick and there is no inflammation apparent at all. Not in the least. The tissues at the back of your throat are, of course, somewhat reddened by your recent bouts of discomfort, but that is to be expected. Your lungs seem uncongested – certainly no fluid in there that I can hear. You breathe with the clarity of a high wind coursing through a vast canyon. I would, however, recommend you refrain from smoking cigarettes and try as best you can to keep away from smokey atmospheres. And look after yourself in other ways. Avoid being wet, especially your feet. Wear galoshes if out walking in the rain and carry an umbrella or waterproof hat.'

Flecker left the surgery in high spirits. The doctor had confirmed what he himself believed. He strolled through the streets with a lightness of step he had not experienced since returning. As soon as he reached the *pension*, he sat down to write to Hellé.

He was cured, he told her. His larynx was perfect, his throat generally red but in good condition. He added, to offset any other quibble she might be considering, that he was spending several hours every morning on his Turkish and dedicated his afternoon to writing. Furthermore, he wrote, in answer to her worries about their finances, he was being as miserly as he could be, counting every shekel and penny and sou. His *pension*, he assured her, was the cheapest in the whole of Islam, his room the most meagre accommodation within its walls. He was quick, however, to point out that it was comfortable, if spartan, and warm and cosy, and an ideal one in which he could regain his health.

The sun was warm and, as Flecker walked up the river valley, the Sunday morning bells of the English, Jesuit and German churches competed with each other, the German the most strident and clamorous.

He kept to the pathway on the west bank of the river which was wider than that opposite. Once he was past the French Girls' School and the convent of the Sisters of Nazareth several small flocks of sheep and goats appeared, grazing on the hills around, but only once did he find it necessary to shoo them out of his way.

The trees were well leafed with new green appearing on the twigs, and as he passed below the small village of Hazimiye an old woman appeared from the buildings and, coming down the hill at a surprisingly quick pace, offered to sell him oranges from a basket clutched under her arm. Flecker purchased two, put one in his jacket pocket and, biting a hole in the skin, sucked at the other as he walked. The juice was sweet and the flesh pulpy; it scorched his throat as he swallowed.

Gradually the hills loomed larger around him and he

became lost to his thoughts as if the growing river gorge were focusing his mind in on itself.

Only a year ago, he and Hellé had walked this way, picking wild flowers.

'A year!' he exclaimed. 'Just one niggardly year.'

He looked up at the hills ahead. Perched on the top was Areiya and, beyond it, Abadieh; he remembered going there with Cumberpatch. He cast his eyes back to Areiya. Up there, out of sight from his vantage point in the valley, was their house. They had been happy there. The black and white puppies had lived with them and Anela, their housekeeper. All now gone from his life. He had written so much there – and failed his damnable examinations. And it was there Lawrence and Dahoum had first visited them.

So much had happened in the year since he had last trod the river bank.

Now he was back, alone and ill – no, he told himself, better and fitter. Still alone, though. Hellé was lingering in Paris in order to kill off the Malta fever. Lawrence was lost in the dunes and wastes of the deserts with his boy. Beazley was distant and older. Yet he now knew Marsh and had him looking after his work. His poetry was included in the most successful anthology for decades. Monro had only recently written to commission an article of him, and *Hassan* was being read by a producer, thanks to Marsh.

But also he was now thoroughly ensnared. The Foreign Office would not release him. He could obtain no other work. Hogarth still wanted him to work with Lawrence and Fontana. He was not earning enough money to buy his way out of the Consular Corps. With the approach of the examinations once again, his future looked bleak.

His progress up the river valley was a series of optimistic revelations during which his step quickened or pessimistic realisations when he slowed and absent-mindedly kicked at loose stones on the path.

By the time he was well in to the gorge his thoughts were once again with Hellé. No matter how hard he worked at his writing or slogged at his Turkish she was never far from his mind. At night was the worst. As he lay in bed, his hands pressed to his groin or folded between his legs, he thought of her and wanted her, wanted her so very badly.

At noon he rested upon a boulder at the bottom of a steep ravine before turning back towards the city. He could just see a tiny portion of it around the bend in the valley. The rains had washed soil down the ravines from the hillside high above and on this richer earth wild cyclamen were growing, their waxy petals and dark green leaves out of place amongst the coarse grasses and low herb-like bushes.

He picked a small posy of the flowers and looked around for wild orchids or anemones, but it was too early in the year for them.

The only sound to be heard was the gentle lap of waves upon the shingly sand and an infrequent snuffle from the donkeys somewhere up the beach in the darkness. Every so often Flecker thought he could hear voices, but they were in his imagination. His nerves were taut and his palms sweating despite the breeze blowing off the sea. The tide was coming in and, with the wind, would aid the men rowing ashore.

'How much longer?' he whispered.

'Twenty minutes. Not more.'

'Are you sure . . . ?'

'Yes, Roy. Quite sure.'

He looked at his companion. Lawrence was wearing a dark coloured *keffiyeh* and a black cloak. His face, tanned from his weeks in the desert, was only partially visible in the starlight.

A night bird wheeped softly up the beach and one of the donkeys snuffled again.

'Here they come,' Lawrence muttered. 'Dahoum's seen them.'

He poked his head forward and squinted into the darkness.

Flecker strained his ears and heard over the sluicing lap of the waves a harsher, slapping lap of water.

No signal came from the boat. Lawrence, to guide them in, struck a vesta but let it blow out before the phosphorous could ignite the wood.

After another five minutes a shadow appeared on the sea and increased in size as it drew nearer. It was a ship's lifeboat, the white sides of which had been smeared with grease and soot. The sailors bringing it inshore had muffled the rowlocks of their oars with hessian. As the keel scraped and ground on the shingle a dark figure jumped from the boat and waded ashore.

'Lawrence?' The figure extended its hand. 'Sub-lieutenant Morrissey.'

'No.' Flecker shook the offered hand, then pointed to the apparent Arab standing next to him. 'I'm Flecker – from the Consulate. This is Lawrence.'

'Identification,' the officer demanded quietly.

'Certainly.' Lawrence agreed. 'I live at Number 2, Polstead Road, Oxford, a predominantly red brick abode, semi-detached, with a small walled garden at the rear containing a few mature apple trees. You may reach Polstead Road from Woodstock Road . . .'

'Right, sir.' The officer's voice was tense.

'Can we get on with it then, Morrissey?' Lawrence said impatiently. 'We can't loiter here and it'll take us a good couple of hours to get back to Beirut.'

Two sailors held the boat against the beach while the

remainder unloaded the boxes, carried them over the sand to where Dahoum was standing with the donkeys harnessed to two carts and loaded them under the Arab boy's instruction.

Within twenty minutes the boat was emptied and had vanished back out to sea. Flecker stood by the carts as Lawrence meticulously smoothed the sand, obliterating the sailors' footsteps. This done, he and Dahoum walked down to the water's edge and scuffled about, then walked back again.

'There we are!' Lawrence said softly. 'Two fishermen casting night lines. An astute observer will see they were unlucky and landed not a single sardine. Now' – he looked at Dahoum – 'to complete the subterfuge.'

From beneath the seat of one of the carts the boy produced a parcel wrapped in cloth. He tossed it to Lawrence who caught it and handed it on to Flecker.

'What's this?'

'Well, my dear Roy, you can hardly travel on a donkey cart dressed like a . . . like a city gent of the stockbroking persuasion; those clothes of yours were fine for a walk into the countryside last evening, but they are hardly fit dress for our triumphal return.'

Flecker untied the knot made of the corners of the cloth and opened it to discover a complete set of Arab clothes.

'Right. Off with those old togs and on with the new,' Lawrence commanded. 'Bundle your civilised rags into the parcel and give it to Dahoum.'

Flecker undressed. The breeze was still cold but he hardly noticed it as he removed his jacket and jersey, his shirt and trousers and socks. Finally he was left in his underpants. He made no move to re-dress. He could feel Lawrence looking at him, studying the curves of his body, assessing the strength of his muscles; he felt both embarrassed and honoured, his nerves flexed to breaking point.

Lawrence made the first move. He came over to Flecker and said, 'Let's get you into your desert costume. We're not draping you about for a pretty portrait on the verandah at Areiya now. That was a dress rehearsal. This is the first night.'

With skilful, impersonal hands, Lawrence helped Flecker dress, tucking in the clothing, tightening the waistband of the trousers, folding the *keffiyeh*, adjusting the *ogal* and arranging the outer cloak so that it fell in the correct manner. When he was done, he stepped back to admire his handiwork.

'You'll pass muster, Sheikh el-Roy. Still,' he added, teasingly, 'we'll soon find out because it can't be long to dawn. Just don't shout out, "Walk on, my son!", if the donkey dawdles to nip at a wayside thistle!'

Lawrence and Flecker climbed aboard the first cart and Dahoum took charge of the second. They turned the donkeys around and set off at a walking pace, the wooden wheels and rigid axles seeming to find every rut and pothole in the seldom-used beach track. When they crossed the railway track, the cart creaking and straining over the rails, Flecker wondered if they were going to make it back to Beirut. Their load looked light – Dahoum had secreted the boxes under a pile of kindling wood and cut brush – but it was heavier than such a vehicle was accustomed to carry.

Flecker considered the necessity for all this subterfuge: previous deliveries had simply been landed at the docks in Beirut. Now, however, he had received a coded memorandum from London to the effect that there was a customs official watching all diplomatic cargo arrivals, surreptitiously opening and then skilfully re-sealing crates destined for the British and American Consulates. Disclosures of stationery supplies or jars of

Oxford marmalade were unimportant. And he was not stealing anything, just seeing what was being imported and presumably reporting on his discoveries. If he found arms it would be another matter. The British had to be seen to be neutral in the area. Importation of arms might imply they were secretly siding with the Shi'ites, or the Druses, or the Maronites.

He sat hunched forward not only because that was how Lawrence sat but also because it provided him with added protection against the cold. Once they were above the beach and on to the coast road the breeze stiffened to a wind.

'Always colder just before dawn,' Lawrence said, sensing his companion's discomfort. 'As soon as the sun's up you'll see the temperature rise quickly, quite dramatically. Then you'll be glad of these robes; they'll keep you cool when it's hot – and warm when it's not . . . You'll see. Keep the folds turned inwards.'

Flecker did as he was told and soon felt the warmth growing. He also discovered that, by hunching himself forward, his spine ceased to hurt at every bump in the road, the surface of which was little better than that of the beach track.

Several times he cast a glance over his shoulder and on each occasion saw the outline of Dahoum and his donkey and cart.

Just before day-break the night seemed to blacken. In the deeper night, Dahoum disappeared from sight and Flecker, straining to hear his cart over the squeaking and rattling of his own, failed to locate him by sound.

'Dahoum's got lost,' he whispered to Lawrence.

'No. He's there,' Lawrence replied with certainty.

A pencilled line of un-darkness appeared upon the contours of the hills to their right and, soon, without any grandeur or suddenness, dawn appeared. It was a gradual process until at last one realised that the night was over. Seared winter weeds coated with dust materialised at the side of the road. Boulders and stones took shape on the hillside, and the sea, formerly a black and still expanse, now moved and turned dull grey.

At the first hint of daylight a bird began to chirrup. Soon it was joined by others until the whole world, immobile except for the odd bush twitching in the air and the rippling sea, was filled with the whistles and cheeps of waking birds. Not one could be seen, but they were all heard.

It was not long before they came across another cart heading towards them. The cart itself was empty; seated upon it was an old man accompanied by a child. Their mule moved with plodding steps, its head down and its eyes only half open. Lawrence raised his hand in salute as they passed and the old man returned the gesture.

'One thing I love about Arabia,' Lawrence said, not looking at Flecker but keeping his eyes on the grey scarred rump of the donkey between the shafts.

'What?'

'Somnambulist mules!'

Lawrence laughed softly to himself.

It was not long before they encountered another cart. This time it was piled high with hay and the donkey pulling it was wide awake. The owner of the cart was not riding with the hay but walking by the side of the donkey.

Once again Lawrence raised his hand, but he also spoke in quick, fluent Arabic. Flecker attempted in vain to follow the words. The Arab replied with a quick response and then both he and Lawrence laughed.

'What did you say?' Flecker enquired when they were well out of earshot.

'I asked him why he was walking when the day was

so young. I'll lay a wager he's the only one we shall see on foot with a cart.'

'What was his reason?'

'He said he preferred to catch fleas from his donkey rather than act as host to the myriad of fleas and ticks infesting the hay.'

From ahead of them came the sound of a steam locomotive on the coast line. Soon it came into sight, a small tank engine gouting balls of smoke from its funnel and pulling a short train of a dozen freight cars to the sides of which a number of free passengers were clinging.

'We don't speak from here on,' Lawrence advised. 'And we'll keep to the coast rather than try to cut through the town. Easier, I think . . .'

As they ambled onwards, the traffic on the road increased. At eight o'clock they passed through the small town of Damour, the scent of brewing coffee and wood-smoke drifting from the cubic mud buildings to tease them. Women in black walked in front of them, pots of water upon their heads and, in the centre of the settlement, men were starting to erect rickety stalls for a morning of trade with passers-by and villagers coming down from the hills to buy fish caught on night-lines.

Flecker was in a state of permanent excitement. He had expected the tension to relax after a while, after they had met and passed muster with the first few Arabs they came across, but this was not the case. He realised it was not what he was doing that was keeping the tension alive – this was not a mere matter of creeping around on a partially built railway line with one German engineer as a threat – but whom he was doing it with.

Lawrence did not look at him, paid him no attention whatsoever, yet his presence electrified Flecker. He wanted to keep looking at him, try to catch his long face in profile against the now bright day, but he dared not. He wanted to get closer to Lawrence: not just sit closer but be closer. He wanted to share not just the excitement of gun-running and spying but also that of living.

Certainly, they were in an inherently dangerous predicament together. Everyone around them was a potential enemy: had the carters to whom Lawrence gave a brief greeting known what lay under the kindling, they would have killed them for their cargo.

Lawrence, sitting relaxed upon the cart, moved to its motion and occasionally flapped the reins against the donkey's back to remind it to keep going. He was seemingly bored. Flecker realised this kind of activity was commonplace to him, and yet there emanated from Lawrence an inexplicable power. Flecker remembered how he had felt that first time they had met, how Lawrence's eyes had held him and how weak he had felt in their gaze.

They arrived at the Consulate just after one in the afternoon. The guard at the gate was ready for them and allowed them immediate access. Once they had unloaded the carts, and Lawrence and Dahoum were on their way, Flecker strode up to his office in his Arab dress, with the parcel of his own clothes underneath his arm.

Robbins, recently returned from leave, saw him in the corridor and called out to him, 'Hey! You there! Where do you think you're going?'

Flecker ignored him.

'*Kiff!*' Robbins ordered and then, seeing one of the messengers at the far end of the passage, shouted, '*Æmsik hæzæ æl ragol!*'

At this point Flecker halted and turned. He dropped his bundle of clothes and made as if to reach for his dagger. Robbins, walking briskly after him, stopped dead in his tracks.

'Morning, Robbins,' Flecker said cheerfully as he watched the other's face quickly blanch. 'How was your leave?'

For a moment Robbins's face was utterly devoid of expression. He was nonplussed by an Arab not only knowing his name and personal details but also speaking in the King's English with an immaculate accent.

'Who the devil are you?' he said at length, regaining his composure and trying to look as imposing and magisterial as he could.

Flecker removed his *ogal* and tugged the *keffiyeh* aside.

'Flecker! Good God! Why on earth are you got up as a camel driver?'

'Donkey driver,' Flecker corrected him, adding nonchalantly, 'just been to a fancy dress do.'

He continued on his way down the corridor, his robes flapping behind him like a don's gown. He mustered all the dignity he could by cutting, he supposed, a dashing figure just as Lawrence did; but he caught his sleeve on the handle of his office door and Robbins guffawed, much to Flecker's annoyance.

It was not good news. Indeed, the mail he found on his desk upon his return was demoralising.

His mother had written at length – and not for the first time in recent weeks – a strongly worded letter criticising his behaviour, his apparent flightiness, his stubborn intransigence, his inability to face reality and his lack of purpose. His father had written similarly but in a more cautious style and with a more careful use of epithet. He received a negative report from Gabbitas Thring, the educational agency to which he had written

– in a last vain hope before leaving Britain – for a teaching position in any public school possible, and he received no letter at all from the Cambridge University appointments board. Worst of all, however, was a letter from Marsh. The first two acts of *Hassan* had been returned as uncommercial.

Flecker was devastated, his one opportunity for a major literary success dashed in an instant. He sat quietly in his room, his face in his hands.

So much had rested on Marsh's ability to influence a producer. Not only would Flecker have made a major literary coup but he would have established himself as a dramatist, would have had a play staged in London, would have earned much needed money from it.

Everything, he realised in his misery, came down to his finances. The hidden subject underlying his parents' letters was money: he was deeply in debt to his parents, to whom he regularly appealed for support to see him over 'a current rough patch'. Hellé wrote of her financial problems in Paris and regularly implored him to be frugal. Any escape from the service was dependent upon his being able to settle his bond. *Hassan* could have paid it off. Now, the play was rejected.

He wrote immediately to Marsh, his opening sentence summing up his acute anguish:

Many thanks for your long-expected letter, very welcome as being from you, despite a certain amount of disappointment.

As he sat back and looked at the sentence, he marvelled, as Lawrence had done, at his capacity for understatement, then continued by asking his correspondent to submit the manuscript to the verse playwright, John Drinkwater, and if he showed no interest to return it. He wrote that he wished England could have hot Februarys so full of flowers as the Lebanon was now, admitted to writing some new poems and to having nearly reached the end of his re-writing of *The King of Alsander*.

He folded the letter and sealed the envelope.

The manuscript of *The King of Alsander* was piled on the table before him. To one side was all that was left to be re-worked. He stared at it as if it was an incubus just crawled over the lip of the table, some dark and malevolent creature spawned to sit on his brain and squash it.

For a moment, he loathed it. There seemed no point in continuing. It had a publisher, but what was that worth? A few paltry quid if it sold well enough to earn him royalties, a few guarded reviews by friends, a few dismissive reviews by others. He was not even sure if, in its new form, it was worth publishing. It was an odd and strange story, not one to fit into any of the current genres taking the fancy of book-buyers. It might be good or, there again, it might be abysmal. He could not tell.

In desperation, he struck out at the manuscript. It tottered but, like a thing with its own will, it refused to fall off the table. This infuriated him further. He flung the nearest object to hand at it – a small pocket edition of Browning's poems which he read nightly, sure within himself that he would one day be just as great a poet.

The book flew over the top of the manuscript sheets and hit the window shutters, one of the covers jamming between the slats so that the book hung, inside out, against the bars of daylight like a bird struggling against the wire of its cage.

Flecker gazed across the harbour. A steam packet was slowly sailing around the end of the mole and, at the landing place, there milled about the porters and ship's agents, chandlers and victuallers, those welcoming arrivals and those bidding others farewell. By the water's edge were piled cases and trunks and boxes emblazoned with shipping line labels.

'You mustn't be downhearted,' Lawrence declared, folding his newspaper in half and wedging it under his empty coffee cup. 'And you must stop this habit of looking at ships arriving from who-knows-where. Your time will come.'

'Not soon enough,' Flecker replied morosely.

'What! You don't mean that . . .' Lawrence touched the sleeve of Flecker's blazer. 'Look at these new poems of yours.' His fingers moved to the sheaf of papers and tapped them. 'These are good stuff; you're sure to make an impact with them. Your new book will be your best yet.'

'Perhaps I ought just to slog away at bloody Turkish and resign myself to being marooned in this God-forsaken country for ever, like some castaway or a Jonah in my own private whale.'

'Jonah had no friends,' Lawrence observed.

'Hellé is in France.'

'But I am here.'

Flecker moved round in his chair, turning his back on the landing place and the steam packet which had now passed the end of the harbour wall and was drifting towards its berth.

'I am sorry, Ned. I just wasn't thinking.'

'You let too much worry you, Roy. Allow things to happen to you. Don't try to shape your own fate but that of others – then yours will become entwined with theirs and all will prosper. A lonely journey through life is hard to ride,' he ended solemnly.

'Isn't your journey like that?'

'It may be,' Lawrence admitted, 'but I've chosen it

so. I like that loneliness sometimes, that complete abne-
gation of responsibility for everything except for one-
self. Yet that is in itself a paradox, for one is always
responsible for something, for someone else. An idea,
perhaps. A person. In my case, a people – the Arabs
with whom my fate is inextricably involved now.' For
a moment, and against his advice to Flecker, Lawrence
himself cast a glance in the direction of the ship. 'But
then I have someone to share my journey with . . .'

The ship's horn sounded a long blast which echoed
around the harbour, bouncing off the fronts of the
buildings.

As they left the table and Flecker paid the waiter,
Lawrence said, 'It'll all work out in the end, Roy. No
need to fret.'

He walked on slowly as the waiter fumbled in his
apron pocket for change.

No sooner had Lawrence spoken than Flecker saw in
his mind's eye Hogarth's letter: 'Everything has a way
of working out.'

'You'll be coming up to Carchemish when I get back
there?' Lawrence asked as Flecker caught up with him.

Flecker nodded. 'Yes,' he said, 'I will.'

'Excellent. I've a little jaunt we might go on together
to find a very beautiful statue. Well north of Carchemish. Only a rumour, but worth following up. A Hittite
deity flanked by lions. Those were the days, eh, Roy?
Lions in Syria!' He paused, then went on, 'And you can
bring these fine poems of yours with you. Your novel
too, if needs be. You can sit upon the tip of the vine
with the birds at your feet and write your songs just as if
you were one of them, immortalised for ever in coloured
tesseræ.'

As they made their way along the road towards the
Consulate at the end of the headland, Ras-esh-Shami-

yeh, Lawrence paused by a tree and looked about them before speaking.

'Were the guns sent on without any problem?'

'Yes, the boxes went three days ago on the railway. I sent two men with them. We've received word from Aleppo they arrived in good order and without any difficulty.'

Lawrence smiled amiably and walked on.

Hellé's letter was as captious as one from his parents. She attacked him for borrowing more money from his father and wanted to know how much he was in debt to his family. She accused him of being capricious and illogical. She reproached him for being inconsistent, and she finished off by saying if this was what he was going to be like for the rest of his life then she did not relish the thought of having to be with him. She had not, she reported, the strength to traipse after him continually. The only respite from her criticisms was when she added that she thought he was not one who wanted a woman following him about, that she was in a bitter frame of mind as she wrote and that this would assuredly pass.

He fell into a pit of despondency at her carping. Despite Lawrence's encouragement and his own inexhaustible yearning to write, he had been slipping into periods of black depression, a melancholy he could hardly bear. His every letter home, to his parents or to Hellé, was barbed with moral blackmails – he did not want to die alone in Syria, he was being driven insane by Beirut, he was feeling himself falling ill under the mental exhaustion of swotting away at his Turkish, he was weakening with sheer lassitude, he was drowning his sorrows in his work but to no avail, he was suffering terrible paroxysms of wretchedness and despair. He added, depending upon to whom he was writing, that his wife could not be expected to suffer the Middle East any longer, or that his parents were driving him to this hell of distraction.

It was not until the last Sunday in February that his letters to Hellé took a temporary upturn. In his letter that day he reported he had finished *The King of Alsander* and was greatly relieved by the completion.

In none of his letters home did he mention Lawrence.

The dry wind periodically whipped sand off the top of the hillock, showering it down upon them. Flecker kept his eyes closed to mere slits, his mouth and nose protected by wrapping one corner of his *keffiyeh* across the lower portion of his face and hooking it into his *ogal*. Lawrence had done likewise but Dahoum, ahead of them up the slope of the hillock, had not. They followed him, placing their feet exactly in his footsteps.

At one point they stopped abruptly. Dahoum, his head just breaking the horizon above them, had seen something and ducked, his hand pressing down as signal for them to halt. Flecker sat, his buttocks moulding into a patch of loose sand through his Arab robes. Lawrence, above him, touched him on the shoulder with his foot and held up a hand, opening and closing his fingers twice – a ten-minute wait.

Flecker understood and lay back against the slope of the hillock, closing his eyes. This gave him no relief, for the late afternoon sun, striking the hillock at almost right-angles, still shone directly into his eyes, the daylight merely replaced by the pink shadow of the blood in his eyelids. Instead, he sat up and lowered his head so the front of his *keffiyeh* acted as a peak over his eyes. The wind was dropping and he could keep his eyes open now so long as he remained alert for gusts.

Below, in the trough between the hillocks, the ground

was littered with a mixture of sand, pebbles and larger stones; here and there a scrubby shrub pushed through the rubble, its hard leaves thin and barely green.

Looking in either direction down the hillock valley, Flecker could see nothing that was, or even had been, alive except for the stunted shrub. The area was scourged and dismal, utterly without hope. It was, he considered, a graveyard for stones. The surface of the moon could be no less welcoming. He thought of the great famine in the Bible, the blighting of Egypt, the seven years of good and the seven years of lean: this area of southern Turkey, he reasoned, had had seven hundred years of lean, seven thousand even. That the great civilisations had been born here, that this was the crucible from which the human race arose to its present glory and power, was beyond his comprehension.

The landscape in which he sat was so much a mirror of his own predicament: one thorny weed struggling against the accumulated odds of a harsh and unfeeling world. The drifting sand was Dufferin and Their Lordships' indifference. The stones were those cast at him by his parents.

Seven good years and seven bad: if the occult cycle of seven by seven was true, if this was the pattern of existence, how long he wondered had he to wait for the period to end? And what – the realisation suddenly terrified him: he had not considered it before – if this period was his seven rich years? If this were the case the seven bad would be bad indeed.

He was writing – well and in quantity. His muse seemed so alert, so full of vitality. There was not a morning when he did not awake with his mind brimming with ideas, corrections for lines he had written the day before, outlines for new poems or entire stories. The plots for whole verse plays unwound in his head.

Yet, if his life was a desert, what was the good of all this creativity? It came to nothing.

Suddenly, near the stunted shrub, his eye caught a tiny movement. He concentrated on the spot but nothing happened. For a moment Flecker wondered if the remaining heat of the day was giving him hallucinations. He had never suffered from heat-stroke but he knew the symptoms. If he was now ailing from it he would be a considerable burden upon Lawrence and Dahoum. A risk, in fact.

He twisted round sharply and looked up. His companions were just below the line of the hillock. Lawrence had removed his *keffiyeh* and Flecker noticed how well the colouring of his hair matched that of the sandy soil. He might have had his body deliberately designed for desert camouflage.

Moving his head quickly did not cause any dizziness. His eyes did not roll and his eyesight seemed unaffected. He turned back again and, as he did so, another movement occurred.

Again, it was insignificant. It happened only for a moment and seemed, for that split second, almost jerky.

Once again he fixed his attention on the spot, but nothing moved until he did. As soon as Flecker shifted his foot, something moved. It was as if his shoe was connected by an invisible string to a little ghost, a desert djinn hiding near the shrub.

Flecker lowered his head, keeping his eyes on the point of the movement. It occurred again. He raised his hand slightly. The movement happened once more. Intrigued, Flecker slid the last six feet down the hillock and stopped just by the stones. As he had approached the shrub, the movement had not recurred.

Leaning forward, Flecker started to move his eyes up and down the patch of stones. He could see nothing but the stones and wondered if what he had been watching was not a movement but a changing of shadows. The small valley was itself in indirect shade now, lit only by the sunlight shining upon the sand and stones against which, from this new vantage point, Lawrence and Dahoum seemed to be glued like flies upon a buff-yellow wall.

Then, as he was considering this alternative explanation, he suddenly saw a small lizard. It was so immaculately coloured in uneven greys that it matched the stones around it perfectly; its patterning completely broke its outline.

The lizard stood like a reptilian mimic of an Old English bulldog, its legs staunchly stuck out like those on a Jacobean table. Its head was flat, but its eyes were larger than those of a common skink. Its tail tapered and disappeared under the stone from which it had emerged.

Flecker moved his hand. The lizard was motionless. He kept quite still and after a minute, the lizard quickly opened and closed its mouth. The invisible string had been severed.

Whether it was the marvel of this perfectly formed creature so expertly adapted to its home which so perplexed Flecker, which so captivated him, or the sheer miracle that anything was alive in such a barren landscape, he could not tell. He watched it for a minute, during which time the lizard slowly extracted the rest of its tail from beneath the stone and opened and shut its mouth twice more.

Just as Flecker was about to return to his place on the hillock above the lizard darted forward. It moved so rapidly Flecker's eye could not follow it and it took him several seconds to relocate the reptile. When he did, it was standing as it had before but, from between its thin lips, there protruded and twitched a brown grasshopper.

Flecker shifted himself. The strings were reconnected. The lizard, at his movement, whisked away, its body moving fluidly over the stones. When it reached the bottom of the next hillock it jinked aside and scampered up it, leaving a track like a stitched hem in an area of wind-blown sand pointing to where it disappeared over the summit.

Immediately Flecker was filled with a feeling of optimism. The desert was harsh and cruel, a land of painful extremes, a place of hopelessness into which the damned were forced, into which the unwanted were driven to starve or die of thirst and madness. And yet, in the middle of it, there lived successfully these creatures. They had decided they would not die but would make the desert their own. They had developed a fortitude, a forging tenacity for life. Nothing was going to prevent them from attaining the fruition of their achievements.

As the lizard was to this desert, Flecker thought, so was he to the desert of the Levant Consular Service, to the Foreign Office wasteland, to the desolation of the literary world which rejected his plays. He would survive. Adapt. He would get out of the bleak valley in which he was incarcerated. He only had to do what the lizard did – take the obstacle at a run and go up it to the end, without stopping.

The sand and loose stones above him started to whisper. Lawrence and Dahoum were slipping down the slope at speed.

'Follow us, Roy!' Lawrence hissed as he reached Flecker's side. 'For God's sake, don't lag.'

They ran down the valley of stones to a point where the trough between the hillocks met another at right-angles. Lawrence ran to the right, Dahoum and Flecker following close upon his heels. They sped through a patch of the low shrubs, Flecker's robe snagging as he went. He heard the material rip.

Ahead they were presented with a Y-junction between two smaller hillocks. Lawrence did not hesitate, but took the left-hand option. The new valley into which they had entered curved and no sooner were they around the corner than Lawrence halted by three large boulders, set in a triangle. He dived between them and Dahoum and Flecker copied him.

'What is it?' Flecker asked breathlessly.

Lawrence put a finger to his lips.

From the sand before them came a phutting sound. Flecker peered cautiously around the side of the boulder and saw a small plume of dust hanging in the air ten feet from him. As it hung there, he heard a snap like someone cracking a knuckle.

There came another spurt of gravelly soil, nearer to the boulder, and another knuckle crack.

Lawrence removed his revolver from his belt. Dahoum also tugged his pistol from inside his robes. Both of them handed their weapons to Flecker. It was only then that he realised they were being shot at.

'Stay here!' Lawrence ordered: 'Follow us if we are taken.'

Without speaking, Flecker nodded.

'Lie low.'

Flecker knelt closely behind the rock, his cheek pressed to the stone. In each hand he now held a gun.

Then, together, Lawrence and Dahoum stood up, waving their hands above their heads.

Lawrence shouted something, but he was already out of the triangle of rocks and his words so indistinct Flecker could not have understood them even if his Arabic lessons had been better learned. Then, from the direction of the Y-junction, Flecker heard other voices raised in anger. For a few minutes there was much yelling, then the sounds died down.

Flecker waited a few more minutes before cautiously quitting the cover of the rocks. He followed the two sets of footprints to the junction and there he saw his companions had met seven others who were dressed not in Arab slippers but in military style boots. At once he felt an awesome apprehension creep upon him. There was only one army that could arrest them – the Turkish Army. His sense of foreboding was further increased by his finding, on a stone near where he imagined Lawrence had stood, what looked like a drop of blood. He rubbed his finger into it and his skin was smeared crimson.

The shadows deepening, he tucked the firearms into his belt and set off following the footsteps. They wound out of the area of scrubby, rock-strewn hillocks and into a region of more rolling country, keeping after a few hundred yards to a well-used path winding its way towards the river which it reached in about a mile and a half.

The soldiers and their captives – for Flecker assumed both Lawrence and Dahoum had been taken prisoner – were making good progress, walking quickly. Their footprints, where the soil was dusty, showed their toes biting deeply in their haste to get on.

As the sun touched the horizon the land turned a soft orange in colour and the temperature of the air began to drop so obviously that Flecker, sucking in his breath to keep going, could taste it growing colder.

The twilight did not last long and, just as it got too dark to see the footprints, Flecker heard from far ahead the calling of children's voices and the playing of a musical instrument. At that distance, it sounded exactly like a tin penny-whistle.

Other paths joined his own. From their size and

number Flecker assumed he was drawing near to a sizeable human settlement. Topping a low hill he saw the river off to his left, wide and slow and dark in the late evening half-light. Ahead of him was a small town.

He sat beside a boulder to assess the situation, at a loss as to what to do. He could hardly enter the town, ask where his friends were and expect to remain free himself. If there was a substantial garrison in the town, there would be little chance of getting near to Lawrence without detection. Furthermore he was thirsty and his throat was sore from the exertion of walking quickly. Eventually he decided at least to go into the town to glean whatever information he could.

The smoke from cooking fires hung over the narrow streets and lanes and, against the now starlit sky, rose the domed roofs of the houses. Doorways were open, people attending to the last chores of the day. They ignored him in his Arab robes, active about their own business.

Outside one house an old man was giving fodder to two mules. There was no one close by and Flecker decided to approach him.

After a traditional greeting, he asked in Arabic, 'Where is the *caravanserai*? I have travelled far today.'

His heart was in his mouth, his Arabic far from perfect. He spoke huskily in an attempt to disguise his poor accent and it scoured his larynx to do so.

'Traveller, welcome,' the man replied, standing up from where he was spreading the fodder on the ground. 'The *caravanserai* is but small; you will find it close to the mosque.' He waved his hand in the general direction of the town centre.

'What town is this?' Flecker chanced asking. 'Is this Birejik?'

The man laughed briefly.

'You have come from the north?'

Flecker nodded.

'Then you have not been counting your steps. Birejik is farther to the south yet. This place is Halfati.' The man looked shrewdly at Flecker for a moment. 'Is your business in Birejik?'

'My business is in Aleppo,' Flecker replied truthfully. The man turned back to his mules, checking the tethers, then asked forthrightly, 'Are you one of the deserters?'

Flecker did not understand the word and his worry must have shown.

'Are you one of those who have run away from the army?'

Somewhat relieved at now understanding, Flecker replied, 'No. I am a merchant. I trade in silk and go to Aleppo to arrange a purchase of fine . . .'

'You need not worry,' the Arab interrupted. 'We are not against you. Have you eaten?'

Flecker thanked the man profusely; yes, he had eaten but he would be grateful for a drink. Perhaps a little goat's milk?

The man called in to his house, and a small girl appeared almost immediately with a jug from which Flecker drank.

'Are there many soldiers?' he enquired, wiping his mouth, careful to use the correct hand in Arab fashion.

'No, but there are patrols in the area. Reservists' – Flecker failed to translate this word also – 'have escaped and are being rounded up. They do not wish to fight and die; it is not Allah's war.'

'Where do the soldiers come from?'

'Birejik, Urfa – where there are barracks.'

'They stay here, too?'

Flecker had to ask although to do so might compromise him; it seemed to him he was making too many enquiries of a military nature. Yet he had to know where his friends might be held, but he did not want to seem curious. The old man remained undaunted.

'Close to the *caravanserai* . . .'

Bidding the old man farewell and uttering further thanks for the milk, Flecker walked into the centre of the town.

Every step took him deeper into the territory of enemies. The increasing sense of danger prickled his every nerve until each movement he made seemed to risk drawing attention to himself. Several times he felt in his waistband to ensure that the pistols were out of sight.

This was no jaunt like his drive with Cumberpatch to Abadieh, the policemen saluting along the road, the two of them representatives of His Britannic Majesty's Consular Service in The Levant. He was now an Arab traveller in a torn robe, two modern and loaded firearms secreted about his person, searching in what had seemed a small town – but now took on the formidability of a metropolis – for two friends who were certain to be locked up in one of its thousands of rooms.

He reached the square before the mosque. The minarets towered above like lances waiting to angle down at him. The *caravanserai* was, as the old man had stated, to one side of the square, a low building with a larger than normal archwayed entrance. Before it stood groups of men talking, exchanging travellers' gossip. Mingling with them were a number of Turkish soldiers.

Flecker's every sinew tightened. With deliberate steps, he walked towards the *caravanserai* and passed through the knots of talking men, picking up snatches of their conversation if it was in Arabic and noticing with horror how many were speaking in Turkish.

Some elders were seated on forms against the wall of the *caravanserai*. A few held antique rifles of eastern design, with curved butts and long barrels bound with brass strips and decorated with filigree silver or bronze patterns. All sported curved daggers in their cummer-bunds.

Joining the end of one of the benches, Flecker leaned forward and rested his forehead in his hands as if he was tired. This was not entirely a charade; he was exhausted now, the tension sapping his strength almost with every breath. However, he was seated in such a way that he was not likely to be drawn into conversation and could eavesdrop on the talk around him.

For the first few minutes he could understand virtually nothing. Yet, as time passed, first words and then phrases came to him until, ultimately, he was able to catch the gist of much of what was being said.

The Arabic was not difficult but the Turkish was and he cursed himself for having been so lax at his studies. If he had applied himself when posted to Constantinople, if he had studied harder, if he had spent more time revising and improving his grammar ... His vocabulary was not bad – of that he was aware, for he could now appreciate a good deal of what was reaching his ears – but he was highly dubious about his abilities to converse in the language. He did not have even a rudimentary skill with construction.

Pushing his anxieties to the back of his mind he concentrated upon the immediate problem: he had to discover Lawrence's whereabouts.

The crowd was animated. Conversation ranged over a wide number of topics – he identified talk of mules and donkeys, the price of cotton, the standards of the *caravanserai*, the condition of the road north and the crossing point of the Euphrates at Kizilin, the availability of fodder and the breaking-in of horses. The Turkish soldiers – there were only four of them in the crowd – walked to and fro, chatting hospitably with the travellers, occasionally asking them innocent questions about their journeys. Yet Flecker knew what they were really about: he shared a similar mission. They were also after information.

One of the soldiers asked several of the travellers if they had had any problems on their journeys. Had food or mules been pilfered from their camp? he inquired. Or had they met, for example, anyone on the road who had begged for shelter or seemed lost? Most answered in the negative and continued with their own conversations, but one or two owned they had experienced an unusual chance encounter. One man admitted he had had a goat stolen but, in answer to the soldier's keen enquiry as to where this had occurred, he was vague and said it was some days before and he couldn't recall the place. Towards Kölük, he said – somewhere well up-river.

After a while the gathering began to thin. Some men made their way into the *caravanserai*, others disappeared into alleyways or down the roads leading from the square. They were heading for eating houses. The smells of cooking meat and spices began to mingle with the perfumes of burning wood.

The soldiers lingered a little longer, standing together and conversing quietly. Then they approached the bench on which Flecker was sitting. He was alone upon it; the old men with their guns had departed. He wished he had had the foresight to leave when they did, but it was too late now. To get up might arouse suspicion.

The soldiers sat next to him and talked animatedly. They spoke so quickly Flecker could understand nothing of their conversation.

Suddenly he realised he was being spoken to and he looked up. As he did so he realised it was a mistake, an awful mistake. He should have pretended deafness.

'*Nerede?*'

Flecker grunted. He recognised the word – *where*.

But where was what? He hadn't heard the original question.

'*Nerede?*' the soldier repeated. He was a non-commissioned officer of some sort, a revolver in a holster on his belt. His comrades carried rifles but no side arms.

'*Hayir,*' Flecker mumbled. '*Henüz bilmiyorum . . .*'

The soldier turned away from him, exclaimed briefly in a mocking and disgusted tone and the others laughed.

Flecker made no attempt to go. It was better to be left alone than perhaps be questioned again should he try to leave. Evidently the soldiers considered him a fool. He had to agree with them – he was a bloody fool to have remained when the crowd of men departed.

He pondered on his chances of shooting his way to freedom. He could, he felt, get his guns firing more quickly than the soldiers could their rifles. Yet he had hardly ever shot a side arm and had certainly never tried to kill anyone. The thought filled him with horror. He had no idea if he could actually do it; if he succeeded, what would be the point? He would be no nearer to discovering his friends' whereabouts.

For ten minutes he sat by the soldiers. The sweat was running down his back, despite the chill of the evening, trickling into the cleavage between the cheeks of his bottom. He felt his brow oozing perspiration. The barrels of the guns dug painfully into his groin.

At last the soldiers stood up. The form creaked as they rose, the wood easing. Flecker felt his muscles give in much the same manner. The soldiers set off across the square at a leisurely pace. Flecker watched them by the light of lamps in doorways and hanging upon a stall near the gateway to the mosque. As soon as they were out of sight down a side street he left the bench and walked quickly around the perimeter of the square. If he followed them, he reasoned, he would eventually discover where their local billet was and there, he prayed, he would also discover Lawrence and Dahoum.

The street down which the soldiers had disappeared was darker than the square. A few doorways were open, but the light they cast was insufficient to illuminate more than a few feet on either side. Half-way down the street three donkeys were tethered to an iron bar mounted in the wall of a house.

Using the donkeys as cover, Flecker moved along the street as rapidly and as silently as he could and crouched down beside them. They twisted their ears in his direction but gave no other sign of his presence.

From his new position he could see the last of the soldiers entering a gateway where a sentry stood, his rifle leaning against the wall beside a stool. Over the gateway was a painted board on which Flecker could just make out the Turkish crescent.

As soon as the sentry turned away Flecker stood up and walked down the middle of the street, his heart pumping hard. He passed the sentry, who ignored him, and turned into a narrow alleyway which ran down the side of what he assumed to be the military post.

It was dark in the alley, the only light coming from the stars and from a grid at near ground level towards the rear of the building.

Carefully watching where he laid his foot for fear of making a noise, Flecker edged along the alleyway until he came to the grid, a barred window rather like a cellar coal-chute for a London town house. As he drew near to it he kept himself pressed in to the wall. Instinct rather than training warned him not to present a profile to anyone who might glance down the alleyway.

He knelt beside the grid. If the bars were loose he might be able – later, when the soldiers were sleeping – to get into the building and look around. He moved his head so that just one eye could peer in.

The room was below ground, a large cellar-cum-dungeon with a mud-brick roof and walls. The floor was of beaten earth. One lamp burned brightly where it hung from a bracket on the wall by a heavy wooden door. To one side of the room was a palliasse thrown on to the ground; on it sat Dahoum, hunched forward, his hands and ankles trussed.

In the centre of the room was a table upon which Lawrence was spread-eagled face downwards, his wrists and ankles tied to the four legs. His clothes had been thrust up over his torso and he was naked from the waist down, his buttocks ashen in the lamplight.

The door opened. Flecker moved back from the grille and lay down on the soil of the alleyway, his hand feeling smooth round pellets of dried goat dung. He drew back from the light but remained where he could see in, pulling his dark *keffiyeh* around his face to reduce the glow of the lamp upon his features.

A Turkish officer entered the room accompanied by two of the soldiers from the town square. He stood alongside the table and spoke to Lawrence. His voice was not loud but it was harsh, his words coming in sharp bursts.

Lawrence twisted his head in an attempt to face the officer and replied to his Turkish in Arabic.

The officer barked a retort at him, his subordinates stepping smartly to stand across the table from their superior. One of them produced a bucket from under the table and splashed a dibber of water over Lawrence's buttocks. Lawrence did not speak, but Flecker could see his fists bunch.

The officer shouted at Lawrence who again made no reply. It was then Flecker noticed the officer was holding, tight against the leg of his trousers, what looked like a riding crop.

Once more the officer shouted at Lawrence, but

Dahoum abruptly replied instead, his voice pitched high
with fear. The three soldiers looked at him in unison,
then one of them quickly walked to his side and, bending down to him, slapped his face hard twice. Dahoum
fell silent and looked at the ground. The soldier then
grabbed him under the chin and raised his head; Flecker
could see the fingers digging into Dahoum's cheeks.

'*Onzor!*' he exclaimed, pointing his head in Lawrence's direction.

The officer, once he was assured of Dahoum's attention, slowly raised his arm and brought the crop down
on Lawrence's buttocks. Flecker saw the weal form.

'*Bir!*' he counted.

He thrashed his arm down again.

'*Iki!*'

Lawrence did not so much as flinch. His fists even
relaxed.

'*Üç!*'

Flecker watched with shared agony as Lawrence was
rhythmically whipped, his emotions in torment and his
mind, like a schoolboy's, ticking off the numbers as the
officer counted them out.

Yet, at the same time, he was excited as he had never
been, even with Hellé when they made their special
love, by the primitiveness of the scene below him, the
sheer cruel beauty of the crop rising and whisking
downwards, the music of its whistle and the bleak slice
of the shadow of the officer's arm upon the wall.

'*Yirmi besh!*' the officer finally exclaimed and lowered
the crop to his side, taking care not to let its bloody
leather shank touch his trousers.

He spoke again, then stirred his crop in the bucket.
At another order, one of the soldiers emptied the water
over Lawrence's buttocks as his comrade untied the
knots fastening his ankles and wrists.

Lawrence made no effort to move until the soldiers

had left the room and the bolt noisily slid across the outside of the door.

Flecker moved quickly to the grille and, hunching there, threw in a handful of gravel and goat droppings which spattered on the floor of the cellar. Neither Lawrence nor Dahoum noticed them.

Lawrence eased himself off the table and hobbled over to Dahoum whose ropes he untied. Then he lay on the palliasse next to Dahoum, face down. His robes had covered him once more as he stood but now, Flecker could see, the pain of even the weight of the material hurt Lawrence and he moved gingerly on to one side, Dahoum cradling his head in his lap.

Once more, Flecker hurled a fistful of grit and goat turds into the room. This time Dahoum looked up.

'El-Roy!' Dahoum said quietly to Lawrence, but loud enough for Flecker to hear.

Lawrence struggled to his feet and limped over to the window, his face just below ground level.

'Roy?'

'Yes. Are you all right?'

'Just had six of the best from the headmaster of this Dotheboys Hall,' Lawrence declared, smiling and filling Flecker with relief.

'I counted twenty-five,' Flecker replied quietly.

'So did I. What a British education does for one, eh?'

'Who do they think you are?'

'Deserters . . .'

'Tell them you're British,' Flecker hissed. 'They can't do this . . .'

'I suspect they know I am. This is a bit of revenge for Woolley's arrogant behaviour, I'd guess . . .'

The bolt in the door was sliding aside. Lawrence moved swiftly and painfully to the palliasse, and Flecker dropped to his belly in the alleyway. A guard entered the room with a jug of water, a wooden drinking vessel and two small oranges. He said nothing but put them on the table; then he saw Lawrence's trail of drips of water and blood leading from the palliasse to the window bars. He asked Lawrence a brief question and Lawrence replied in Arabic, gasping for his breath. The soldier shrugged and left.

'Leave things to me,' Flecker whispered loudly through the grating, slipping away down the alleyway before Lawrence could caution him.

The officer sat behind a rickety desk, both his hands splayed out on the top. Flecker was reminded momentarily of Cumberpatch when he had broken the news of his failing the examination. If only, Flecker thought, he had worked harder at his Turkish. He could use it now.

'*Ingilizce biliyor musunuz?*' Flecker asked, his voice as quiet and as unemotional as he could manage.

The officer shook his head.

'*Hayir!*' he muttered.

'*Fransizca biliyor musunuz?*'

'*Oui. Je parle français un petit.*' He pointed to a chair. '*Asseyez vous, monsieur.*'

The officer sent his orderly out of the room to fetch two cups of coffee. He then began to question Flecker, but was immediately interrupted. Flecker was determined to maintain the initiative.

'*Je suis Monsieur Fontana, l'ambassadeur diplomatique de La Grande-Bretagne dans le bureau consulaire à Aleppo. Vous avez en custodie un homme Anglais . . . Avec beaucoup de respect, je demande . . .*'

As diplomatically as he could, yet as forcefully as he dared, Flecker demanded the release of Lawrence and what he termed 'the Arab boy with him, his manservant', both detained because of a misunderstanding.

They were, Flecker reported, both searching for a statue, from their archaeological dig at Carchemish, for which activity permission had been given by the Turkish authorities.

For twenty minutes, receiving only gruff replies in French from the Turkish officer, Flecker pressed his case. Finally, the officer held up his right hand to silence him.

'Your French is good, Monsieur Fontana,' the officer said in good English, 'and you plead your case well. But I cannot release them; it is a matter for the court. If they were deserters, as I believed them to be, then I should have released them in the morning. But they are not . . .'

Flecker disguised his surprise at the officer's command of English. Instead, he grinned in what he hoped was his most disarming fashion.

'You have played games with me, sir,' he said, still smiling.

'And you with me, monsieur. Tell me, why are you also here and dressed as an Arab?'

'I came to help find the statue. I am interested in ancient matters. As for wearing Arab robes . . . Do you know the saying, "When in Rome do as Rome does"? I am wearing these clothes as they are the most practical for travel in the desert. We have been journeying with men from the desert tribes: the Bedouin.'

The officer considered Flecker's statements for a moment before speaking again.

'I accept your reasoning but I am still unable to allow your countrymen to have their freedom. It is most irregular and only irregularities . . .'

His voice petered out and he shrugged, his hands rising from the table then falling again. Flecker immediately recognised the path their discussions would now take and began to consider his possessions, what he was wearing and carrying.

At this point, the orderly returned with a wooden tray bearing two cups of sweet, thick, black coffee accompanied by two glasses of murky water. Flecker drank the coffee, his head reeling as the muddy liquid ran down his throat. It was the first drink he had had since midday, except for the old man's cup of goat's milk, and his throat was parched: in the tension of events he had not realised it.

For an hour, he and the officer talked. Flecker complimented him on his English, on his French, on the efficiency with which his troops had mingled in the square. They discussed the success of the German railway, the Hittites and the Assyrians and, as the officer put it, the curious British greed for the acquisition of anything over a thousand years old.

Gradually, like two wary animals padding around each other at the extremities of their territories, they came to an agreement. It did not, Flecker remarked after the deal was struck, involve him parting with anything old. The officer laughed uproariously and Flecker handed over his pocket watch and Dahoum's shiny silver pistol.

'You may receive the prisoners in the morning,' the officer said. 'Just before dawn.' He stood up and slipped the pistol into his pocket where it dragged the material down with its weight.

Flecker spent the rest of the night beside the donkeys in the street, huddled against them for warmth. He dozed fitfully but did not sleep, his throat throbbing once more and his whole body occasionally racked with short bouts of shivering.

Arriving back at Carchemish, Flecker spent the whole

of that evening massaging Lawrence's back and bathing his wounds, dabbing them with diluted tincture of iodine. Not once did his patient wince at the stinging of the lotion which stained his white buttocks a blotchy brown.

The weals had ceased to be inflamed but were still very tender. The few scabs which had formed had been repeatedly rubbed off by Lawrence's Arab trousers which had become so encrusted with dried blood that Flecker had thrown them away.

'It was awful. I was watching through the window and could do nothing . . . nothing at all.'

'It matters not,' Lawrence said quietly, the flames of fire dancing on the mosaic beside where he lay on a folded blanket, his head resting upon his arms.

'But it was so . . .'

'These things happen,' Lawrence went on. 'It is not the first time, nor will it be the last.'

Flecker made no reply. For a moment his mind was empty of thought and then the realisation came to him. His hands stopped massaging and Lawrence craned his head as far round as he could.

'You understand, Roy,' he said, 'I knew you would.'

My darling little Pussy, [Flecker wrote]

This is just a line to say that I am well, struggling hard with my Turkish – even to the point of seeking practical assistance – and writing as if the devil was after my pen if not my soul. I'm certain the poems are shaping into the best I've ever written and the new book will be the crown so far of my poetic outpourings.

There is not much happening here in Beirut. The wild flowers are glorious once more this year and yet, when I see them, I sometimes long to see bluebells towering over them or primroses poking their little faces through. What I would give to see a snowdrop pushing through the leaf litter of an English wood!

I cannot wait for you to arrive. Cable me this instant with your itinerary and the name of the ship. I shall write to every rock above water that you pass.

Your loving yearning Tigerrr!

He sealed the letter in an envelope he found in the chest in Woolley's room where they kept the money for paying off the workmen at the dig, and inserted it in another envelope on the flap of which he wrote in block capitals: RAFF: TO BE POSTED IN BEIRUT. PLEASE.

The sun beat mercilessly down outside. In the shade of the building a camel was resting; every so often it snorted, snuffled asthmatically and belched. Fifty yards off, four mules lackadaisically stood in the heat, their outlines hazed. Far away towards the railway line, a mirage of water hung silverish in the air.

Flecker and Lawrence lay on the two beds in Woolley's room. The heat was oppressive. Both men were naked, Flecker lying on his back, Lawrence on his front.

Throughout the night Flecker had been coughing spasmodically. Lawrence had twice come into his room with a Roman glass beaker of warmed milk and it had soothed Flecker's throat, if only temporarily; within thirty minutes of drinking he was coughing again. He was certain he was running a temperature but it could have been put down to the heat.

Lawrence broke the silence of some minutes. It was almost too much effort to speak in the heat.

'Do you know, Roy, the Pathans have a particularly nasty torture – on the North West Frontier. It's guaranteed to drive a man out of his mind in an hour.'

Flecker made no reply, but Lawrence knew he was listening.

'They get a large iron box about three feet square

with a few one-inch diameter holes drilled very close to the lid. They place it in the sun until it is too hot to touch and then they put a prisoner inside it. Naked. His feet are on the hot metal below, so he cannot stand still, but if he touches the sides they blister him; so he has to hunch up. He cannot sit, for there isn't room and his arse would get scorched. The air is stifling and, even if he wanted to, he can't get his face near the air holes. It takes considerable fortitude to survive.' He paused. 'Most die.'

The camel shifted against the side of the building, its hide rubbing on the mud-brick wall.

'We are not unlike a Pathan captive, eh, Roy?' Lawrence continued.

'Sweltering in our little box,' Flecker replied. 'At least we can touch the sides.' He, too, paused. 'And each other.'

He stretched out his hand and brushed his fingers against Lawrence's side. His skin was slick with sweat.

'I wasn't thinking just of this room,' Lawrence remarked. 'Do you remember that conversation we had – when was it? So long ago now. About being trapped . . . ?'

'Yes, I remember.'

'Well, that's how we are. Caught in our own little boxes. We cannot be other than what we are. We can change our colour and our uniform, disguise ourselves as much as we like – yet, under the skin, we are fixed as an image on a photographic plate. We may fade in time, but we never change.'

A far-off shout reached them and Flecker saw, through the doorway, a boy approaching the mules.

'I should love to escape from myself,' Lawrence went on. 'Be a completely different person. Not just dress in Arab clothes, but be an Arab. Then, when I was tired of that, I could transmute myself into being someone utterly different – a bishop, or a bank manager, or an airman. In short, I'd be a chameleon of a chap. . . .'

'Are you not already that?' Flecker suggested. 'You're an archaeologist, a fellow of an Oxford college, a spy and an Arab. Isn't that enough?'

Lawrence laughed briefly.

'I am also a masochist, a convinced misogynist . . .'

The mules were braying, complaining at having to move in the heat. The boy was hitting them with a short stick.

'I'm unable to get away from this. Sometimes I hate myself for what I am, yet I cannot reject it, cannot slough it off like a snake and have a new, shiny, pristine skin. And sometimes I like it – the sheer anguish of the sorrow and the consummate loveliness of the aching . . .'

For a long moment neither of them spoke. The mules disappeared from sight in the direction of the river.

'Do you read Swinburne?' Lawrence asked suddenly.

'Yes.'

Flecker knew to what Lawrence was referring, to which of Swinburne's poems he was alluding. He began to recite from it.

> A beautiful passionate body
>   That never has ached with a heart!
> On thy mouth though the kisses are bloody,
>   Though they sting till it shudder and smart,
> More kind than the love we adore is,
>   They hurt not the heart of the brain,
> O bitter and tender Dolores,
>   Our Lady of Pain.
>
> Thy skin changes country and colour,

Lawrence went on, quoting from later in the same poem.

And shrivels or swells to a snake's.
Let it brighten and bloat and grow duller,
    We know it, the flames and the flakes,
Red brands on it smitten and bitten,
    Round skies where a star is a stain,
And the leaves with thy litanies written,
    Our Lady of Pain.

Later, as the sun lowered, they dressed and walked along the river bank. The wide Euphrates drifted by deceptively quickly. Only in the central current did the muddy water swirl with apparent action.

'A war is brewing,' Lawrence said, scuffing his toe in the soil and flicking bits of gravel into the water. 'Hogarth told me as much. The Germans are getting too big for their boots.'

Flecker watched the ripples of the gravel speed downstream and disappear.

'What will you do, Ned?'

'I'm to stay on here. Work with the Arabs, give Johnny Turk a hard time. We need intelligence officers in the field – or, rather' – he kicked a larger stone into the river – 'in the desert. That's what they call a spy now, an Intelligence Officer . . .'

'I shall apply to serve with you,' Flecker announced.

Lawrence smiled and put his hand on Flecker's shoulder.

'That wouldn't do, Roy. It won't be a picnic. There will be no mosaics and no sweet boys, though Dahoum will stay with me, that much I know. You must stay by your wife. Risk nothing. After it is over, it will be up to you and her to start anew. Have your children, Roy . . .'

Lawrence turned his face away, letting his hand drop to his side. Flecker felt an immeasurable sorrow flood through him like a rapid and mortal disease.

'Ned?'

Yet Lawrence made no answer. He just stood looking across the muddy, swirling Euphrates at the eastern shore.

10

Beirut: the second week of March 1913

The light was so bright when he awoke he thought at first he was still in his dream, staked out in the desert with a Turkish soldier leaning over him, the sun in his hands, directing it straight into his victim's eyes. To one side of the soldier stood Lawrence, his arms hanging limply by his sides, dark smears of blood on the backs of his hands like stigmata.

The sheets against Flecker's belly and beneath his back were cloyed with sweat. His arms were damp and chilled where they lay on the topmost sheet. His hair and moustache itched with sweat, his joints ached and in his ears hissed an unending sibilant sizzle.

He forced himself up, thrusting with his elbows. His skin was sore in the bend of his arm where the sweat had collected during his restless sleep. As he moved upward, he banged his head on the temperature chart suspended from the white enamel bars of the bed-head.

Reaching behind, he unclipped the chart and studied it. His temperature had remained steady at 104° for the last twelve hours.

A nurse appeared around the corner of the ward carrying a tray on which she balanced a number of tumblers half-full of medicines. As she passed the foot of his bed Flecker tried to call for her attention but could not. His voice was almost entirely gone. However, sensing that he was trying to call her, the nurse stopped just past his bed and returned.

'Yes, Mr Flecker?' she asked, sliding her tray on to the table next to his bed.

'I need a drink,' Flecker croaked, his words barely audible. 'My throat . . .' He pointed to his mouth and, in dumb show, raised an imaginary glass to his lips.

'I'll be along when I'm able. Just be a little forbearing, Mr Flecker,' the nurse assured him, holding him forward with one hand while punching his pillows into a softer shape with the other. 'Just wait a moment or two.'

She went down the ward and disappeared behind two screens erected around the bed of a newly admitted patient.

Flecker leaned over the side of his bed and felt with his hand beneath the table. After several fumbling attempts he succeeded in grabbing hold of his pencil and notepad. Even the joints in his fingers felt stiff and old.

By now he was wide awake, yet the hissing still zizzed in his ears. He pressed his hands to the sides of his head to try to contain the pressure in his skull. It was no use. The hissing continued, but it seemed now to be outside his head. He looked at the window. The panes were awash with rain and small pellets of hail bounced on the deep-set sill.

He began to write, his hand shaky at first but becoming a little more firm. Yet his fingers tired almost as soon as he began.

The words seemed to calm his whole body. Once they began to flow they came with a fluency which pleased him, with which he was becoming strangely accustomed – for these days, he thought, he no sooner had to grasp a pen or pencil than his mind began to work, the words tumbling out almost effortlessly. It mattered not what he was writing – a poem draft, a revision of a stanza, a loving, mildly rebuking, teasing letter to Hellé, a har-

sher and more direct letter to his father, a joking, hopeful note to Marsh or another literary friend, even a
consular report – the words still spilled free of him as
if they had a life of their own.

My dear Rupert,

I am writing – it seems the course for me these days – from
my sick-bed in hospital, having been consigned here in a
carriage a few days ago. I contracted a fearsome cold on my
chest and lost my voice completely, as the result, I suspect, of
spending the night recently sleeping in an alley in a Turkish
town with only a few donkeys for companions and mutual
warmth. The nights, as I am sure you must know, can be
parky in the desert. Don't believe all you hear about the hot
sands! They are only hot for a twelve-hour at a time.

It was all a bit of an adventure and I found it fascinating
– can say nothing more as it was all 'government business' –
but it left me in the grip of this awful cold and laryngitis.
Even if you were here, by my bed, I should have to write to
you. The doctor orders me silent as a mouse.

Would it be that you were here by the bed!

I am not my usual hearty fellow and all that. This Eastern
Land has me down in the dumps. I can see no way out of it,
which is what is worse. I'm trying all sorts of wheezes to
make it out but to no effect. The CU appointments board
might get me a teaching post. I've got my name in with
Gabbitas Thring too, but I would fain not wind up my days
as a schoolmaster in a tired little establishment somewhere in
the West Country, thrusting the classics at reluctant boys and
struggling to mark their illegible essays on Homer. I could
transfer to another consular department but – O! that prospect fills me with such dolour I really do not want it. The
best thing would be to get out of it altogether.

My wife is in France at present but due to leave any day
now to join me. That will, I know, lift my spirits higher than
summer clouds – those high, thin ones that fleece over England
at the end of a summer's day, tinged with pink like impure
marble. Here there are none of those clouds. Either the sky is
a scorching blue or it is hazy with heat and blowing sand.

Siroccos are bad at present. Or else they are thunderous clouds like omens from the Old Testament threatening to flood the world. Even as I write, a cataract of rain is sluicing down the windows of my ward.

I am in the dumps, dear Rupert. Nothing seems to work out.

As you will know from Marsh, I have a new book of poems on the way. It's called *The Golden Journey to Samarkand*. It is, I think, a solid title, one that will catch the eye and draw the mind. None of your stodgy *Forty Poems* or *Lines from an English Meadow* or whatever. I think the title is as important as the contents, don't you?

Only God Himself knows how the book will fare. Fair, I do hope.

If only there was some way of making my living by my pen. I know I am not Spenser or Pope, but I am sure there must be a niche for me in English letters where I could snuggle down and do the odd piece that would bring in a crust for Hellé and me every so often.

These past months have been hell on earth without my wife here to coddle and support me. Her absence has had me dancing from slough of despondency to trough of despair and back again with hardly a molehill of joy in between. I seem to pass my time writing poems and reading, and studying for accursed examinations I am certain to flunk. *Hassan*, my play, is being turned down at every submission. My novel, now with Goschen, *The King of Alsander*, is a quaint piece and due out next year. I cannot start to think how it might be received for it is not a common book. It's a poetic tale about all the powers that be. I shall write and ask for a copy to be sent to you.

I do so miss England: the mists and cool bright sun, the roll of green hills and the scar of the cliffs of Dover. I do so also miss being able to talk with people. Real people of the literary persuasion.

There is one out here, T. E. Lawrence – an Oxford man – with whom I get along famously. We work together from time to time, for he is an archaeologist and we poor consular men have to look after the welfare of those with more exciting lives. Exalted, even! He is a man of learning, a dear sweet youth with a fine ear for poetry and a tongue that would charm rocks to sing if they were so commanded by him. He dresses *à la mode* in the desert, in burnouse and flowing headgear – called a *keffiyeh* – and carries a revolver stuck in his belt like an American outlaw. He also knows of you, dear Rupert, and your poetry.

He is a free agent in the dunes of the desert and I am a prisoner in this bed and this job. How I wish someone would come and shear the shackles! But I am afraid I'm too entwined now ever to be set at liberty. I feel like an old elm that stood in my father's garden, leaning with the wind, dropping inch by inch with every storm, wrapped about with ivy and fit only for a gardener's axe.

I think often of you and Marsh in the cosy nest you have together in Raymond Buildings and treasure in my memory my last evening there with you both. Do give him my warmest regards.

You may write to me, as you know, care of The British Consulate, Beirut. I shall not be tied to this bed of sweat and discomfort for much longer.

Ever thine,

He signed the letter 'Roy' and folded it over, carefully aligning the corners of the paper before firming down the fold with his thumbnail.

The nurse arrived with a glass of tepid water for him and held it to his lips. He sipped at it with relief and then lay back upon the pillows, the letter in his hand.

11

At sea, Beirut and Brumana, and Switzerland: March – June 1913

His two letters to Hellé reached her when the ship upon which she had embarked at Marseilles, the *Lotus*, berthed at Alexandria. Although he had written in an almost jocular fashion and his second letter stated he was now out of the hospital, she had been terrified at his news. He was, she believed, sure to have understated the seriousness of the situation: a loss of voice and a hospital bed were, in his circumstance, no small matter. She went straight to the purser to ask when they would be sailing. His answer was non-committal – they would not be leaving port for another day and a night.

During this delay she tried in vain to send a telegraph to Flecker, then sought a boat which would be departing sooner and sail faster. There was none. When finally the *Lotus* sailed Hellé was in a frenzy. She slept fitfully and spent her waking hours pacing the decks as the coastline slid relentlessly by on the starboard horizon, a dull smudge between the sea and the sky.

When at last Beirut appeared on the starboard bow and the ship's engines began to slow, her excitement and dread mounted. Her mind was a turmoil of irrational fears: he might be too ill to meet the ship; he might be dying. She feared the worst and went quickly to her cabin to complete her packing not only in readiness for disembarkation but also to busy herself, to keep her hands active and her mind occupied with other than just the one thought – Flecker's health.

There was a knock on the cabin door.

'Purser's information, madam,' the steward announced. 'We are unable to land passengers in Beirut. The vessel is under a five-day quarantine order. Cholera has broken out in Alexandria. Passengers due to land in Beirut are to remain with the ship to Tripoli and back again.'

He closed the cabin door and she heard his knock again further down the passageway outside.

She sat down heavily on her bunk. *'Mon Dieu!'* she swore quietly and then, her tears beginning to run on to her cheeks, she said, 'Oh, my Roy . . . My Tiger . . .'

After a quarter of an hour she dried her eyes and opened her cabin door, going up to the smoking lounge. There, seated at one of the leather-topped desks, she quickly scribbled a note to Flecker and searched for the purser to arrange for it to go ashore with the agent. This done, she went out on deck and stared longingly at the city lying under its heat haze. Somewhere in that jumble of houses, below those hills, her husband was lying in his sick-bed waiting for her.

As she peered at the shore, her thoughts heavy with sadness, a small boat detached itself from the dock area and began to row out to the *Lotus*. From a small staff in the prow fluttered the Thomas Cook's flag. Distractedly she watched it approach, paying it only casual notice until a figure stood in the stern of the boat and began to wave frantically. Her attention caught, she studied the figure for a long time before she realised it was waving to her. It was Flecker.

'I've permission to remain with you during the five days' quarantine,' he explained as she welcomed him at the head of the ladder slung over the ship's side; he had clambered up it with an attaché case in one hand and had not so much as got short of breath.

'That's wonderful!' she remarked and clung to his

arm as he went to the deck officer and presented his boarding pass.

Once in her cabin, he hugged Hellé tightly, feeling the soft contours of her body moulding to his own. He kissed her repeatedly and ran his hands over her back, his fingers loosening the buttons on her tunic. When she was naked, he laid her on her bunk and undressed himself. The ship was soon under way again and, as it met the swell beyond the harbour, it began to roll gently, pushing him slowly from one side of her to the other.

The night sea air was cool, blowing off-shore and carrying with it the occasional faint scent of indistinguishable blossoms. They sat side by side on deck and he told her of his illness, making light of it. He had, he said, only been in the hospital a few days. It was not serious; the doctor, he declared, would not have admitted him had she been in Beirut to nurse him. As soon as he had spoken, he feared she might take his remark as a rebuke but it was no use attempting to retract it.

He had, he went on, written many new poems since they had last been together and he longed to read them to her. Additionally, he had learned a lot more Turkish and had taken a few practical lessons in the language, but he did not elaborate on the circumstances of his so-called lessons. He informed her he had rented them a little house in Beirut – not as beautiful as the one at Areiya but suitable for the time being. It would not matter, he said, what it was like as they were together and their surroundings were unimportant; yet he quickly went on to say that they would not remain long in Beirut. He was certain they would be out of it in months. For good. Something was going to turn up. He just knew it.

He went to the deck rail and looked down at the sea wisping by in white fronds under the moonlight. She joined him, slipping her arm through his.

'The sea smells so fine, so clean. The ozone does me good,' he said quietly. 'I wish someone would invent an ozone machine.'

'You made me very worried, Roy. I was so scared after I received your note. And in pencil . . .'

'The nurse didn't like us using a pen in bed – in case it marked the sheets. I wrote all my letters in pencil. An awful bore . . .'

'I thought it might be because you couldn't hold a pen tightly. The lead was so faint.'

'Nothing to lean on in bed. Only my knee.'

She knew it was an excuse, but pressed no further.

'The sea air does smell good,' she agreed.

He looked up from the waves vee-ing out from the ship's hull and stared at the thin line of coast. Faint lights shone distantly where there was a small fishing village and, on a headland, a lighthouse beacon shone.

'Let's go to the other side of the ship,' he suggested. 'I don't want to have to see that bloody shoreline. How I long to be seeing the last of it as it slips over the horizon of my life!'

They walked by several other couples standing at the rail and passed the last of the lifeboats where it hung from its davits. Half its keel was freshly painted white and gleamed in the arc of a nearby bulkhead lamp.

'That's better,' Flecker said as they reached the other side of the ship and sat in two deck-chairs beneath another lamp. 'If we look out now we shall see Greece and Cyprus, Italy and France and, beyond that, England. In the other direction, beyond the coast, all we should see would be desert as far as Fair Cathay.'

He lay back in the chair and closed his eyes.

'Do you know what I can see?' he asked.

'No. What?'

'I can see the spires of Oxford and, right in the middle, the dome of the Sheldonian.'

She closed her eyes.

'I can see the towers of Notre Dame and the dome of Sacré Coeur de Montmartre. And the Seine idling by beneath the bridges of Paris.'

After a while, during which time she wondered if he had dozed off, he said, 'I have one poem to read to you. I brought it with me especially. Will you hear it?'

'Yes,' she answered firmly.

He opened his jacket and took a folded sheet from an inner pocket.

'When the fever dropped, I found my mind working on a poem. I didn't actually make it; it made itself inside me and then came out when my mind was less frenetic. I think it's the best I've written in a long, long while.' He looked around furtively. 'There's no one coming?'

Hellé shook her head and he began to recite.

Would I might lie like this, without the pain,
    For seven years — as one with snowy hair,
Who in the high tower dreams his dying reign —

    Lie here and watch the walls — how grey and bare,
The metal bed-post, the uncoloured screen,
    The mat, the jug, the cupboard, and the chair;

And served by an old woman, calm and clean,
    Her misted face familiar, yet unknown,
Who comes in silence, and departs unseen,

    And with no other visit, lie alone,
Nor stir, except I had my food to find
    In that dull bowl Diogenes might own.

And down my window I would draw the blind,
    And never look without, but, waiting, hear
A noise of rain, a whistling of the wind,

And only know that flame-foot spring is near
By trilling birds, or by the patch of sun
    Crouching behind my curtain. So, in fear . . .

He stopped and looked at her. She was sitting upright in her deck-chair, her back straight, her hands resting in her lap. She was sobbing. He could not hear her yet he could see her shoulders moving as she cried, silently, like an embarrassed mourner at a graveside.

'My Pussy,' he whispered, leaning over to her. 'What's wrong with my little pussy-cat?'

She shook her head.

'*Rien*,' she replied. '*Rien*.' She looked at him. 'Roy,' she whispered, looking into his eyes, her roundish face glistening where the tears had run down her cheeks, '*je t'adore, mon petit Tigre*.'

She dabbed at her eyes with her silk handkerchief, crumpled and still damp from her earlier tears.

'It is such a sad poem. Is it really how you thought?'

'Yes. I suppose I still do.' He paused, then went on, 'You know, when I'm ill, it's sometimes quite beautiful. Except for the pain.'

She brightened a little.

'Isn't the pain also beautiful?'

'It's not that kind of pain. It's not sharp, it's not ecstatic, not loving. It's deep in the body, nagging. It's not in the soul, like . . .'

'I know,' she said soothingly, putting her hand on his, comforting as if he were her child. 'I know, Roy.'

He woke in the early hours of the morning and thrust his hand under her arm as she lay by his side, pushing it through until his palm cupped her breast. The bunk was narrow and they were pressed against each other.

When she woke she turned over, his hand sliding across her chest.

'Can't you sleep?'

He shook his head, then asked, 'Who is in the next cabin?'

'No one. There was a Miss Salter, but she left in Alexandria.'

'And the other side?'

'We're the last cabin in the passageway.'

He slipped out of the bunk and fumbled in his attaché case.

'What are you doing?'

She sat up, the sheets falling to her waist. The moon was low, shining through the porthole, casting a round circle of grey light on the cabin wall which moved slowly up and down to the motion of the ship.

He did not answer her question in words. Instead, from his case, he took out a thin leather belt from which the buckle had been cut and the length halved by it being tied double in the centre with twine.

She swung her legs over the panelled side of the bunk and stood naked upon the cabin carpet.

'Is there the room, do you think?' he asked.

She nodded.

Flecker lay on his front on the bunk, his face turned to the porthole. The ship altered course and the moon illuminated his features.

Hellé swung the belt in the air, flicking it across his bare buttocks. He did not move but a spasm ran under his skin. She swung the belt again, not hard but with a flick of her wrist so that the tips of the leather caught him and left little red marks on his flesh as if he had been pinched.

While she swung the belt and whipped it back across her, he thought of Lawrence in his dungeon stretched out before the Turkish officer, of Lawrence lying naked on the mosaic floor, of Lawrence orating Swinburne and of her, standing naked behind his back, her breasts heaving and swinging and her plumpish arms driving the leather downwards, making his heart beat faster and faster and his breath come in gasps.

Beirut:
Sunday

My dear Ned,

I am at my wits' end.

I jut cannot put my mind to my studies and there is no way on this earth I can pass muster in the examinations – my umpteenth attempt at the blighters – now less than two months off.

Whenever I think of sitting quietly, I either think of you or I find my brain filling with the turmoil of words that make poems.

It is as if I have within me a vast pot-pourri, a sort of jumbled thesaurus from which words spill out in the most beautiful ways. I am writing frantically and the wonder is that much of it is so very good. I look at it after the first lines are down and I think, did I write this? I am also translating (not Turkish!) some Albert Samain and Jean Moréas . . .

After H. and sleeping all night with those mules I was very ill and sent to hospital. But now I am better. Hellé has arrived in Beirut and we are living in a small house I have rented in the city. It is not as pretty as our house at Areiya and we miss the puppies, but it is otherwise home.

In the quiet hours, often at night if I cannot sleep for the wild dreams and marvellous words tumbling about inside me, I think of you, of C. and our adventures together. I miss you very much.

Thine ever and ever,
Roy.

The doctor folded his stethoscope and placed it in a black lacquer box which he dropped into the drawer of his desk, sliding it shut with the palm of his hand.

'You seem in fine health, Mrs Flecker. I can find no trace of the Malta fever lingering. Your lungs are clear and your heart is sound. Your blood pressure is also normal. I suggest you dress yourself now.'

'Thank you,' Hellé said. 'I am relieved for, as you know, I must stay fit to care for my husband.' She paused before asking hesitantly, doing up the buttons on her blouse. 'How is he?'

When the doctor spoke it was with the reserve she had expected.

'I had supposed you would take this opportunity to ask after him in his absence and, in truth, Mrs Flecker, I am concerned. You are aware his temperature has been going up again lately and that he had a brief spell in hospital a few weeks ago. I fear we may see a marked relapse in the near future.'

He looked at her face. It was a study of blank terror, her cheeks drawn and her eyes almost glazed as if she was not listening to a word he was saying.

'I can make a few suggestions,' he continued, 'which I would suggest you follow. Now – you reported to me he was breathless and suffering from considerable lassitude upon your return from Tripoli. That he had, as I recall, to lie down upon reaching the house you are renting . . .'

She nodded.

'And it was a hot day?'

Again, she nodded. 'Stifling, doctor,' she added as further confirmation.

'Of course, the heat is a part of his problem; it exacerbates the condition a great deal. You have yourself pointed out that the sea air, cooler and less laden with dust, suited him better on your five-day enforced cruise up the coast; well, this is the nub of the matter. He should really be away from the heat as much as possible and in cleaner air. A more stimulating atmosphere. You should, I feel, relinquish your house in the town and move to the mountains. I might suggest Brumana. It is high up, some fifteen miles by road from the city. There is a good hotel there in which you could comfortably reside. A distance from the city, as I say, but as your husband has only to visit the Consulate a few days a week, I feel this would be no hardship. The road is good . . .'

Hellé nodded once more.

'I agree,' she said. 'I shall mention this to my husband instantly upon my return. It is so hot where we are – a one-floored house in which the wind cannot circulate. The air stays so still . . .'

'Excellent! Move to Brumana, Mrs Flecker. I am certain the change of climate will assist your husband no end.'

She walked back to the house, arriving a little after noon to find Flecker seated at the table he used for his writing. He was dressed in just his trousers with a towel draped about his shoulders. As she entered the room he did not look up but carried on writing furiously, his pen-nib scratching the page.

'Is this not better!' he exclaimed suddenly, not so much as glancing in her direction but gazing at the paper. 'Much better! I've re-worked a bit of "The Painter's Mistress" and it is . . . Listen!'

She sat on the chair by the door, still behind him.

> And still I hear each sound that falls,
> The wood that starts in the sun's heat,
> The mouse astir among the walls,
> While down the summer-smitten street
> A cart rolls lonely on: the hush
> Tightens: I hear the flickering brush.

He sat upright in his chair, stretching his hands before him.

'Is that not a considerable improvement on what it was?'

She rose and stood next to him, her hand on his shoulder, peering over at the paper.

'It is,' she answered. 'It is much improved.'

Yet she did not remember the first version from which this had been drawn. She remembered less of his verse, her mind now preoccupied with his illness and their predicament.

'I'm going to do a bit of Turkish now,' he announced and folded up the paper, slipping it into his notebook. 'Later, I'll show you some new poems for the book.'

She went into their bedroom and seated herself at the dressing-table, taking from her writing compendium a sheet of cream-laid paper. For a few moments, she composed herself as she always did before writing to his mother. Letters to his parents required such tact and planning. It was not that she was being devious, just careful.

Yet she could not bring her thoughts to focus. As soon as she considered what to write and how to couch her phrases, her mind expanded, burgeoning with the catalogue of problems that beset them.

Early every morning, before the other guests were about, Flecker rose and went out to sit on the terrace of the hotel. Around the edge flowered pink acacias in low stunted bushes; they undulated in the first breezes, the freshly opened petals waxy and delicate. If the gardener had been at work, there glistened drops of water on the leaves and blossoms, the crisp new sunlight spangling in them.

In the peace and quiet, before the sun grew hot and the day filled with human activity, he wrote, working on foolscap sheets or in his notebook. If the breeze was troublesome he weighted down loose pages with stones or his glass of orange juice.

As he worked, Hellé watched him. He bent over when he wrote. It was not that his back arched but more that his head pushed forward. His hand sometimes wrote several complete lines without pausing and, when he did stop to allow inspiration to come, he let his hand and pen remain hovering over the point at which it would next write.

There was, she thought, an economy in his methods. It was as if he were loath to waste effort, knowing somewhere deep in his soul he had only a finite reserve of energy upon which he could draw.

His poetry was quite superior to what he had written before. Even his translations from the French or Latin were sharper, more precise, less self-indulgent. He seemed suddenly to have come to grasp the difficult task of carrying a rhyme scheme successfully across from one language into another, a technique he had sometimes foundered upon in the past.

And yet his new-found poetic power, his newly dis-covered awareness and his driving urge to write was, she knew, brought about at the expense of his physical strength.

It was as if, even unconsciously, he sensed his time was now as finite as his energy.

He did not admit – he probably did not realise, she thought, as she did – that he was dying. Yet he was.

There was no time span on it, no way of saying he had another month to live, or another year. He was not under such a precise death sentence. But she was only too aware they would not spend many more years together. Even if he was successful in leaving Beirut now, if a sudden windfall paid off his bond . . . If the university appointments board or Marsh or Gabbitas Thring suddenly offered him a secure living in England, he would be hard put to accept it immediately. He would need to recuperate, probably for months, before he could undertake new responsibilities.

Paradoxically, she considered, his illness seemed to be the spur his creativity needed. When he was fit once more, his writing might deteriorate and she worried that might be as crushing a blow to him as his being ill.

He had something in Beirut to fight. He had the consular examinations to contend with – although there, she had to admit, he had all but surrendered – the heat, the pain in his throat and lungs, the animosity of his masters in London, the acrimonious and critical attitude of Cumberpatch. Once back in England, all these would be removed. The stimulus of opposition would no longer be there to press him on, and she wondered if he might survive the cosy protection of a teaching post in the soft countryside of the shires.

For a moment, looking down on him from their bedroom window, sitting on the terrace with his back ramrod stiff but at a slight angle, she conjured up an image of him in an academic gown, a mortar-board on his head, the tassel swinging as he walked, small boys deferentially calling him 'sir' as he passed and nodded to them in an aloof, paternal manner. Under his arm he was carrying a sheaf of exercises and several leather-bound volumes, a blue and maroon marbled notebook and a leather wallet of pens and pencils. The grass behind him was as trimmed and as smooth as the felt on a billiards table and a mulberry tree was in full blossom, squatting in the middle of the lawn like a beautiful mushroom. Perhaps, she thought, he was not a schoolmaster but a college don and the exercises were dissertations.

Suddenly he turned and looked up at her, as if some instinct informed him she was gazing down on him.

The emerald grass of an English university quadrangle dissipated into the brown, patchily green grass of a hotel terrace in the Lebanon.

He waved, just once. She returned his wave and went back into the room, her heart immeasurably saddened by her thoughts.

When later she joined him on the terrace, he was eager to show her a new translation he had been working at, he claimed, since before first light.

'Henri de Régnier,' he explained. 'I was reading him last night and his words swam round and round in my head before I fell asleep. He says so much of what I feel. It's as if he and I were somehow joined by some sensory bridge . . .'

'What have you been working on?' she enquired, wondering if her enthusiasm was just a little too forced.

'Listen. He's speaking of bees which kill, the kind that hunt flesh, not nectar: "Drink, swarm of war, stream from your plated hives and cull death's dust on flowery-fleshed fierce lives . . ." He speaks of the "brazen boom of bees" and – I should never think of that! We English – so insular! For us, bees hum and buzz and hiss and zizz. For him, they boom like cannon. They are cannon. Every projectile, every bullet, is a vicious insect. Isn't that a stunning metaphor, Hellé? And what can I manage in my little poems, eh? Drums that boom, rose-round lips that blow battle horns, tottering catapults pulled by slaves.'

He looked across the terrace, over the acacias, to the hills bathed in morning sunlight.

'My poetry's old. My wars are fought with swords and ballisters. I haven't a gun in my mind . . .'

He sat quite alone in the shade of the cedar. No other guests were about in the grounds. The servants were all about their afternoon work; Hellé was in Beirut. He had dealt that morning with a file of dispatches sent from London, Aleppo and Carchemish: there had been little for him to do other than pass on the information contained. The messenger from the Consulate had had time only for one cup of coffee before Flecker was through and was able to hand back most of the papers for forwarding. He had only to put in an occasional appearance at the office, every three days or so, to check on shipments of artefacts or to send off messages which should not be seen by others.

Only one item had required his longer attention. It was a brief letter from Hogarth. He was, he wrote, pleased with the way things had gone, grateful and glad Flecker had not only used his initiative but also displayed a degree of courage in the Halfati affair. He went on to state that Flecker's precarious state of health was of concern to him. He was afraid it might jeopardise the operation. To this end, he was transferring much of Flecker's responsibilities – for the time being only – to Fontana, drafting in an extra man to help with the everyday running of the office in Aleppo. Flecker was not, Hogarth was at pains to point out, underlining his words in mauve pencil, to assume he was dismissed. But he was, similarly, not to worry for the time being about doing other than that directly requested of him by Lawrence or Fontana. And he was not to be anxious about the future. 'It will all come out in the wash,' were his closing words.

The letter raised Flecker's spirits. Although nothing stated in it was definite, it gave him hope. Someone in a high place, someone in the labyrinth of Whitehall, the catacombs of government corridors and closed offices and muffled words, was looking out for him. He was not alone.

When he looked up from re-reading the letter for a

fourth or fifth time, the hills were shrouded in an after-noon heat haze. The acacia blossoms were wilting; the gardener had liberally saturated the ground but no vestige of the water remained. Only a smooth scar left by the splashes marked the dust and earth. Even the goats and sheep on a nearby slope seemed immovable, mere cut-outs pasted to the hillside.

How he hated this country! Its heat, its dust, its filth of animal dung in the streets. In London, horse dung was cleared away – in the main thoroughfares, at least. In the lesser byways, the rain sluiced the ordure down the wide grilles of the gutters. Here there was no rain and the dung remained, drying and disseminating in foul powder which drifted on the wind. The sirocco blew endlessly, it seemed to him. And the people fought – over a difference of gods, over the rights to a camel, over the ownership of three sand-dunes and a stagnant sump of green water under a siccative palm. They were, to him, a despicable lot.

These thoughts in his head, he decided to take a stroll, despite Hellé's strict instruction that he was to remain in the vicinity of the hotel and to keep to the shade out of doors where the air would be cooler, more bracing.

Taking a light straw hat from their room, he set off from the hotel, keeping to the road along the top of the hill in the direction of the village of Baabdat. He gave himself the goal of reaching the settlement three miles away. It would take him until evening, if he was to keep to a leisurely pace.

At first, the sun was pleasantly warm; a breeze blowing from the direction of the sea cooled him. He did not hurry and, by the time he arrived at the junction of the road with a track leading westward, he was no more tired than if he had taken a comfortable turn around the hotel grounds.

Beside the junction, a high point on the road, and under a tree leaning inland from the incessant pressure of the sirocco, there sat a young boy. He was whittling a stick with a dagger, carving from it a stylised statue of one of his goats which wandered to and fro on the hillside below.

Flecker perched himself next to the lad, nodding a greeting to which the boy replied with a dip of his head and a flash of his eyes. The boulder where Flecker was seated was polished smooth by generations of cloaks and coats and trousers.

As the boy carved, the white shavings from his piece of wood strewed the ground around him. A small, nondescript bird repeatedly approached with jerky, cautious hops to snatch a peeling of wood and fly off with it down the hillside. Flecker watched it go until it was invisible.

After their initial acknowledgement of each other's presence, neither man nor boy spoke. The boy was deft with his knife and rapid. The carved goat quickly took shape, even to its stubby horns and laden udders.

Flecker did not look at the boy but away across the hills towards the sea. He day-dreamed about the goatherd, thought of him naked in a grove of stunted, gnarled olives, his skin like the white whittled wood, glowing and smooth against the distorted trunks, his youthful muscles and hips, his rounded buttocks and his short curly hair in contrast to the land around him. And he thought of how the landscape was so ugly and yet the boys so beautiful, the boys who would soon be men as twisted and barren as the desert, the unyielding, callous sun.

Into his reverie intruded a white devil, a virginal Baal with horns which mocked him and thrust upward to pick his eyes out on their points.

The boy was offering the finished goat to him: it was

a skilful carving, even down to the dip in the centre of its back and the whiskers on its chin, stroked into the wood with thin, deft knife-strokes.

The boy did not speak. Flecker held out his hands, cupped as if he was about to drink from a spring, and the boy gently laid the goat in them.

'*Shokran*,' Flecker said very quietly. '*Shokran gæzilæn*.'

'*Æfwæn*,' the goatherd replied.

He leapt from the rock and ran down the hillside towards his flock, leaping from boulder to boulder like a fleet-hoofed goat himself. Flecker watched him go with an unmitigated sadness.

Rested, he stood up and placed the carving carefully in his pocket. He decided to change his plan. Instead of going to Baabdat, he settled on making Jouret el Ballout his destination.

The track went along a ridge for a little way, then disappeared over a small rise. It was easy walking, the breeze still drifting up the valleys. At the rise, he halted and looked down the valley ahead of him. On a slight promontory to the south was a stand of pines.

They were stately trees, unbowed by the winds, with no others in their vicinity. With deliberate steps, he left the track and walked towards the pines.

Once more he was a schoolboy on holiday at Bournemouth, running on the sands, building a castle which the tide demolished if the sun did not crumble it first — even then, he considered, the sun had been there to confound him. He could see his father walking across the beach in his Sunday best, his priest's collar tall and tight at his throat and his hymnal and Bible clasped to his side. He could hear his mother calling him but he could not see her. And he heard his sisters teasing and taunting him, their laughter cool and delicious.

'Oh, God!' he said, quietly. 'Will I never see that blessed shore again? . . .'

His head throbbed and he dropped to his knees below the pines, thrusting his fingers into the spiny carpet of needles, picking them up and smelling the pungent perfume of the sap. He scrabbled about and gathered a dozen or so pine cones.

He tossed them in the air, watched them bounce once upon the needle cover and then lie like dead things.

He gazed up into the branches. The high sun penetrated the thick cover in only a few places, bright and almost frigid star-like sparks of light.

He got to his feet and gazed about like a man suddenly coming to discover himself in the very centre of a dream in which every action, movement and sound was exact and indescribably real and yet, at the same time, he knew it was a fantasy.

He put his hands to his face and found his cheeks wet with tears. He smeared them over his chin and then looked at his hands as a murderer might stare upon bloody fingers.

'Claire!' he called suddenly. 'Claire!'

The pines absorbed his words.

'Claire! I'm sorry.' His voice was pained, racked with the anguish of a guilt long since pressed away to the dark reaches of his mind. 'I didn't mean to hit you. I didn't mean to bang you into the lamp-post. I didn't mean to cut your head. Joyce! Joyce! I'm sorry . . .'

No one answered him. The pines soughed in the breeze.

'Mother, don't sigh like that,' he scolded the branches, turning slowly, his arms spread out and his dark, Semitic features giving him the look of a lesser messiah in a high collar and tropical suit. 'I can't help it. I am what I am. I am what you made of me, what you shaped of me. I am you, mother. And father . . . I'm sorry I couldn't take the faith to heart. It wasn't for lack of trying. And now . . . Now I'm so lonely and want to come home.'

When he left the pine copse his collar was chafing on his neck. The salt of his tears had dissolved some of the starch and he fumbled with the stud to relieve the painful itching. His hands felt weak.

Abandoning his goal of Jouret el Ballout, he returned up the track, his breath catching. He had not realised the way had been downhill. By the time he reached the polished rock he was breathless and exhausted. He collapsed on to it and bent forward, sucking in great gouts of air. He was sticky with the effort of the climb.

When his breathing was less laboured, he felt in his pockets and took out a propelling pencil and a much folded piece of paper. He opened it out – it was a tariff sheet from the hotel; the reverse was blank.

Sitting on the boulder, he began to write. It wasn't a poem – at least, he thought it wasn't. It had no metre as such, nor rhyme scheme, and yet it tumbled from him as readily as the most beautiful words he had ever written.

She knew as soon as she was ushered into the surgery. It was not as if the doctor was going to be giving her any unexpected news, but the intensity of his words struck her cold. He had no sooner shaken her hand and bade her be seated than he began.

'Mrs Flecker, I will come directly to my point, for I know you will not want me to beat about the bush and, besides, I am sure you must know what I am going to say.'

She nodded imperceptibly, her hands clasped in her lap.

'Your husband is seriously ill. His propensity for

bronchitis and laryngitis has been of concern to me for
some time – since he came to be my patient here in
Beirut. Now, however, I am more than aware that his
illness is chronic and I can see no immediate respite for
him so long as he remains in this climate. I would
ask you how his health is now you have moved to
Brumana.'

'It is little changed,' Hellé reported. 'He is easier in
his mind and his breathing is lighter at nights, but
otherwise he still suffers from his sore throats and
coughing fits. If he exerts himself he is quickly breathless. But perhaps that is due to the altitude?'

She looked at the doctor. His face was set and she
could tell what he was about to say.

'I believe you are not at such an altitude that it should
have any effect,' he replied. He closed his folder and
placed it upon his desk.

'Have you noted, Mrs Flecker, any other changes in
your husband? Not necessarily in his physical health.
In his behaviour, perhaps? In his peace of mind?'

Outside, the sun blazed down. From the street below
she could hear the call of a tinker and the jingle of
harness.

'He is happier,' she said at length. 'At least, I believe
so. He seems at peace with himself, although he is
worried about his pending examinations.'

'Is that so? I had heard . . .'

Hellé smiled gently and stared at her hands.

'Perhaps, in the secrecy of the surgery, the truth may
come out,' she said. 'In fact, he cares not for his examinations. His future hangs by them but he seeks to escape
his job . . .'

'He is writing?'

'Oh, yes!' she exclaimed, her face rising and filled
with an almost girlish excitement. 'He writes every day,
sometimes for hours on end: his poetry, his articles and

his letters. He is translating much from the French. His own poetry is so very good, too. The ideas just seem to pour from him . . .'

Just speaking of his writing made her happier; yet when she gazed into the doctor's face it was apparent he was not sharing in her joy. If anything, he was alarmed.

'I see.' He paused. 'How long has this new wave of creativity been in evidence? A year? A month?'

'Ever since I returned from Paris.' She thought for a moment, then corrected herself. 'No, since my husband left me in Paris. He concentrated on his writing in my absence. When I came out he was able to show me much work. He's completed his novel and is now preparing a new book of poems.'

'I see,' the doctor repeated pensively. 'And since you moved to Brumana?'

'All the more so.'

The doctor sat in a leather armchair beside his desk. From his waistcoat pocket protruded the red rubber tubes of his stethoscope and the silvered handle of a tongue depressor.

'Mrs Flecker, I will be quite blunt with you. Your husband has consumption.'

The very mention of the word made her feel suddenly weakened: it was as if someone unseen had drawn a cold steel blade down her spine.

'It has developed from his chest ailments,' the doctor continued. 'He has weak lungs and should never have come to this climate. It has aggravated his condition very severely. I can only suggest you begin to take steps to leave the Lebanon – indeed, the Middle East – altogether. I would strongly advise you seek to gain your husband's admission to one of the sanatoria in Switzerland which specialise in the cure of such diseases. They do wonders there. Might I suggest you consider

Leysin? I can give you a solid recommendation to a hotel and doctor there capable, I feel, of being most admirably suitable.'

For a whole minute she sat quite still. She was not really concentrating upon what the doctor was saying and yet his every word registered in her mind.

'How long do you . . .' she began.

'One simply cannot tell. Some months, perhaps. Maybe a year or two. Of course, it is possible for a complete cure to be effected in Switzerland. It will be necessary for your husband to remain away from any hot and dusty climate . . .'

The doctor leaned forward, his hand resting on Hellé's. It was warm and dry. She studied it for a moment, the light brown hairs and the dark veins running just under the skin, the trimmed, square nails and the signet ring on the little finger.

'I must say, Mrs Flecker, I fear . . . When a consumptive reaches the further stages of the course of the disease, his senses seem to become heightened, his abilities of perception increase and expand. It is as if the mind is preparing for the glories of the next world.'

Hellé felt the tears stinging her eyes and, fumbling in her bag, found a handkerchief with which she dabbed at her cheeks.

'I am sorry, Mrs Flecker, but I must say I think it is imperative your husband leave Beirut at the earliest convenient moment. There is little time to be wasted.'

The horse was old and not really up to the journey to Brumana. The carriage rattled and creaked and the driver, though he did his best to coax all the speed he could from the animal, was adamant, as they entered the beginning of the Beirut River valley, that the drive would take over three hours.

She waved her hand at him dismissively and said, '*Eh bien!* Very well. Do your best.'

For the entire journey she tried in vain to think logically of the problems ahead. They would be losing his salary. He would have to resign his post and thereby forfeit his £500 bond. His health was poor and worsening by the day. The Swiss treatment, though deemed effective, was expensive. She could not borrow from her mother and she could not consider attempting to borrow yet more money from his parents to whom they were already deeply obligated: even if the money was not expected to be repaid, there was at least a considerable moral debt there.

She had her jewellery. It would not fetch a great deal but it would provide some money. There was the house in Athens – still unsold – and she wondered if she might be able to obtain a loan against it.

And there was always his writing. His novel might sell better than expected and provide an income in royalties. His verse might also start to receive greater notice; after all, his more recent poems were quite the best he had written.

It was then she remembered the doctor's words – that those in the last stages of consumption had their awareness heightened beyond everyday conceptions. His poems, she thought, were the last bright rays of his life.

The room was in total darkness. She reached for the light switch and was about to depress the little brass knob on the end of its stalk when an awful dread struck her. She stopped her hand, her fingers gripping the switch, and listened. It was silent in the room. Nothing stirred, not so much as a cockroach, not so much as a dropping petal.

One day, she thought, she would come to their room like this and he would be dead. He would be lying on the bed, his head to one side on the pillow, one hand resting over his body, the other flung out and holding a sheet of paper – like the painting of the dead Chatterton, the boy poet cut down by death before his time.

A noise interrupted her train of thought. It was a faint hissing.

She switched on the light.

Flecker was prostrate in the chair by the desk. His arms hung by his sides and his legs were splayed before him. His eyes were shut, his face was ashen and, in the glaring central light hanging from the ceiling rose, his flesh was tinged with grey. His breathing was shallow and slow.

'Roy!' she almost shrieked.

He opened his eyes.

'My Pussy!' he muttered, barely audible. 'You've been so long . . .'

She put her arms under his own and tried to help him to his feet. He was a dead weight. She struggled to get him to the bed and when he was lying down she rushed to the wash-basin and soaked her handkerchief in water, rubbing his face with it.

'You've been so long,' he repeated.

'The carriage was slow. The horse was old and the driver was unable to use the whip on him. He found every hill a terrible struggle and it took nearly four hours. I left the city at half-past two . . .'

She prattled on, conscious that she was saying nothing, afraid of a silence coming between them.

'I went for a walk,' he admitted weakly. 'Along the road.'

'When?'

'After luncheon . . .'

'That was exceedingly foolish of you. The air is less

bracing in the middle of the day and it was' – she spoke passionately and angrily like a mother infuriated with a miscreant child – 'sheer folly. You have been told not to go out in the sun like that.'

Her chiding failed to disguise her true emotions.

'My Pussy is angry with me,' he pouted, his face crestfallen in imitation of a child's.

'Tigers do not,' she said emphatically, 'go out in the heat of the day. They lie in the shade like lions and wait until dusk. It's at night they go on the prowl.'

'Do we prowl tonight?' he asked, struggling to raise himself on his elbows.

'We shall see,' she answered in an aloof and teasingly mocking tone. 'Tigers who don't do as they are told are locked up in their cages . . . .'

She kissed him then on his forehead. The skin was burning with fever and his hair smelled of the dust of the roads.

'I wrote a poem,' he confessed proudly.

'Is it enough that you risk your health – frail as it is – for a poem?'

'For this one, yes – it was.'

He pointed to the table and she crossed the room.

It was written out on a single sheet of paper. There were few corrections to it; it was as if he had written it virtually word-perfect from the start.

'It's called "Brumana",' he said, 'after this place. It's about some pine trees that prompted me to remember . . .'

She began to read but then sat in the chair he had vacated, and just gazed at the opening lines:

> Oh shall I never never be home again?
> Meadows of England shining in the rain . . .

'Oh, Roy!' she said gently.

*

That evening, his strength sapped by his walk, Flecker fell to sleep soon after he had drunk the cup of beef tea Hellé had had sent up to him in their room.

She dined alone, paying little attention to her food, picking at it and moving it around the plate until it was cold. The maître d'hôtel approached her, a worried expression on his face, but she assured him the meal was perfectly all right; it was just that she was not hungry.

At nine o'clock she stepped on to the hotel terrace and settled into a chair left outside by another guest. A waiter brought her a glass of chilled Chablis which she sipped periodically.

Her thoughts were less confused now than they had been in the carriage and she began to formulate a plan. First, she would go to see Cumberpatch with Flecker's resignation from his Vice-Consulship, pointing out that he was leaving the service through ill-health. She would, additionally, request a disability settlement. Second, she would visit the Thomas Cook office in Beirut and see what the availability was for passage to Naples or Marseilles. At the same time Flecker would write to all his contacts, informing them of his resignation and the reasons for it, and requesting their assistance. She was certain someone would help them: there was Hogarth, of whom her husband said little, Edward Marsh and Rupert Brooke, Harold Monro and Goschen, the publishers. Perhaps, she considered, Lawrence could do something; he might have friends in Oxford who could work for her husband, get him a junior teaching post in the university. And, she went on thinking, her spirits rising by the minute, they had so many irons in the fire – the teaching agency, the university appointments board. That he was consumptive would militate against him obtaining a schoolmastering position, but once he was cured that would be no obstacle.

333

By the time she had drunk her glass of wine Hellé felt pleased. There was a way, she was sure of it. Matters would work out for the better. On hearing footsteps behind her, she half turned in the chair. If it was the waiter, she decided, she would order another glass of wine before retiring. It would help her sleep.

On the terrace stood Flecker. His hair was dishevelled, and his collarless shirt, some of the buttons unfastened, was only tucked in on one side of his trousers. His fly was open, his feet bare. His eyes were staring.

'Hellé,' he whispered.

'Roy!'

She did not know what to say.

'Hellé,' he said again, his voice husky and grating. 'I . . .' He sucked loudly, his chest trying to expand but little air entering it. 'I can't . . .'

The maître d'hôtel appeared, summoned by an indignant guest who assumed a drunk had gained access to the public rooms.

'Disgraceful!' the complainant loudly commented as the maître d'hôtel walked towards Flecker.

For his part, Flecker was standing erect, weaving slightly as if about to lose his balance, fighting to stay vertical. Hellé was frozen in her chair.

'Sir!' the maître d'hôtel began, placing his hand firmly on Flecker's shoulder. 'I must ask you, sir . . .'

Flecker seemed about to collapse under the weight of the hand upon him. He did not crumple to the floor but seemed to shrink.

The complainant, an Englishman in his late fifties, a merchant from Beirut, rushed forward to help the maître d'hôtel who was propping Flecker up.

'. . . breathe,' Flecker gasped.

Together, the two men carried Flecker between them through the lobby and up the stairs to his room. Hellé followed them with slow, measured steps; already, in her mind, she was following the cortège.

His bed-sheets were sodden with sweat, his pillow stained with saliva. They laid him on the bed and departed, the maître d'hôtel having smoothed the sheets flat and replaced the pillow-cases with clean ones from the hallway cupboard, the merchant apologising for the fifth or sixth time for his assumption that Flecker was inebriated.

'No, he is just a very sick man,' Hellé explained, 'and, please, there is nothing to apologise for.'

When she got into the bed the damp patches of perspiration were cold to the touch: goose-pimples rose on her thighs and arms. As she drifted into sleep beside him, Flecker moved his hand and, finding hers, gently held it, his fingers interlocking with her own.

Flecker was shown from the room; as he left, he cast a glance at her which she read as neither worried nor questioning – it was merely submissive. He was yielding, she believed, to what he knew to be the inevitable.

'I'll be down in just a moment, dearest,' Hellé said. 'Just a word about myself . . . Nothing to be concerned about. A little woman's matter . . .'

Flecker nodded slowly, falteringly. His mouth opened but no words came out.

The door closed behind him and neither she nor the doctor spoke until the sounds of his footsteps had diminished.

'It is utterly imperative that your husband leave Beirut at the earliest opportunity. I was more than concerned at our last meeting but I am now gravely anxious. Not a day may be lost. You must book passage on the first available vessel. I shall telegraph ahead to Leysin . . .'

She shook the doctor's hand and thanked him for

having looked after her husband, her voice tremulous.

'You will need much courage, Mrs Flecker. I believe you will find it. In the end, I am sure it will all be for the better.'

As she reached the door, but before she opened it, the doctor spoke again.

'One last point. It is a crucial aspect of the treatment that your husband not be frightened or depressed. Keep up his spirits at all times. His state of mind is as important a part of the cure as the mountain airs.'

When she reached Flecker, waiting for her in the carriage, he anxiously asked her, 'Are you all right?'

'Yes, quite,' she replied, trying to be cheery. 'And so are you. We are leaving Beirut as quickly as we can.'

Brumana,
Beirut,
Lebanon.

Dear Ned,

I am so sorry.

My wretched illness has forced me to leave Beirut for ever and ever. The doctor demands it.

I feel I have let you down, let DGH and RAF down, let the side down. Isn't that a typical admission of a public schoolboy?

We sail in a few days – 19 May, to Genoa. Hellé has got us on an Italian steamer. From there we go to Leysin (Switz.) where I am to take the cure.

I have written to DGH to explain it all. No doubt Cumberpatch will write too.

Even my pen is still at present. But not, I pray, for long.

Your loving Roy.

Leaning on the polished wooden rail, Flecker watched as the steam launch chugged its way back to the shore, its wake white and its plume of gouted smoke from the short, brass funnel drifting off to the south.

'At last,' he said quietly. 'We are rid of Beirut at last.'

Hellé gripped his hand firmly, as if he were a child and he might slip overboard.

'No,' she promised, 'we shall not again visit this land.'

After a moment's hesitation, he said, 'I shall miss it. There are its beauties: the cedar trees and the rock roses in the mountains. Areiya was beautiful, wasn't it?'

She nodded. The ship, as if in affirmation, sounded its steam siren, the booming clarion call echoing over the sea.

Somewhere in his memory Flecker heard another ship's horn and a distant voice came to him, asking, 'You'll be coming up to Carchemish? I've a little jaunt we might go on together . . .'

And somewhere on the shore was the café and the table at which they had sat and, to the right, was Ras-esh-Shamiyeh where they had walked together.

'I wrote some fine poetry here. Some damn fine poetry. I made a few friends. I met Lawrence . . .'

Another blast from the hooter interrupted him.

'You will write much better poems in the cool air of the Alps,' she assured him.

No sooner had she spoken than the irony of her statement struck her: the better his poetry became, the nearer to death he would be.

The anchor chain was up and the ship, imperceptibly, was getting under way. She looked at him and smiled. He turned to her, his face solemn and drawn. Then he faced the shore again and stood gazing at it as it began gradually to shift and move astern.

At sea, off Tyre.

Dear Hogarth,

You will, I am sure, have received word from our Consul in Beirut and, I trust, my own letter sent in the bag.

Please forgive the brevity of this letter. I am writing en route to Alexandria and am not myself in body although, in spirit, I feel buoyed up with optimism and anticipation.

I have handed over all business to Fontana in Aleppo.

It is fortunate that nothing of any significance is pending. The last delivery went off smoothly and I have had word from Lawrence that he received it and it has been passed on with no problem. Another three crates are on their way from Enfield but I have succeeded in having these diverted to Cairo to await your instructions.

Once again, I cannot say how much I regret having let you down.

Quite what the future holds for me now I cannot say. Any assistance you can arrange over helping me to meet my financial obligations will be greeted at this end with much gratitude.

Please forgive my writing. My hand is somewhat shaky and it is an effort to write.

Yours,
J. E. Flecker.

PS: I shall ensure this letter reaches you through official channels in Egypt.

For three hours the steam derricks rattled and hissed and clanged over his head. Stevedores and deck-hands shouted orders, bellowing at cross purposes in Arabic, French and Italian, while the din of cargo loading into the holds reverberated through the ship.

Flecker dozed fitfully, the porthole wide open, Hellé glad they had a cabin which did not look over the dock. If that had been the case they would have had to keep the thick glass oval tightly shut as a precaution against pole-fishers. However, by mid-day the heat in their cabin grew stifling. Flecker could not breathe and Hellé, worried to her wits' end by his wheezing, turned for help to the only passenger with whom she had spoken, an American missionary who shared her table in the dining saloon. He was not, he stressed, a medical man but he suggested Flecker stay ashore for the duration of the ship's stop in port: perhaps, he suggested, they might stay in an hotel.

'I fear we cannot afford it,' Hellé admitted, close to tears. 'We have only just enough money to get us to Switzerland. My husband is going for the cure . . .'

The American silenced her with a kindly and compassionate smile.

'It would be my great honour, madam, if you would permit me to pay for your stay in the hotel. I'm sure the Lord would not mind my utilising some of His wealth in such a cause of charity.'

Hellé began to demur but the missionary would hear nothing of it and he immediately arranged for a carriage.

Once at the hotel, only a few minutes' drive from the dock, Hellé called for a doctor. Shortly afterwards there arrived a young Englishman dressed in an immaculate white tropical suit and carrying a brown Gladstone bag. He rapidly examined Flecker and placed a thermometer under his tongue; he had to leave it there for three minutes, for Flecker's gasping threatened to upset the reading. At last he removed it and studied the mercury.

'One hundred and five point eight!' he exclaimed. 'A serious fever. I must advise you to consider disembarkation. I am frankly dubious of the wisdom of continuing on your voyage. You are under a great pressure of trauma at present and to further exacerbate your condition . . .'

Flecker lifted his hand to the doctor's sleeve.

'If I . . . as a poet,' he said weakly, 'were to use such words, I should never again see the light of print.'

339

The doctor laughed.

'Very well. I speak in professional riddles,' he acknowledged, 'but I'm no poet. In plain truth, Mr Flecker, you are far too ill to travel.'

'We must,' Hellé said flatly.

'That's as may be. But I believe . . .'

'If my fever drops,' Flecker asked, 'will I then be able to return to my journey?'

The doctor grudgingly agreed.

'In that case,' Flecker said with determination, 'I shall see that my temperature drops.'

The doctor gave Flecker a sleeping draught, refused a fee for his call and, as he left, handed Hellé several vials of murky brown liquid, stressing upon her the exact dosage. She returned to the room and surreptitiously put these in her handbag, but Flecker spied her doing so.

'What's that?' he enquired.

'Medicine.'

'What medicine?'

'Something to ease your pain and the oppression when we return on board.'

'What is it?'

She made no answer.

'What is it?' he insisted.

'Laudanum.'

He grinned feebly. 'I shall write good poems with that,' he retorted softly. 'Lots of reds and royal blues and golds, like Coleridge . . .'

He drifted suddenly into sleep and Hellé, relieved that at last he was resting, fell into a fitful sleep herself in the chair at the foot of his bed.

With every violent movement of the ship his limp body shifted in his bunk. She had tried to cushion him with pillows brought by the steward but these presented another problem. In his delirium his head kept rolling to one side, and she was afraid he might be smothered.

The strong opiate helped him. She diluted it with more port wine and it eased his discomfort but, when he was not fully asleep, it also increased his ramblings. He slid or half-rolled as the ship ploughed through the storm, speaking in a gruff voice, sometimes strident and dictatorial and at others soft and wheedling.

Some of what he said she understood: 'Line three, verse two . . . change it to "sorrow" . . . oh! Sorrow be good to me . . . is that you, Raff? . . . the mound at Carchemish is a Hittite city . . . Have you seen the Little Shrine?' At times, however, he was incoherent, mumbling and working his mouth as if in agony. Several times he ground his teeth together or clenched his jaw, every muscle in his neck striated as if he were suddenly an old man. Once he tried to sit up and almost shouted out, '*Onzor! Bir! Iki! Üç! Yirmi besh! Yirmi besh!*'

She kept his temperature down with ice-cubes from the ship's cold room and, at all times, she ensured the swivelling ventilator over his head directed its blast of air upon his face. For some days she barely slept at all herself, fighting to keep awake with cups of coffee and beef sandwiches heavily laced with Colman's mustard.

In transit – Genoa,
Italy.

Dear Ned,

I recall little of the voyage from Alexandria to Naples. In Egypt I fell very ill, was taken like a member of the aristocracy to the best hotel in the city – on the corniche, no less! – paid for by a kindly passer-by on life's long road – and attended by a doctor with a penchant for elongated diction. His middle name was hyperbole. He gave me laudanum and I had wonderful dreams across the Med. I came on deck when we hove to off Catania and lay like an invalid in a deck-chair. It was so good to see Civilisation's Shores once more!

By Naples, I felt – comparatively speaking – quite restored and we went ashore to the Gambrinus and had a real bean-feast. The food on board the ship wasn't bad but it can be monotonous. Not that I saw much of it! The restaurant was more a treat for Hellé than it was for me.

Merely inhaling Dante's air has sparked my spirits. I feel ready now to go to Leysin and get well quickly.

As you can see, we are at present in Genoa, having taken a fortnight to get thus far from Beirut. It seems like an aeon. From here – tomorrow – we go by train through the Simplon tunnel to Aigle in the Rhône valley, and then by funicular to Leysin.

I am still very weak, tire easily and cough a lot.

Just before Genoa, we sailed past Leghorn. I thought of Shelley burning on the beach there, like a beacon through time lighting my way. Morbid!

I will write again from the heights of Switzerland and health.

Remember me, do, to Dahoum.

Your loving Roy.

The main street was thronged with invalids. They appeared to outnumber the seemingly healthy by at least two to one. Those not confined to bath chairs walked with slow, deliberate steps, their faces to the ground as if, Flecker thought, they were playing the pavement game – step on a crack and a bear will come out and get you. Except, in their cases, it would not be a bear but an angel of death. Before the many small hospital buildings – more like large private houses – and châlets lining the way from the funicular terminus were row upon row of beds or divans on which lay, for the most part, children. They were well bundled up against the cold air in mufflers, rugs and blankets, mittens on their hands, their peaky faces stark against the gaudy patterns of their coverings. They watched the newly arrived sick disembark from the funicular and move towards the town centre in search of accommodation. Flecker noted, with a chill in his spirits to match that in the air, that few people seemed to be taking the funicular down the mountain and of those who were queuing to board it none was ill.

'Perhaps they are all cured,' Hellé remarked in reply to his observation. 'Some people are sure not to be lucky enough to return, but they are those whose disease is far worse than yours. Many of these people have bad blood, complaints of the bone and marrow, diseases of the brain and nerves. You have but a weakness to strengthen rather than a disease to eradicate. You, my darling Tiger,' she finished imperiously, 'are not in the same class.'

'Perhaps they are,' he answered, echoing her opening words but without her optimism.

By the time Flecker arrived at the Hôtel Belvédère he was depressed and moody and checked in to the hotel – it was so-called although it was in truth a rest-home-cum-hospital – with a look of apprehension and bewilderment on his face which considerably upset Hellé. Conscious of the Beirut doctor's parting words, she succeeded in disguising her emotions.

'Just a few months from now,' she said lightly as Flecker's cases were placed in his room, 'and we shall be in England. Your book will be in all the shops and we shall be so busy looking for a new job for you that all this will be just a bad dream.'

'Nightmare,' he retorted sullenly.

'At the end of every night comes the dawn.'

'All my dawns are going to be bleak midwinter ones. I'm going to spend the next umpteen weeks waking alone. How do they expect anyone to get fit here without a ray of love in their life?'

'We shall have that. I promise . . .'

She left him then – for the Belvédère did not accommodate healthy 'guests' – and began her search for rooms, finding a vacancy in a cheap boarding-house at the other end of the town. She was obliged to secure the least expensive lodgings possible, for the tariff in the Belvédère was one of the highest in Leysin: she had decided before they left Beirut that Flecker was going to get the best service and cure possible.

The routine of the Belvédère was not what Flecker had expected. The patients were allowed to do as they pleased. If they wished, they could leave for a walk about the small town, go to one of the small local restaurants or cafés, stroll into the surrounding woods and hills. They were obliged to be present in their rooms every day at a set hour to be visited by their doctor who, in a tender but detached way, examined them, asked after their health over the previous twenty-four hours and usually passed some comment of mild encouragement. He dispensed no drugs, save for minor ailments – the main medicine of the place was the air, not what might be poured from a bottle. His most important elixir was his encouragement.

Flecker spent his mornings in the hotel loggia set aside for those residents undergoing open-air treatment. He sat in the bright sunlight and read or corrected the proofs of his new poetry collection which had reached him some weeks before.

Sometimes he just lay back and relaxed, his limbs growing almost weightless, his mind drifting away in disconnected thoughts.

Every daydream was like a long sequence of poem fragments: Cheltenham and the Cotswolds or the hills of the Lebanon, the pines of Bournemouth and Brumana, the sand-dunes near Poole Harbour and those near Carchemish, the Thames and the Euphrates, Syria and Surrey . . . People came to him in his quiet reveries

– Lawrence and Hogarth, Dahoum and Brooke, Marsh and Monro, his mother and Hellé's. And words jumped up at him, neatly typed out as if he were watching them pumping from the platen of a typewriter. Some he recognised and some he did not.

Hellé and he spent the afternoons together. They talked or rambled about Leysin for the first few days, but after that they simply sat side by side and read or relaxed. After the tribulations of Beirut Hellé savoured the luxury of doing nothing.

The frequency of Flecker's coughing fits reduced somewhat. They did not cease, but they racked him less, and although he was still weak he believed himself to be gaining in strength. His letters to his parents and friends brimmed with optimism. To Lawrence he wrote that he was soon to be fighting fit again, ready to 'take on every Hun in Persia and demolish their arrogant schemes'; to his parents he was immensely better but still weak; to Marsh he admitted his health had broken down in Beirut but that he was spending the summer in Leysin where, after but a week, the 'marvellous air' had set him 'well on the way to convalescence'; to Brooke he barely mentioned his illness – he could get news of that inconvenience from Marsh – and wrote primarily of his hopes for his new book of verse and the fate to befall *Hassan*.

Hellé worried secretly about their finances but even this burden was soon lifted. Flecker's parents telegraphed they would pay the sanatorium fees; the Foreign Office put him on half-pay for three months pending a medical board assessment in August; Hogarth wrote to say 'matters of a fiscal nature are in hand' and he was not to worry. Even the threat of the Turkish examinations was removed in a letter saying these would now be dropped from consideration in any appraisal of Flecker's future career prospects. Similarly, in view of his financial situation, Their Lordships waived the matter of the bond.

With such anxieties removed, Flecker began, for the first time since they had left Beirut, to concentrate hard on his writing again. On 5 June he and Hellé walked to the small post office in Leysin and mailed off the proofs of his book.

'*The Golden Journey to Samarkand,*' he said proudly, as Hellé stuck the stamps on the package. 'I think it sounds so fine.'

'It is!' she assured him, joyful in her mind that this piece of encouragement was not merely part of the prescription for his treatment. 'It's the best book you've written yet.'

With his anxieties removed and Hellé's approval of his work, Flecker's spirits soared.

12
Switzerland:
June – September 1913

Distant thunder rumbled in the mountains to the east,
beyond Col de la Croix and over the peaks of Les
Diablerets, shrouded in a mantle of ominously dark
clouds and reverberating with each dull clap.

All night the storm had hung over the mountains,
occasional jags of lightning illuminating the slopes.
Flecker had spent much of the night sitting at his open
window watching the display, his emotions a mixture
of peace and exhilaration. There was something so
powerful in the storm and yet, at the same time, strangely amicable. He believed that if he were to walk far
into the Alps, stand beneath the storm clouds with his
head bare and his arms outstretched like a Christ, no
harm would come to him. In fact, he felt, if the lightning
were to strike him it could rid him of his illness, clear
his whole body in one massive, tingling bolt of heavenly
electricity, leave him vibrant and alive.

In the morning the mountains still loomed sinisterly
under grey clouds, but Lac Léman to the north-west
was bathed in sunlight. It was as if Switzerland, the
home of the chronically ill, were in the grey twilight of
sickness whilst the mountains of France were in the
glow of health.

'Paradise and purgatory,' Flecker remarked as Hellé
joined him at the Belvédère.

'What do you mean, dearest?'

'You said Leysin was another cycle for Dante to add

to his tales of the Inferno. Today it is. The mountains are in dismal hell and the plains are paradise. Old Nick's grumbling away up in the peaks.' He waved his hand dismissively in the direction of the valley leading to the Col du Pillon. 'Over there. Hades above the earth.'

She laughed. 'He's far enough off,' she decided. 'He won't bother us.'

'I'm in his bloody desmesne, though,' Flecker retorted, his voice suddenly glum and bitter. 'They say Switzerland is a land of cuckoo clocks. So it is. They squawk out their count of hours remaining . . . It's a home for invalids. Look at them.'

Around the hotel loggia were lying or sitting the immobile patients. Their pained or bleak, blanched faces showed that they were those with few days of life remaining.

'You aren't one of them,' Hellé said quietly.

'You know what they call this place? God's Waiting Room. It's just an ante-room to the everlasting here-after.'

'You aren't going to be here for long. Does one not only pass through purgatory? You're just in a state of limbo, dear Tiger.' She took his hand and held it tightly. 'You are not waiting, you're passing through. Come, let's take our constitutional.'

They left the hotel and strolled through the town to the top of the steep hillside from which they could gain a good view of the eastern end of Lac Léman. The thunder continued but the clouds rolled back as they walked, bathing the mountainside and the pines in sun.

'Do you know what I did last night?' he asked.

She shook her head and, letting go of his hand, placed her fingers on his shoulder.

'I wrote. The first true poem since Brumana.'

She stopped abruptly. He did not, and her hand fell from his shoulder.

'Roy, that's wonderful!' she exclaimed. 'Quite, quite wonderful! You see, you *are* getting better.'

'I am.' There was a powerful confidence in him. His eyes were bright, like a child's, wide with amazement and realised pleasure. 'I'm sure of it. Certain! I feel stronger. My bones feel tougher, my blood races. I feel alert and vital. I'm sure I'm improving. The air here does do me good.'

'A new poem! You must show it to me.'

'It's for you.' He took a folded piece of paper from his coat and held it out to her. 'You thought I had forgotten.'

'Forgotten what?' she enquired, accepting the paper and unfolding it.

'Today,' he said. 'Your birthday, my sweet little Pussy. This is for your birthday. What else can I give you?'

Her fingers ceased unfolding the paper and she smiled sadly. Her lips quivered. He stood next to her and put his arm about her, standing before her and blocking out the sunlight from her face.

'Don't!' he whispered. 'There's nothing to cry about. And it is a good poem, too. It has no title yet. Just "For Hellé" . . . Read it.'

But she did not hold back from crying, her shoulders twitching with each sob, her hands folded against her breasts, pushed there by his closeness.

'You read it, Roy,' she said finally, her words coming in short gasps.

He took the sheet of paper back from her and they walked slowly on, keeping to the side of the mountain. Above were steep slopes going up to sheer rock; below were trees and the Rhône valley and the distant, shimmering lake.

I have seen old ships sailing; still alive
On those blue waters lilied by the seas
That still can tell the caverned Cyclades
The charm which heartened Peleus to his dive
That day he left his tower upon the coast
And drove right down across the darker swell
His ivory body flitting like a Ghost
And past the holes where the eyeless fishes dwell
Found his young mother thronèd in her shell.

He looked at her, but Hellé was walking with her face
averted, looking out over the valley to the French mountains and the western sky.

And all these ships were old,
Painted the mid-sea blue or deep sea green,
And patterned with the vine and grapes in gold.
But I have seen
Pointing her shadow gently to the west
And imaged fair upon her mirror bay
A ship a little older than the rest
And fading where she lay.
Who knows. In that old ship – but in that same
(Fished up beyond Phracia, patched as new
and painted brighter blue)
With patient comrades sweating at the oar
That talkative, unskilful seaman came
From Troy's fire-crimson shore
And with loud lies about his Wooden Horse,
Wrapped in his eloquence, forgot his course,
It was so old a ship – who knows – who knows,
It was so beautiful – I watched in vain
To see its mast split open with a rose,
And all its timbers burst to leaf again.

She propped the poem against the mirror in her tiny
room at the boarding-house. About her, on the floor,
were stacked the cases and trunks in which were stored
the possessions they had brought from Beirut. The

brightly coloured baggage labels from their voyages across the Mediterranean seemed almost to mock her. She had sorted all the luggage through and removed only the barest of essentials for their everyday use. The remainder would have to wait until settled times, and England.

For the third time she read the poem through, her lips mouthing the words. In the mirror above the page she could see her eyes, red with weeping.

She did not look at her reflection, turning her face aside as soon as she caught sight of herself, as if she were embarrassed by her appearance.

'I mustn't cry again in front of him,' she told herself once more. 'I mustn't. I simply must not.'

She folded the poem and slipped it into her leather writing compendium, placing it safely in the document pocket which had a securing flap.

The poem safe, she brushed her hair and wiped her eyes, rinsed her face in the wash-basin and lightly applied some make-up to her cheeks before going down to supper in the cramped dining room where the talk was always of the weather and the state of the franc, the recovery of the other guests' dying relatives and lives lived far away from Leysin.

> Hôtel Belvédère,
> Leysin-sur-Aigle,
> Switzerland.
> 1 August

My dear Ned,

It is high time I wrote you a proper letter, not one filled with miseries and disjointed phrases, garbles and gabbles. Ever since I arrived here I have been in a state of inner bedlam, thinking one thing one minute and one thing the next. But now . . . That's all behind me!

I am in fine fettle, finer than I've felt since I left those ragged shores of Lebanon. Indeed, looking across the mountains here, listening to the dull plonking of cow-bells and watching the clouds rise, expand and disappear like bad dreams, I feel I was born here. The air is crisp and cool and dry. When the sun shines it is bright and cool, a searching light rather than an all-consuming one. After the Levant, I understand what those Scottish Presbyterians mean by fire and brimstone!

And, Ned, I'm writing again. Poems. And ideas crowd in on me. I have had notions for short stories and songs – even, maybe, another novel. And my books are coming along. The proofs of *Golden Journey* went back long ago and – lo and behold – now I have the finished article and am sending you a copy under separate cover. It does look good. The publisher has done a wonder with it and I pray it will do well. There have – I have my reports and spies out in London – been few reviews, but one in the *Globe* is good to topping even though the critic doesn't like a golden *journey* and would rather have a golden *road* – to which I may bow when I use the poem, as I intend, in the last act of *Hassan*. Which is not doing well, alas! I cannot get a theatre interested in it at all.

But so what, when I'm writing again? Not a lot. I wrote a pretty piece for Hellé on her birthday and am pleased with it beyond all measure. I've worked on it a bit and it is the finer for it. And I wrote some good stuff before we left Beirut.

One of these was a curious piece, even for me. It was prompted in my mind by a strange dream I had. The doctor had prescribed an opiate for me to calm my nerves and soothe my throat. It was a weak prescription but it gave me some wonderful reveries! One day I read through Daguerches' *Consolata Fille du Soleil*. I then saw a Chinese army leaving a city, the weird Oriental banners flying and the gold and scarlet robes of the Mandarins at the head of the column. The soldiers carried those bizarre pikes with curly blades and long sweeping scimitars like Kubla Khan. And from the walls of the city hung the bodies of the tortured, their blood as red as the Mandarins' silks and just as shiny. Their flesh was white as shrouds.

The dream gave me such a tingle of excitement! The colours were so bright, so real, as if the moving painting of the scene was not yet dry, the colours recently applied and the varnish fresh.

When I woke, I drafted the poem and worked upon it for several days. I cannot bring myself to not send you a version of it:

TAOPING

Across the vast blue-shadow-sweeping plain
The gathered armies darken through the grain,
Swinging curved swords and dragon-sculptured spears,
Footman, and tiger-hearted cavaliers.
Them Government (whose fragrance Poets sing)
Hath bidden break the rebels of Taoping,
And fire and fell the monstrous fort of fools
Who dream that men may dare the deathless rules.
Whom dire example even now can show
Where high before the Van, in triple row,
First fiery blossom of rebellion's tree,
Twelve spear-stemmed heads are dripping silently.
(On evil day you sought, O ashen lips,
The kiss of women from our town of ships,
Nor ever dreamt, O spies, of falser spies,
The poppied cup and passion-mocking eyes!)

By these grim civil trophies undismayed,
In lacquered panoplies the chiefs parade.
Behind, the plain's floor rocks: the armies come:
The rose-round lips blow battle horns: the drum
Booms oriental measure. Earth exults.
And still behind, the tottering catapults
Pulled by slow slaves, grey backs with crimson lines,
Roll resolutely west. And still behind,
Down the canal's hibiscus-shaded marge
The glossy mules draw on the cedar barge,
Railed silver, blue-silk-curtained, which within
Bears the Commander, the old Mandarin,
Who never left his palace gates before,
But hath grown blind reading great books on war.

Dreaming of Samarkand

Now level on the land and cloudless red
The sun's slow circle dips toward the dead.
Night-hunted, all the monstrous flags are furled:
The Armies halt, and round them halts the World.
A phantom wind flies out among the rice;
Hush turns the twin horizons in her vice;
Air thickens: earth is pressed upon earth's core.
The cedar barge swings gently to the shore
Among her silver shadows and the swans:
The blind old man sets down his pipe of bronze.
The long whips cease. The slaves slacken the chain.
The gaunt-towered engines space the silent plain.
The hosts like men held in a frozen dream
Stiffen. The breastplates drink the scarlet gleam.
But the Twelve Heads with shining sockets stare
Further and further West. Have they seen there,
Black on blood's sea and huger than Death's wing,
Their *cannon-bowelled* fortress of Taoping?

What do you think of this? I allow it isn't my greatest poem
yet, to be sure. I am critic enough to know it and man enough
to say it to myself. Yet I feel it is a fine fragment and I find I
so relate to it. It says so much of life, of us . . .

I miss so very much our opportunities to be together and
share adventures. And, dare I say it, share our love?

Love is such a strange and odd emotion. I love Hellé surely.
She has made me live as I never did before with her petting
and her – you know what! And yet I have such love for others.
There have been those others, too. Jack B., whom we both
knew and who is such a masterly poet should he turn his pen
that way . . .

And you.

How strange it is, sometimes, I think to myself, that we
men should love those of our sex. Not just like friends and
love as comrades but really love, want to feel the caresses
from, the kisses of. And the cuffs, in our case! And yet, there
again, is it so strange? Did not the Greeks love masculine
beauty? And the Romans? And do not still the Arabs with
their pretty boys? And you with yours?

How I sometimes – especially now I am here, like a coughing eagle in its eyrie – envy you both your safe closeness in the desert. If only I had been stronger. Not only my lungs and my arms, but myself, too. My soul, if you will.

I know it cannot ever be between us, save in words and poems . . . Casual glances across a room. (I dreamed the other night that we meet, decades hence, in an Oxford senior common room: me in my crusty gown and wing collar, looking like a dishevelled country parson, and you in yours with your muscles moving under the loose folds of black.) Yet that is enough. To know the love is there is just enough.

And Taoping!

I'm sure my own poppied cup helped the poem. And I think of your rose lip blowing on the battle horn. Perhaps on my battle horn before we muster for war. The war of love, maybe.

But I am rambling. And that is no good for a sick poet soon to be cured poet and schoolmaster in the shires. Ramble once and the boys know you for a fisherman after red herring. (I taught a little while, once. After coming down from Oxford: I was at Mill Hill which I hated and later in Yorkshire where they worked me like a pedagogic cart-horse. Did you know? I expect so . . .)

It is not just the colours in that poem. Looking through it now, to assure I make no blunders in the copying out, it is the sounds, too. The swish of the whips and the grunt of straining slaves.

In some ways, I am so like that Mandarin. Never left my palace, only know of war from books.

But I have been to battle with you. That night on the embankment returns to me sometimes, sets me all a shiver, I can tell you. *'Hast du etwas Ungewöhnliches in der Nähe gehört?'* and then *'Nein. Gar nichts. Vor fünf Minuten hab' ich einen Hund gehört.'* Thank the gods for dogs, eh, Ned! So much of our times together sets me all a-shiver.

It was such a wonderful game we played! Yet looking at it now from my high perch in the mountains I wonder on the morality of it all. I think I am now considering it as I never did in Beirut.

Hogarth's grand game and we the pieces, eh? Beat the

Germans at their railway, queer up the Frenchies' interests when the chance comes along. Arm the Arabs. And for what? In the end, aren't we doing what the Mandarin does? Laying waste? I wonder if, one day, we shan't inadvertently turn similarly against the Arab, side with the Frenchies or the Germans or the Jews or the Maronites or whoever it pleases us to foster in friendship.

Politics is a funny business. I think, now I am away from it, it was one of the reasons I so despised the work as a VC. I never really understood it. Not really. It always seemed so underhand somehow. Immoral, almost. Why knock the Frogs? They are our friends. And the Germans – the Kaiser himself is blood-related to HM The King. It's not as if they are bloody Bulgars seeking to stomp their heavy flat feet all over Greece.

I know DGH regards it as a vital human activity. Diplomacy is for him a glorious chess match and the countries of the world are his squares.

Ha! Dear Ned, I ramble again.

Perhaps I should put it all into notes and make a novel. Strive at it, once I'm clear of sanatoria named as hotels, deathbeds called morning couches. Mourning, more like. I'm sure it would all make a most thrilling yarn.

What do you think?

Anyway, you can see from this long meander of waffle that I'm perking up no end. Every now and then I cough a bit but nothing like I did in Beirut. In a week or so, Hellé and I are going to set out on a few expeditions together. To Montreux, perhaps, on the lake.

This morning I watched the lake so far below and off some kilometres to the north west. The waters were as dark as . . . . Black on blood's sea, maybe? Huger than Death's wing which I am, I know, plucking bare – feather by feather. How I hear him scream as the flights come out to make my quills!

All my love, dear Ned,
Ever thine,
Roy.

Their favourite walk was one which took them beyond the point, on the outskirts of the alpine fields around

Leysin, from which they could first gain a wide panorama of the Rhône valley and the lake beyond. The mountain ridge running down from the peak of Tour d'Ai above Leysin towards the town of Aigle below was forested in conifers, with outcrops of rock appearing from time to time in the trees. A path from the edge of the fields followed the contour of the mountain round the ridge and into the small steep valleys beyond. It was seldom frequented and Flecker guessed it was an old track that had once joined Leysin with the hamlet of Corbeyrier half-way down the mountainside, fallen into disuse since the building of the funicular and the road.

The trees had been felled to form several clearings and in these spaces thrived patches of alpine flowers, their white and delicate faces bright in the afternoon sunlight. The rocks were patterned with lichens of deep mauve and royal red, garish yellow and sombre grey. In the shadows of the conifers flitted silent birds and, on occasion, Flecker fancied he saw the shadows of deer.

Because the path maintained the curve and lie of the land, there were few taxing climbs to be made and Flecker found the walk not in the least tiring. Convinced that the cure of Leysin was having its effect upon him, he insisted each day they venture further, the turning point on their walk being marked by a small cairn of pebbles he piled by the side of the path. Their next walk had to reach at least the marker of the last.

'Right!' he announced as they arrived at the pebble heap of the day before. 'You see, I am mending almost by the hour. This stack was reached with me quite breathless yesterday. Today' – he pushed his hands against his chest and pressed them in and out as if to bellow his lungs – 'I am no more breathless than I was when we set out.'

'Indeed, you're not wheezing in the least,' Hellé

357

agreed. 'And your cheeks are rosy as apples and your eye bright as a button.'

He smiled at her and kicked the pebbles, scattering them on the path and sending some spattering into the trees below.

'You sound like my mother,' he chided her. 'Or a nanny.'

'I heard your mother say . . . I wonder why buttons are bright.'

'Because they are made of mother-of-pearl and stand out against the black bodices of elderly ladies.'

She laughed. 'How much farther do you feel able to go today?'

'As far as the horizon,' he declared confidently. 'I shall set off from here and my next stone pile will be atop Leckhampton Hill. I may not arrive there today, I grant you, but I shall get there soon. And we shall no longer walk in the jagged, sharp mountains of Switzerland but on the curving hills of the Cotswolds, with the villages not huddling in the valleys like scared mice but curled like cats, purring with contentment.'

He took her hand and they continued along the path for some way before reaching a recent clearing. The stumps of the felled trees were still white and the shavings on the ground were fresh. He bent to pick up a handful and was reminded suddenly of the beautiful goatherd on the road between Brumana and Baabdat. They were tacky with semi-congealed sap; the goatherd's had been dry. He touched one of the stumps and the sap stuck to his fingers. When he smelled them the perfume was thick and resinous.

Beyond the clearing the path was almost indistinct. Evidently the foresters were its only regular traffic.

'Do you think we should go further?' Hellé asked cautiously. 'It might be dangerous.'

'Nonsense!' Flecker retorted. 'These old tried paths are as safe as houses. Let's press on.'

'Remember you have to go back. Your pile of pebbles, when you make it, marks only the day's half-way point.'

He ignored her and set off through the trees, pushing low hanging branches aside with his hands and holding them for her, breaking himself off a switch which he toyed with as he walked.

For ten minutes they walked along the path in the twilight of the conifer forest. Neither spoke. Small birds darted ahead of them but nothing else moved. They saw no direct sunlight, save the occasional prick through the canopy of the trees, until they reached an outcrop of rocks which led up the mountainside above them as far as they could see. At this point the path crossed what had once been a stone slide from high above, perhaps the site of a long-forgotten avalanche.

'I don't think we should go on,' Hellé said, looking at the path where it wound, barely visible, between some massive boulders.

'Very well,' Flecker acceded. 'But let's not return yet.'

He stepped off the path and climbed with an agility that surprised her to a rock twenty feet up.

'Do be careful, Roy!'

'It's flat here,' he announced, standing on the rock. 'It's a shelf of rock.' He waved his thin stick in the air, cutting an arc against the sky with it. 'I can see the whole wide world. Come up.'

She started to scramble over the stones, the leather soles of her shoes slipping.

'I can't.'

'Come on. Of course you can. If I can in my condition . . .'

He dropped his switch on the rock platform and came down the rock slide. Taking her wrist in his hand, he pulled her up, giving her instructions as to where to place her feet.

'Like a minuscule amphitheatre,' he remarked at last. 'A flat stage of rock with a horseshoe of boulders all round and . . .'

She had moved to the wall of rock at the rear of the platform, standing there and looking at her feet.

'Look at the view, Hellé. Have you ever seen anything like it?'

Across the valley rose the mountains of France, Dent d'Oche, Cornettes de Bise, Pic de Morcian. To the right lay Lac Léman and, in the far distance, Lausanne and the mountains beyond. To their left the Rhône ran narrowed by peaks and below them lay the river with narrow fields on the banks.

'Quite stunning,' she allowed, her voice quiet with terror. 'Let's sit. I am afraid to stand.'

They sat side by side, back from the lip of the platform, their spines against the rocks, and did not speak. After a while Flecker moved and lay down upon the stone, placing his hands beneath his head and closing his eyes against the sunlight.

'Shall we be getting back?' she suggested. 'We shouldn't be caught out in the darkness. It would be the end of us.'

'Can you think of a better way to die? To be at one with nature?'

She made no reply but put her hand on his arm.

'Besides,' he went on, 'it isn't that late. We can return in under an hour and it's more than an hour to the sun starting to touch the peaks.'

Gazing at the view before her, her hand resting on his arm still, she said softly, 'I love you, Roy. You will always remember that, won't you?'

'Of course.'

He blinked against the sunlight.

'You won't forget this when we are apart?'

'No'.

'And you will always love me, won't you, Roy?'

He sat up, taking her hand.

'What nonsense is this? You know I shall.'

He twisted around and knelt before her, kissing her cheek; her skin was cold and damp. He ran his other hand down her face, his fingers tickling her neck and then toying with the buttons of her blouse. He pushed his fingers between the folds in the material, worming in through her undergarments until he met the skin of her breasts.

'Not here, Roy'.

'Why not?'

'We may be seen . . .'

He laughed quietly and asked, 'By whom? Some chamois on an upper slope? An eagle riding the mountain air? I'd gladly be seen by an eagle.'

'What about people on the path?'

'Who?'

'Or looking up from the valley?'

It was then she remembered once kissing Petros on the mountain-top when she was fifteen, how he had said the summit was the safest place, for no one could see them. And how the electricity had sparked down her back!

'We are merely two small rocks from below and, in any case, who can see over the lip of the rock?' Flecker's words broke into her thoughts. 'Of course, the population of Lausanne can see if they all have star-gazing telescopes.'

She pushed his hand away and began to undo her own buttons.

'Then we shall be two stars,' she said with quiet determination.

When they were both naked, she asked, 'Do you really want me to?'

He nodded and lay upon his front on the stone. It was warm from the sun and he could feel the afternoon's warmth washing over his back, dissolving into his skin and warming his blood much as she would.

She rubbed the twigs and dried buds from the thin stick he had brought from the forest.

'Are you ready to growl, dear Tiger?'

He nodded again, stretching out his arms.

Now, she thought, he was entirely hers. There was no one else, no woman, no man, no boy.

At each tiny swish of the stick, at each sting upon his skin, he could see in his mind's eye Lawrence, Dahoum, the mound at Carchemish, the desert, the boots of the German engineer, the donkeys in the alleyway at Halfati, the cellar in the military post, the sailors coming ashore on the beach, the slaves pulling their machines of war across the plains before the city of Taoping. And into each smart the sun branded its warmth and his heart pumped harder and harder against the rock until he feared the whole mountain would shake with him.

The envelope bore three low denomination stamps. The postmark was smudged but Flecker could see it had been mailed in Aleppo. He slid his finger under the flap and tore impatiently at it. The writing paper within was yellowed as if it was an ancient parchment, the weave cracking where it had been folded against the grain of the water-mark. He tugged it flat and it split a little way along the crease.

Turning up the wick in the lamp and holding the letter in both hands as if it was not made of paper but of delicate porcelain, Flecker read it through rapidly. It was undated and bore no address:

362

Dear Roy,

I have your letter safely to hand. It came in one of the bags up from Beirut but a day or two ago.

Your poem 'Taoping' is a fine one and I think you belittle yourself admitting to its not being your greatest. In truth it is not, but it is not far short of it. Perhaps, as you allow, the medicines are aiding your muse.

Dahoum and I are struggling on. The weather at the site has been beastly – oppressively hot and with the sand blowing sometimes for hours on end.

Roy, you must not think so much of me. Or of the business in which we have plied our trades. Or the world in which we live. We are but a part of a huge order, a vast machinery which structures history, both our private one and that of all men. We cannot question it. Let your mind ignore these vexings.

Forgive my brevity. I've but a short moment in which to set my reply down. We head north again just after dawn. I shall post this en route to you. The embankment is finished, the bridge progressing at a steady rate.

I do trust that you are improving and that Hellé is well in the circumstances. It cannot be but hard on her to have to nurse your every whim. A sick poet is a demanding creature, I'll be bound.

> Yours,
> Ned L.

Flecker refolded the letter and slipped it back into its envelope. A huge void opened in his spirits and he felt hollowed out. Lawrence had hardly mentioned the poem or Flecker's concerns – love, sorrow, beauty, friendship: none was there.

He wondered if, in his answer back, he should again press home the thoughts, the love, the doubts he had proclaimed in the hope of eliciting Lawrence's perceptions; then it occurred to him that, perhaps, Lawrence had not received his long letter. In replying, his mind must have become muddled with another earlier letter. After all, he was busy, travelling about so much, having so much responsibility for the archaeological dig, for the spying. Yet no sooner had he formed this excuse for his friend than he realised this communication had mentioned the poem. There was no doubting that Lawrence's brief letter was a response to Flecker's much longer one.

He had so wanted a lengthy letter from Lawrence, more a discourse on his points, an exchange of views, a returning of his love even. He so missed the opportunity to talk with Lawrence, to simply be with him. And yet the reply he had received was blunt, bleak almost. It was as if he was speaking but the other was not listening, or found his words boring and demanding not so much attention as polite dismissal. What course of action he should take when next writing he did not know; he considered chastising Lawrence for his brevity, criticising him for his apparent rejection of his concerns, pleading with him as a lover might to be more forthcoming. Whichever option occurred to him seemed inappropriate and, in the end, he decided that he would himself put aside any thoughts on the letter and continue in his own writing as if he had not received it. A one-sided conversation, he thought bitterly, was better than a silence.

Turning over in his bed, Flecker pushed the letter under the volume of Paul Fort's verse which lay beside his tumbler of drinking water. Then he coughed and pressed his handkerchief to his mouth. As he took it away from his lips he dared not look at the linen to see what marks had appeared upon it.

For a while he studied his notes on Paul Fort. He had been toying with the idea of writing a critical study of the poetry and the more he read the more he believed Fort to be underestimated and unjustly ignored by the literary world. It was not that he was an unknown writer, simply that he was not as lauded as Flecker believed he should be.

His attention began to drift from his notes. He wanted to review them, re-assess his ideas, but he could not: the vision of Lawrence intruded upon him.

At last, his eyes tired and his throat rough, he put the sheets of notes down on the counterpane of his bed and lay back upon the pillow. He closed his eyes and was soon breathing heavily in a troubled sleep.

Just before midnight Hellé entered the room to see that Flecker was comfortable. He had slipped sideways on his pillow and his head was lolling to one side. A damp patch stained the pillow-case where he had dribbled saliva in his sleep. She moved him over towards the centre of the bed and he half-woke, snuggling down under the sheets which were damp and cool. She punched the pillow with her fist to loosen the down inside.

'Will you have a sip of water?' she asked him softly.

He shook his head and raised his hand upon the coverlet in a sign of refusal.

'I'll just tidy your notes,' she whispered, 'so that things are in order for you to start work in the morning.'

He grunted his acknowledgement and sighed. She knew he was once more asleep.

She dimmed the lamp, screwed the top back on to his fountain pen and shuffled the papers into a neat sheaf, lifting the book on the bedside table to use it to weigh them down. He liked to have his work at hand when he awoke. It was then she saw Lawrence's letter, recognising immediately the handwriting on the envelope.

How he had received the letter without her knowledge surprised her. She assumed that the maid must have given it to him during the morning when she was out and it was time for the bedroom to be cleaned.

Hellé leaned over the bed. Flecker was breathing

lightly but evenly. His eyelids flickered in response to a dream. His fingers twitched ever so slightly. Filled with misgivings, she took the letter out from the envelope. The writing was faint in the low lamplight but strong enough for her to read it without straining her eyes.

She had no idea of what Flecker had written to Lawrence; all she knew was that the letters he sent to his friend were bulky. He used up a lot of the writing paper pads in his correspondence to Lawrence and she could feel the size of the letters when she took them to the post office. However, reading between the lines of Lawrence's reply, she could guess what her husband had written. It was enough for her to see Lawrence's suggestion that Flecker think less of him, enough for her to sense the tone of the letter.

She put it back in the envelope and arranged it beneath the book of poetry just as she had discovered it. The sheaf of notes she put into the pages of the book.

As she left Flecker's sick-room, Hellé knew she had won and, as she undressed in her own tiny room, the chill night prickling her skin, remembered the walk they had so recently taken along the forest path. On that rock platform she had owned Flecker.

She examined her body in the looking-glass, twisting her hips from side to side, the shadow from the lamp accentuating her breasts, the dark notch of hair below her stomach, the curve of her buttocks. She pressed her hands along her belly and upwards, lifting her breasts. Two stars, she thought: she and Flecker were two bright stars in their own firmament.

What the battle had been exactly, she was not sure. It had been a fight for Flecker's affections, perhaps, or a struggle to assert herself: possibly, it had been a contest with Lawrence or with that in the world for which Lawrence stood, the masculine forces against which all women are perpetually in conflict. Yet, whatever the nature of their bout, she knew she was victorious, that now she had Flecker exclusively. The threat Lawrence had posed – either in reality or in her imagination – had passed.

Montreux

My dear Ned,

I feel very active. Eagerly restive and longing to get a move on with things. We have moved from Leysin down to Montreux – I was getting so depressed up there – and, after a few days at a *pension* at Territet (just outside Montreux) have shifted a kilometre or two to the Hôtel de Glion, Glion-sur-Montreux. It looks to be a most suitable habitation.

I came here once as a callow youth aged 19 and pondered my future at the place. The cycle has turned. The wheel of fortune has come around again and I'm back, ready to start another decade anew.

I'm doing so much! *Golden Journey* is faring well, I am told, and I have started to re-work my play – *Hassan*, in case you have forgotten. Have also begun a study of Paul Fort's poetry. It is high time he was brought to critical attention and gained thereby the publicity he so deserves.

I've even begun to re-write the National Anthem!

I assume you saw – perhaps you did not – an article on it in *Poetry and Drama*? It is a feeble set of lines. The music is good, but the words! They are an insult to the Royal Family and I have set about writing a new version, strident and patriotic, glorying and – well, you can guess.

Now that I am back in the lowlands I can see how horrid Leysin was. It wasn't just the row upon row of dying who so sapped me of spirit. Those alpine meadows and the endless dark firwoods . . . I enjoyed them at first but, after a while, they started to pall. It was like residing next to acres of un-cut coffins. Here, the lake is clear and the air less sharp.

I find my emotions wavering somewhat. At times, I like the Swiss. The doctor at Leysin, in his impersonal way, was pleasant enough and the hotel staff amenable. But overall the Swiss are a stodgy and rapacious lot, vulgar in themselves and further ignobled and decivilised by the hotel society. They eat too much chocolate. They are avaricious and greedy and they sing the most ghastly folk-songs, yodelling with all their might as if seeking to gargle with air. They speak bastard French and worse English. Or bastard Italian, depending on where you are. They are materialists of the first order and have, I believe, as much interest in poetry as the bullock has in the butcher's welfare.

You can see from this I'm getting back on form!

Enough of this. I miss you, my dear fellow. Why not plan to visit me when next you head for England's shores? I am not so far off the beaten track. It merely seems that way.

Ever thine,
Roy.

The visitor, who arrived within a day of the notice of his coming, was not at all what Flecker had expected. The telegram from London had simply stated a Mr Crossett would be visiting him and he therefore reasoned that he would be an innocuous civil servant.

By accident, the cable had been sent to the Hôtel de Glion but the Fleckers had moved again to the mountains, to the Sanatorium Stephani further up the Rhône valley at Montana-sur-Sierre. Crossett had gone first to Glion, only to be told he had yet another fifty kilometres to his meeting. It did not put him in the best of humour; his time was precious.

It had been anticipated that Flecker would attend a medical board hearing in mid-August, but he had written to the Foreign Office to say he was still too ill to travel to Britain; he offered to tender his resignation, if it was to be demanded, but stressed he felt he would be well again at the end of the year and ready to return to full-time employment. This was deemed unnecessary and his term of sick leave was extended for another three months.

Mr Crossett, he assumed, was travelling out to see him to assess his future usefulness to the service. At

first, Flecker assumed this was his only object, but he
was soon disabused.

The two men met in a secluded corner of the hotel
foyer, tea being served to them by an elderly waiter.
Crossett, a tall and austere man in his middle age with
broad shoulders and a military bearing, did not speak
as long as the waiter was in earshot.

'I am here, Mr Flecker', he began their meeting after
the most cursory of formalities, 'to discuss with you a
few factors arising from your past service. And I shall
come directly to the main purpose of my visit. I must
return to London within the day; your moving without
notification has severely disrupted my plans.

'Their Lordships ask me to confirm your leave of
absence is extended and that this is to be regarded as a
mitigation on their part. This, however, is not my concern. I am here to question you about your attitudes
towards your role in the Consular Service. Certain
doubts have arisen.'

Crossett placed a briefcase upon the low table by his
chair and opened it. From within he took several sheets
of paper tied together with a green treasury tag.

'Will you kindly look over the enclosed, Mr Flecker?'

Flecker took the sheets and held them in the light of
the lamp.

Each page had a red rubber stamp embossed upon it,
over which someone had scrawled a signature and a
date. At the foot of each sheet was another stamp con-
sisting of boxes and headed: 'When read, initial and
circulate as indicated.'

Upon each page were typed, spaced paragraphs under
a common cipher – 'JEF/TEL/DGH/Ops Syr 1913'. He
read the first paragraph with horror:

It was such a wonderful game we played! . . . I wonder on
the morality of it all . . . Hogarth's grand game and we the

pieces, eh? Beat the Germans at their railway, queer up the Frenchies' interests when the chance comes along. Arm the Arabs. And for what? In the end, aren't we doing what the Mandarin does? Laying waste. I wonder if, one day, we shan't inadvertently turn similarly against the Arab, side with the Frenchies or the Germans or the Jews or the Maronites or whoever it pleases us to foster in friendship . . . Politics is a funny business. I think, now I am away from it, it was one of the reasons I so despised the work as a VC. I never really understood it. Not really. But it always seemed so underhand, somehow. Immoral, almost. Why knock the Frogs? They are our friends. And the Germans – the Kaiser himself is blood-related to HM The King. It's not as if they are bloody Bulgars seeking to stomp their heavy flat feet all over Greece.

He flicked over the pages: they contained other frag-ments of his correspondence to Lawrence. Some state-ments were underlined in red pencil, others in blue. The red underlinings were annotated with footnote reference numbers, but none of these was attached by the tag.

'I think . . .' Flecker started to say, but Crossett inter-rupted him.

'Would you mind turning to the last page, Mr Flecker?'

Flecker folded the sheets over and read, with dread, the only paragraph on the page:

Perhaps I should put it all into notes and make a novel. Strive at it, once I'm clear of sanatoria named as hotels . . .

Beneath his own words was a flurry of notes in red ink. Flecker tried to read these also, but Crossett leaned over and took the papers back.

In Beirut Cumberpatch had intercepted his personal post to London, to literary friends and magazine edi-tors. However, Flecker had assumed that his letters to Lawrence would have been beyond the reach of censor-ship going either, when he was in Beirut, through the sealed diplomatic bags or, since his departure from the Lebanon, in the ordinary public mails. He realised then that someone in the Consulate in Aleppo was opening and scrutinising correspondence.

'These notes,' Crossett said, 'where are they?'

'Th–they aren't,' Flecker stammered.

'I'm afraid I do not understand.'

'There are no notes; I have taken none.'

'In your files in Beirut, Mr Flecker, carbon copies of some messages are missing.'

'I did not always make carbons.'

'You are instructed – standing orders . . .'

'I know that,' Flecker admitted, a hint of exasperation in his voice, 'but – well – I didn't always. Sometimes there wasn't time.'

'It takes no time to carbonate a copy.'

'Be that as it may,' Flecker said, 'I have no notes.'

'What of this novel?'

'There is no novel.'

'Yet you claim to be writing again.'

'I am. Poetry. Plays. Critical articles . . .'

'Critical of what?' Crossett butted in.

'Of poets,' Flecker rejoined. 'French poets, English poets. I am writing literary criticism.'

'And the plan for your novel? Surely your novel has a plan?'

Flecker cast his eyes upward for a moment.

'There are no notes, there is no plan, there is no novel. Not even an outline, not even an idea. I simply said – wrote . . .'

'The idea exists here.'

Crossett shook the papers slightly and returned them to his briefcase.

Flecker fell silent. His shoulders ached and his throat was sore, his head throbbed.

Did Lawrence, he wondered, know of this tampering

with the mail and, if he did, did he condone it, or accept it as merely another part of the official procedure, another aspect of the political game? He pondered the possibility of Lawrence being now one of 'them', the faceless bureaucrats, the power-mongers, the controllers of destiny – but he could not believe it. Lawrence would not turn in such a manner. Perhaps it was Hogarth himself who had ordered the interception of the mails.

Suddenly, Flecker was very annoyed and yet also very ashamed that his special love, his most private of feelings, was common knowledge. There was, he knew, nothing to be ashamed of; there was, he sincerely believed, nothing unnatural in love between men. Yet, nevertheless, he felt humiliated.

'Memoirs?'

'I beg your pardon?' Flecker said.

He had not been listening, had been wrapped in his thoughts. This man from Whitehall, and many faceless Whitehall officials, had been reading his letters. All his secrets were out – his love, his dreams, his private hopes and fantasies.

'Memoirs. Have you written any memoirs?'

'I have not,' Flecker answered belligerently. Then he calmed his voice. 'Look, Mr Crossett, I have no plans to use anything in a novel. I have no intention of writing articles about anything. Or memoirs. I do not keep a diary, only a verse notebook . . .'

'May I see it?'

Flecker left the table and went upstairs to his room. He made his way along the corridor, the rain tapping dismally on the windows. As he approached his room he noticed, at the far end of the corridor, a man walking away from him. He was wearing a deerstalker and a cape and Flecker laughed inwardly – Mr Sherlock Holmes was on the case against him.

'The Miscreant Poet', he considered, might make a

good title: 'The Samarkand Vice-Consul' was even better. It would be a story of gun-smuggling and intrigue, of plot and counter-plot revolving around an innocent caught up in the dirty underworld of political subterfuge.

Inside his room, just as he was taking his notebook out of the drawer in the dressing-table, he noticed his comb and clothes-brush had been moved and placed behind the tray on which he kept his studs and cuff-links. Someone had pushed the dressing-table accoutrements back towards the mirror in order to make a space. In the left-hand drawer his handkerchiefs had been disturbed.

As he returned down the stairs, Flecker was angry but kept his temper under control. To lose it would be to give Crossett an advantage. He had to keep cool and collected.

'I assume your accomplice will prove to you I keep my word,' Flecker said icily as he handed over his note-book.

Crossett made no reply but gave Flecker a disparaging look. He flicked through the notebook, then said, 'In affairs of the state, Mr Flecker, there can be no chances.'

'Are you implying I am a mountebank?'

'I am ascertaining you are not, Mr Flecker. That is quite a different matter.'

'I feel I do not agree with you, sir.'

'That is of little consequence to me.'

Crossett handed back the notebook. The waiter approached them to enquire if they required more tea and tut-tutted loudly when he saw they had not yet drunk their first cup.

'I must ask you, Mr Flecker, to sign an undertaking – as a gentleman and an Englishman – that you will not, at any time, impart to any person or persons other than those authorised by His Majesty's government,

373

and in the presence of any person or persons whom you know to be a member or members of that government, any knowledge, detail, fact or concept with which you have come in contact during your time in His Majesty's service, or which may have come to your attention or realisation subsequently. Furthermore you are requested to undertake not to record, publicise, publish either in truth or in disguised form – such as in a fictional account – store or retain any knowledge, detail, fact or concept appertaining to any matter concerning the operation of His Majesty's government and any sub-sequent government of the British Isles.'

Flecker made no immediate response. His mind was in confusion. His employers did not trust him: he was considered little better than an alien spy. And yet they had spied upon him, had tampered with his private correspondence, had searched his room.

His silence, misconstrued by Crossett, prompted him to add, 'You have no choice in the matter, Mr Flecker.'

'That was not what I was considering,' Flecker retorted angrily. 'It goes without saying that I will accept such an undertaking; it is one I am already bound to in my own thoughts, without there having to be a legal document to the effect.'

Crossett softened a little.

'I am delighted to hear it. And, frankly, regardless of the reports I have read of your service record, I was myself under no illusion at all that you would refuse.'

He removed from his briefcase another sheet of paper which he put on the table.

'I have my own pen,' Flecker said sharply as Crossett reached for his inner pocket. 'After all, I am a professional writer.'

He signed the document and pushed it away from him.

'What would you have done had I refused?'

'Any subsequent course of action would not have been in my control,' Crossett said ominously. 'That would have been up to people of less diplomatic persuasion. It does not bear thinking about, I assure you.'

As Crossett placed the document in his case, Flecker noticed the initials on the leather were 'HFD'. So, he thought, the man's name was false. He wondered in the light of this how much veracity there had been in his words, how much of what he was yet to say would be the truth and how much expedient lying.

'Now,' Crossett said, picking up his teacup and sipping the lukewarm liquid, 'in recognition of your having signed this document, I am charged with giving you some good news. But first I must remind you of the gravity of your recent act. There can be no revocation of the document; it will stand as long as you are alive.'

'I appreciate that.'

Flecker beckoned to the waiter and ordered a glass of water. His throat was painful now.

'Good. Now, I have this for you.'

From the inner pocket of his coat Crossett produced a sealed envelope. He handed it to Flecker who tore it open.

Dear James, [he read]

You will receive this by way of a messenger sent out through the FO. You will not have been given it before signing the document he offers you which I trust – I know! – you will sign without demur. You are that good sort of chap.

In recognition of your services and in view of your present predicament, I can make you an assurance. Your sick leave is extended to the end of the year: this you will know by now. If necessary it may be extended further beyond that time, but concentrate on getting well; this you do not know and are not to know yet, if you understand me. After that, if you are still ill or unable (unwilling) to serve further, your resignation will be accepted, your bond officially waived and you will receive an immediate and, I think, adequate life pension. This course of action is not, I might add, a common occurrence. (Never mind the complexities that lie behind it – thank your friends for that . . . you will be well looked after.)

This letter is not for you to keep. The messenger will take it. And you may report its contents *to no one at all.* I stress that most emphatically. To do so will be to jeopardise this pension and possibly embarrass your patrons in the matter.

Rupert is – as you may know – in Canada and sends his best regards. I pray it will not be long before we all see you here, fit and hearty and versifying madly.

Yours, et.
E. Marsh.

Flecker read the letter again, slowly. One phrase stuck out: 'You will be well looked after'.

How many times that sentiment had been expressed to him, he thought. Fontana had assured him at their first meeting in Aleppo – 'They'll see you all right,' he had promised. Hogarth had written that things had a way of working out – that it would 'all come out in the wash'.

'I must have that back, Mr Flecker. And the envelope, if I may.'

Upon receiving them Crossett screwed them into a ball and, after dropping them in the ashtray upon the table, set light to the paper with a match. When the ball was reduced to ashes he crushed them into powder with the teaspoon from his saucer.

'What of the carbon copy?' Flecker asked wryly.

'Of this communication there is no copy,' said Crossett without so much as a hint of a smile.

The view depressed him. From his window he could see only the other wall of the Rhône valley smothered, as he put it in every letter he wrote save those to his parents, with dead-green firs and grey blasted rocks. The narrow Val d'Anniviers ran into the mountains opposite but gave little relief to the alpine scenery. Flecker felt as if he was imprisoned by the mountains, the first snows of the winter demoralising him further.

He wrote feverishly but now was displeased with much of his output. His French translations lacked vitality, while his free translation from the Latin of the sixth book of the *Aeneid* was exciting to him and aroused encouragement from those to whom he sent fragments, but it was not, he believed, his best work.

He grew embittered with himself. His writing, despite the growing acclaim for his new volume of poetry, was being turned down or held on to by editors, preventing him from sending it elsewhere and earning from it – the *Fortnightly* retained a long article on Paul Fort but made no decision about publishing; *The Nation* rejected 'The Old Ships', Flecker's working of Hellé's birthday poem; *Poetry and Drama* seemed no longer to respond to his work, preferring the writing of the younger, more futurist poets.

They had need of the money. Flecker's father sent them enough to make up the difference of his being on half-pay, but Flecker abhorred being dependent on his parents. As long as they held the purse-strings they could call the tune of his life and his father was anxious he seek reinstatement in his diplomatic career. He could not be told of Marsh's letter, and this irked Flecker.

As a part of his father's demands the Fleckers had to account for each penny or so spent. Hellé was obliged to keep a daily petty cash account in which every item of expenditure was accurately noted. Every so often this had to be submitted to Cheltenham for approval.

'It's like having to report back to head office all the time,' Flecker complained. 'Anyone would think we were running a company, not fighting for our lives in a land of cacao-eating Philistines. It's as if we were getting their money for high living. The only height around here is the bloody altitude.'

'They have to be careful,' Hellé cautioned, 'it is their money and they want to know it is all going to pay for your health again. They don't want me to be flitting off to Geneva to buy new dresses with it.'

'I wish you did,' he retorted. 'It would teach them a bloody lesson. "Two shillings and fourpence three-farthings – Roy's meals in Montana" is really "one fine bottle of claret with lunch at the Trocadero, Geneva." I'd like to see their damned faces!'

He began to relapse, his coughing fits becoming prolonged and frequent, racking his body with their intensity. He grew more morose almost by the day.

In his presence Hellé continued to maintain a brave face. She smiled and joked and mildly chided him, encouraged him over his work and offered constructive criticism of what he did manage to write. All the while she planned the future with him, pointed out the vast array of hope and opportunity which was developing.

Yet, secretly, in the new room she had rented for herself as soon as they arrived, once more apart from his, she wept and sat alone for hours.

Montana
Switz.

My dear Ned,

I am only writing a brief missive to you. I feel too despondent to write much these days. My cough has returned with a vengeance and I feel in low spirits.

We are now at Montana-sur-Sierre surrounded by thousands of feet of fir trees. I feel like a lost northern troll, or some trapped and ugly beast of Swiss mythology – if the Swiss have mythology. I doubt very much they have the imagination to design a tram ticket.

We are still hopeful of things coming right. I have approached a friend about writing advertisements. They seem to be money for old rope – and good money, too! My writings are being rejected all over London. I'm suddenly too old-fashioned, I think. I need to write new stuff like your namesake – one D. H. Lawrence. But I can't.

As soon as the coughing subsides – as surely it will – I think it was brought on by the shock of going from Leysin to the lake, then back up here – we are 1400 metres up! – I will return to normal and get back on the mend.

I think of you often.

Ever thine,
Roy.

What difference did it make? he thought, as he walked with halting steps to the post and telegraph office in Montana to purchase a stamp. They knew already.

His love for Lawrence was a documented fact, not merely in letters stored in a suitcase or a box in the house in Carchemish but in buff manilla dossiers in Whitehall. His feelings for others, men of his standing and thought, his brothers in creativity and emotion, no matter how taboo they might be, were a fact. He could not hide it.

He looked at the envelope in his hand. The air trapped it in, the words he had spoken in pen upon the sheet would next see light of day in the room with the mosaic. The next fingers to touch where his had scribbled would be Lawrence's.

But then, he considered, would they? And he grew embittered and hated those who controlled him – the crass Cumberpatches and Crossetts of this world. Was it, he wondered, his friends who were prying into his life? Was it Raff who was the opener, the censor, the eavesdropper?

With a hand shaking as much with anger as with the chill of the late September mountain air, he stuck the stamp upon the letter and flicked it into the post-box.

13
Montana and Locarno, Switzerland: January and Spring 1914

It was snowing lightly as Dr Flecker stepped from the funicular at the Montana terminus. He had his overcoat buttoned to his neck, and a comforter forced in between his neck and the collar of the coat. His black hat was quickly speckled with snowflakes and, despite the wide brim, so was his moustache. He stood on the platform and cleaned his spectacles: they were steamed up with the moisture of breath in the car. Behind him was Mrs Flecker, her black dress damp at the hem from walking through the snow between the Sierre railway station and the funicular. Her boots were too damp, the leather dulled. A porter, burdened with their cases, waited for her to step on to the platform.

'Frankly, I am relieved to be out of that cramped compartment,' she said, her voice subdued but nevertheless supercilious. 'One has no way of knowing what germs might be lingering in there. The passengers . . .'

At the barrier, Hellé was awaiting them. The fur collar of her overcoat glistened with melted snow and her shoulders were wet. She had been waiting for an hour; the train from Geneva had been over an hour late due to the weather.

'My dear Hellé,' Dr Flecker greeted her, his hand outstretched. 'How are you? There was really no need for you to come and meet us. I am sure we could easily find our lodgings by ourselves and just as readily discover the way to you both.'

Mrs Flecker, moving from behind her husband, also shook Hellé's hand. She did so firmly, with a tighter grip than her husband's, her face set in a half-smile which could have been interpreted as a reaction to the chill of the air and snow, now falling more steadily.

'Hello, sir . . . Mother . . .' was all Hellé could say. She knew the smile for what it really was: there was no love lost between daughter- and mother-in-law.

As they waited for the porter to find someone to help him with the baggage, a group of winter sportsmen pushed past them, their voices loud and brash, their German accents guttural and coarse. Their own porters carried polished wooden skis and ski-poles, banging them into Mrs Flecker who reacted with a stern stare which prompted a ribald aside from one of the skiers, much to his friends' amusement. They left the station to hail a horse-drawn sled.

'So gauche!' Mrs Flecker remarked with considerable annoyance. 'So terribly continental . . .'

Under different circumstances Hellé would have had difficulty in suppressing her mirth.

'How is Roy?' Dr Flecker enquired a moment later, as their own sled moved slowly across the snow, the horse's breath pumping in gouts from its nostrils.

'He is little changed since I wrote to you. He has had a serious relapse. His coughing is worse, his throat very raw and the lozenges he so hates seem not to be having more than a temporary effect. His attacks are worst in the evening and he shakes so; he cries then because he cannot stop . . .'

She rubbed her finger along beneath her eyes. Her own tears, prompted by the freezing air as much as her unhappiness, were icy upon her cheekbones.

'Do not distress yourself, my dear,' advised Dr Flecker, his voice neither kind nor cruel but merely detached, like a distant relative at a funeral. 'The Good Lord has it all in His hand. We must trust in Him . . .'

'The doctor informs me this relapse makes all the more slender his chances for a complete recovery.'

Hellé wanted so much to say he had spent far too long in the Middle East, that he should never have returned there the previous winter. He should have resigned from the Consular Service then, paid up his bond and be done. She wanted to accuse his father of intransigence, his mother of narrow-mindedness and a lack of foresight. Suddenly his degeneration was their fault – at least in part – and she believed they knew as much. Why else, she wondered, had they come? Surely not in answer to the pathetic pencil note their son had appended to one of her letters and set of accounts, asking if they might visit him. It was not affection that brought his unemotional mother all the way to Montana-sur-Sierre in mid-winter. It was guilt.

As the sled glided over the snow in the street, bumping as it crossed the ruts made by other vehicles, Hellé's dislike for her mother-in-law – which she had so long suppressed – rose to her mouth like bile. She hated the woman, her lack of compassion, her stubborn and narrow Anglicanism, her utterly despicable Englishness.

Within her clothes, despite the cold, Hellé was hot with anger. In her fur gloves, her palms perspired. She so wanted to speak her mind, to accuse them of their penny-pinching ways, to challenge them with her assertions that they had prolonged her beloved husband's illness, had made it worse, had ruined his chances for recovery. Already that week she had spent more than £5.10.0 on medicines alone. In a year that would amount to fifty per cent of his Foreign Office bond. If he lingered on, struggling to write and to live, fighting his own guilt that he was a burden upon them, they would soon spend the equivalent of the bond in drugs alone. In addition there were sanatorium fees, doctor's fees, transport, her own lodgings . . . how she longed to fling these facts before them, allow full rein to the temper – the European, the *continental* temper – she harboured deep within herself.

Yet she could not. To sour relations now would threaten them both. They needed Dr Flecker's money. And to cause unpleasantness now would be to ruin the visit for her husband. He could not cope with more family animosity.

She dropped the Fleckers off at their lodgings and went on in the sled to the Sanatorium Stephani. She found her husband sitting up in bed with a thick woollen shawl about his shoulders, the window open several inches. He was reading.

'This really is turgid rubbish!' he exclaimed, his voice weak and croaking. 'I can't think why Marsh gives it such plaudits . . .'

She took the book from him but did not look at the cover.

'It's negative tripe. Has no guts, no fire, no emotion. It is just a long, horridly real haze of tedium. It has no vulgarity in it but it is vulgar, common. The lives of coal-miners! Hardly illuminating stuff! It's a mean and spiritless story about mean and bloodless characters . . .'

'Enough!' She laughed lightly but her eyes were dull. 'What is this you so berate and growl at, my loving Tiger?'

She rearranged his pillows and tugged the shawl closer to his throat.

'D. H. Lawrence – one of the new poets,' Flecker said begrudgingly. 'He's published a novel, *Sons and Lovers*. It is quite devoid of human beauty. He demeans the dignity of the working classes, shows the civilisation of industry as squalid. His people are not in touch with the raw edge of life, simply existing . . .'

He picked the book up from where she had laid it, studied it briefly and then tossed it on to a chair.

'Have my parents arrived?'

'Yes. They will be along shortly. Your mother is resting after the journey. The Geneva train was well overdue. The weather . . .'

'The damnable snow! God, how I hate this black and white country. Black trees, black rocks, black souls and white snow – layer upon layer of it cavorted upon by loud-mouthed buffoons on slivers of varnished willow.' He paused. 'Is that the wood they use for their ridiculous footwear?'

She shrugged and said, 'Don't be so tetchy, dearest.'

'I can't help it. I feel so miserable . . .'

She leaned over him, kissing his forehead. It was cold and waxen.

'Enough of the air for a while,' she ordered and shut the window.

'When will they come?'

'Soon.'

He lay back and closed his eyes.

'I am so utterly exhausted. I'll sleep for a bit before they arrive.

His mother was quick to show her disapproval of her son's sickroom. No sooner had she kissed him, more dutifully than lovingly, her husband shaking his hand, than she began her criticism.

'Roy, this room is terribly small for the price demanded. I would have thought better could have been found elsewhere in the town.'

'When the winter is over, that might be possible,' Hellé told her. 'At present it is not. The winter holiday-makers are wealthy persons and the tariffs rise as long as there is sufficient snow for skiing or tobogganing. In the winter the invalids here take second place. They are often not the richest of people and so must take what they can . . .'

'That is quite monstrous,' declared Mrs Flecker. 'Something should be done about it.'

She turned to look around the room and then out of the window at the view across the valley.

'How are you feeling in yourself, my boy?' Dr Flecker asked, sitting at the edge of the bed.

'Better today, in truth,' his son replied, rubbing his eyes at the weak sunlight that, for a moment, came into the room around his mother's bulk. 'I've been very low with a fever, temperature fluctuating towards evening each day. My throat is poorly most of the time and I feel utterly lacking in vitality. Lassitude is the order of the day. Yet, in fact, my mind is still running on. I am writing . . .'

He fell silent. Discretion was called for, he felt.

'And your medication?'

'I have to suck these atrocious lozenges and there are others in the cupboard. We bought the cupboard,' he cast a glance at it, 'because I could no longer bear staring at the serried ranks of bottles and jars and potions and pills parading on the dresser top.'

His mother turned back from the window as the sunlight faded.

'Switch the light on, Hellé dear,' she commanded and, as the room was better illuminated, she went on, 'This room really is an awful mess, Roy. So many books and knick-knacks. It looks like a street market. What is this?'

'A Hittite statuette, mother. It came from northern Syria where I . . .'

'Northern Syria. I see.' There was considerable

disapproval in her voice. She picked up the statuette, cursorily looked at it and put it down again. 'No doubt the climate there was even worse than in Beirut.'

'Scrub desert,' Flecker confirmed. 'But I had to go there in the course of my work . . .'

The statuette and mention of his duties in the north brought back to him a brief, vivid memory of Carchemish. He saw the mosaic floor and the antelopes set for ever in timeless tesseræ: and they in turn reminded him of goats. Beside the statuette was the goatherd's carving he had been given at Brumana. He saw the bird zip in for a shaving but its flight turned into his mother's hand picking up the carving, examining it without any sign of interest and replacing it.

'And all these pictures,' his mother continued, running her finger along the frame of one. She studied the spot upon which the statuette had stood and then the thin grime of dust on her finger. 'Really! This will not do. Hardly a room for a sick man. There's dust everywhere. Domestic dust can be just as inflaming to the delicate tissues as desert dust. Does no one ever clean this room?'

'A maid visits it daily,' Hellé informed her. 'She dusts and sweeps the floor . . .'

'Then she is a slovenly woman! Any maid in my employ who let this get by would be instantly dismissed. You must take a firm hand with her, Hellé. Complain to the management and see she is discharged if her work does not improve.'

Hellé nodded, deciding simply to agree. That a complaint might have them instructed to leave, rather than the servant, was a distinct possibility. Even such a small room could be used.

'Where do you reside, Hellé?' her father-in-law asked. 'In this establishment?'

'I have a room elsewhere, not quite' she wanted to

drive the point home to Mrs Flecker 'as large as this one. But I spend most of my time here. Roy is in need of almost constant nursing attention at present and so I stay with him most of the time. I sleep in the chair at night and spend my days here. We read and I help him with his work. I leave for my meals unless he is very bad, in which case the porter brings me up something light on a tray.'

'What are you writing, my boy?'

'I am translating Virgil. And writing new poems.'

'You seem to be getting quite famous,' his father announced. 'Your new book is being talked about — and not just at home amongst the masters and staff at the school. Your publishers have several times asked me for a photograph of you for the newspapers. One newspaper actually wrote to me direct. And that edition, *Georgian Poetry*, in which you were represented, has sold remarkably well.'

'Yes, I know.' Flecker lay back against his pillow. The meeting was tiring him. 'Marsh has written to me . . .'

He wanted to tell his father about Marsh's secret letter but he knew he should not; Marsh's warning was a serious one, and he was loath to risk his future income. Yet at the same time he longed to tell his father he need not be reliant upon him for the rest of his life.

'I have earned a little money from it, too,' Flecker admitted after a moment. He reached for the bedside table and pulled out an envelope from between two volumes. The exertion caused him to cough roughly several times, his shoulders heaving with the effort.

'Such dust . . .' his mother muttered, and clicked her tongue disapprovingly.

'I should like you to have this,' Flecker said, offering the royalty cheque to his father. 'Please put it to good use . . .'

His father took it, looked at it and handed it back.

'You retain this, my boy. I think you should have the fruits of your own labours on this occasion.'

'You might consider putting it towards the rent on a better room . . .' his mother began, but her husband cut her short.

'Buy yourself something with it to while away the hours,' Dr Flecker advised.

Everywhere there were butterflies. Azure, cobalt, turquoise, sapphire: large with spots like distant planets upon their wings. Their antennæ twitched. Their clockspring tongues unfurled and sipped the air. Their spindle legs flexed and bent. When they closed their wings behind their backs the undersides were gold, bronze, copper-hued. When they flew they looked like the leaves of birch trees dancing in a stiff breeze – yet golden. When they glided they looked like flakes of gold leaf drifting on still sunlight.

As soon as he woke his first action was to reach for paper and pen. Hellé was still absent.

> When the whole sky is vestured silken blue
> With not one fleece to view,
> Drown your deep eyes afar, and see you must
> How the light azure dust
> And speckled atoms of the polished skies
> Are large blue butterflies . . .

His hand ached, his head reeled. The books seemed to lean in on him. The Hittite statuette grinned broadly like an evil imp.

He shut his eyes . . .

It was a noontide field. There were few flowers in the meadow. Somewhere, far off, a dog barked. It was the kind of bark a dog makes when it sees the prospect of a flung stick or a marrow bone. The field gathered itself into a storm of blue shards. The butterflies rose, higher and higher. The blue of their wings became the sky, the gold of their wings the sun.

And the dog stopped barking and became the rumbustious laugh of a skier in the street outside.

Much to the annoyance of Miss Schor, the old family nurse the Fleckers sent out from England to tend their son through his relapse, Flecker insisted on spending much of his time playing the zither he had purchased with the cheque from Marsh.

'Mr Flecker,' she proclaimed with no slight annoyance, 'the noise that instrument makes is quite as bad as the cacophony at Ladysmith. I was at that siege – and the relief thereof – in the war against the Boer, and I know! The sound of rifle fire is no more soothing than your strumming. I would rather face another outbreak of typhus than another unmelodious concert from you! At least with typhus I can offer succour to the sufferers.'

Flecker smiled benignly but ignored her. And she was in no mood to ban him the instrument. It was, in her opinion, better he be playing it than taxing his brain with his incessant reading, writing or concentrating on being read to by his wife.

Understanding the need to keep her charge's mind as eased as possible, Miss Schor did not remove all the ornaments from Flecker's room. She was reluctant to upset him, for when he was nervous his pattern of sleep was disrupted and he grew insomniac and restless, easily exhausted and quick to succumb to coughing fits. She did give autocratic orders to both the manager and the maid, the effect of which was that the room was properly cleaned daily under her own supervision and subsequent inspection. If the dusting and polishing and sweeping did not meet with her approval she was quick to demand it was re-done – and immediately.

On occasion, Flecker was allowed out as a change from his dreary existence in the room: the nurse was anxious he should be kept away from his books whenever it was possible. He was cerebrating far too hard, in her opinion.

When he went out he was bundled up in scarves and blankets and coats, a woollen balaclava round his head – Miss Schor had had it with her in Russia and, she was keen to assert, it had saved her ears from severe frostbite on more than one occasion – and taken for a sleigh-ride through Montana and along the road to the nearby alpine village of Crans.

He did not enjoy the scenery, the snow crisp under the runners, the sky laden with the next few inches of it; but he did enjoy the warm scent of the horse and the jangle of bridle and bell, the perfume of leather and the sound of the horse snorting, the plumes of its breath in the sub-zero air.

A copy lay by his hand. He picked it up – *The King of Alsander, J. E. Flecker.*

'Aren't you excited, Roy?' Hellé asked. 'It's out at last. And the reviews are good.'

'Yes, I am,' he answered but with no expression of exhilaration. 'And they are. But I'm not pleased with it. I wasn't in it at the end. And it won't sell; I can tell.'

'Oh, that's nonsense! How can you foretell the sales?'

She took it from him and opened it as if to start reading.

'Don't,' he said. 'It's just a pot-boiler, a corny tale. Another Ruritanian adventure. Not as good as *Prisoner of Zenda*, nor as gripping. A mere pastiche, a shabbily contrived imitation. I wanted it . . . I don't know. I don't think I know what I wanted from it. Except maybe some reputation as a novelist – and a bit of cash. And I know it won't sell because the readers will see through it. If I can see through it, and I made it, then anyone can. I was blinded by the wonder of it, but they . . . And I'm not blinded now. I know a paltry book when I see one; I get them sent to me often enough!'

'You shouldn't be so self-critical,' Hellé remonstrated, replacing the volume on his bed. 'It's a good story. If it was not, the publishers would not have accepted it.'

'Perhaps. But it won't make me money. It won't make my reputation.'

With a sweep of his arm he knocked the book on to the floor with the sheets of paper upon which he had been writing.

'Enough of it! I am simply just not making an impact. All my work now is shallow and trite, hardly a shadow of my former output. I know it's in me, I know it's there, but it won't come.'

'Hush, dearest Tiger,' she whispered. 'These are not your kind of growls.'

'Don't hush me!' he retorted petulantly. 'I get enough of that from Nurse Boer-War. And I know the truth when I see it. Your molly-coddling has no effect.'

He deliberately picked up his pen and dropped it on the floor where it clattered on the boards.

'Don't fret so, dearest.' Hellé retrieved the pen and put it on the table. 'This feeling will pass . . .'

'How can it?' he said despairingly. 'I know what's what in the world. I've been passed by. The literary world doesn't want my writing any longer. They want the morbid miner-tales of David Herbert Lawrence, the meandering piffle of the futurists. Look at the last edi-

tion of *Poetry Review* . . . My God! What a mess that
magazine is. Look at that Ezra Pound. Disjointed jottings of the lesser variety. Why? His poems look like
the notes taken by a court stenographer. They need to
be written up into poems, for they surely aren't finished.
Yet he publishes them and Monro, who ought to be
begging me for real poems, takes him as seriously as if
he were born on Parnassus and suckled by wolves.'

'What of *Hassan*?' Hellé said. 'That is good, it has a
grand chance. You have signed the contract on that.
Mr Basil Dean's keen on it. And – well! Sir Herbert
Tree might even play the part. What more could you
want, dearest?'

'Dean's rearranging it,' Flecker replied crabbily. 'He
will get twenty-five per cent of the earnings for his
work, and he will not be starting on the script until
April at the earliest. He can't be so keen if he can put
it off.'

Hellé answered his objection with, 'Theatrical people
live differently from us. They have different priorities.'

Flecker shrugged.

'I'm tired now,' he said, 'and I want to sleep.'

Miss Schor entered and gave him his medicine,
removed the zither from his bed and tidied the room.

'Don't wake me until morning,' he ordered. 'Tonight
I am going to sleep well. And I want one of you to get
a date from the doctors for my next escape from this
damned white-snow-and-black-fir mountain prison.'

He was staring at a hillside. It had not a vestige of snow
upon it and it was this, he thought, which had first
drawn his attention to it. It was shimmering under a
baking sun, the grey and mottled rocks wavering in the
heat. The shadows were short and the sky above the
rocks was brilliantly, deeply, royally blue. There were

low bushes between the rocks but no trees of any significance – and no firs.

He shifted his ground. Now he was gazing up the
hillside and the horizon was above him, the line of the
mountain against the sky.

Half-way up the hillside, from the rocks, appeared a
man. He was some way off but Flecker could make out
his every feature plainly. He had short, wavy hair the
colour of which was burnished brown against the hot
rocks. His face was oval, with a short chin and sensuous
mouth; his nose was slightly long and his eyes wide and
large. He was wearing a dark jacket of homespun and
a white shirt, the wide collars of which stood up behind
his neck.

Flecker called out to him but did not understand the
words that he himself was mouthing. The figure replied
in a clear voice.

'Mortal brother,' he said, his words ringing as if in
cold air, 'since you too love the stony hills and seas of
Corinth with every scorching breath you suck . . .' His
voice faded momentarily then became lucid again.
'. . . the divine shore from which Apollo led me to the
caves of death.'

Without reason, Flecker raised his hand. The figure
did not acknowledge him.

'You are the inheritor. The future lies with you.'

As suddenly as he had appeared, the figure was gone,
and from the very rocks around him another, deeper
voice came to Flecker. It seemed to issue from the very
earth at his feet, the air around him. He wondered for
a moment if he was dying and this was God.

'Be still, brother poet! Shelley fancies much. He is so
used to dreaming such grand designs and universal
plans that even these Elysian fields cannot contain him.
Be still and join with me.'

He could not see the speaker and yet a vision of him

came to Flecker. He appeared not unlike the first spirit: he wore the same style coat and shirt and his hair, though darker, was of the same length and curly cut. His eyes were too wide but, it seemed to Flecker, had less of the manic stare. His lips were full and he was, Flecker considered, the more handsome of the two. As he turned, he limped. A roll of thunder sounded in the cloudless sky and he disappeared.

Then Flecker heard his own voice, saying, 'I seemed to fall from sleep into a deeper sleep and a veil came over me which was made of Shelley's hair shot through with rose and gold. The gold glowed deeper and the rose burnt red and I saw running and rustling at my feet the rivers of a golden sun bleeding scarlet as though wounded in some last great fight. A huge lake of blood and fire burst in through the window and the mountains became islands . . . Hymettus and Parnassus. Olympus, even.'

A hand smoothed his brow. It was Hellé's. A voice spoke to him urgently. It was Miss Schor's. A warm wind blew over him. It was the blood of Byron and the blood of Shelley.

Montana-sur-Sierre,
Switzerland,
22 March, 1914

My dear Marsh,

I am writing very briefly to ask a favour of you, if I may be so bold. For once, you will be no doubt pleased to note, this has nothing to do with my literary estates, as I now tend to think of them.

With regard to my – how shall I put it? – pension fund, I write to ask if you would be so good as to arrange for any monies to be paid into a bank account with Martin's Bank at Temple Bar, in the name of Mrs Hellé Flecker.

I assume that the pension, or a pro rata percentage of it,

will continue to be provided after my demise for the support of my dear wife.

I do apologise for burdening you with this request. For obvious reasons I am unable to see to the matter myself and cannot approach any other to act on my behalf.

Yours, with every best thought,
Roy.

For hours on end that night it snowed heavily: so much so that, by morning, the roads down to Sierre were impassable, the funicular halted by drifts. It would have made little difference for snowfalls on to the Genève-Milano main line had closed the service. Flecker was despondent and restless the whole day, edgy to be gone, quietly ranting against the blizzard which had piled snow against the window of his room, plunging the interior into a grey and murky twilight.

His depression, which for the sake of his cure it was so important to alleviate, was the cause of Hellé's decision that they should move on; it was also advised by the imminent rise of the rent of their lodgings. Every hour, he ordered Hellé to go downstairs to the manager to discover whether or not the funicular was running yet. Every time she reported it was not he grew angry.

'This snow – it's worse than any disease. We are packed and ready to move. My room looks as bare as the interior of a sarcophagus; my pictures are off the walls; my books are packed. And I have to lie here waiting. For what? For the spring to come and thaw this clot of sky? In England the woods will already be pulsing with bluebells. The snowdrops will have died. The daffodils will be out. Here there's not a blossom in sight. Only the ink-stain of fir upon fir smothering the mountain-sides.'

'Be patient. I am told they're clearing the way already. The road is being shovelled and the main line to the

Simplon Tunnel is being ploughed open. Earlier, when I was out walking, I saw the plough train pass down the valley.'

'How you can walk in this abomination I do not understand! It saps my strength . . .'

He tried to write, to read, but he could not concentrate and when he dozed he did so fitfully and with much tossing and muttering.

Finally, on the last day of March, they left the sanatorium and went down the funicular to Sierre and there transferred to a comfortable train heading for Italy. Flecker's spirits rose as soon as he saw Hellé holding their reservation tickets.

'We are off now at last?' he asked.

She nodded.

'Good! Not a moment too soon. I have had quite enough of the Swiss.'

The train moved slowly out of the station, the track running alongside the Rhône. Flecker leaned his elbow on the compartment window and watched the black surface of the river. When the train crossed the water on a bridge of steel girders, the wheels echoing hollowly beneath the carriage, Flecker asked hopefully, 'Is this the border? Are we in Italy now?'

Hellé laughed and teased him.

'No, we are not in Italy yet. It will be some time before we get there – at least an hour or two. You must be patient and sit still. You're like an impetuous schoolboy going on an outing. Read your book.'

'When shall we be in Italy?'

'Half-way through the Simplon Tunnel. The border runs along the mountains and we shall be going under them. Read your book.'

He started to read but fell asleep, his head against the wooden pillar of the window. When the train entered the tunnel, Hellé let him sleep on, making sure the windows were tightly shut, the compartment door firmly closed and the ventilator in the ceiling fast against the fumes and stagnant air under the mountains. Despite her precautions, the taint of sooty smoke leaked in and she was obliged to stuff her best handkerchief into the ventilator slats.

Flecker did not wake until the train was slowly steaming down the Valle d'Ossola. He rubbed his hand against the glass of the window and peered out through the hole he had made in the condensation. All he could see was a thin river tumbling over stones, the sides of the valley covered with trees indistinguishable in the dying light of the afternoon.

'Switzerland,' he muttered contemptuously. 'Shall I never be rid of it?'

'Valle d'Ossola,' she said.

He made no reply, sunk in his thoughts, his face glowering at the view.

After a few minutes, he announced, 'I am going to stand in the corridor. My legs are aching with inactivity.'

She opened the door for him, the runners squeaking as it slid aside, a cool blast of air sweeping in over her feet.

'Do not stay for long, dearest,' she advised. 'It is cold out there and you should not . . .'

'Hush, woman!' he interrupted. 'What difference does it make? In there the spirit is cold, out here the body is cold. At least some natural harmony is established.'

He closed the door behind him and leaned against it, his coat pressing against the glass. Hellé let her eyes shut; she was so tired her eyelids hurt.

Suddenly the door was thrown open and she woke from her brief semi-doze with a start, her hands automatically going to her face as if in protection or exclamation.

'Hellé! Hellé! Look!'

She stood up and followed his gaze. The train was passing several small islands, dark against the water around them, small lights winking on one in the twilight: against the rapidly growing night pricked the pinnacles of a palatial mansion.

'Borromee!' Flecker shouted against the din of the train, its brakes beginning to whine. 'Lake Maggiore! *Lago Maggiore!* We are free at last!'

He hugged her close and, together, they remained in the corridor as the train halted briefly in the station at Stresa.

As it pulled out, the locomotive humping great clots of smoke and sparks on to the breeze coming off the lake, Flecker said loudly, 'Did you hear that?'

'Hear what? Everything is drowned out by the engine.'

'No – in the station. Did you not hear it? Wasn't it utterly beautiful?'

'What?' she asked again.

'Italian! Dante's language. Boccaccio's tongue. They were speaking Italian.' He was jubilant. 'When I am better we shall live in Italy. We shall take a house in the bandit-infested mountains and live like peasant lords. And have a flat in Rome to use for visits to the theatre. And we shall drink wine incessantly from our own vines. It shall be an old house with beautiful paintings and sculptures, a Roman emp . . .'

He coughed once and stopped talking, yet his spirits did not diminish.

All the while they waited on the platform at Gallarate for their connection through to Locarno – Flecker wrapped in scarves, and with Hellé's fur gloves on his hands, his feet cosseted in a travelling rug – he listened intently to the porters, to the ticket inspector, to the other passengers alighting from or boarding evening trains, or waiting.

Hellé watched his face by the light of the platform lamps. His eyes were bright, his features alert, his movements quick and his voice, quiet when he spoke to her, firm and assertive. It was as if merely crossing the frontier had brought about a partial cure.

After an hour they boarded a northbound train on the lake-shore line. It was a local stopping service, but Flecker did not mind. At every halt he got up from his seat, looking eagerly out of the window at the little villages clustered around the stations with their platform lamps glimmering, at the people climbing down from the train into the blocks of light cast by the carriage windows: and always in the background was the black expanse of the lake. Nearing Locarno the lights of the town shimmered upon the water and the last few miles they had to make in a horse-drawn landaulet went by quickly.

> Pension Rheingold,
> 8, Via dei Fiori,
> Locarno,
> Switzerland.
> Thursday 3rd.

My very dear Ned,

As you can see from the above, we are moved to a new *caravanserai* nearer the plains.

It is still in Switzerland, the land of the damned and the damnable, but in another part, so to speak. Hereabouts the language is Italian, the way of life is more italianate, the people in the streets are more human and here are fewer places where you can buy chocolate. There is not a single skiing buffoon in sight, although I dare say if one wanted to see them – to laugh or rant at them – I am sure there are some passing through the railway station.

The change of air – and, more importantly, people – has wrought a massive change in me. I still feel weak in the limbs and chest but in spirit I am recharged, a positive voltaic pile of energy. I've had some good news, too. One Mr Raphael is going to turn my novel into a play for which I get 25% of the take!

I am confined, still, to my bed. The doctor here insists I remain indoors and this is not really agreeable as I was hoping to get out and about a bit.

We are a little lonely here, in truth. We know no one. Even in Montana-sur-Purgatory we were friendly in a passing way with a few folk. Here we are in a German pension and seldom even see or hear our fellow inmates – which I suppose is one up on having them hollering like dairymen at dawn outside one's window. We are promised a few visits from friends. Leonard Cheesman (did you know of him in Oxford?) is to call in. So is Frank Savery, another old Oxford comrade with whom I climbed roofs and did other such undergraduate excesses and who now works in the Legation in Munich. There is word that Basil Dean, working on *Hassan*, may visit us also . . .

Why do you not come, too? Will not the digging season be over for you soon? Will you not be heading back to London to report?

We are easily reached. By train from Milano – there is a direct line through Como and Lugano. Or you could take the romantic route and steam up the lake on a little paddle-boat. Rather like the Isle of Wight ferry but more sedate and not packed with trippers of the worst sort.

Do come. I so want to talk with you again about so many things I cannot write about . . .

Telegraph us if it is at all possible.

> Ever thine in love and the desert sands,
> Roy.

The sunlight streamed in to the room, dust particles moving in the eddies of air it warmed. Flecker watched them, his fingers tapping edgily upon the wadge of paper on the bed beside him. As each column of dust rose his eyes followed it and, as soon as it disappeared from the sunbeam, he shifted his stare to the next.

Gradually, entranced by the dance of the dust, his mind began to wander. The butterflies of rich blue which he so often saw drifted past him, their wings lazy and the transparent windows in them glazed with veins. They moved and, as they did so, they became first vague, soft-feathered birds, then horn-coated dragons with wings like bats and hooked scales. Several had reptilian faces, several the visages of fleas or mites. One had the face of a tarantula.

From their viewpoint, Flecker saw himself lying on his sick-bed. He was dressed in gold cloth. Around his head was a garland of primroses so pure as to be as white as mountain butter. And as he watched himself he saw his body rise, burst through the ceiling of his room and arrive at a shining place where his feet trod butter-white flagstones and the air was filled with incandescent sound.

He ran his hands over his body. There was no pain. He pressed his chest, the balls of his thumbs forcing into the flesh. He felt nothing. His throat was clear and, for just a moment, he joined in with the singing – for the sound, he knew now, was the music of voices – and every note rang true.

Gazing around, he saw clouds the shape of faces, the shape of cathedrals and churches and monasteries. A man came towards him with a copy of his book of poems; he knew it was his, yet he could not recognise the binding nor know which of his collections it was that the figure held. The man was both positive and yet vague. Flecker could not tell what he was wearing, yet knew he was not naked. As he passed him by, the man spoke, but his words were in a language Flecker did not understand.

Then quite suddenly the singing ceased. As it did so

the light began to fade and the flagstones turned wet as if rain was falling. Then they became rain and fell in grey sheets. But the sun still shone.

The rain became the dust and the dust danced in the sunbeam and Flecker felt the pain return to his chest and the soreness to his throat.

He was adamant. Hellé tried desperately to dissuade him, but he would not be turned.

'I will not meet anyone in this sepulchre of a room, surrounded by moribund German zombies and ... I will simply not. And that is an end to the matter.'

'But you are unwell. You cannot ...'

'No!'

He spoke emphatically, as loudly as he dared before the level of pain in his throat reached an unbearable pitch.

'But ...'

'But nothing. I am determined. Now get me my clothes, for the love of God! And not all that invalid clobber of scarves and overcoats and blankets and hats and mufflers and gloves and longjohns and fur and wool. I want a suit out. And a shirt with a normal collar and a dark tie and ordinary socks with ordinary elasticated suspenders – not those groin-high woollen things which make me itch and feel like a sheep – and a handkerchief in my pocket and a normal man's hat on my head. I will allow a waistcoat, so take out the brown tweed. And I want ordinary shoes with a bit of polish on them, so get the maid to buff them up a bit. I will take a scarf – the brown one, to go with the tweed – but I shall only put it on if I feel the need.'

Hellé stood resolutely at the foot of the bed and made no sign of obedience.

'Will you do this?' he asked despotically. 'Or do I

have to get out of this damnable bed and struggle about for myself?'

'You cannot go out. You are too weak, too ill at present. You need to recuperate more. You know what the doctor . . .'

'Blast the doctor! I've had enough of doctors. I want a bit of self-determination now. So will you?'

Still she did not make a move.

'Please.'

He did not wheedle. His voice was not cajoling or ingratiating. It was not pleading. It was simply requesting, and the one word weakened her resolve.

'How long for?' she enquired.

'Give me just an hour,' he said. 'I know I am not strong; I know I should not go out; I know all of this, but I just cannot bear to be in here when . . .'

'Very well,' she conceded. 'One hour. Not more. If you are not back in ninety minutes I shall come and fetch you, be assured of that.'

She unbuckled the straps over the largest suitcase and started to rummage in it, removing the articles of clothing he requested and laying them out on the bed. When she was done, he swung his feet out from beneath the blankets and, seated on the edge of the bed, began to remove his pyjamas. Then he stopped and rebuttoned the striped jacket.

'I want to wash,' he declared. 'I smell of bed and sickness.'

He got back into bed as Hellé left the room to order a hip-bath. The maid arrived twenty minutes later with several ewers of hot water and the tub. It was placed on the carpet by the bed and the water poured in, the room filling with steam through which the sunlight cut channels like staircases of light.

Flecker undressed and lowered himself into the water. It was very hot; he winced and moaned as he submerged himself. Then, lying back against the tall end of the bath, he allowed Hellé to pour water over him with an enamel mug, soaping his body and sluicing off the suds. He leaned forward: she rubbed his back and he felt her fingers slipping soapily between his buttocks. When she washed his belly, he closed his eyes, sensing her fingers pressing between his legs.

'It has been a long time, dearest,' he said quietly. 'You don't mind?'

'No. But then, yes, I mind. I want my Tiger. Often. But . . . when you are better. Think then of the fun we shall have when your strength is restored.'

'Do you remember Leysin?' he asked. 'The rock beyond the forest?'

'Yes.'

'We shall be like that again, shall we not?'

'Yes. I promise we shall.'

When he was washed, she dried him thoroughly with a huge towel warmed in the sunlight, and he dressed himself. He had difficulty with the studs on his collar and she fastened them for him.

'What time is it?'

'Two o'clock.'

'I have only thirty minutes . . .'

She went with him to the front door of the *pension* and saw him into the carriage.

'The driver will wait for you,' she said, 'so do not send him off. You must return by four.'

Flecker nodded and climbed into the carriage. The driver tickled his whip over the pony and the carriage creaked as the springs shifted.

It was, Flecker thought as the wheels lurched over the cobbles, the first time he had been out on his own for months. He now realised how dependent he was upon Hellé and, momentarily, the thrill and terror of being without her overwhelmed him. It was, he thought, like the first time he had ever travelled alone, as a boy, on the train.

The carriage passed through the town to the lake shore, turned at a junction and halted by the kerb. The driver made no comment to Flecker, who lowered himself to the pavement and looked around. Behind him was a row of waterfront buildings and, across the road, the lake. Far out on the sunlit surface one of the steamers was plying southwards. The smoke from the vessel's funnel hung like a stain in the still air. The sun upon Flecker's neck, his hands and his face felt so good. It was undiluted, he considered. It was not filtered through the window-pane and the dust drifting endlessly in his room.

Beside the lake were a number of tables set out by a café in one of the buildings. Flecker could smell roasting coffee. Some of the tables were occupied by couples or groups of men: at the end table farthest from him was seated a single figure.

The person was sitting erect and apparently staring out at the lake, at the steamer and the hills beyond. Flecker knew before he took a single step from beside the carriage that it was Lawrence.

He had taken only a few steps when Lawrence moved round in his chair and saw Flecker. He got quickly to his feet, yet did not leave the table.

'Ned! Dear Ned! How very good it is to see you.' There were tears in Flecker's eyes, partly from emotion and party from being unused to the bright sunlight. 'I knew you would come and when the telegram arrived . . .'

His words tailed off. They shook hands then and Flecker embraced Lawrence, his arms around him. Lawrence's remained for a moment hanging at his sides, hesitant: an observer at one of the other tables would have recognised his reserve as British, but no one paid them any attention. Very briefly Flecker kissed Lawrence on his cheek, Lawrence's fair stubble rasping lightly upon his lips.

'How are you, Roy? You look well.'

'It's a trick of the light.' Flecker smiled slightly as he sat opposite Lawrence across the small wooden table. 'I am not anywhere near good health. The doctor in Montana recommended a change. The doctor here decrees the air of Locarno is not good for me. Between the two is the Simplon Tunnel.' He laughed briefly. 'So I am caught between the devil and the deep blue lake.'

'Are you on the mend?'

A waiter came out from the café and approached their table.

'*Posso esserle utile, signore?*'

'*Due caffè,*' Flecker ordered.

As he spoke, for a split instant they were back in Beirut and the lake was the eastern Mediterranean and the hills were those of the Lebanon.

'Your letters have kept me regularly up to date with all your enterprises,' Lawrence said when the waiter had left them. 'You seem to be flourishing. Your play on its way to the stage. Your novel about to metamorphose into a play. Your poetry being so well received.'

'Much of my new work is rejected. I am not a fashionable writer, I have too much of my muse interested in artistry and skill. I'm not one of your put-it-down-as-it-occurs boys and to hell with a neat rhyme and a strict, controlled metre. The magazines are full of the new Futurists. I'm an old Futurist myself.'

He laughed and it set him off coughing, the first fit he had had since mid-morning. It did not last long but it left him sapped of strength.

'Do you have medicine?' Lawrence asked anxiously.

Flecker nodded and took from his coat pocket a small

twist of paper from which he removed one of his lozenges.

'These things,' he said with heartfelt asperity, holding it up for Lawrence to see. 'They taste of acid and hatred.' He put it in his mouth and shifted it to one side with his tongue. 'They are so vile they pucker the inside of my cheek in minutes and the taste lingers for ever. If they could put blasphemy into a bonbon, this would be it.'

Lawrence smiled and the waiter appeared with their coffees on a tray. He placed them on the table and Flecker paid the bill, insisting Lawrence put his money away.

'This treat is for me,' Flecker insisted, 'so I am paying for it. To have you here is worth far more than a cup of coffee. If I were Croesus I'd be hard put to pay the full value of our time together.'

'I am sorry I didn't reply as often as you wrote,' Lawrence apologised. 'It wasn't always possible. You know what life is like at Carchemish.'

'Tell me of it. What have you unearthed? What have you discovered or achieved? I want to hear every detail.'

'A good deal, in fact. Woolley's been back and we've dug out three new sites of well above average interest. A lot of Roman stuff – pottery, some coins, glassware, a bit of a knife. In fact, some rather nice goodies. All shipped off to London through Aleppo. We've managed to get a line out through Latakia – Raff fixed it up after you left. It wasn't on before, but now – I think he's greased a few palms.' He reached into his pocket and produced a small wooden box about three inches square. 'This is for you.'

Flecker accepted the box with eager anticipation. It was crudely made, the wooden sides knotted and obviously hand-cut with a sharp blade; the lid fitted badly. He opened it. Within, nestling in sawdust, was a tiny bowl not two inches across. Very carefully he removed it and placed it on the table. It was made of creamy-coloured clay and contained in its matrix many fine, dark flecks. Asymmetrical, it leaned slightly to one side.

For a moment Flecker was taken back to the first time he ever opened one of Lawrence's shipments, to the first object he removed from the grass and straw of the Euphrates. That had been a bowl of a similar colour and texture, with gritty fragments in it. And it too was so light, so fragile, so miraculous.

'That was made before the potter's wheel was in use,' Lawrence said. 'It is not Hittite but older. Much older.'

'Did you get it in Carchemish?'

'No, I bought it in Turkey. Near Samsat.'

'Where is that?'

'Far up-river. Further north of Halfati than Jerablus is to the south.'

'You've been so far?' Flecker asked with amazement. Lawrence winked.

'All in the line of duty.'

'It's very beautiful. Thank you. It will have pride of place in my room.'

'Keep the box,' Lawrence suggested. 'It'll be useful for transporting it when you move back to Britain.' He paused, then added, 'Dahoum made the box – from driftwood in the river. He said it is his gift to you.'

'How is he?'

'He is well. In Aleppo at present – watching over something for me,' Lawrence answered enigmatically.

For a few minutes Flecker studied the bowl, twisting it in his fingers, feeling the history of it move into him like the warming sun. When he had put the bowl back in the safety of the box, he unbuttoned his jacket. The sun was hot and he felt flushed by it.

'They opened my letters,' he said. 'Did you know?'

'Not at first, but, yes, after a while. Hogarth told me they would.'

'They know everything. Or can guess it.' Flecker's voice became tense. 'That I love you. What we did. What I think about . . . about everything.'

'It doesn't matter,' Lawrence consoled him. 'We have friends.'

'Those friends were the ones who opened the letters – or ordered it to be done.'

Lawrence made no answer. He sipped at his coffee and watched the thinning smoke from the steamer drift to the surface of the lake.

'They only do it to protect themselves. What you write of a personal nature is of no import to them.'

'Not so. I was visited by one Mr Crossett. He had copies of the letters – or parts of them. He wanted the carbons of dispatches I sent to you, or to London; he said they couldn't find them in the files. I said I hadn't kept any, it was too risky; that I'd been told to keep our operation very quiet. He accused me, as near as makes no difference, of being a bad Vice-Consul, ignoring the rules. I was a good officer . . .'

'Don't worry about it. I know all about it – about Crossett and the offer and Marsh's note to you and Hogarth's moving in the background to secure an extension of your sick leave. It's the nature of the game, of our game.'

'Is it only a game?' Flecker asked pensively. 'Just a pastime like dominoes or backgammon or chess . . . ?'

'To them it is.'

'What is it all for? I see no point in it – the manoeuvrings and angling for position, the accumulation of power. What can you do with it? The individual, I mean. If Britain gains a railway to Baghdad, or France a port on the coast of Cathay, or Germany an oil well in the Persian Gulf . . . What does Hogarth get from that? I understand how the country gains something, or loses something. But the man behind it all . . .'

'He gains the knowledge that he has moved the path of history, that one day someone will say, "Hogarth stopped the railway". Isn't that what we all do? Isn't that why you write, Roy? So that, a hundred years from now, someone will read your words and say "That is how I feel" or "That is what beauty is to me"? All of us want to make a mark upon eternity.'

Flecker drank his coffee – it was cool enough now not to hurt his throat – and beckoned to the waiter to fetch two more before he continued.

'And you, Ned? What do you want? Someone to say "Lawrence dug up this statue" or "Lawrence foiled the German railway"?'

For a moment Lawrence made no answer. When he did, it was brief.

'No, not that. I think I'd like people to say that I was for the Arabs. I'd like them to think of me when they speak of Burton and Doughty.'

'But what will you have achieved?'

'I don't know,' Lawrence replied candidly. 'I've not achieved it yet. But I shall. In years to come I shall accomplish something great and be known for it.'

The waiter served the fresh cups and removed the empty ones. Again Flecker paid the bill, refusing to allow Lawrence even to touch his wallet.

'War is coming,' Lawrence confided, his voice low so it might not carry to the other tables. 'In a matter of months we shall be at war with Germany. And, when it comes, it will be a bloody and long war, for so much is at stake – national prides, trade, the future of the industrial base of Europe.'

'Are you sure?' Flecker asked.

'Oh, yes. Utterly. And when it comes the smaller nations will be caught up in the maelstrom. For this will not be a regional war; it will rage over the whole of Europe and any country which has been colonised will be sucked into the storm – British East Africa and German East Africa, the French colonies . . . And those countries where we and the Germans are struggling for power will be embroiled, too. Like Syria, Mesopotamia, Turkey, Iraq – they will all be lands on which we fight out our grand designs. That is why I want to remain with the Arabs.

'I love the Arab – his way of life, his courage, his tenacity to survive against all the odds. He lives in the most inhospitable land, yet is at one with it. He understands his universe. How many of us Europeans can say as much of our worlds? So, when the carnage starts and the bugles blow, I want to be with the Arab.'

'On whose side?' Flecker queried. 'Your own, or theirs, or the British?'

Flecker wondered for a moment if taking sides would have any relevance. He recalled Cumberpatch's conversation in the carriage on the way to Abadieh. It was the Europeans who had established the *senjak* of the Lebanon, the Turks and the British and the Italians and the Germans and the French who manipulated it to suit their purposes. Siding with the Maronites, the Druses, the Shi'ites. Covertly – or overtly, as the situation dictated – supporting the Arab cause, the Zionist cause, the imperial or socialist cause. And he heard Cumberpatch's voice for a moment, saying, '. . . unless we carry on meddling. You know, Flecker, I sometimes wonder . . .' He had, Flecker remembered then, deliberately stopped in mid-sentence.

'In truth, all three,' Lawrence said after a moment's thought.

'That is the difference between you and the others,' Flecker said. 'You face the truth and accept it. You tell it. For Hogarth, the whole damned business is so devious. It is deceitful and evasive and underhand. Hogarth hates the Germans – he sends you and me to spy on them and undermine them – yet he dined personally with the Kaiser only last year. And our policy is to support the French, yet we are ever quick to jump in in their place to exercise our authority on behalf of the Maronites. I saw that once at first hand from Cumberpatch . . .'

He stopped talking. Out on the lake the smoke had totally dispersed but another steamer was coming into view, bringing with it a new pall.

'The French must be curbed . . .' Lawrence began.

In his mind, Flecker heard Lawrence's voice echo: 'Nothing worse than a Frenchie in the windpipe. Best thing to do with the French is spit them out.'

'They are our friends!' Flecker cut in. 'How can we try to weaken their position when they are our allies? It's immoral. If I was to do this to you, or you to me . . .'

For a moment Flecker wondered if Lawrence had connived in the opening of his mail, but no sooner had he thought this than he cast the notion aside – yet he remembered pondering upon it once before. In a manner of speaking Lawrence was one of 'them', the masters, the makers of the rules and the movers of pawns. He might well be but a minor player, Flecker considered, but he was still someone with the power to direct at least a part of the design of the play.

'Indeed, they are our friends,' Lawrence said, severing the train of Flecker's thoughts, 'and, when the war comes, we shall need them as never before. But that is by the way in the game. As for you and me – that's different. We are not countries.'

'Every man is an island,' Flecker observed.

Lawrence smiled and drained his coffee.

'That's as may be, but even men – as islands – change

their shores under the tides of history. This is one of the reasons I must stay with the Arabs; they will be under attack more than they are now. The Turks want to suppress them regardless of their common religion. The Germans want to exploit them. The French want to manipulate them. And, of course, there is the Zionist movement behind it all wanting a homeland in Palestine. The Israelites want to return from the corners of the earth whither they have scattered to inherit their "birthright". To do that they will have to displace the Arabs. And we shall help them do so, no doubt, and I shall have to play my part in it, because it is the way of the game . . .'

He sounded tired and sad, like a man worn down by care, his spirit eroded by brutalities. The steamship on the lake sounded its whistle once and the whoop echoed from the hillsides.

'Do you remember the harbour in Beirut?' Flecker asked.

'I recall our sitting drinking coffee beside it. Do you remember the morning spent running guns up the coast road?'

'I shall never forget it, not as long as I live.' He stopped abruptly, then continued, 'Which I doubt will be long now.'

Lawrence made no attempt to disabuse Flecker of his statement. Instead, he asked, 'Have you written everything you want to?'

'Of course not. If I lived to a hundred I should have things to write about. The sunlight on English grass, rooks wheeling over winter trees, the sound of the wind in the Cotswold valleys – things like that.'

'Then you will not die yet,' Lawrence stated categorically. 'You've too much to accomplish first. Too much to write. Just as I shall not die yet, for I have not achieved my purpose. When that time has been reached, then I shall die – either by my own hand or by some freak of chance as best befits the end of an active life.'

A sparrow landed on the edge of the table, shifted its beady eyes from one man to the other and then flitted underneath to search for crumbs. Finding none, it flew off to perch on the railings overlooking the water and cheeped once.

'I am ready to die,' Flecker decided. 'I have not written myself out, but I accept I never shall. A year from now, two at the most, I shall be dead. Only the words shall live after me.

'God is ready for me.' He chuckled. 'Listen to me! Isn't that an outmoded thing to say? You can tell I'm no longer a fashionable thinker.' He became serious once more. 'And I have given Him much thought of late. My father, as you know, is an Anglican priest and I was brought up in the Church although I seldom paid it much heed. Now, however, I have thought of it. Islam, the religion of might is right, has perhaps pushed me towards Christianity. There is so much wrong with Islam. It's a religion based not on love but on . . . The Turks fight the Arabs, Muslim against Muslim. True, Christians have fought Christians often enough but not now, for our religion is based on love.

'I admit to finding myself drawn more towards the Roman Church than the puritanical Anglican. The magic has gone from the English Church, but lingers in Rome. My mother would get very batey if she knew . . .' He laughed at the prospect and coughed once.

Somewhere in the town, a clock chimed the hour. Flecker counted off the strokes.

'I have to go,' he said. 'I need to return by four and it is that already. The doctor visits me between four-thirty and five.'

'I will accompany you back,' Lawrence declared. 'After his consultation we can continue talking. I have much to tell you yet. About the Germans mucking up their labour force – once more! – but this time starting a gun battle, about the house and the dig . . .'

'No, I will return alone. My lodging isn't big enough for a cosy chat. It's a gloomy place and I do not want its miserable darkness casting shadows over us.'

'Then I shall meet you here tomorrow,' Lawrence offered.

'I can't. I'm not allowed out of my bed, in truth. This excursion was a special one for me – the first time I have put on clothes in more than a week. My especial outing – which is why I bought the coffee.'

Flecker stood up. His movement was slow, almost sluggish, and he toppled the chair behind him on to its back. Lawrence picked it up as Flecker shuffled away, his steps positive but small, like those of an elderly arthritic.

'You will write to me, won't you?' Flecker asked. 'Tell me about the Germans.'

The driver of the carriage – aware that he was obliged to return his fare to the Pension Rheingold by four, and seeing him rise from the table – tapped his pony with the reins and turned the carriage towards Flecker where he stood on the cobbles.

'Ned,' Flecker said, the carriage drawing slowly nearer, 'I love you.'

Lawrence took Flecker's hand. He held it as if to shake it but did not, then he placed his other hand upon it.

'Be careful in all things, Roy. Get well and write more poetry again. Keep dreaming of your Samarkand.'

'I never stop dreaming. Much of my life now is a fantasy.' He paused and looked directly into Lawrence's eyes. 'And you know, Ned, words are so like the desert sand. They shift . . .'

'Your time will come, dear Roy. Everything has a way of working out.'

'Yes, my time will surely come,' Flecker replied.

Tears welled from his eyes and ran down his cheeks, some soaking into his moustache. He could say no more.

Lawrence let go his hand and Flecker climbed painfully into the carriage. The driver again tapped the flanks of his pony with the reins and the vehicle moved off, jolting over the road surface and squeaking as before.

As the carriage turned from the lakeside to enter the town streets Flecker, despite himself, cast a quick glance towards the café. The groups were still seated at the tables. No solitary figure was there except the waiter clearing the table.

Flecker lay in his bed. A spider was weaving its web in the corner of the ceiling above his head; it was the first insect he had seen for months. In Montana and Leysin, he thought, it must have been either too cold for them or too high.

It was not a big spider. Its leg-span was barely that of a farthing.

A farthing! How good it would be to be once more in England with pounds and shillings and pence and halfpence and farthings. 'That will be one-and-sixpence-ha'penny, if you please!' he heard the young assistant in Blackwell's Bookshop demand. Indeed, it would be good to be away from francs.

He leaned over the edge of the bed and rummaged in his clothes. From his trouser pocket he removed the money left over from his outing and put it on the bedside table for Hellé to collect. Then he picked the money up again and counted it to see how much his visit to

Lawrence had cost. The coffees had been more expensive than he had expected. At the time he had not counted, had not scrutinised the bill. They had to be so very careful with money: he was never allowed to forget it.

He looked again at the spider, which had more than half completed the web. Soon, Flecker thought, it would be finished and ready to snare flies or midges. When the weather warmed, he was told, the lake produced swarms of them.

The spider was as restricted as he and Hellé were. It had to make do with one web, in one place; it could not go out and hunt its prey, but had to wait for it to blunder into the web.

'Just like life. Just like poetry,' Flecker said aloud. 'I weave my web and wait for words to get entrapped. It's all a matter of trapping the truth. So much of human existence is reduced to the grasping of truth.'

Truth, he thought: it was true he was ill, true he was in Locarno, true he was dying. It was true he had been to Carchemish and dug in the mound, wriggled about on a railway embankment. It was true he had failed his exams. It was true he had written poems and a so-called novel. And yet he recollected Lawrence once telling him that truth was what one thought it was. When the time came to judge what was true and what was false he would know it. All he had to do, Lawrence had said, was think of Carchemish and the mosaic, of him and Dahoum, of the desert night and the burning sun.

He closed his eyes and saw them again, although he was unable to form an exact picture. His memory was fading. Yet what he saw so nebulously and felt so intensely he knew to be the truth.

*

Locarno, Switz.

My very dearest Ned,

You cannot imagine how good it was to see you last week. Our meeting quite set me up again, although our parting was so painful. I do earnestly pray it will not be our last.

I am writing to your parents' home in Oxford in the hope that, in this way, it will not be scrutinised by others, but if it is – then to hell with that!

After our talk I gave many hours to thinking what passed between us about 'the game'. And I feel such shame at having been a player. I am a patriotic sort of fellow and not one to put his mother country down. (If there is a war a-brooding, I must make certain I am fit enough to join in and fight.) Yet I still feel shame for what I have done.

Why can't people speak the truth? Be open?

I must have been a poor Vice-Consul although I think I was better than many. I was a business-like official and completed my responsibilities with efficacy. I was not the dreamer-poet who can't face up to realities. And I must have been a damnably poor spy! I conducted my part with competence, but I fear I was not up to scratch – what spy questions his masters!

And I wonder just how good a poet I am. My work is still turned down. I have so many irons in the fire – *Hassan, Alsander* as a play, other possible commissions coming my way, the odd book to review – but the more I jiggle them about in the coals the more I think the fire has gone out.

From day to day, sometimes from hour to hour, I waver from the pinnacles of gay, abandoned, unreasoned optimism to the cavernous Hades of pessimism. One day I think I shall be Poet Laureate – the next I doubt I shall make a clerk in a dreary City office, trapped like a pig in a poke and snuffling with the smoky fogs of November.

This pendulum swing of the spirits is a part of my disease. I know this. (I've not been told it – there are as many lies hanging in the air about me as there are in dossiers in Whitehall. But these are kindly lies . . .)

I wonder, dearest Ned, if this world is the place for me. Or you. We are too rich of spirit – cast in too pure a human gold

– for all these chicaneries. That war you prophesy, the Arabs, the Turks, the Germans . . .

Write to me and tell me of your German shoot-up. Tell me about Oxford and who you are meeting and what the Hittite goodies look like in their glass cases in the Ashmolean. Tell me if Blackwell's is still selling books – not turned over to dispensing guns!

We move from Locarno soon. The air is not good here. We go back to the mountains, our address to be Hotel Buol, Davos Platz, Switz.

I must stop, The light is failing.

Ever your loving,
Roy.

He held the razor tightly between his fingers. His hand was not shaking, as it often did when he had just woken, but he was wary of nicking himself with the blade. Whenever he did cut himself the wound, no matter how tiny, bled profusely and Hellé had to dab it with peroxide to force it to scab.

The most difficult part was shaving around the ends of his moustache. If he removed too much his moustache became lopsided and he was loath to trim it.

He had soaped his chin, but the lather was thin. From his left cheek protruded one of the bristles from his shaving brush; it was long overdue for replacement but Hellé, going to a barber's in the town, had been shocked by the prices being charged and insisted he use his present brush until it was, as she put it, bald to the point of appearing positively professorial.

He removed the bristle and was about to commence shaving when, for the first time in weeks it seemed, he saw himself in the mirror.

Usually he paid little attention to the image. He shaved quickly, for the bathroom was cold and he did not want to catch a chill. His hair, when it was brushed, was brushed by Hellé. When he bathed, she washed him. But he wanted to shave himself; it was a matter of manly pride.

The reflection in the mirror, however, had little about it of which to be proud.

He did not shave but wiped the lather away with the hot flannel. He was profoundly shocked by his appearance. His eyes were sunken and dark-rimmed; his cheeks were sallow and his hair looked dry and brittle like the bristles of a hearth-brush. His skin was tensed as if stretched over a frame.

'I look like a damned Oriental!' he exclaimed. 'I look for all the world like one of those shagged-out creatures in the employ of the China Missionary Society.'

He held up his hand. His fingers still gripped the razor; the knuckles were prominent and the sinews ropelike and taut. The razor became a rope deck quoit; he dropped the implement into the basin with a clatter.

'Hellé!' he shouted with anguish. 'Hellé!'

She rushed along the corridor from the bedroom, wrenched the door handle and pushed into the bathroom beside him.

'What is wrong, dearest?' she asked anxiously.

'Shave me!' he commanded. 'From now on, you shave me. If we can't afford a barber, you do it.'

Hellé spent the morning massaging his back.

Leaving his bed only to go to the lavatory – during which time, in order not to disturb him unduly, Hellé re-made his bed – Flecker's muscles ached and his legs were weakened.

For the journey to Davos he had to be fitter. It was a long way and they could do little of it by main-line train. Much of their travelling would be done on narrow gauge railways, and yet more time would be spent in carriages.

As she rubbed oil into his back, pressing her hands firmly into his skin and kneading him as if he was dough, he fell into a doze.

At first he occasionally grunted and she ignored the noises, assuming him to be moaning at the discomfort or pressure of her hands. After ten minutes, however, he began to speak. His words were only partly intelligible.

'November,' he muttered, 'so damp and fogged . . . And Leckhampton glowering in the gloom like . . .' His speech slurred. 'The elms play violins . . . And nurse . . . Claire! Joyce! I'm sorry.'

As Hellé stopped her massage to reach for the oil, he moved his arms. They were by his sides, but he slid them up until they were at right-angles to his body. She looked at his face pressed against the pillow; his mouth was awry but he still spoke, surprisingly clearly.

'Pines . . . Brumana and Bournemouth . . . And the goatboy with his chips of flesh.'

His hands twitched.

'Ned? Ned?' he uttered, his voice suddenly louder. 'The pain is in my side . . .'

She rubbed his ribs where they met his spine. Despite being bed-ridden for so long now, he had not put on much weight. She could feel his bones, the condoyles of his vertebræ, the smooth bow of his ribs, the angled curve of his shoulder-blades.

'Hellé?'

She wondered if he was speaking from his sleep.

'Yes, dearest?'

'Is the door locked?'

She knew what he was thinking, that he had returned from his dream of words.

She wiped her fingers on a hand towel and slid the bolt in to the hasp. He heard the sound and tried to roll over, but she stopped him with her hand.

'No,' she said in soft command. 'You just lie there, dear Tiger, and growl.'

He was walking across dunes of sand. They might have been at Bournemouth but they were not — of that he was quite certain. The sun was beating down with the power to bleach stones. Ahead of him — as if to prove him right — appeared a *wadi* in which three camels were tethered. Nearby a black Bedouin tent was pitched.

As he drew nearer an old man came out from the entrance to the tent and offered him a cup of goat's milk. When he had drunk his fill, the old man presented him with a camel.

Mounted upon the camel, Flecker set off across the desert. The sun was as strong as ever, but he seemed not to be affected by it. Even when he removed his *ogal* and *keffiyeh* the rays did not even warm him.

Through a rapid transition of day and night, he rode onwards, never stopping. The camel, like himself, needed no rest, no refreshment.

They were following a road of sorts. There were signs of many other vehicles and animals having gone before them: Flecker recognised the tracks of motor vehicles, the hoofprints of horses, sheep, goats, other camels — even the straight lines of sleigh runners. By the wayside were the signs of travellers' camps — aggregations of animal dung, campfire circles filled with charred twigs and grey ash, shallow depressions where tents had been erected.

After a long journey, which tired neither Flecker nor his mount, he saw in the distance a rampart wall around a small city. As he came closer, the road ceased to be made of sand but instead was of yellow stone which shone polished in the sunlight.

The gates of the city swung open – huge wooden gates studded with iron bolts.

A multitude ran out and lined the road. They were silent and, as he passed, bowed to him as if he was Alexander the Great returned from triumphs beyond all imagining.

Beneath the archway of the gate stood a small party of what he assumed to be official welcomers. He reined in his camel, made it kneel and slid from its back.

It was then he saw the group consisted of Fontana and Hogarth, Cumberpatch and Robbins, his father and Dufferin. They bowed to him. Behind them stood Marsh and Rupert Brooke who stepped aside to allow him passage.

Beyond the gate, upon a snow-white marble dais, sat Lawrence. He was dressed in purest gold and by his side stood Dahoum, holding a palm leaf like an Easter pilgrim to Jerusalem.

'Hello, Roy,' he said, grinning, 'I told you your time would come. Welcome to your destination!'

Flecker gazed about himself at the wooden buildings with their carved balconies and low-pitched roofs. Through a doorway he could see a courtyard in the centre of which stood an olive tree.

'Aleppo?' he asked.

Lawrence laughed his quiet laugh.

'Samarkand,' he replied. 'This is Samarkand.'

Hellé returned to the room after dinner that evening. He was sleeping peacefully and she had thought it safe to slip away and eat her meal at a table rather than from a tray balanced on her knees at his bedside.

He was happier in himself than she had seen him for some time. Frank Savery had been staying in Locarno and had talked every day with him, insisting on coming to his room. They had read to each other, discussed poetry and religion, Islam and Christianity, Flecker's dislike of the Middle East – and Savery mocking him in a friendly way over his dislike but pointing out how much of his poetry reflected the beauty and mysteries of the region – and spent some time criticising Flecker's most recent work. They studied the reviews of *The King of Alsander* and *The Golden Journey to Samarkand*.

When Savery had left to return to his post in the Legation in Munich, Flecker's spirits had remained buoyant. Relieved at this temporary turn, Hellé believed she could allow herself an hour off duty.

The room was in darkness when she returned. The curtains were open, but there was no moon. Only a faint panel of light shone on the ceiling, cast there by the windows of a house opposite.

She did not switch on the light. Instead, she struck a match and lit a candle stub she kept on the table to read by at night.

On the bed, by his hand, his notebook lay open. His pen had fallen to the floor and the ink had stained the carpet. She picked it up, thankful the stain was small and partly disguised by the pattern.

Carefully she lifted the notebook and read it.

When the words rustle no more,
   And the last work's done,
When the bolt lies deep in the door,
   And Fire, our Sun,
Falls on the dark-laned meadows of the floor;

When from the clock's last chime to the next chime
   Silence beats his drum,
And Space with gaunt grey eyes and her brother Time
   Wheeling and whispering come,
She with the mould of form and he with the loom of rhyme:

Then twittering out of the night my thought-birds flee,
  I am emptied of all my dreams:
I only hear Earth turning, only see
  Ether's long bankless streams,
And only know I should drown if you laid not your hand
  on me.

She closed the notebook and put it on the table.

Her hand, touching his to put it under the warmth
of the blankets, caused him to flinch slightly. Then his
fingers turned and closed on hers, so tightly the pain
brought tears to her eyes and she gulped in her breath.

He relaxed his grip and she bent over to look at his
face. He was asleep, totally asleep and barely breathing.

She tapped the manuscript into order, but one sheet in
the centre stubbornly refused to slip into place and she
removed it. It was the end of *Forgotten Warfare* and
she read again his words as they had been re-typed.

To think that it was with cheerful anecdotes like these that I
had hoped, a white-haired elder, to impress my grandchildren!
Now there's not a peasant from Picardy to Tobolsk but will
cap me with tales of real and frightful tragedy. What a race
of deep-eyed and thoughtful men we shall have in Europe
after the war – now that all those millions have been baptised
in fire! But for my little memories I can keep at least this
distinction – the unearthly beauty of the East. I mean the
adjective. A man may find Naples or Palermo merely pretty:
but the deeper violet, the splendour and desolation of the
Levant waters is something that drives into the soul.

She fastened all the pages together with a steel springed
clip and thrust them into the envelope. Then, in her
strong hand, she wrote on the front:

'To:
G. Bell & Sons, Ltd.,
Publishers,
York House,
Portugal St.,
LONDON WC'

Maison Baratelli,
Davos Platz,
Switzerland.
Monday 4 Jan. 1915

Dear T. E. Lawrence,
    I am writing but briefly to let you know that my husband
and your dear friend died yesterday afternoon at 3.20pm.
    He is laid to rest in the Anglican church here in Davos.
He will not be buried here beneath the snows he so hated
but in England, in his beloved Cotswolds. I am making the
arrangements now.
    Towards the end he spoke of you and bade me send you
his love. Then he was delirious once more as he had been
and he muttered off and on.
    His last words were 'Is it all nonsense? What I've been
saying – is it all nonsense?'

Yours etc.,
Hellé Flecker.

A Selection of Arrow Books

☐	No Enemy But Time	Evelyn Anthony	£2.95
☐	The Lilac Bus	Maeve Binchy	£2.99
☐	Rates of Exchange	Malcolm Bradbury	£3.50
☐	Prime Time	Joan Collins	£3.50
☐	Rosemary Conley's Complete Hip and Thigh Diet	Rosemary Conley	£2.99
☐	Staying Off the Beaten Track	Elizabeth Gundrey	£6.99
☐	Duncton Wood	William Horwood	£4.50
☐	Duncton Quest	William Horwood	£4.50
☐	A World Apart	Marie Joseph	£3.50
☐	Erin's Child	Sheelagh Kelly	£3.99
☐	Colours Aloft	Alexander Kent	£2.99
☐	Gondar	Nicholas Luard	£4.50
☐	The Ladies of Missalonghi	Colleen McCullough	£2.50
☐	The Veiled One	Ruth Rendell	£3.50
☐	Sarum	Edward Rutherfurd	£4.99
☐	Communion	Whitley Strieber	£3.99

Prices and other details are liable to change

ARROW BOOKS, BOOKSERVICE BY POST, PO BOX 29, DOUGLAS, ISLE OF MAN, BRITISH ISLES

NAME...

ADDRESS ....

....

....

Please enclose a cheque or postal order made out to Arrow Books Ltd. for the amount due and allow the following for postage and packing.

U.K. CUSTOMERS: Please allow 22p per book to a maximum of £3.00.

B.F.P.O. & EIRE: Please allow 22p per book to a maximum of £3.00.

OVERSEAS CUSTOMERS: Please allow 22p per book.

Whilst every effort is made to keep prices low it is sometimes necessary to increase cover prices at short notice. Arrow Books reserve the right to show new retail prices on covers which may differ from those previously advertised in the text or elsewhere.

Bestselling Fiction

☐ No Enemy But Time	Evelyn Anthony	£2.95
☐ The Lilac Bus	Maeve Binchy	£2.99
☐ Prime Time	Joan Collins	£3.50
☐ A World Apart	Marie Joseph	£3.50
☐ Erin's Child	Sheelagh Kelly	£3.99
☐ Colours Aloft	Alexander Kent	£2.99
☐ Gondar	Nicholas Luard	£4.50
☐ The Ladies of Missalonghi	Colleen McCullough	£2.50
☐ Lily Golightly	Pamela Oldfield	£3.50
☐ Talking to Strange Men	Ruth Rendell	£2.99
☐ The Veiled One	Ruth Rendell	£3.50
☐ Sarum	Edward Rutherfurd	£4.99
☐ The Heart of the Country	Fay Weldon	£2.50

Prices and other details are liable to change

ARROW BOOKS, BOOKSERVICE BY POST, PO BOX 29, DOUGLAS, ISLE OF MAN, BRITISH ISLES

NAME...

ADDRESS..

....

....

Please enclose a cheque or postal order made out to Arrow Books Ltd. for the amount due and allow the following for postage and packing.

U.K. CUSTOMERS: Please allow 22p per book to a maximum of £3.00.

B.F.P.O. & EIRE: Please allow 22p per book to a maximum of £3.00.

OVERSEAS CUSTOMERS: Please allow 22p per book.

Whilst every effort is made to keep prices low it is sometimes necessary to increase cover prices at short notice. Arrow Books reserve the right to show new retail prices on covers which may differ from those previously advertised in the text or elsewhere.

Bestselling General Fiction

☐ No Enemy But Time	Evelyn Anthony	£2.95
☐ Skydancer	Geoffrey Archer	£3.50
☐ The Sisters	Pat Booth	£3.50
☐ Captives of Time	Malcolm Bosse	£2.99
☐ Saudi	Laurie Devine	£2.95
☐ Duncton Wood	William Horwood	£4.50
☐ Aztec	Gary Jennings	£3.95
☐ A World Apart	Marie Joseph	£3.50
☐ The Ladies of Missalonghi	Colleen McCullough	£2.50
☐ Lily Golightly	Pamela Oldfield	£3.50
☐ Sarum	Edward Rutherfurd	£4.99
☐ Communion	Whitley Strieber	£3.99

Prices and other details are liable to change

ARROW BOOKS, BOOKSERVICE BY POST, PO BOX 29, DOUGLAS, ISLE OF MAN, BRITISH ISLES

NAME...

ADDRESS...

....

....

Please enclose a cheque or postal order made out to Arrow Books Ltd. for the amount due and allow the following for postage and packing.

U.K. CUSTOMERS: Please allow 22p per book to a maximum of £3.00.

B.F.P.O. & EIRE: Please allow 22p per book to a maximum of £3.00.

OVERSEAS CUSTOMERS: Please allow 22p per book.

Whilst every effort is made to keep prices low it is sometimes necessary to increase cover prices at short notice. Arrow Books reserve the right to show new retail prices on covers which may differ from those previously advertised in the text or elsewhere.